Amber

May you see your flash

Michel Prince

MICHEL PRINCE

rebel ink press

Publisher's Note:
This is a work of fiction. All characters, places, businesses, and incidents are from the author's imagination. Any resemblance to actual places, people, or events is purely coincidental. Any trademarks mentioned herein are not authorized by the trademark owners and do not in any way mean the work is sponsored by or associated with the trademark owners. Any trademarks used are specifically in a descriptive capacity.

ISBN: 9781937265571
First Print Edition

10 9 8 7 6 5 4 3 2 1

Cover Artist: Carl J. Franklin

Rebel Ink Press , LLC
Printed in The United States of America

www.rebelinkpress.com

Chrysalis

Dedication

Dedicated to my soul mate, guardian angel and husband Reggie. Thank you for putting up with and supporting every crazy dream I've ever had.

My niece Ashley for helping set up the technical stuff, you are truly an artist.

Bette for editing. (I had to fragment the sentence just for you.)

A special thanks to my angel readers and cheering squad: Anita, Angela, April, Kari Heimer, Scott, Kristina, Anne and my sweet niece, Heather.

Finally, for JP. Thanks for giving up 'mommy time' so I could pursue my dream. I'll always be there to support yours.

Chapter 1

The chocolate colored skin on his clean-shaven head glistened with sweat from football practice. Was it smooth to the touch, I wondered, or would little prickles of hair scratch my palm? I became entranced by a drop of sweat sliding down his neck, under his collar, and I could only think what I wouldn't do to follow that trail to its end.

His sleeveless t-shirt stuck to him, defining his chest and his biceps were exposed, showing he had the perfect horseshoe that comes from hours of lifting. No way could I get my hands around his arm and have my fingers touch, but part of me just wanted to try.

He was joking with a few other players as they crossed the gym to go down to the locker room. As he reached to push open the door, his t-shirt road up, revealing his abs and upper hip. The tie of his football pants was already loosened. I stopped breathing. I had seen him walk through the gym before, but something about seeing part of his body that had always been covered sent my private fantasies into overdrive.

My head flew to the side as a thousand pinpricks exploded like fireworks across my left cheek. The unexpected assault came from a volleyball sent special delivery by one of the senior players.

The white-leather facial was followed by a snotty "knock it off." I couldn't tell if it was her voice or my mild concussion distorting her voice into a screeching noise.

"What did I do?" I asked in vain.

It wouldn't have mattered. Waking up this morning in *her* neighborhood and having the audacity to come to *her* school was enough.

"Don't even think about it, Soft-Meat," Sharyn Johnson growled as she crossed over to me, her eyes burning into mine. "He ain't no damn coconut!"

I turned away, not wanting the confrontation and realized maybe I wasn't as good as I thought at sneaking looks at him. I looked back at the faux oak double swinging doors that lead to the boy's locker room, but he was out of sight. The rest of the team was passing through the door now.

"A cocoawhat?"

Having lost what had become my vision of perfection, I wanted an explanation from Sharyn.

"A coconut. Black on the outside, white on the inside and water on the brain. He don't mix. The last thing he's thinking about is some pasty ass white girl with an itch to piss off her daddy."

She picked up the ball that bounced off my head as I stared at her in amazement. It's not that I'd never gotten the vibe from her that she hated me for reasons other than my setting skills, but for her to put it out there like this was...Well...Unparalleled.

Oscar Jeffreys was a senior. Correction, Oscar was *the senior*. Captain of every team, class president. I heard he completed an Eagle project, though at the time, I had no idea what that meant. He was the guy every girl wanted and only one girl ever had. Mya Thompson, last year's queen of everything. She went away to college a few weeks ago. Rumor has it theirs was a mutual break up. They were "taking a break." As a result all the girls on the team were dying to take her place. It was the only thing my volleyball team talked about in the locker room.

"Leave her alone, Sharyn!"

Kelly March came to my rescue, again. Kelly was a junior and had been in my older brother's class in elementary school. Caleb was the fourth child in our family, but everyone called us Irish twins. I used to think we were twins because we did so much together, but I was ten months younger. He died right before my tenth birthday.

At five-foot-nine, Kelly wasn't the biggest girl on the team, but she carried herself as if she was. She never picked a fight, but she ended many.

"Up your game instead of tryin' to tear down someone else's," she bit at Sharyn.

Sharyn stalked off, slamming her ball into a wall with all her might.

"Ellie, I know it's hard not to look at him," Kelly said, always the queen of the obvious. "But, really, you're a sophomore so keep him for your fantasies. I've never seen a senior/sophomore relationship that didn't end in heartbreak or pregnancy. It's usually both."

There it was! I was not getting pregnant. My family was the unmitigated study in failure. Being the youngest of five very different children, you'd think people wouldn't know what to expect from me. Instead, they saw me as another one of the Chisholm children, destined to make the same mistakes as my siblings. I was never given any credit that I might have learned from their mistakes instead of being doomed to repeat them. I was just another problem someone would eventually have to deal with.

This is why I lived in the world of movies. My real life never made sense to me. The families and friends in movies had what I considered normal reactions to situations. Audrey Hepburn was my favorite actress, but I was currently on a Doris Day kick. If you want an idealistic reality, watch a Doris Day movie. She had enough spunk to not be a pushover, something I always looked for in the heroine.

I avoided attachments that could pull me down. Oh, I had a few friends, but outside of volleyball, I wasn't about to get too involved. Involvement meant attachment and attachment meant someone would have to get to know me, and worse yet my family. I had this grand idea, if I went away to college, I'd say I was an orphan. No brothers or sisters. No family to speak of. Alone. Hey, it works in the movies, right?

So that's me. Head down, push through and hope to survive. And of course keep Oscar Jeffreys for my fantasies. Plus, Sharyn was probably right about one thing. What would Oscar want with a pasty white girl?

Mixing did happen in our school, but not with someone like Oscar.

Our game would start soon. It was the first of the season. Looking around the gym I needed a landmark to regain my focus so I zeroed in on the twelve banners of the other schools in our conference. Our banner was the largest, white with blue print and silver trim. The fierce head of a cougar growled in warning in the center.

The same cougar growled in the center of our pine court. The white lines for the volleyball court defined the boundaries, as well as the ten-foot lines. Blue lines cut through our court for the three-point line of the basketball court.

"All right, Cougars, shag the balls and get over here."

Coach Marks' high voice stood out. She had been coaching for five years. Her blond hair was cut short. In a suit, she always seemed to look so uncomfortable. The tight, black pinstripe pants looked short and the sleeves of her jacket were too long.

Not that I was a fashonista. Far from it. I was probably the only one in the school who would prefer a uniform to having to figure out what to wear. Jeans and a t-shirt until it got colder. Then I added a hoodie. Kelly tried to get me to dress up more, but for me that usually just meant adding a sweater.

We snatched all the balls and put them in our basket and threw it in the corner. Finding a spot on the bench, we waited to hear who Coach had in our lineup.

The bleachers rose at least thirty rows behind us, all the way to the windows at the top of the gym. If this had been the boys basketball opener, the stands would have been packed. Oh well, the less witnesses, the better for me.

But even with the small number of fans, I was nervous. In the stands, little sisters and brothers looked bored and annoyed with having to be there. Maybe a few grandparents were sprinkled in, but mostly it was moms and dads. Minus mine, of course.

"March, you serve first. Sands, Johnson, Kendall, Zupfer, Chisholm, you're setting opposite Johnson," Coach informed us as we stood up to run out on the court as our names were called.

We were using a pathetic, junior-high level 4-2 offense: four hitters and two setters. Coach Marks said it was that way until I proved myself enough to run a 5-1. That scared me. Then I'd run the whole floor by myself. Being five-foot-three, I was just too short to be a hitter. With a 4-2, I could be taken out when I was in the back row. If I stayed in, I'd have no responsibility other than defense.

Volleyball had always been a sport that appealed to me in a deep way. I could hit the ball as hard as I wanted, grunt, run and yell "mine" without consequence. There was little cost to the sport, so I never had to worry about trying, fruitlessly, to get money from my parents. Earning a spot on the varsity squad as a sophomore was next to impossible, but I'd done just that. This was the main reason Sharyn hated me. I was her competition for her position, team setter.

I was hoping to grow, but no girl in my family was over five-foot-seven. When I started playing volleyball I focused all my energy on being a setter. My parents wouldn't pay for me to join a club team and they wouldn't bring me to practices or games. I had to wait until school could take care of transportation to join a sport. I babysat all summer to pay for my jersey, shoes and kneepads. This was my happy place, I just wished I didn't have to fight with anyone to stay here.

"Good luck, snot face."

That could only come from my new best friend, Jordan. He was a freckle-faced redhead who lived two houses down. He was too gangly and uncoordinated to play any sport, but he seemed happy to cheer me on. We'd met over the summer. His family moved in to the Jensen house, which sat empty for a few years. The Jensen's son was with Caleb when he died. I don't think they ever got over the guilt of that. I'd only known Jordan since June, but there was something that seemed trustworthy about him. Must have been the eyes, green with slight specks of hazel. We stayed up for hours talking about my family and our lives. He understood when I was with my family, I felt alone, adrift in an ocean with no land in sight.

"Thanks, loser," I said punching him in the shoulder.

"Mr. Franklin, can you please be a line judge?"

Coach learned that she could count on Jordan, too. This was our first game, but he'd helped a lot during our preseason practices.

"Yes, ma'am," he replied.

"Jessie Smith's our other line judge. Go talk to her and get set up."

Jessie was cool. She was a sophomore who I had been with in elementary school. Jessie hadn't even made the JV team, but she told Coach she would be the JV manager. She tried to help out on Varsity wherever she could. It was a good way to earn points with the coach for next year.

The refs blew the whistle and we set up. I was standing directly next to Mary, a junior and outside hitter. Blue and silver glitter adorned her mahogany brown eyes and her black hair was pulled up into a tight ponytail. We had to switch positions so I could be in the middle by the net once Kelly served. Luckily, we'd won the coin toss. We were playing the Bears, a decent team from Eagan. They were set up similarly, but I could tell by their setter they had converted to a 6-1 offense. That let me know they were better prepared and their setter could actually spike the ball.

The setter controls the floor. She's supposed to get the second hit and decide who finishes it off. One mistake and I could be sent back to JV. I wished now I hadn't pushed myself so much this summer. What was the point? I wasn't above spending a year on JV.

My stomach was already tightening. I turned my head and saw Kelly standing almost to the wall. With the volleyball extended in front of her, she looked me in the eye and winked. The knot in my midsection eased as she refocused her eyes on the ball then the other side of the net. Two steps and she jumped while throwing the ball high in the air. Right as she hit the height of her leap, her right hand made contact.

Slam. Kelly's serve was loud as I got into my spot. Mary backed away from the net and everyone was low and in position waiting to see what would happen to the serve.

"Aaaaaaaaaaace!" We all came together in the middle of our half of the court slamming our hands down. Kelly got us on the board by landing a perfect serve right on the backline of the court. The other team's back row was blaming each other, which I thought played in our favor. If their team was breaking down this early in the game, we might have a chance of creaming these guys.

I set up Mary and Steph and easy passes led to easy sets, as they hammered home some great spikes. Then a shanked ball from a dig ended up hitting the ceiling and being called out.

The other team served a few times. We didn't make any major errors, but they gained back some of our lead. Finally Mary spiked the ball to get control back on our side. We rotated position on the possession change. I was stuck serving, my least favorite part of the game and one of the reasons we still ran a 4-2. No jump-serve for me. Kelly promised she'd teach me if I could ever get enough control. My weak serve barely cleared the net, falling gently over and setting up a perfect situation for the other team.

We ended up winning the first game 25-14 but we lost the second game 21-25. As the third game was nearing its start, Coach told us to not give up.

"Play hard. This is our house and we're not going to lose this match!"

We served first and Kelly gave us a nice start to the game. Then we were met with disaster! The Bears slammed down a spike that Sharyn dug for and although she missed the ball, she ate the floor when she did it. Blood was everywhere. She bit her lip and split her chin and the game was paused for an injury time-out. The school janitor came in to clean up the blood and Coach substituted Laura for Sharyn. Laura was a good hitter so I didn't know why she didn't play more. Then I realized exactly why.

"Ellie. We need to switch to a 5-1. We just don't have the depth to put in another setter."

Her voice sounded as if it was in a tunnel. She grasped me by both arms and barked, forcing me to lift my eyes from the floor.

"Look at me!"

Looking up at her, I felt like a two-year-old being scolded by my mother.

"Ellie, you're the best natural talent I've seen since college. You can do this. Run the floor!"

I shook my head to try to stop the echoing as my stomach cramped. I rubbed hard on my stomach, hoping I could release the gut wrenching pain. What was she thinking? Me run the floor? I took a deep breath and looked across the floor to Jordan, who was giving me the thumbs up and making a whiney face mocking Sharyn. If nothing else he made me smile. Kelly came from behind me and placed her hands on my shoulders.

"We got this," she said.

Only a few minutes removed from Sharyn's injury and still everything seemed as if it was moving in slow motion. It felt like it took an hour to walk to my position. Shaking out my hands, hoping my fear would go with it, the Bears setter looked at me and smirked. She knew she was older, more experienced. What was I doing? Was I crazy? I closed my eyes, reminding myself that I'd worked hard for this. This was my position.

I could still hear Sharyn screaming on the bench. Her parents were there to help get her settled down, fighting over whether they should leave now for the emergency room or wait until the end of the game.

I don't know where I found it, but somewhere deep inside I found the courage to step up to the situation. I kept telling myself it was just practice. The ball went back and forth a few times. The score was now tied 25-25. We needed two points to win. Betsy served us up an ace which was great. No pressure. If she could do that one more time, we would win.

Slam! The ball went deep into the left hand corner. *Pass, set, get low, get low, get low, here comes the spike.* Kelly dug the ball, but it came off her arms wrong. I ran to where it flew my eyes trained on the ball, refusing to let it get away. This was my job! I had to get this ball and set up for the kill. Yelling "mine, mine, mine" at the top of my lungs, I ran across the floor. Finally catching it on my fingertips right by the stands, I did a back set, yelling "5-2, 5-2, 5-2," letting Mary know it was coming to her and low at that. I felt myself falling backwards. I knew I had to turn, but the arch from my back getting it to Mary was enough to upset my center of balance. I fell back in time to see her slam home a spike that went right through the defenders' block and hit between the left and center back players. They both dove, missing the ball and ended up hitting each other.

Our bench erupted. I scrambled to get myself off the floor and this was when I realized I truly never fell. Someone's strong hand was holding me on my low back above my waist. I lifted my head. Oscar's deep brown eyes were like a warm inviting macchiato begging me to fall forward to him. My legs were straddling one of his own.

He slowly pulled me up so I stood upright, but he kept his hand on the small of my back. His hand was so massive it fit across the whole of my back. I clutched his shoulders for balance and to let him know he could let me go. But he kept looking in my eyes. If I didn't turn I'd be eternally lost in his.

"Aahh…thanks. I think I got it from here."

"Great save. Lucky for you I was here to save your life."

I never heard his voice before, it was deep and comforting.

"I never knew anyone who died from fallin' on their butt," I replied.

The other girls pulled me as his hand slipped from behind me. I looked over my shoulder and saw him talking to some of the other football players, his eyes keeping watch on me. We lined up to shake hands and echoes a chorus of "good game." Coach was telling us to get rest, finish our homework and hit the showers. Not necessarily in that order.

Chapter 2

Showering in the locker room wasn't an option. Yes, it's petty, but I barely filled an A-cup, my legs still weren't defined and no matter how many crunches I did my stomach had no definition.

Instead, I went to the locker room, took off my game shoes and kneepads shoved them into my locker then quickly grabbed my warm up suit. Somehow I could block out my uniform shorts during a game, but once the game was over I got a sudden rush of insecurity. I should be happy we'd opted out of the bun huggers that were basically underwear made out of more durable fabric, but to me, the skintight biker shorts weren't much better. I pulled on my Payless shoes my mom thought were appropriate for varsity sports, threw my bag over my shoulder and headed to the gym.

At the end of the bleachers Jordan was waiting to walk me home. He currently was under the delusion he was 'my great protector'. Really, I think I weighed more than him soaking wet.

"Ready to go?" he asked, knowing I'd prefer to stay here and run drills until midnight.

"I guess so," I sighed.

As we crossed the gym someone yelled my name.

"Ellie." The voice was so low, all I could think was I had forgotten a biology assignment for Mr. Lester.

I turned to see Oscar. He knew my name? He wanted to talk to me?

"Hey, Ellie right?" he asked. "I think you owe me something." His eyes smiled at me.

My face instantly scrunched with confusion. He must have mistaken me with someone, anyone, but looking behind me, all I saw was the wall. "Excuse me?"

"Ellie, sophomore phenom setter that doesn't look where she's going. That's you, right?" His eyes were laughing although he tried to keep a straight face. "Remember? I saved your life. You owe me."

"A…I…um." My fingers twitched. Could he be any more perfect? His voice was deep like a voice over guy, but the tone was soft. Oh no. My knees were getting weak. I needed to run. "I'm not sure what you're talking about."

I grasped Jordan's left arm and started to walk out of the gym before I made more of an ass of myself.

My left arm suddenly had something monumental wrapped around it and my grip on Jordan was lost as Oscar spun me around and I landed face first into the center of his abdomen, his six-foot-seven frame towering over me. I could smell Irish Spring and I realized I was sweaty and half of my ponytail had fallen out.

Why hadn't I asked Kelly to French braid it so I might have had a chance of looking decent? Oh yeah, I know why, because in a million years I never thought I'd be talking to Oscar Jeffreys. I was content watching him from afar. He held me slightly away from him so he could look at me. I kept my head down. At least I could tell him I was flushed from the game and not because his touch was setting off goose bumps up and down my arms and legs. Thank God I put on those warm ups! I didn't know what was happening, but I wished Jordan wasn't standing right beside me as a third wheel.

"We were just leaving and we really need to get home soon or our parents are going to ground us," Jordan said, putting his hand on my shoulder. His touch was never going to cause a shiver, but at least it calmed me down.

"Um, yeah, I gotta get going now," I said, still not looking up.

And that's when I felt his hand on the small of my back again. It felt as if everything else went away, like his hand was a blanket covering my whole body. I looked up, like someone was slowly pulling a string at the top of my head, my eyes taking in his heather gray t-shirt that hung loose at the abdomen, but still defined his chest and shoulders. His neck was long and his face was perfection. Smooth skin, strong jaw and full lips.

"Well, I certainly wouldn't want to get you in trouble. If I were to drive you home, would that give me a few minutes to talk to you?"

His eyes locked on mine and my mind froze, unable to answer.

"Um..sure. Ellie, I'll wait for you by the door," Jordan grumbled.

I could hear only hear the two of us breathing. Everything else was just like the hum from a fan.

With my hands on his chest, I tried to balance myself as well as keep a little bit of distance. My brain was finally thawing.

"What is it you want?" I asked, trying to be as cute and innocent as I could be, utterly failing in my attempt. I knew what I hoped, but I expected it to be about another girl, maybe someone on the team. There's no way he could possibly want anything to do with me. The dumb, pasty, white girl who was, yeah also a sophomore.

"Well," he said as he slowly let me go and allowed a bit of space between us. "First, I'd like to drive you home."

I nodded yes. Hadn't we already agree to this? "How many conditions are there?"

"Second, I wanted to know if you'd want to go get some pizza after the game Friday night. A bunch of us usually go to Pizza Luce's after the game, win or lose, but especially when we win," he smiled. "I'd take you now, but it seems you have a curfew."

Damn that Jordan! My parents wouldn't notice if I never came home, let alone if it was two hours after a game. They have no concept of sports. They've never even been to a game, ever.

"Um, a, well, yeah I could do that. But I'd need a ride because I don't have a car." My mind was racing as I tried to process what he was proposing. We walked to catch up to Jordan then made our way to Oscar's car.

"Meet me outside the locker room after the game. You're going to the game, aren't you? It'd be a shame to miss it. We're playing North and we always beat them."

"Yeah, I guess I can do that," I said, uncertain of myself. Part of me was screaming, *it's a trick, he couldn't possibly like you. This is some hazing prank he's playing on you.*

Oscar opened the front passenger door for me and Jordan pushed the seat forward and jumped in to the back. The look on Oscar's face change from one that'd won a challenge, to anger, causing a shiver to run down my spine. Quickly his smile returned warming me as I slid into the front seat.

His car was a primer gray, 1969 Ford Mustang Fastback. The leather seats were worn out, but the engine sounded strong. Too soon I was showing him where to turn, as I only lived four blocks away from the school in a modest split level home.

Even though Saint Paul, Minnesota, was a metropolitan area, our home was nestled in the tight-knit neighborhood of Rondo Park. With early 1900's houses, it was one of the oldest neighborhoods in Saint Paul, after the historic Crocus Hill of course. Ours was one of the newer houses on the edge of the neighborhood that was put in after the city widened Interstate 94.

Jordan tapped his foot against the back of my seat the whole ride home, annoying me because my seat was shaking. I swear to God, I think he was trying to get me to turn around and punch him in front of Oscar. When we pulled up outside my house, I bent forward so the back of the seat would move forward allowing Jordan to get out. He jumped out, thanked Oscar for the ride, and waited for me to get out, but I turned to Oscar.

"Thanks for the ride. I guess I'll see you Friday."

His right hand reached out catching my left wrist, pulling my face within an inch of his mouth. I could feel his breath tickle my lips and the cool smell of mint floated in the space between us. "I just wanted to say I really enjoyed catching you today. Please feel free to fall around me anytime." His voice was low, as if he wanted this moment to be just between us.

It took all my strength to pull myself up I was drawn to him, as any girl in the school would be. Thoughts came screaming at me again, *sophomore-hazing, coconut, pregnancy, you're plain, he's perfect*. "I better get in so I can go on Friday," I said, keeping up the ruse that my parents cared.

I rushed out of the car so fast I hit my head on the ceiling and I could hear Oscar laughing as I rubbed my head and walked to the door.

I put my key in the lock and turned around. I saw Oscar smiling as I quickly stepped into the house and closed the door. I heard his car pull away fast. My back pressed hard against the door, my heart pounded as I slid to the floor to contain my excitement.

It was the first time I'd come home without instantly feeling dread. Usually I felt a crushing sensation, like someone was watching me. I stayed with Kelly any chance I could. Even when her parents were out of town, I felt safer at Kelly's house than I ever did in mine. It was as if I was an intruder in my own home.

When I finally pulled myself together, I walked downstairs to my bedroom and threw my bag on the floor. Kicking off my shoes, I started to take off my warm-ups. I'd recently gotten my own room since my oldest brother, Levi, finally moved out.

Levi, the second child was tall like my dad and had a strong chin and huge arms, totally out of proportion to his body. He was like a football player on top and a basketball player on bottom. He tried almost everything in an attempt to change his mood. And because of him, the expectation for me was that I was supposed to be drinking, smoking or doing drugs in some fruitless effort to escape the reality that was my life.

I was headed to the bathroom, but something made me turn around. I could make out the outline of a head in my window and a shudder rushed through me, causing my breath to catch and my heart to skip a beat. A knock at my window made be jump, but actually calmed me. The problem with a split-level home was being stuck in the lower floor. In my case, Jordan was always popping by. Usually

I didn't mind it, but tonight I just wanted to shower and bring myself back to paranoid as opposed to tripping psychotic. I opened the window, but plopped on my bed keeping my back to him to let him know I didn't care what he wanted.

"What's up," I asked.

"Nothing. Just wondering what's with you and Mister Wonderful?"

"I don't know. I think he was just trying to be nice."

"Right," Jordan said. "Because seniors are so nice to sophomores. You know how many of them have smacked me on the head, tripped me…I even got a swirly the last time I tried to go to the bathroom. Give me one reason he's talking to you besides trying to get some? He's going to use you and throw you away."

That made me turn around and face him. His eyes were fierce and full of hate.

Had I been wrong? Was he jealous of Oscar? Did he think he had an exclusive line on me? What was upsetting me most was his comments were exactly the same thing I was thinking myself. He was making my point, the point, I was trying so hard to suppress. What would the most sought after guy in the school want with me if not to use me?

"Really, I don't need this, okay," I said, trying to fight back the tears. "Can I just talk to you tomorrow?"

"Fine! But watch out for him, I promise you he's up to no good."

I let the water heat up as I tried to figure out what just happened. Oscar couldn't want to go out with me. I pulled out my ponytail and brushed my hair that Kelly compared to crushed garnet because of its slight reddish hue.

As the mirror started to fog up I stared at myself. I couldn't come up with one good reason to refute Jordan's warning. Oscar's interest had to be a bet. I had the body of a normal ten-year-old, which wouldn't be bad if I wasn't fifteen. No one ever thought me special or pretty. People rarely thought of me at all. Surely Oscar made a bet with some other guy that he could score with me by Friday. That's it! Yep, not a chance he could possibly want to go out with me because of me. He didn't even know who I was. Then again I couldn't help thinking about all the stupid teen movies I'd seen, where the loser ends up with the stud. I wonder if Jordan would count that as a reason?

My mind ran through a mental checklist of what Oscar could possibly want from me. What could he know about me? Grace! He had to know Grace. She graduated last year. Grace, third in line for the family debt. With her soft curls and teal eyes, my sister, was a beauty who knew it and used it for all it was worth. She used boys and men to get what she wanted in life. She'd turned her body into an ATM card. A quick swipe and the push of a few buttons, and Grace could get whatever she wanted.

And Jennifer was infamous. Oscar expects sex. That's it. Nothing more. I wasn't going to the game and it certainly wasn't going for pizza.

Content with my decision I hopped in the shower. Shampooing my hair, I could feel the soap flowing down my back the small of my back where his hand had been…So secure… No! It was a joke. A trick! No one like Oscar could ever want someone like me.

I grabbed the body wash and started to clean my body. I thought about the smell of Irish Spring and what he'd do if he were helping me in the shower. I imagined hands slowly going over my shoulders as he gently kissed my neck.

Stop it! No matter how bad I wanted it be, this wasn't real.

I turned off the shower, dried myself off and brushed my teeth, stormed back to my room, slamming the door just to get out some of my anger.

Aaaaaahhhhhh! I hated my family! They set me up. If Jen hadn't given it up to every guy who said 'hi' to her, if Grace wasn't one breath away from being a prostitute. If my sisters were even remotely normal, I might've had a chance at a normal relationship, not with Oscar maybe, but with someone. If I wasn't spending my time having to make up for their mistakes my life would be different.

Maybe I could just fall into what they expected. Sleeping with Oscar wouldn't be so bad. He's gorgeous and he seemed nice. I could do worse. No. No. No. That's exactly what everyone expected me to do. Get drunk and sleep with everyone. Drop out of school and become another mooch in the world. But I refused to do that. I'm going to do something with my life.

I plopped angrily on my bed to finish my history report just as my black Nokia phone vibrated, signaling I'd received a text.

I meant it. I couldn't place the number. *Wrong #.* I replied reaching for a book. *Doubt it.* Okay. Now I was confused.

Who RU?

UR savior.

Okay, prank text.

Don't have 1.

Yes U Do.

Who RU?

UR savior.

Okay, this was getting annoying. *Whatever loser.*

Y Loser?

Not gonna reply 2 stranger.

Oscar. UR savior.

My heart stopped. Literally stopped. I tried to focus on something in my room, but everything was blurring together. The only thing I could make out was his name. How the hell did he get my number?

U there?

Yeah.

I meant it.

Meant what?

U can fall on me.

OMG! Breathe, Ellie. Breathe. This is so not happening.

? my #?

I had to know. Only a handful of people had my number and none of them would give it out.

Angels work 2gether.

Okay, so that was cute. A smile started to cross my lips. *Stop it, Ellie,* I told myself. This isn't real.

UR angel?

Halo's crooked.

LOL. Don't need savior.

All need savior.

Who's, urs?

U.

Oh, he's good. My face flushed and my body started to tingle. What were the odds that I was put on this earth to save Oscar Jeffreys? "None," a whisper made my head turn and the tingling stop. No one was in my room. So now I'm hearing voices as well as having delusions of grandeur.

Just then I got another text, this time from Kelly. *Thx 4 save.*

No prob.

? #? I sent to Oscar.

Y u care?

Just do. Then Jordan had to butt in.

L what pg bio ? on.

It'll cost u! came from Oscar.

23

? Oh crap, I thought. No one ever texted me and now there were three people chiming in. I responded to Oscar and not Jordan. I quickly responded to Jordan then, Oscar.

Cost what?

23?

Bio ? not 4 u. I sent to Oscar.

Ok cost 1 date? Who ? for?

No really. And NOYB.

Y NOYB? B-friend.

Y&N.

Huh?

Male friend.

Good.

Y good?

U owe me a date.

No I don't!!! Haven't told who gave #.

Movie? Dinner? Walk?

No really gotta go.

Y?

I $ for bill.

Anytime minutes?

Y?

I like ur voice.

Oh man. I wanted to reply, *me too*, but sent this instead.

Batt dying.

Liar!

Prove it! I texted with confidence, only to receive.

I'll B right over.

Crap. He can't come over. I look like…whatever. He can't come over. I quickly texted.

NO!!! I ran across the room and ripped down my HSM poster, which I should've taken down after seventh grade.

Proved it:)

Ugh! What a brat, I told myself but I smiled. I relaxed on my pillow and enjoyed the moment.

Gotta go to bed.

Offering? Oh God, what'd I just say?

NO!!!!

2 bad:(

G-night Oscar.

G-night Ellie.

I rested my head on my pillow and looked at the crumpled mass of poster I'd thrown on the floor. The tear cut through Zack Efron's face. Not a loss. I never got him. I bought the poster because it was one with Corbin Bleu. His eyes seemed so happy.

Oscar's eyes were amazing. The kind that make you feel safe no matter what's happening in the world. I could never look in his eyes again.

Now I was going to have to replace the empty space on my wall. My walls are covered with movie and music posters. *New Moon, Elizabethtown* for Orlando, *Breakfast at Tiffany's* as all must bow to the great Audrey, and the cover of *Love, Music, Angel, Baby.* The rest were cut from magazines and contained photos of actors, movies and singers I liked. Having all these images on the walls made me feel less alone in my house.

Chapter 3

On the walk to school, Jordan talked about a YouTube video he'd watched the night before. Then he dropped a bomb on me.

"Um, Ellie."

"Yeah."

"I found this last night on Craigslist."

He passed me a printout.

It was an ad for a massage service, but it was obviously someone offering a happy ending.

"Hookers? Really. You that desperate to pop your cherry?"

"Funny. It's your sister." His smug voice was only half as irritating as his smile.

"Excuse me?" I could feel my face flush and my stomach flip.

"Look at the number."

I looked. It was hers. Her cell was only two digits off mine. Why the heck is she doing this?

"You didn't tell anyone did you?" I asked folding up the paper as small as I could and shoving it in my back pocket. I'd have to sneak into the office so I could shred the evidence.

"Who would I tell? You're like the only person I know."

"Right, well, please don't tell anyone. The last thing I need…"

Oscar jumped into my mind. His *too bad* text combined with my family history made me realize that while last night was fun, I couldn't respond to him again. Thank God for Jordan. He seemed to be watching out for me.

The day was a blur of congratulations and whispers behind my back. In second period Jordan sat by me listening to Mr. Lester's lecture on the animal and plant classification systems. Then he leaned over and told me about gym class.

"A bunch of guys were talking about a bet." I tried to block him out. "There's a pool. They get points by sleeping with junior and sophomore girls. Sophomore girls are a hundred points."

A wave of nausea swept over me. So it was a bet. Wouldn't you know. Why had I let myself even imagine Oscar wanted me? Stupid! Stupid! Stupid!

By lunch I was fully annoyed, but at least it was nice outside so I could enjoy the fall day in peace in my favorite spot. The sandwich I packed lacked a lot, but my mom hit up the snack aisle at the grocery store so I had some chips and a granola bar. I looked out across Interstate 94 trying to make the cars turn into a blur of noise and color. I didn't notice Kelly approach until she shook me in an attempt to get me out of my funk.

"Hey, she won't be that mad. Eventually it will heal. It might even make her face look better."

"Huh, What are you talkin' about?"

"Sharyn. I figured that's why you're so upset. You're worried about how bad her face will look and that she's gonna kill you for taking her spot, right?"

I hadn't been thinking about Sharyn at all. That was another problem I have to face in a few days when she was less swollen. When her vanity would actually allow her to come back to school. I was thinking about Oscar, what his plan was, and what he was going for. Why had something in his eyes made me it feel like he was telling me the truth? That he wanted me at his game. That he wanted me.

I realized I was ignoring Kelly so I responded. "Uh no, I'd forgotten about that. I guess I was just enjoying the silence."

"Well, what is it then? You never sit out here without good reason."

She was right. She caught me a few times during the summer and even earlier this year when I was stressed out about trying out for the team. I just didn't know how to tell her about Oscar. She was my friend and had been for longer than just this year. She was like the sister I wished I had. I also knew she wasn't interested in Oscar because she had Max. Another huge football player Max had to be six-four. He was stocky and always wore his hair in braids. And you never saw one without the other.

"Oh, Ellie, I'm so sorry. I forgot," Kelly apologized.

"Forgot what?"

"It's the third."

A wave of nausea swept over me as my head spun. I was nine years old again.

From the funeral on it was all about how Caleb was the good child, better than all of us, as if his death destroyed any hope for the rest. Most mothers would have clung to their children tighter, but mine became even more distant, especially with me.

Caleb was riding his bike on the railroad tracks. He didn't hear the whistle. Paul Majors, the anchor from Channel 11, called it "the tragedy that has the whole neighborhood in tears tonight."

Following the funeral I was curled up in a ball under the dining room table. I had to wear an itchy, green velvet dress from Christmas that I hated. The stiff lace on the neck and sleeves must have been created by someone who worked in psychological torture and detested children. It was over eighty degrees out, but my mother didn't want to waste money on a black dress that would have been comfortable. *It's not like you're going to wear it again before you outgrow it. Your Grandpa's in good health,* she snipped at me when I asked. My head was resting on my knees and I hoped no one could see me under the table.

Black flats. Must be mom by the table. A pair of brand new Nine West heels stood by her. Grace. I didn't know what Nine West meant, but Grace said it was a big deal. I could see Jen's legs all the way up to the knees. She was sitting in a chair across the room. On the phone, again. She'd been fighting with someone because something broke. Teenagers. She was acting like it was some life altering thing. She was such a drama queen.

A pair of patent leather Mary Jane's came up to the table. It wasn't one of my cousins. I could tell because they weren't scuffed. I pulled in tighter.

A little girl in a dark plaid dress with her curly hair pulled back by a black headband lifted the tablecloth and slipped in next to me. She had the smoothest skin. It was the color of mocha. Her eyes were so dark, almost as if they were black, but somehow they were warm and all knowing, as if she was born with an old soul.

"I'm Kelly," her voice was light and airy.

I just looked at her.

"You don't have to talk to me. When Caleb talks about you, he says you're quiet. He told me you were here."

"That's not funny," I growled. How dare she?

"I'm not trying to be mean. But he did."

"This is his funeral so I don't know who you were talking to, but it wasn't him."

"Don't you believe in spirits? I do." Her eyes were sparkling and she was picking lint off her dress. The tiniest pieces were almost invisible. "They're all around us, you know. Good ones and bad ones."

A felt a shiver run down my spine remembering the figure that seemed to haunt our house. I wasn't stupid enough to tell anyone, but I often saw a shadowy figure that looked like a guy wandering through the house. Who knows how long he had walked through this old neighborhood? He would stare at me and I'd get scared. Maybe it was because I'd never seen his face. It was more like a dark shadow. I hadn't seen Caleb, but the regular ghost hadn't been around as much either.

"Why'd he talk to you and not me?" I asked.

"Maybe he didn't think you'd believe he was real. When he was alive, we were good friends. Last year we did that plant project together."

"The one that was about light and water and stuff?"

"Yeah," she smiled. "He says you're his favorite sister."

I swallowed hard. A lump formed in my throat. I didn't want to think about how close Caleb and I were. My brothers and sisters already abandoned me in my mind. Grace and Jen wouldn't play with me and Levi slept all the time.

Caleb started to do the same in the past six months. His new friend Dawson Jensen had been stealing him from me. And he was mean. Anytime I would try to join in their games, I got yelled at and they threw rocks at me. Before he met Dawson, Caleb had never cared that I was a girl. I *hated* Dawson.

But this Kelly girl was Caleb's friend and she didn't seem mean.

"Is he here now?" I asked looking around.

"No. He had to go. He's got a story to read right now."

"A story."

"It's kind of a long one. He won't be able to come back again. But he wanted me to help you."

"Help me?"

"That's what he said. He didn't know why, but he said I had to look out for you since he couldn't anymore."

"He was my twin."

"Did you have a secret language?"

"No." I hung my head in shame. We should've created one. "He knew what I was thinking all the time though."

"That's cool. I don't have any brothers or sisters."

"Oh."

"Would you be my sister?" Kelly asked.

I had friends, but only at school, not anyone outside of school. I didn't want anyone to know about my family.

"I don't know."

"It's just Caleb and I were really good friends. And now I've lost him. I didn't have many friends and you're his twin."

"Maybe. Caleb and I liked to make forts and sleep in our family room. Would you like to sleep over?"

"Yes. We could watch *Cutting Edge*. Have you ever seen that movie?"

"Yeah, it was on *Disney* last month," I said, excited at the thought of returning to a place of make believe where my reality would make sense.

"My mom bought it for me. It's my favorite. I love ice skating."

"Me too. At least I think I would. I've only gone once."

"Maybe my mom would take us to *The Depot* when they put the rink in this winter. You can rent skates there."

My heart was racing at the thought that Kelly wanted to take me skating. No one had ever taken me anywhere.

Two days later Kelly spent the night. We stayed up all night watching movies and talking. It was my tenth birthday, but I didn't tell her. No one in the house remembered.

Shaking myself from the memory of Caleb, I looked at Kelly.

"I'm the worst sister ever."

"Why?"

"I forgot it was the third. I haven't even been thinking about Caleb at all."

"That's a good thing. You're not wallowing in the memory of Caleb. You're living your life and that's what you're supposed to be doing."

"I guess."

"You've stumped me. Why are you out here?"

"Okay, promise you won't laugh?" She nodded and a weird look crossed her face. "You remember when you shanked the ball and I ran over to the stands."

"You really don't have to remind me how you saved me. I know, I owe you for that one." She hated owing me.

"That's not what I'm talking about," I said, shaking my head. "Did you notice what happened after I set the ball?"

"Yeah, Mary killed the ball and we won."

"Did you see me?" I said emphatically, trying to get her to focus.

"Not after you set it. I was just so excited…"

I could tell by the look on her face she was catching on. "Didn't you fall on Oscar Jeffreys?"

"Not exactly. I was falling backwards and he caught me," I said, bringing my hands to my face.

"Nice way to slide into first."

She nudged me and had a slight smile on her face. I glared at her and she got serious.

"So what's so bad? I swear you get embarrassed so easily. You're in a sport, he's in sports. He understands these types of things happen when you sit in the front row."

"It was after, on my way home. He stopped me in the gym and asked if he could take me home so we could talk about Friday night."

"What?" She was shocked and I knew why. Mya, the beauty queen, all around wonderful person, was just down in Chicago at Northwestern.

"He wants me to go to the game, and then for pizza with everyone afterwards," I sighed. "But you know me. I can't shut out the voices in my head telling me I'm an idiot. Did you give him my number?"

"No. Why would you think that?"

"Who else would?"

"Not me but…Oh, I'm gonna…" she said. "Are you mad about it, because I'll kill him."

"Oscar?"

"Max! He stole my phone on the way home."

"The number isn't the issue. I think Oscar's just using me to check off one more person he's screwed."

"What do you know about him, really?"

"Him? I don't, but come on, Kel. I'm a skinny little white girl. Sharyn's right."

"So you have no love for my brothers?" Kelly picked in her attempt at an urban accent.

"You know I don't care about that."

"Then what? What about him screams, 'I hate white people.'"

"Nothing. But he's perfect."

"And…"

"I don't know. That's all."

"Why would he only be trying to sleep with you? He's not one of the guys I warned you about."

Kelly had told me about 'the Magnificent Seven'. They trolled the halls, brought girls home and ran trains on them. Kelly only knew of four of the guys since the group always replenished its numbers in the fall. The boys in my class would be the new recruits I'd have to look out for.

"Why else would he want me? The only thing I have going for me is my virgin status."

"Why are you selling yourself short? You're a great person. You deserve happiness, too, you know."

"Do I? Name one person in my family that has happiness, real happiness, not just the fly-by-night kind."

"That's no excuse," she scolded.

"I'm 15 and I look like I'm 10. There's not one part of my body that could appeal to him in any real way. Have you heard of any bets going around?"

"No! Isn't your birthday Sunday? You'll be 16 and I think he has a summer birthday, so really, you're only a year apart."

I shook my head at her for trying to make something seem obvious that wasn't.

"If you're really worried about it, don't go, on Friday. Stay locked up in your own little world forever. You've got Jordan."

I rolled my eyes at the thought.

“I just don’t want to fall into what’s laid out before me. I want something better. I want to make the right choices. I can’t see how this could possibly be one.”

“Let me play devil’s advocate. What if he really does like you and you pass on him. You’ll forever have his face in the back of your mind as a what if. I know you’re strong enough. If the situation isn’t going the way you want it to, you can stop.”

“Can I? Can I really stop in the heat of the moment? When has that ever happened in my life?”

“There’re different kinds of heat. If you would’ve stopped in the heat of the moment during the game, we wouldn’t have won. You would’ve paid attention and seen where the ball was going and called it dead. Instead you dove headfirst and made the right decision. You can do that here, too. It’s not like sluttiness is a genetic trait. I think it’s more nurture than nature and you’ve been able to repel your nurture pretty well.”

I decided I’d think about Kelly’s advice although I could hear Jordan in the back of my head. The first bell ending lunch went off as I got up, shook off some leaves and dead grass from my pants, and marched back down the hill toward school.

“Trust me you’ll make the right choice. Either way, I’ll be there to support you.”

Kelly left me with a hug and ran back to catch Max before his lunch break started.

As I walked to geometry, a thousand thoughts bombarded my brain. What was I going to do now? I played out a hundred scenarios, some funny, some sad, my face changing with each one. A mental pro-con constantly ticked in my head. The next two days were much the same. I was there physically, but mentally, I was somewhere else. I snapped out of it for practices, partly because I had to now that I was in charge. I had to make calls and move people around.

And partly because I knew Oscar would be coming through the door each day after his practice. Every time I heard the door open, my head would turn. When Oscar would come in, I'd see him then turn away, but I couldn't refocus until I looked again. He always smiled at me. Usually he would keep up the conversation he was in, but his eyes wouldn't leave mine until I blushed and turned away again.

When Sharyn came back Friday, her face was still quite swollen and a big piece of a gauze was taped to her chin. Most people would have made fun of someone in her situation, but the look of pure hate in her eyes kept everyone at bay.

On Friday we ended practice playing queen's court, a game in which teams of two or three challenge to become queen of the court. We rotated between teams hoping our team could stay in as long as possible. The losers ran laps based on the number of queen's points.

I was teamed with Kelly and Mary. Flanked in such good company, it should've been easy to dominate, but we were having problems from the start. By the second round we'd caught our stride and were finally racking up points. No one could stop us. Mary and Kelly had perfect passes, I'd set to one of them, then hear a loud slap of the ball spiking the floor and that was it, the match was over.

As happy as Coach was that we were doing so well, it meant the others were doing poorly. By the last play, we scored ten points in total. I looked at a sign on the wall that said fifteen laps equaled a mile. I had a feeling we'd pay for that sooner or later.

We shagged balls while the others ran and it wasn't long before a loud bang caught everyone off guard. About twenty players from the football team were coming through to get ready for the game. I saw Sharyn slow down and lower her head to hide her mangled face.

Oscar was listening to his iPod his eyes focused on the person's feet ahead of his. He looked up and saw me looking at him. He winked. I looked down at the ball in my hands and tried to focus so the knots in my stomach would release and I could breathe.

Suddenly that blanket was there again. Oscar put his hand on the small of my back and leaned in to talk to me. I could hear *Whoop that Trick* blaring from his ear buds, which were now around his neck. My mind instantly went to the movie and the explanation of the song. I focused on the lyrics, a form of poetry to me. These lyrics were about protecting what's yours even if you have to fight and possibly die for it. I wondered if Oscar thought about the words or just liked the beat. He was getting ready to go into battle on the field. Maybe he needed the motivation to protect the ball with all his might. Maybe he'd do the same for the girl he chose to be his. *Idiot*, I scolded myself.

I looked the other way and saw Sharyn glaring at me. When I turned back, Oscar whispered in my ear, "I can't wait until tonight. I really want to talk to you and find out who you are."

I felt his breath on my neck and my eyes fluttered. That was it, my cue tonight was going to end in disaster. Trusting him would be hard enough, but trusting myself as every nerve in my body was reacting to his touch at once, no way. I turned my head and his mouth was right next to mine. I took a step back so I could speak. "I can't go tonight."

His stood straight up and looked at me like he was a pouting child who'd just lost his dessert. "Why not?" It had to seem louder than it was.

I lowered my voice. "I don't think I can stay out that late." My words came out of my mouth like those of a stumbling fool. "And I don't have any money for pizza. Besides we have to be back here at the school at 8 a.m. We have a tournament."

I tried to come up with as many acceptable excuses as I could. Next thing you know I'd be telling him my grandpa was sick, I heard there would be a snowstorm and I had a shift at a soup kitchen.

"Look, if you don't want to go out for pizza, I understand. I just figured you'd feel more comfortable in a group."

His face showed that he was still a little put off. Clearly no one ever told him no before.

"It's not that I just know that the games go late," I said, still fumbling with the ball, almost dropping it twice.

Kelly shot me a death look, knowing full well my parents wouldn't notice if I didn't come home for a week. Truthfully, I hadn't seen my mom since volleyball started. Come to think of it, I wouldn't even start to worry unless we ran out of fresh groceries.

"Can you at least come to the game? I really want to see you in the stands," he pleaded like a child asking his parents for money as the ice cream man rolled down the street. I knew there was no way he could pick me out of the hundreds of people in the stands so I nodded yes.

"Good. Kelly, I expect you to get her there on time and take care of her."

I looked at her and back to him and wondered what their exchange was really about. I knew Kelly was my friend, but how many people really knew how good a friend she was?

"I won't be a party to this," Kelly said, snatching a ball off the floor.

"Yes, you will," he said, his eyes boring into her. "If you don't bring her, I'll play horrible and we'll lose and then you'll feel guilty all week."

"Really? You think if she doesn't show up, you'll lose," she scoffed. "And you think your performance's really going to make a difference in the game?"

"I'm the starting receiver. If I'm not focused, we'll lose and you know it."

"If that's your idea of a threat you need to work with something I actually care about," Kelly said, tossing a ball in the basket and picking up another.

"How 'bout Max?"

I saw Kelly draw in a breath as she squished a volleyball that appeared to be going flat.

"Does he care if we win or lose?" Oscar continued.

"Fine. I'll bring her to the game, but I'm bringing her right home after. She won't even talk to you."

He flashed that amazing smile at her and turned to me, his eyes sparkling from the win.

"I hope the other team's this easy to convince. I promise you, Kelly, I have only the noblest of intentions," he said, crossing his heart.

"There's a first time for everything," she called after him as he crossed to the locker room to suit up. Almost the whole team had been through by now. I shot Kelly a look, letting her know she'd have to explain herself later.

"Come on. Let's hit the showers so you can get to the game on time," Mary said.

"I've got to go home. I don't have any of my stuff here to shower with anyway."

I ran to the locker room to take off my shoes and kneepads and threw them in my bag along with my uniform for tomorrow's tournament. When I turned around to leave, I saw Sharyn was glaring at me.

"What the hell do you think you're doing, soft meat?" she said, slamming me up against my locker, causing my head to swim. "I told you to stay away from him." Her right index finger was an inch away from my face. "This is my year with him and no SnoBall-wish-she-was-black-lily-white-honky-cracker-whore is going to change that!"

I'd never had so many racial slurs hurled at me at once. My head hit the back of the locker again and pain shot from my neck to forehead.

"I didn't go after him. I don't have him. I don't even know why he's talkin' to me. But you need to back the hell off," I said, regaining my ground.

My body was shaking as I looked up to her five foot seven frame. She was short for our team, but I was considered the midget.

Cranking my neck up sent another shot of pain and I held the front of my head and at that exact moment Kelly stepped between us, her hands holding us apart.

"Sharyn, you're already on the short list for this team. Don't make me report this. You can't blame her for every man that doesn't choose your ugly ass." Kelly's face was nose-to-nose with Sharyn's. "Ellie, get home. I'll pick you up in thirty minutes," Kelly growled, her eyes never leaving Sharyn's. Sharyn's eyes were ablaze with anger. If looks could kill, I wouldn't have made it out the door.

I ran home trying to understand how I was to blame. I never encouraged this. I never went up to even say so much as 'hi'. I never even looked at him. Well, that he knew of at least. If Sharyn wouldn't have hurt herself, she had have been the one he rescued. She'd have run him over. I thought about it and realized no, she wouldn't. If he wanted to date her, he could have. They had been in the same high school for three years. Was I just the newest toy that he wanted to play with?

Chapter 4

I made it home in record time. More out of courtesy than necessity I yelled, "I gotta leave in a few minutes. There's a football game."

The TV blared and something was cooking. The smell stopped me in my tracks. That was odd. No one ever cooked at our house. Looking up the stairs, I saw *she who must be obeyed*, my sister Jennifer, the self-appointed enforcer of the house and procreator extraordinaire.

I took my shower quickly and pulled out everything in my closet. I don't know why. It's not like Oscar was even going to see me in the stands. I found some distressed jeans, a white t-shirt, and my Cougars Volleyball sweatshirt and then pulled my hair up into a ponytail. Not planning on missing an actual home-cooked meal, I went to the kitchen, only to find Jennifer crying over some spaghetti.

"Why are you here?" I questioned, knowing it had to be about a guy.

"Roger kicked me out. He said he doesn't want to be with a fat cow who can't even give him a son."

Roger, my sister's latest man to get her pregnant, had no memory of how big she was going to get. I saw my nieces and nephew. One niece was his daughter Taylor, the other two were from Jennifer's previous boyfriends, or at least we think they are.

"I had my ultrasound today. Another girl."

"Doesn't he know it's the man that determines the sex?" I tried to be supportive, but what did she expect. She'd have another unwanted child, and weren't there enough in this house alone?

"Thanks a lot, like I need that. That'd just make it worse if I told him that."

Her sobs were becoming more animated by the minute.

I got a plate of spaghetti.

"So, where's Mom and Dad?"

Slightly, under control, Jen said, "I don't know. Something about a company meeting out in Woodbury."

My dad worked for 3M and was on the upper end of middle management so he had to put in an appearance at functions. The doorbell rang and I took a huge bite to finish off my plate and put it in the sink.

"Where are you going?" my sister asked.

"Football game," I replied, thinking, *doesn't anyone listen when I talk.* "Kelly's taking me to take my mind off the tournament tomorrow."

That was partially true. I opened the door for Kelly who looked at me, and shook her head.

"You're in Levi's room now, right?"

"Yes?"

"Let's go. It's going to be a little cool out, but I think I can make this work."

"Isn't the game starting soon?" I asked not wanting to change.

"We've got 20 minutes. I think we can take care of you in plenty of time."

In my room, Kelly found a fitted white t-shirt, which showed my stomach if I moved at all. That's why it was in the bottom of the drawer. Then she found a sweater that really was just a cover up, navy with a loosely knit flower pattern so my baby tee would be seen.

"I know it's painful, but please dress like a girl."

She pulled out my ponytail holder along with some hair.

"Ouch."

"Sorry."

"Are not."

"You're right."

I changed my outfit, as she started to brush out my lifeless hair. She took two barrettes off of my dresser and pulled just a little of my hair back behind my ears, securing it with the barrettes. She then dug out some eyeliner, lip-gloss and eye shadow she'd picked up at Walgreens on the way here.

"War paint," I grumbled. "I thought you gave up on that fight."

"I have a new weapon now," she replied, as she flicked her finger, telling me to drop my eyelid or prepare for an eyeshadowed eyeball. "He's tall, dark, handsome…" She giggled.

After five minutes, she said. "There, now you look like a girl."

I turned to the mirror and was shocked. She was right.

"Why do I need to look like a girl?" I asked. "I thought I was going to stay away. Remember, *she won't even talk to you*," I said holding up air quotes. As much as I thought about Oscar the whole week, I was glad Kelly made that condition. I wasn't sure I'd be able to control myself if I was by him in any setting. His eyes and his smile invaded every thought I had. I needed this night to be done with, so he would pass over me. Everything about him made me want to stray from my plan for my life.

"You are, but he can see you from the field, and I found out from Max Oscar's been asking a lot about you since last Tuesday."

Asking about me? Those questions had to be recon for the points Jordan had been talking about. I'm sure that Oscar had been asking about a lot of girls.

"Max and Oscar hung out a few times before, but they'd never talked about any girl. Not even Mya. I guess you made quite an impression on him."

Bewildered, I snagged my keys and we headed to the game.

"Look. Normally, I'd be telling you to run the other way," Kelly said, "but something about the way Max was talking makes me think he really likes you."

A long line was already forming in general admission. Luckily, I had an all-season all-game pass for the year. I really liked basketball and I didn't know if I'd make the varsity volleyball team at the time. We crossed over to the season pass line and got right in. Kelly was leading me to a place I assumed was good for viewing us at the stadium. It was down low, and I realized a few people held this place for her because of Max.

I now realized why Oscar asked her to take me. I saw him scanning the crowd, looking everywhere, then to Kelly's spot. She waved and pointed. A smile spread across his face melted me, and I sat down as I meekly waved too.

A few minutes later a group of girls sat behind us.

"OMG! You were so right," a girl said.

"I told you. He's so f-i-n-e," her friend replied, "Oscar's one, fine black specimen."

My fists clenched. I kept my face forward, trying to appear interested in pregame warm-ups, but my ears were tuning out everything, except their conversation.

"Six seven, two hundred and sixty pounds of pure male. You know what I could do with that?"

"Nothin', 'cuz he's gonna be mine."

"Uh huh. Mya just broke him in last year. I'm gonna train him right."

"You wouldn't know what to do with him. I, on the other hand, would lick him from…"

"Ellie, are you cold?" Kelly asked, shaking me from the conversation behind me.

"No," I replied quickly, so I could get back to ear husslin' on these girls. I turned my head to make it seem as if I was looking at the crow's nest where the announcer was, but really I felt a need to look at them.

Okay, I will never understand why anyone would ever wear high heels to a sporting event? They had to be freezing in their tight ass outfits. I was just jealous. They seemed much more his type. Beautiful and perfect.

"….that'd crush you," the first girl said.

"That's why he'd be on his back. I'd ride him like the stallion he is."

The game started with Oscar running back a touchdown from the kickoff. I guess I did need to be here for him. After he scored he looked right at me and pointed the football. I smiled, embarrassed, as I noticed people were looking at me.

I heard the girls behind me get up to leave. I turned just in time for them to give me a *whatever* look, followed by a scowl.

The rest of the game was more evenly matched. I hated seeing him get tackled, even though he popped right back up. I could just make out his face behind his facemask. It was stern and focused. I also couldn't help looking at the way his pants hugged his body. It sent shivers down my spine, as I imagined running my hands from his chest around his hips and down, resting at the top of his…

"I don't know what you were just thinking about," Kelly said, "but your mouth looks like it's about to bite into something delicious."

"I need a pop. Do you want anything?"

"No, I'm fine. Can you make it there and back without having any more nasty thoughts?"

I rolled my eyes. "Maybe, maybe not. If I don't come back for awhile, don't send a search party!"

I walked up the stadium steps and over to the concession stand. I ordered a Sprite and laid my head against the concrete wall to cool off. The idea of touching Oscar was still foremost in my mind. I tried to block it out, but it seemed it just stayed there taunting me. I figured I'd better get back to my seat just in case Kelly actually did send a search party for me.

Walking down the steps, I heard someone yelling at me, "Chisholm, Chisholm."

I turned my head just in time to get the last of a cup of pop dropped on my head. Sharyn was looking at me. "I'm sure you like having something brown all over you."

I had almost made it to Kelly, and she reacted instantly to my scream from the ice cubes going down the back of my shirt.

"Okay, now you've gone too far."

Kelly was by my side, shoving Sharyn down on the stadium stairs.

"Are you okay?"

"Yeah, just a little wet." Luckily, I picked up some napkins at the concession stand and patted myself down. Kelly was holding her hand out and it was as if this small gesture was enough to hold Sharyn down.

"I wonder why he doesn't want you?" I scowled at Sharyn, keeping the rest of my opinions to myself, I turned on my heels to go back down to our seats to see Oscar one more time before I left. It was the fourth quarter. The game was tied up 7-7. Our defense was holding. I now felt happy that I'd showed up to give him that extra boost of luck at the beginning of the game. Why was I even thinking about that? I wasn't a lucky charm. He'd probably used that line a hundred times.

I turned towards the sidelines and Oscar was looking at me confused. I guess I appeared bad with sticky, stringy hair, the little bit of makeup I'd been wearing is probably smudged. How much had he seen? He smiled at me. I waved, smiled and pointed to the exit, letting him know I needed to go. He shook his head no and held his hands up praying I'd stay.

Suddenly, my attention moved from him to the game. There was a fumble on the field. Max recovered the ball. Kelly was yelling and jumping up and down. When I looked at the sidelines again, he was gone.

Oscar was back in formation. We only had 1:25 left and were on our forty-yard line. The first down burned twenty seconds off the clock; the running back had only gained two yards. Lining up again, the running back made it to another first down, but burned another forty-five seconds. Fifteen seconds remained. Oscar was lined up on their thirty-three. The center hiked the ball, the quarterback fell back, scanned the field, then released the ball just as the other team hit him. The ball flew through the air dark night air. Oscar had defenders closing in on either side. He jumped, caught the ball and landing just inside the end zone. The defenders had him sandwich between them, but Oscar kept the ball tucked. The time clock expired with a loud blare. His body had been so fluid in the air. He pointed the football to me again, as Kelly and I jumped up and down and cheered.

Kelly clutched my arm and started running. I had no idea where we were going, but she seemed to know all the back ways around the stadium. We came out by a tunnel I never knew existed. I heard what sounded like thunder, and I realized the players were coming through the tunnel, cheering wildly. Max picked Kelly up and was spinning her around as they kissed.

Suddenly, I felt the blanket surround me.

"See, aren't you glad you came?"

His hand was on my back again. I forgot I was sticky as he turned me around. His left hand holding his helmet, his right hand pulling me closer.

"What's all over you?" he asks laughing at me.

I lightly licked my lips and said, "I think it's Coke."

"Any particular reason you chose to shower in Coke instead of water?"

"It wasn't my idea. I guess the girl you're dating sees me as a problem."

I could see anger building behind his eyes.

"Sharyn!"

"Yes."

Maybe he was supposed to be hers this year. Had he promised her that he'd be dating her? Was this really her year?

"I'm so tired of that bitch!"

The words caught me off guard. I'd never heard of him swearing.

"I'll take care of her. She just can't get a clue."

"Um, so, what does that mean?" We're not together," I stated blatantly, as I stepped back from his grip, fighting myself as much as I was fighting him.

"Not yet, but eventually I'll win you over."

He pulled my body closer and I could smell him. His sweat was intoxicating. Usually, I can't stand the smell of sweat on boys, but his was drawing me in. Maybe it was the mixture of his sweat and the polyester smell of this jersey, but something was blocking my ability to fight.

I could feel every one of his abdominal muscles pressing up against my chest and face.

"But right now I need you to get in the shower, because you're sticky and I need to get you home. I refuse to get you in trouble." Smiling at me, I could see he was thinking about something. "Just a minute. You said it was Coke around your lips, because I love the sweet taste of Coke." I tried to pull away, but he pulled me even tighter. So I turned my head down. "It's okay," he whispered in my ear as his breath fell upon my neck. "I'd rather kiss you on your terms."

He let me go and I looked over at Kelly, still in Max's arms, talking to each other.

"Max, let's get going so we can meet up at Pizza Luce's," Oscar yelled.

Max dropped Kelly to the ground, her face flushed from the embrace.

"Come on, Coke head, let's get you home." When we reached her car, she couldn't hold it in anymore. "What was that?"

"What?"

"Are you dating him?"

"No. Definitely….no. I don't know what I'm doing," I said truthfully.

My head was spinning as I was fighting myself to decide if I should just let the cards fall where they may or use my better judgment and push away. I climbed in her car and put on my seatbelt. "He said I'll be dating him soon. His arrogance's really infuriating. I guess he's really mad at Sharyn."

"You told him about that?"

"I didn't want to, but he asked and I guess she's been pissing him off lately. I do something wrong?"

"No. It wouldn't matter what you did. She's never going to leave you alone." The last of the crowd finally crossed the street and Kelly pealed out, whipping me around in the car. "Sorry, I just need to get back to pick up Max. You want me to give Oscar a hug and kiss for you?"

"No, thanks. Maybe I'll get up the nerve to do that myself."

Why'd I say that? I'm not going to kiss or hug him ever!

"So you want to go tonight?"

We were at my house.

"No, I need get in the shower and go to bed. You should do the same. We have to be at the school at eight a.m., remember," I said, scolding her like a mother.

Kelly just rolled her eyes at me.

"I'll be good, Mom. And I'll try to find out what Oscar's thinking. Don't worry, I won't let him hurt you."

I had to shampoo three times to wash the pop out of my hair. When I crawled into my bed, I tripped over my niece Adriana. I guess my sister's spending the night. Adriana let out a yelp, but fell back to sleep. I set my alarm for 6:30. Curling up with a teddy bear and wrapping myself in my blanket, I could still feel his hand on my back. A crack in my window allowed the last of the warm summer air to slip into my room, letting me dream of him breathing on my neck while holding me close.

Chapter 5

It was already 7:15, I had been fighting waking up for awhile, falling back into my dreams of Oscar. I rushed around my room, avoiding the small child on my floor, putting my uniform on, throwing on my warm up suit and my street shoes. Upstairs, I was dug around for something to eat. Finally finding a banana and a granola bar, I threw them in my bag with my water bottle.

I ran to the school and got to the bus with five minutes to spare. Kelly was sitting in the middle, she motioned for me to sit in front of her. I threw my bag against the bus wall as I sat down. Kelly looked tired, but not exhausted.

"Did you sleep at all?" I asked.

"I don't sleep, you know that."

"How are you going to play today?" I scolded.

"With an inhuman strength reserved for Goddesses, such as myself," she replied, with her hand on her chest. "Meer mortals, such as yourself with quake in fear."

I rolled my eyes and laid my head against the back of the seat.

"So, you'll never guess what happened last night," Kelly said, whispering to keep people out of our business. "Oscar spent the whole night cross-examining me, about you."

"What was he asking?" I asked nervously. What had she told him?

"Nothing really. He wanted to know what you liked, who you'd dated, when was your lunch…he just wanted to know how to win you over. I've never seen him so intense."

Coach started to count us off and the engine roared to life.

"So what you're saying is he likes me?" The thought thrilled and petrified me all in the same instant.

"What I'm saying is he wants to, but he just wants to get to know who you are. I think he was just a trophy for Mya. He acted like he'd never really had a girlfriend. Just girls that wanted him on their arm." Kelly leaned over the seat, resting her arms on top. "The fact you've been so hesitant with him has been driving him crazy."

"It's only been a week!"

"Not for him. Why do you think that he was at the game? He's been watching you since we were doing two-a-days. He'd stopped in because Sharyn had been calling him and he didn't know who she was." She looked over at Sharyn and let out a quiet laugh. "She'd been picking on you again, so who knows what day it was."

Although it had gotten worse lately, Sharyn has been mad at me since she first saw me.

"Anyway," Kelly continued, "you ignored her and kept playing, then I guess you did some amazing move, and he's been obsessed with finding out more about you."

Two-a-days were the first two weeks of practice. That was the middle of August, when we used to have to do conditioning in the morning and skills in the afternoon. I remembered the football players coming in from the their two-a-days, but it was August and we were sweaty and tired all the time. During that time someone thought I was appealing? I actually did an amazing move!

"Really, you can't see how wonderful you are," Kelly said rolling her eyes. The confusion must have shown all over my face, but what'd she expect? I've never felt worthy. It was one thing to be told you're nothing. It's another to be told nothing.

No "I love you", "good job" or "you look nice in that". I'd felt empty my whole life and to suddenly have someone care what I liked, what I felt, out who I am. I didn't even know who I was. I couldn't see past my own pain of rejection. I put on my headphones as Pink preached to me so I'd never be one of the *Stupid Girls*, as I tried to get all the thoughts of Oscar and this weird idea someone was interested in me out of my head.

A half hour later we arrived in Bloomington for our tournament. We realized we had a bye in the first round, so we had plenty of time to warm up. I'd eaten my banana and cereal bar, but after stretching and a few rounds of pepper, I realized my water bottle was empty.

The hallway was a ghost town, maybe everyone was watching one of the first three games. The water fountain was at the end of the hall, as I started to fill up my bottle, it came over me again. The feeling of security.

He came to my game! His hand was on the small of my back. I froze, except for my head, which tilted slightly back in the direction of his body. The bottle overflowed and water splashed on my shoes, causing me to jump back, spilling a little bit more, but this time on his shorts. I put the top on immediately and laughed nervously.

"Sorry about that. At least it's lower so you won't have to explain it."

I slowly looked up from his thigh to his hips, gliding over his chest and finally to his face, perfect with the sunlight streaming through the narrow window down the hall. He was smiling again, mischief in his eyes. Suddenly, I was against the wall. He caught my free wrist and held it over my head. He bent down to look me in the eyes.

"I need you to let me give you something. Please don't object, but I think you need a good luck kiss. I'm sure you will perform perfectly if I give this to you. Are you willing to let me test my theory?"

My heart was pounding my lips ached for his touch. They tingled, as I hoped for a long, strong kiss. I nodded slightly, closed my eyes and tilted my head up. His free hand gently stroked back a stray hair from my face, then he cupped my head. His thumb stroked my cheekbone. I felt him lean down slowly, my lips burned. I could feel his breath, as he brought his lips closer to my mine.

Instead I felt a soft peck on my forehead. I opened my eyes, crossing them to see him lightly kissing my forehead. I turned my head slightly and as the words were coming out, I tried to pull them back. "What the hell was that?"

He laughed and shook his head, releasing my arm. My lips sore from the rush of hormones that filled them and were now also pulsing through my body.

"Are you ready for that? I thought you'd want a more stupendous moment, the perfect time, something to tell our grandchildren about."

"So now we're getting married and having kids?"

"I don't know, but I'd hate to take a chance. What if I kiss you for the first time like you were just some girl, then down the line that's what we'd have to tell our grandchildren about? Do you not see how your actions can have catastrophic repercussions for generations to come?"

"Well, I'd hate to disappoint our future offspring, so I guess I'll have to wait."

"Oh, now you want to kiss me. I see how you are. If this is the way our relationship's going to go, it'll be hard for me to keep up with you."

"Now we're in a relationship?"

His massive hand swallowed mine with softness and led me back towards the gym.

"Look, we can keep going on like this and waste a month or two dancing around what we know will eventually be, or you can just admit you want me to be your boyfriend and we can get started with our life together."

Our life together?

"So, because no other girl has told you 'no,' you assume that I'd be the same," I said, frustrated he was right.

"No, you're not like any other girl. But," he said, grabbing me around the waist, "eventually, my winning personality will wear you down."

It wasn't his personality that was wearing me down right now. It was the instant connection I felt with him. His hands were strong, but gentle with just the lightest touch. His arms made me feel secure, like I was in a cocoon and no one could touch us. His touch created a world I could've only imagined for myself, but never envisioned could be. So maybe Kelly was right. I could take a chance and let him be my boyfriend, waste a few weeks, until he got bored, and then never have the regret of saying no to him. But this had be on my terms, not his. I was going to control the relationship!

"Fine. I'll admit I want you to be my boyfriend, if you give me a kiss worth remembering." If nothing else, I needed to release the pressure still pulsing in my lips if I was ever to focus on the game ahead.

"Lil' Girl, you're going to drive me crazy, I can see that now," he said, shaking his head at me. "I don't want to kiss you when you're under duress like this."

I was going to drive him crazy? He just said he wanted me to admit I wanted to date him. Now he…Ugh…He was twisting…AHHHHH. I didn't know what I wanted. But wait, lil' girl? Oh no! That wasn't going to fly with me. I hated being treated like a child.

"Did you just call me little…"

He took my head in his hands, as I felt his lips brush mine. I closed my eyes as his hands slipped down my back and he held me close, lifting me off the ground. My arms were around his neck and I felt his tongue slightly parting my lips as I let it enter feeling his velveteen tongue caress mine. I wished the kiss could last forever, but within a few seconds he slowly put me on the ground again. My hands slowly glided down his biceps, stopping to feel the strength behind them. I finally opened my eyes to see him smiling at me.

"Now that, we can tell our grandkids about. Good luck, I'll be cheering for you," he said, releasing me, and turning towards the gym doors as if nothing had just happened.

It took me a minute to catch my breath. "What the…" Ugh, he took control. I hated that, but I loved the kiss. As frustrated as I was with him, I just wanted him to hold me and never let go.

He turned back around and walked towards me. Bringing his delicious lips within a breath of mine, our eyes locked as he whispered sweetly, "you said you wanted me to give you a kiss worth remembering. Tell me truthfully. Will you ever forget that?"

A smile rolled across his face. I used all the strength I had left to not smile.

"I was just trying to do what you wanted," he said. "What can I say? You have me wrapped around your little finger."

I had him what? My mind raced. I asked him? Well, technically I did, but…He had a way of taking control while he tried to throw everything back on me. Maybe I could get him to leave so I could sort this out. I didn't know if I could deal with him all day long.

"You know, we may be here all day. I don't think the championship game starts till five," I said, in an attempt once again to control the situation I put myself in.

"I have nothing else to do and no place I'd rather be," he said.

Damn! I lost again.

The back of his fingers grazed my cheek as he smiled. "It's pretty damn sexy to have a girl who believes in herself enough to know she'll be in the championship."

His right hand slid down my neck causing gooseflesh to rise. As it traveled down my shoulder and he took my hand in his as we walked into the gym. A few feet into the gym his hand started to release mine as he found Max in the stands. Not wanting to let go of his hand, I dragged my pinky finger, locking it onto his. Leaning over, he whispered, "I'll be here all day." His lips brushed against my cheek, causing a shiver down my spine. He let go of my finger and headed over to Max.

I went to my team, focused my eyes on Kelly, snatched a ball and said, "let's play some pepper, *now* please." Pepper would calm me down. Pepper was a great game, just pass, set, spike, dig, repeat. No thinking, repetitive action that I could do in my sleep. I needed to do that or ten minutes of hitting a ball as hard as I could against a wall. My whole body was reliving the kiss. I ached to continue what I'd started in the hallway. Wait, I started that! *What am I doing?*

"I may not be as strong as you think I am," I said, as I set up a ball for Kelly.

"Why's that?" She replied, as she slammed the ball down.

I dug for the ball, almost hitting the floor.

"I asked him to kiss me."

She caught the ball one handed and walked over to me. "You did what?"

I could feel myself blush as I explained how he started it, I asked to finish it, but somehow he still finished, and I was completely confused because I think he was my boyfriend now. She hugged me and told me how happy she was for me.

"I know he'll be wonderful for you and you deserve this," she said.

We looked around the corner and saw the game was just ending on the far court and we needed to get going to prepare for our game.

"Are you going to be able to focus?" Kelly asked, as I was still slightly shaking.

In the stands I saw Max and Oscar in a seemingly deep conversation. Suddenly, they noticed Kelly and I were watching at them. Max winked at Kelly and she blew him a kiss. Oscar smiled, making me melt again.

"I don't know, but if I don't, I may not get kissed anymore," I giggled.

Kelly slapped me on my back.

"What?" I said, holding up my hands as if I was innocent.

"Let's get some serves in," Kelly said, nudging me.

The other teams' games were over. I guess I was still wound up, because I hit the back line. Coach looked at me and I just shrugged.

The games were a blur, but we kept winning. I had my best games ever. I had great serves and my sets were all on target. Around lunchtime, we had a two-game break. I realized I forgot to pack a lunch. I dug around in my bag, hoping to find a few dollars, when I felt something behind me. A hand slid down my right arm and held it tight, spinning me around.

"What's for lunch?" Oscar asked.

"I forgot to pack my lunch this morning. For some reason, I wanted to stay in bed instead."

I turned back to my bag, realizing I'd almost admitted Oscar had been in my dreams all night.

"Just let me find some money. I know I have to have something."

"Come on."

He picked me up by my waist and carried me out of the gym, setting me down once we were outside.

"Tell the truth. You didn't think you'd be here this long, did you?"

"I hadn't really thought about it," I said, adjusting my shirt and righting myself since I had just been turned into a carry-on bag. "I guess I have to chalk it up to being a dumb sophomore."

At the mention of our age difference, I felt a chill through my body. Stupid! Stupid! Stupid!

"You know, having someone around that doesn't know everything is refreshing. Come on, Lil' Girl let's get you some food so you can finish what you've started."

By his inflection, I didn't know if he meant volleyball or the kiss.

At the concession stand Oscar bought me a slice of pizza and a granola bar. We were straddling a bench. I ate slowly so the food wouldn't cause me problems in the next game.

"I'll give you credit. I don't think I could play this many games in a day." A smile crossed his face. "And then you have to still be awake enough to go out with me tonight."

"We're going out tonight?"

"If you're not too tired. Or if you didn't already have a hot date?"

Not likely, I said to myself.

"I suppose I could blow the game so I wouldn't be as tired," I joked.

"But you wouldn't, because you're just like me, too competitive for your own good."

He turned his head and yelled. "Hey Max, you and Kelly want to go out tonight? I thought we'd head down to the mini golf in Como Park tonight."

"Sounds fun," Max yelled back. "Now can I get back to my lunch?" I doubted lunch was what Max really wanted to get back to. He and Kelly had been locked in a lot of lip action since they sat down.

"Whatever man." Oscar turned back to me. "You know this could turn into a death match. I have a feeling you're not going to go down without a fight."

I just grinned.

“Well, that explains why you picked something physical after I spent the whole day exerting myself. How often do you cheat?”

“Hey. I’m being a cheerleader and that’s not an easy job. I don’t know if you noticed, but we’re getting a little bit crazy out there.”

I had noticed they were being loud and obnoxious. It had been hard for me not to laugh.

“You’re doing a great job at that. I was thinking I should talk to some of the cheerleaders and see if we could get you two a pair of skirts,” I said as I reached my right hand across to his. He flipped my hand over and started to trace the lines of my palm. I scooted closer to him so we were just inches away from each other. I could feel the heat of his breath as he slowly brought my hand to his lips and kissed my palm.

A loud noise startled me. A volleyball ricocheted hard off the back wall and was coming straight for me. Oscar instinctively pulled me into his chest, turning my head away from the ball. I felt the ball hit the back of his left arm and it bounced to the floor.

I felt safe curled up like a little girl in this massive chest. His arms wrapped around me, holding me tight. I never wanted him to let go. But suddenly he was gone. I looked over and saw him making a beeline straight to Sharyn.

“Oscar, stop, it’s okay.” I said jumping up and running to stop him from getting in trouble.

“I’ve had just about enough of you.”

Sharyn's face looked shocked and scared. No one had challenged what she'd been doing to me this year. She was good at doing it behind Coach Marks' back. I tried in vain to pull Oscar back by his arm.

"Look here, Bitch, I'm tired of your pathetic attempts to attack Ellie. You drunk, nasty slut!"

He shook me off his arm, bringing his finger an inch from her face. I could barely hear what he said, but it seemed like everyone else had.

"I fell asleep and woke up with you trying to strip my pants off. I never wanted you to touch me, you walking diseased whore."

Through gritted teeth, he laid out his final warning, "You'll leave Ellie alone from now on or I'll make your life a living hell."

The whole team seemed to be watching. Sharyn couldn't go off with her normal barrage of white girl comments to me.

Oscar turned, surprised I was an inch from him as he almost plowed me over.

"I'm sorry you had to see that. I can't stand pathetic, little people. I like you and I'm allowed to do that. Let's go finish your lunch so you can warm up."

I wasn't about to point out I'd finished it as he wove his hand in mine and walked me back to our bench.

Sitting back on the bench he seemed so upset, it made me nervous. I reached a hand up to his face, standing up so I could be face-to-face with him. My nose was touching his as I whispered. "Thank you." I lightly kissed his lips and he started to relax. Sitting down, I turned around so my back was against his chest, my hand moving to his thigh. Laying my head against him, he raised an arm to wrap around my waist and I felt safe again.

"You know what I need?" he asked.

The endless possibilities ran through my head. "No."

"I need you to win this tournament."

"Oh, is that all?"

"No. Then I need you to go home and take a shower..."

"So now I smell?"

"Well, a little," he teased, "but that isn't what I meant. I just want to have you help me put Max and Kelly in their place, then let me take you out so we can be alone."

"I'm not ready for that."

I sat up, afraid I'd lost him.

"First, you physically assault me in the hallway, now you're talkin' about takin' my innocence. I'm not talking about sex."

He pulled me back to his chest.

"You have a one-track mind, don't you? I just want to talk to you. I want to know who you are, I want you to know who I am." He tickled me a on the ribs and said, "I can only date you for so long based on your body!"

Coach came around the corner and told the team it was time to get warmed up. I got my water bottle gently tugged on Oscar's hand. He got the hint and followed me.

"Is there something I can do for you, Lil' Girl, because I really need to get my pom-poms and pull on my skirt."

I refilled my bottle, capped it and turned around.

"Yes, I think my luck has worn off. I could really use a boost."

I smiled more than I had in a long time. I didn't need to ask twice. He grabbed me, lifting me up. I put my arms around him and let him kiss me.

He did want me to win. Walking forward he pinned me against the wall. After what seemed like forever, he set me down, then pecked me on the forehead.

"I wasn't sure which one was the lucky one," he winked and walked back into the gym. It didn't matter if we won as a team, I felt I'd already won him. Maybe my luck was finally changing.

Chapter 6

The ride home was full of cheering. We were riding high on our domination of the court. The year was looking as if it would be a good one. And we got *hardware*. In addition to a trophy, we got medals. Kelly and I decided we should wear them on our date tonight. Maybe Oscar was right. I was too competitive.

Kelly gave me a ride home, when we pulled up, we saw Jordan in his driveway working on his bike. I suddenly felt a pit in the bottom of my stomach. I felt my cheeks cool and Kelly stroked my hand.

"It's going to be okay. He's your friend and he will be happy for you, I promise."

I realized Kelly had no idea how much Jordan tormented me this week. He played off his hatred wasn't because of Oscar, as a person, it was because he was a senior and they're all the same. Jordan tried passing it off he was just 'looking out for me'.

I got out of the car, as Kelly yelled, "thirty minutes or we'll never get there in time."

"Hey did you win?" Jordan yelled, crossing over to my yard.

"Yeah, check out the hardware." I pulled the medal around my neck out of my warm up jacket.

"Too cool. What do you have to be ready for in thirty minutes?"

"Um, we're going to go mini golfing at Como for a celebratory game," I said, trying to get to my door and avoid the conversation.

"The whole team? Aren't you tired? You've been gone all day."

"Adrenaline high."

"Who's going, Ellie?"

"Um, Kelly and a few other people."

"Like who, Max and Oscar?"

"Maybe." I couldn't get my keys out fast enough.

"So now Kelly's helping Oscar score points. Isn't that great? Have you never heard of hazing? Just because Sharyn's more blatant about it, doesn't mean Kelly's not doing it also." He grabbed my right arm forcefully. "Don't go. Trust me, you won't like what happens tonight."

Anger surged through my body as I jerked my arm away.

"Kelly's been my friend for almost six years now. You don't know her. She'd never do anything to hurt me."

"Fine, come back a whore like the rest of your sisters," he said, storming off to his house.

The high of the win and the kisses were now gone. My arm ached from where Jordan's hand had been. A red mark would soon be a bruise. He was really mad at me. I wanted to apologize, but I didn't know what I'd done wrong.

After showering, I dried off and looked at my body in the mirror. I thought about what Oscar had said, '*I can only date you so long based on your body.*' Could he really find me attractive?

The spot on my arm was now a fire red. I was tempted to wear something short-sleeved just to get Jordan in trouble for touching me, but I knew I needed to wear something other than a t-shirt and jeans.

In my room, I pulled on some underwear, a non-sports bra and my best pair of jeans. They were tight in the right areas, at least that's what Kelly told me once. I opened my closet and hoped my fairy godmother had magically put something good in there. I only dressed up on game days, and even that was just khakis and a sweater.

A text from Jordon arrived. *Sorry.*

Can't reply 2 busy bcomin ho.

A slight tap on my door preceded Kelly's normal phrase. "Are you decent?"

"Not really."

She looked at me in just a bra and jeans and said, "Well, that's one way to get across you want him!" Her look changed quickly.

"What's that?"

What's what? I couldn't think of any of my shirts would cause that reaction.

She caught my arm and suddenly I remembered the ache in my arm.

"Oh…Jordan was really mad. He was trying to stop me and he grabbed too hard. It got worse because I jerked my arm away." I sounded like a *Lifetime* movie, the abused woman trying to explain how it was all her fault.

"We have to hide this. Oscar will kill him."

Kelly started to pull apart my closet finding a long-sleeved linen tunic I didn't even know I owned in the back.

"Where'd that come from?" I asked as if Kelly would know how clothes magically appeared in my closet.

She looked at me as if I was mad. "Narnia," she snipped, but wouldn't look at me.

I pulled it over my head, as Kelly started to dry my hair with a towel. She used a headband to pull my hair back from my face, but still allowing hair to flow down my back. I'd considered cutting it, but Oscar had been playing with it during lunch. Maybe I'll keep it. What was I doing, planning my life based on him? I've got to get my head on straight. Kelly draped my medal around my neck for a finishing touch.

"We've got to get going."

Kelly explained Max was riding with Oscar so Oscar could take me home, or I could still ride with her.

We parked and walked to the mini-golf. Max and Oscar were leaning up against the old brown railcar that served as the admissions booth. The railcar's windows all open. Inside, a bored-looking worker read a book.

The guys were tossing peanuts to the chipmunks, which must have lived underneath the railcar. Oscar dropped a peanut as a small, brown and white chipmunk came out, snatched it, and ducked back under the car, only to reemerge when Max repeated the action.

Kelly waved at Max and he nudged Oscar.

Oscar's head rose and I drank him in, knowing at least for right now, staring at him wouldn't embarrass me. As I looked at his brown eyes, broad nose and lips smiling at me, my lips couldn't help but curve upward and tingle in response. I instantly remembered the kiss from earlier that day. His pale peach polo complemented his beautiful smooth skin, which was exposed by two undone buttons. The bulge from his biceps stretched the short sleeves to the limit.

I don't know what we technically were. A couple, a date, two people who both showed up at the same place, but the thought he was my boyfriend, even if it was just for the day made my whole body warm.

"It's about time. We thought you chickened out again."

He must still be upset about me not coming out last night, I thought. *Stop it*, I told myself, *quit trying to read people you suck at it*.

"We had to shower, not just get out of some little skirts."

He smiled and extended a hand, which I happily took. He somehow held my hand tight, while drawing circles in my palm. My whole hand felt light.

Inside the railcar, we picked up our balls, putters and the ever important score cards.

Oscar's other hand gently touched one side of my neck. His fingers slid down the ribbon to my chest then held my medal.

"Really? You guys needed to wear these?"

Embarrassed, I took mine off and shoved it into a pocket.

"I was kidding you. You earned that. You should be proud of what you do." Then he whispered, "I'm just happy you're here with me."

His breath brushed against my neck. I could barely understand what he was saying. Something came over me. His lips were so close to mine. I turned my head and my hand slid onto his cheek. Our eyes met. His eyes were definitely going to be trouble for me.

My brain went into overdrive. When he looked at me, I felt beautiful. I wasn't sure what desire looked like, but right now, looking at Oscar, I had a feeling desire was staring directly at me. And I wanted to be the one to satisfy it. My biggest fear was Oscar could see the same thing staring back at him. I didn't know if I could stop him from returning the favor. Closing my eyes, I gently kissed his lips stopping him from straightening up.

"Getta' room," Max teased.

"Oh, leave them alone or you ain't kissin' me tell the next blue moon," Kelly said, pulling Max away.

"Woman, do you know how long away that is?" Max whined.

"When have I ever made an idle threat?"

At the first hole, I let everyone go ahead, not wanting to admit I'd only played mini-golf once. Oscar figured out I was no expert when I started to line up my putt. He slid in behind me and swallowed me with his massive size. He placed both hands over mine and whispered. "Nice and easy." He brought my arms back just a little bit and I tapped the ball. Luckily, the fairway was at a downward slope, so the ball landed just a few inches from the hole.

"That's it. You don't need my help anymore. There's no way I'm going to let you win this one."

Trying to feign innocence and vulnerability, I reached for his hand and gave him the look I'd seen my sisters use a hundred times. "I don't know if I could do this without you." I realized I wasn't being myself, but what I thought he wanted. It disgusted me. I wasn't a pathetic helpless girl he could take care of. He looked at me with a weak smile, but his eyes looked disappointed, like I'd just crushed the idea he had of me.

At the next hole Oscar came to help me and I said. "No. I can do this. Don't worry about it." The words come out in a biting, upset way. I wasn't mad at him, but at myself. I wasn't helpless, I wasn't innocent, well I was, but I'd seen the game played out between my sisters enough to know the rules.

With each hole I stood farther and farther away from Oscar. Kelly and Max kept sharing silent worried looks between then. By the ninth hole, Kelly was at my side.

"What happened? I thought you liked him? You're being a completely rude bitch."

I didn't know how to tell her. I couldn't even get it straight in my head.

"What's going on?" Kelly asked.

"I can't explain it. I'm not mad at him, just myself."

My throat felt like I had acid running up it.

"You're going to have to figure something out. You're upsetting him."

She turned to face the boys. "Hey, why don't we call it? I don't really feel like playing the back nine anyway."

Relief washed over Oscar's face, like he'd been let out of a bad blind date after the first drink. I knew Kelly would be driving me home and there was no way to explain to him I hadn't meant to be a bitch. I did this all the time, beating myself up, but it always seemed to be taken the wrong way by others. My face betrayed me and made them think it was their fault. I reached my hand to touch his back, in an attempt to see if I'd really been that bad, but he shrugged it away. There was no way I could fix this. It was probably for the best. It could never end well anyway.

Kelly grabbed Max and ordered, "We're going. Oscar, you can take Ellie home, right?"

This was more of a statement than a request. I could see his eyes cut to her.

"Kelly, it's fine. I can go with you," I said, not wanting to be a burden on anyone especially him.

Kelly pulled me off to the side and snipped. "Fix this! He liked you. Not the fake you, but the real you."

She had a hand under my chin, so I couldn't look away.

"You haven't blown this yet, but *you* need to fix it. Even if you don't end up together, don't let him think this was you today."

She stormed off with Max, her hands flailing in frustration. If Max didn't hate me before, I'm sure her snapping about how stupid I was for the next hour should seal the deal.

I turned towards Oscar, but couldn't look him in the eyes. He motioned to where his car was downhill.

About half way there was a playground. I ran ahead and jumped on a swing. Oscar walked over, dragging his feet like they each weighed a ton. I rested my head against the chains, with my eyes staring at my shoes. Tears welled up and my throat felt like I had a bad case of strep. He wrapped his hands around mine on the swing chains and knelt down so we were face-to-face.

I looked up, warm tears were running down my cheeks. My stomach flipped and I had the worst case of verbal vomit in my life.

"I'm sorry, I didn't mean to be, I don't know, it's just I don't know what you want, but I want to be it."

My throat tightened and I was losing my breath, but I couldn't stop talking. As long as I was talking, he had to still be by me. "I only know what my sisters did, but I don't want to be like them. They disgust me and so I'm constantly fighting with myself to not be useless like them. I get mad at myself and everyone thinks I'm mad at them and really I just have these voices yelling at me in my head." The words came faster yet. "I'm not helpless, I'm strong, I make my own way, but I'm scared at the same time scared of being hurt.''

I finally breathed in just long enough to start another barrage of me telling Oscar things I hadn't even told Kelly.

Then his lips found mine. His hands moved up my neck and he ran his fingers through my hair. My lips parted slightly. His tongue touched my lips. I let go of the swing, putting my arms around him. He fell back and I was on top of him. My legs straddling his body and I could feel his stomach muscles tighten. Suddenly, I found my competitive streak again. His fingers tugged on my hair, as we fought for control over the kiss. I wanted to be the aggressor. I slowly licked his lips as he opened his mouth, our tongues touched, and my body pulsed with electricity.

He rolled me on my side and pulled away, but our foreheads were still touching. "This is why I wanted to talk to you. I don't know you well enough yet. All I know is I can't have you wet-eyeing me."

His hands were so soft as they wiped away my tears. He kissed my forehead and I sat up.

"I'm sorry I acted so stupidly. Really, it would probably be better if you left me alone. I'm crazy. The damn voice in my head is always telling me I'm doing something wrong or I need to stop."

I looked down at him, lying on his side, looking up at me. His eyes weren't judging me, but understanding and processing what I was saying.

"Look," I began, "I didn't have some crazy bad life. It's just ordinary, but for some reason, I always feel like someone's out to get me. Every time I get something good, either it leaves me or I chase it away, thinking it can't be true. I'm impulsive, but I try to pull back before I have any long-term regrets."

"What regrets are you worried about?"

"You make me … I can't … " *Whew*, what was I supposed to say? His every touch made me want another. Just one glance melted every muscle in my body. His scent after the game made me twitch in places I didn't know could twitch. Part of me felt animalistic when I was around him, wanting to grab, bite, claw, suck … okay not helping me figure out how to say …

"Well, you see...I'm afraid that I won't be able to stop myself and I'll sleep with you before I'm ready, and I don't know why I just said that."

I buried my face in my hands.

He slowly pulled my left hand away from my face. "So, I'm something good?"

I cut my eyes to him. Out of everything I said, he focuses on that, or maybe he was trying to be cute. Either way, when my eyes hit his, Oscar had a look of joy.

"I don't want you to do anything you'll regret. I didn't go out with you in an attempt to get some. If I wanted a quick piece of ass, I'd return Sharyn's call. Well maybe not her. Have you seen her face?"

I laughed and he continued to wipe my tears.

"Look, it's getting dark. Can we go somewhere to talk?"

He stood up holding his hand out to me. I grabbed it and he pulled me up with no effort. He wrapped his arm around my shoulders and kissed the top of my head.

The inside of his car was stuffy and the radio was turned down low. Oscar pulled me closer to him and I rested my head on his right shoulder. His hand was running through my hair, twisting a strand at the end.

"This is better. Ellie, you're beautiful,"

I scoffed and he covered my mouth with his finger.

"This isn't up for discussion. You're beautiful, strong and intelligent. You bring so much to the table. That makes you someone anyone would be lucky enough to love and be loved by you. I'm not saying I love you. I'm saying you're someone I could see myself loving. Every girl I've ever dated has been the same, weak and insecure. If I learned anything this summer it was that isn't what I want. I wasn't looking for anyone, but I saw you."

My mind raced. Mya was so strong, how could she ever be seen as weak?

"But what about Mya?"

"Mya? Mya, was a joke. She saw me as someone who'd make her look better. She was so insecure. She knew her beauty was only on the outside. If I wasn't worshiping at the altar of Mya, she'd punish me. I never loved her. Half the time I didn't even like her. I tolerated her because she filled time. I realized I wasted a year, but then again I didn't. She made me see everything I didn't like. Who I want in my life and who I don't."

He brought his other hand up and stroked my cheek.

"You're not what I thought you'd be," I admitted, a little ashamed of assuming.

"Is that a good thing or a bad thing?"

"Good. You know stereotypes."

"I'm the first black guy you've dated?"

"You're the first guy period. I didn't mean black stereotypes … "

"Wait…I'm the first guy you've dated? How's that possible?"

"You're funny."

"No, seriously. Guys have wanted to date you…"

"Nope. You're the only one. Were you dropped on your head as a baby?"

He laughed at that.

"Okay, then what stereotypes did you mean?"

"Male ones. All guys want something. Sex in some form. They don't listen to what I want. They just say what's expected to get what they want. But then again, maybe you're just saying what I want to hear and I'm falling for it."

"That's a theory, but I don't think you're weak-minded."

"I hope you're right."

"Look, I prefer being the exception as opposed to being the rule."

"I like that."

What I liked was thinking that I could be the exception. That Oscar could actually make me the exception in my family.

"So is that why you don't sag your jeans and keep the stupid stickers and tags on your hat, like the rest of the idiots at school?"

"I don't sag because it's uncomfortable and looks dumb. You know, I saw a guy in a wheelchair at Target with his belt around his thigh."

I had to laugh at that.

“And I don’t need people to see I have a brand-name hat or the size of my head. But let's look at the most important part…It proves you’ve been looking at me.”

“Nope, never saw you before Tuesday. Sorry to burst your bubble.”

“So it’s just since then you’ve been obsessed with me? That’s okay. I don’t mind that I’ve been in a one-sided relationship for a month now.”

“One-sided?”

“Me, looking at you, all the time.”

I felt my face get hot as fire and my eyes shot to the floor. I started to count the pebbles around the black floor mat, when something obscured my view. Oscar’s left index finger was under my chin and moved my head like it was on a dowel and weighed no more than a feather. Oscar’s face was perfect with the glow from the stereo illuminating his cheeks and lips. But his eyes were the best, deep brown with light dancing around the irises, circled by what had to be the softest lashes in the world.

“Now you need to tell me some more about you. What’s the problem with your sisters?”

“You’re doing it again.”

“Told you I was exceptional.”

If nothing else, he had no self-esteem issues.

We talked for two hours. It was like he broke down all my usual walls.

"I can't believe I told you that! What is it that makes me tell you everything?"

My face turned towards his. With the lightest touch, he pushed back a strand of my hair and tucked it behind my ear.

"You can trust me. I want to be your friend more than anything."

My hand was on his thigh, so I pushed myself up to kiss him. He slowly moved his hand down my neck, gliding over my chest and down to my hip. I could feel the warmth of his hand through my shirt.

His hand moved under my shirt, he brushed so lightly on my skin if it weren't for the heat of his body, I'd have thought I was imagining it. His lips moved slowly along my cheek then down my neck. With one brush of his lips against the crook of my neck I was alive. I could feel his tongue tracing circles, sending shivers down my spine. I returned the favor, kissing his neck. My hands slipped under his shirt then glided down his chest so I could feel his perfect abs. I found the notch at the bottom of his throat with my lips and I was hit by the cool, fresh smell of his cologne.

Now both of his hands were under my shirt. They slid up my back pulling me closer as my lips returned to his. He slowly released me and started to push me back to the passenger seat.

"Let's stop while I still can."

My face was flushed, my body aching to continued to be touched.

"I think I should get you home."

I fell against the back of the seat and closed my eyes, trying to calm myself. The engine roared to life and I could feel the car pulling away from the curb. My house was only a few minutes away. The clock on the radio said it was just after eleven. I could catch the end of Saturday Night Live. That should calm me down enough to sleep.

"Hey, what window's yours?" Oscar asked as we pulled up to my house.

I pointed to the back one on the lower level.

"Why?"

"Oh, just wondering. So Grace's is the front one?"

"Yeah, and my parent's room is over there," I said, pointing to the second level of the other side of the house. "Would you also like to know what year it was built and if we have stainless steel appliances?"

"Can I come over tomorrow? We could watch the game together. The Vikings are playing at noon."

I had nothing planned. It was just my birthday, nothing special. Spending the day with Oscar would be the best birthday present I'd gotten in years.

"Um, no, nothing special, just going to hang out and do some homework, as long as that won't distract you from the game."

"No. I'll see you at noon."

As I approached my door I realized he hadn't pulled off so I unlocked the door and went in waving as I entered.

The house was quiet I guess Jennifer was back with Roger. My stomach grumbled and I realized I really hadn't eaten all day. I made myself a sandwich and poured a glass of apple juice and I carried my feast down to my room.

Colbie Caillat was the musical guest on SNL. She sang *Fallin' for You.* I danced and thought about Oscar. The night couldn't have ended more perfect. I pulled off my jeans and shirt and dug through my drawers. *"I want you all around me ... I think I'm fallin' for you."* I sang along. I found a pair of shorts and a tank top. With only the light from the TV, I tossed my clothes into a hamper and removed my headband. I dug to find a ponytail holder that wouldn't irritate me during the night and I pulled my hair back.

Bouncing on the bed, I finally laid down and took a bite into my sandwich. Then there was a tap on my window.

Chapter 7

I reached up with one hand and slid my window open, not moving from my position on my bed.

"After what you did to me today, I don't know if I'll ever speak to you again. Look at these bruises!"

I thrust my right arm up in the air.

"If this screws up my game, I'm going to beat you like the redheaded stepchild you are." Like a little kid who wasn't going to give up their wubbie, I said. "And secondly, I don't care what you think about Oscar. He makes me happy and he's going to keep making me happy. I'm not going to allow anyone to screw this up for me, so until you've something positive to say about Oscar I…I don't want to talk to you."

With that, I slid the window closed.

There was another tap on my window. I slid it open again.

"Who the hell laid a hand on you?"

Oscar's voice was quiet, but angry. I sat straight up in my bed and turned slowly to see his face. I crossed my room to shut the door.

"I thought you were someone else," I said.

"That's obvious. How many people come to your window at 11:30 at night?"

"Usually no one, but since we were out so late I…I…I figured you were Jordan coming to apologize. I haven't been replying to his texts."

"Why did he hurt you?"

The monotone pace to his questions was more unnerving than anything.

"He thinks all seniors are alike, and I guess he's been getting picked on a lot."

My mind raced as I tried to remember how to remove the stupid screen from my window.

"No. He. Hasn't. I put the word out two weeks ago, he wasn't to be touched, because he's your friend."

"Look, let me figure out this screen and you can come in and we can talk."

"I don't know if I want to come in."

My fingers were shaking, making it harder to maneuver the screen out.

"I was just coming to tell you I forgot to give you something, but now I don't know if I will."

"What? I told you that Jordan was my friend, he lives two doors down, sometimes he comes down and we talk through the screen. He's never been in my room."

With a sigh, Oscar took off his shoes and slid his legs through the window. He stepped on my bed, then laid down. His legs hung off the end of my bed, so he pushed himself up so he was sitting against the wall.

I closed the window and he gently held my right arm.

"This looks like more than a bruise. Are you sure he didn't hurt you more?"

His fingertips were running up and down my arm. I could feel the hair on my arm raising.

Suddenly, I realized I was alone. In my room. With Oscar! He was on my bed.

"It's just a bruise. Look, Jordan has been riding me all week, saying I'm just a bet. Is there some game where sophomores are worth a hundred points?"

Part of me was still questioning Oscar's motives and part was trying to makeup an excuse. I needed him to let me know I was more than just a pawn in some game being played for his amusement.

"Stuff like that, he's just looking out for me."

"From now on, I'll be looking out for you," he informed me and grabbed my waist, pulling me on top of him. It's amazing what body heat can do to a person. I closed my eyes for a second and breathed in deep. My whole body relaxed.

“I only have a few minutes,” he said. “My curfew’s twelve, but I wanted to give you something. This will make it real, you know.”

He reached in his pocket and pulled out his class ring. “I assure you I’m not trying to score points off you.”

It was all the confirmation I needed.

I felt the weight of it as he placed it in my hand. It was silver with a beautiful pale green stone encircled by *St Paul High School*. I was rubbing a finger over it.

“I was born in August,” he said.

On one side, the ring was engraved with *2010* and a football, a basketball and a runner’s shoe. On the other side, it said *Oscar* with a strange symbol.

“It’s a Fleur De’ Lei. The symbol for Boy Scouts,” he informed me.

“You’re a Boy Scout?”

“Yeah, I’m finishing my Eagle. It’ll have it done by next month. There will be a big ceremony and everything.”

“You’re a Boy Scout?” I laughed at the thought of him walking old ladies across the street.

“Yes. Exception remember,” he sighed. “Look, my mother was very active in scouting. She got me through Cub Scouts and set me up with this troop. She died of cancer two months after I crossed over from Cub Scouts to Boy Scouts. A few days before she died, I was planning a camping trip, my first with the troop. I came in her hospital room in my uniform after a meeting. Pride filled her eyes as I told her everything we'd planned. She smiled at me, she was so excited about my plans. The only thing she wanted me to achieve is to become an Eagle Scout. She died a few days later. No one expected me to go camping. My dad handed me a letter from her before her funeral. It said *if I skipped the camping trip she'd understand, but let it be the last one you skipped because of me. Don't let the fact that my life has ended be a reason to end yours. Scouting will make you the man I see when I look in your eyes. Remember a Boy Scout's brave. You can mourn me, but I want you to live to become an eagle and fly high. I love you and will be with you eternally."*

His face was sullen and I thought I heard his voice crack.

"At her funeral there was over a hundred scouts in uniform to pay their respects. How could I turn my back on that kind of love and devotion? I attended the camp two weeks later. I just wished my dad had been more involved because if it wasn't for scouting, I don't know where I'd be now. He's still not gotten over her death."

I was playing with his ring I could almost fit two fingers in it.

"Now I'm telling you things I shouldn't be."

His hand wiped across his cheek and he stood up.

"I guess we're made for each other, but Lil' Girl I need to get going or I'll be grounded."

I looked over at the clock, it was 11:45. I started to pout.

He picked me up and said, "Well this has been a very emotional day. Can we try just having one easy one?"

"Probably not, but I warned you," I said as he kissed me gently and my arms wrapped around him.

"That you did, but something tells me you're worth it."

He squeezed through my window. When he got out he crouched down and kiss me one more time.

"Promise me something."

"I'll try, what is it?"

"First, keep your curtain closed when you're changing your clothes or I'll let you do something you'll regret."

Oh my God. He saw me changing, he saw my body, but wait, he didn't mind looking at it. I'd noticed I was starting to curve a little bit.

"You didn't see me… "

"Dancing," he said with smile. "Yes. I heard you, too. I hate to tell you, you're not going to make it to Hollywood Week."

Oh my God. He saw me naked, well almost naked, singing and dancing. I could feel my face flush with heat. Shoot me now. His voice stopped my inner voice,

"And don't open the window to anyone, but me."

This he said in a such serious tone, it caught me off guard. I didn't know how I was going to accomplish that without a fight. I just didn't know if I could make Jordan understand.

Chapter 8

The sunlight was streaking through the window into my bedroom. Yet another reason to pull my curtain closed. My body ached from the tournament. I rolled out of bed and headed to the bathroom in search of ibuprofen. I could hear someone in the kitchen moving around.

Pills in hand I headed upstairs to investigate. It was my mother of all people. Ever since Caleb died, it was like I was invisible to her. She had never been really close to me, but Caleb's death just exacerbated the situation. I broke a banana off from the bunch so I could take my pills. She sat down at the table with her bowl of cereal and looked over at me.

"Oh, I didn't see you there."

"I just came up."

She was only in her late forties, but her face seemed to always look tired and stressed, making her look older. The photos in our house showed a young and happy woman who was pretty. What scared me was she reminded me of myself. I'd look at her face, trying to catch a glimpse still in her. Her hair was grey with only a trace of the chestnut brown. Her eyes were a cool blue grey, but even they lost their sparkle.

"Jordan was here earlier. He wanted you to call him when you woke up."

I really didn't want to talk to him. The idea of having a confrontation about what happened last night and Oscar's request made my gut hurt. The clock suddenly caught my eye.

"It's 10:30 already! I gotta get ready. Um, I have a friend coming over to watch the Vikings game in the family room. Is that ok?"

"You're going to have to watch it in your room. Jennifer is moving everyone back in, at least until she has the baby. She lost her job and can't afford her apartment anymore," my mother sighed. "No one's going to hire her when she's pregnant."

That was such a copout. Jennifer was barely four months along. She could get a job at a fast food place. She just didn't want to try. I couldn't understand that. Why wouldn't you want to try to stand on your own two feet? How could she ever be an example of anything to her children? Even if she moved in here Target and Wal-mart were less than three blocks away. What a loser! She could get a job if she wanted one.

"At least we'll have someone to cook every night. You know I don't know why you never learned how to cook. You were always at Jennifer's side when she was cooking."

I couldn't believe the nerve. What kind of mother complains because her children didn't cook for her? I don't remember the last time she used a stove.

"Um, it's a guy coming over."

I thought that might change her mind about having her now sixteen-year-old daughter in her bedroom with a guy all day. *But no, that'd mean she'd have to care.*

"Then please stay in your room. The last thing Jennifer wants to see today is a guy, even if it's just Jordan."

"It's not Jordan. It's…um…my…boyfriend."

"And…" My mother said looking at me as if I was an idiot. *As long as he was male she didn't want to see him, got it.*

Remembering the products of men my sister totes around with her, I stopped in my tracks.

"Where are they going to sleep?"

"Grace is moving in with a friend in Uptown. So the kids are using her room and Jennifer is moving into your room."

"No, she's not! Why can't she move into the office?"

"I can't give up my office."

"Why not? You don't even use it. You just want it to say you have one," I stood my ground, my fist clenched. "I finally got my own room and I'm not giving it up!"

"Why are you being so selfish?"

"I'm selfish? How am I selfish? Do I have a room I never use, but I keep to myself? Do I spread my legs to every guy that looks at me twice so I can be a leech to my family? I'm not giving up my room and that's final!"

The one thing I could count on with my mother was I wasn't worth the effort to her to fight with. I was exhilarated by this sudden surge of power. I didn't know where it came from. I never stood up for myself or talked back to anyone. It was like I went to bed a five-year-old and woke up twenty-five.

"Fine. I'll see what I can do. They're going to be here later this afternoon. I'll talk to Jennifer."

I think even I could figure out how to dress for a day in my bedroom with my boyfriend. But seeing as how much my mother seemed to care I might as well be in there naked.

Deciding against my naked theory I pulled out some shorts that were a little bit small, but I didn't think Oscar would mind, he might even enjoy them. The soft cotton shorts had *Baller* on the back and a tiny volleyball on the right front leg. I put on a tank top, but threw on a to cover my bruise. Then I picked up my room. I arranged some pillows from the family room on my bed to turn it into a couch. It was then I was distracted by Oscar's ring on my nightstand. I toyed with options on how to wear it. Some girls wore them on a chain other girls wrapped string around the ring so it'd fit. The doorbell rang, but it was only a quarter after eleven.

A chain from a necklace I picked up at a thrift store was on top of my dresser; I snatched it and slid the ring on it. I took the stairs two at a time and opened the door just to find Jordan. Great! *As if today couldn't get any worse.*

"Really! This is really happening, isn't it?"

"Please don't start. Why can't you just be happy for me?"

"You do realize your new, black football-playing boyfriend's initials are OJ and you're white."

"You do realize in your scenario you're Ron Goldman."

Jordan shuffled his feet nervously and looked away.

"This is what you want?"

"Yes," I said, trying not to let my voice crack.

"Then I'll accept it, but I won't like it."

"Fine, just keep your comments to yourself and we can get along," I said, trying to set clear boundaries.

"Can I come in? I have something for you."

He brought his hand from behind his back and handed me a gift bag. I'd been so mad about Jennifer moving in I'd forgotten my birthday. It appeared my mother had too.

"Thanks. You can come in for a few minutes, but Oscar's coming over and I'm already having a bad day. I don't want the two of you fighting."

"What happened?" He said, walking into the entryway as I dug into the gift bag.

"Oh nothing. Jennifer's just moving back in with her brood. My mom wants me to start sharing a room with her, so we had a fight."

"Doesn't she have an office?"

"Thank you! My point exactly."

As much as I wanted to be mad at him, he understood me on a level others could not. Often he could finish my thoughts. He gave me a volleyball key chain and a Justin Beiber CD. All I could think was please say he isn't wanting me to listen to *Baby*. If nothing else, he knew me well enough to understand I would know what he's saying.

"Thanks for this. I'll definitely use it," I said about the key chain.

He leaned in to give me a hug, but it felt weird and I tried to keep my distance.

"Just remember I'm here for you when he breaks your heart."

"What did I just say!" I pulled away and glared at him.

"Sorry. It's just a habit."

"It's only been a week. How can it be a habit?"

"It's only been a week, how's he already your boyfriend?"

He had me there. My relationship with Oscar was fast, but it just seemed right. Kelly said he'd been after me for a month or so. The roar of a grey mustang pulling up in front of my house caused my two worlds to collide.

"You better go. He saw my arm and isn't very happy with you."

"Why?"

"I have a bruise," I said, looking at him as if he were an idiot.

Jordan looked shocked.

"I'm sorry, I didn't mean to hurt you."

I looked over his shoulder and shook my head slightly at Oscar to let him know I was handling Jordan. He seemed to understand me, it was as if we were already creating a secret language between us.

"Well, you did. Thank you again for the presents." I stepped forward, opening the door wider to usher him out. He turned and saw Oscar, a sigh escaped Jordan's lips. He left, running across the Miller's yard to go home.

Oscar walked to the passenger side of his car. My hand was on the door, my right leg bent and my head tilted as I waited to see what Oscar was doing. When he turned around, he had a bouquet of calla lilies. He walked up sidewalk to me.

"Happy Birthday," he smiled, kissing me on my cheek. He had done his homework.

"Thank you," I said, taking the flowers. "We're going to have to watch the game on the TV in my room. I hope that's okay. It's been a long day already. I'm so glad you're here." I took him by the hand and headed downstairs, closing the front door with my foot. When we got to my room I closed the door and set down the flowers on my dresser.

"I'll have to find a vase, but I just don't want to go out there right now."

"So what did you get for your birthday?"

That was a normal question, I supposed. I should've had something to report.

"Jordan gave me a CD and a keychain." I knew what would be coming next.

"And your family?"

"Have you ever seen *Sixteen Candles*?" I asked, trying to shrug off the pain of being forgotten. He just looked at me strangely.

"Watch it sometime and you'll understand. My mom wants me to give up my room so my sister can move in with her three kids for the next six months to a year."

His eyebrows raised.

"They don't really celebrate my birthday around here."

"Aren't you lucky I bugged Kelly to find out enough about your birthday to know to bring you a cake?" I hadn't even notice he had a cake in his other hand behind his back. It was small, but perfect, even personalized.

I think I was seven the last time I had a birthday cake. My mom picked it out of the grocery store's bakery freezer. I'd really wanted the Barbie one, but my mom chose the cheapest one. The whipped cream topping melted before we were home and it didn't even say Happy Birthday, let alone *Happy Sixteenth Birthday Ellie,* like this one from Oscar. This one even had a little Matchbox car on top.

"I'm very lucky, but what's with the car?" I asked, as I stood on my tiptoes and pulled his head down to kiss him thank-you. Suddenly, he picked me up, so I wrapped my legs around his waist. His hands held my butt and I realized how short my shorts were, his hands were touching the bare skin of my upper thigh. He walked over to my bed and set me down. With his back against the wall, pulled me in between his legs, wrapping his arms around my waist. I leaned against his chest and I was safe.

"The car's a good luck charm for your driving test. Are you taking it tomorrow?" Oscar asked.

"I'm not taking the test," I said.

This is why I don't let people in my life; I hate sounding pathetic. Oscar's arms held tighter, making me feel like I was in a safe place, so I decided to try to explain.

"I didn't take driver's ed this summer and it's not like my parents will let me drive anywhere anyhow."

"Oh, okay, but you are going to get your license, right?"

"Let's not ruin this day."

I turned around to see his face and knew I'd have to explain even more.

"I'd need a parent to sign for me to get a license and I just don't see that happening. They haven't even let me get a permit."

I reached for the remote my nightstand and turned on my TV, scanning the channels for the game. Oscar's arms around me made everything perfect. We watched the pregame show. I wasn't sure how blatant Oscar was being as he rubbed a finger or two against me. Wherever he touched, my skin buzzed, making me think my skin was a little kid, throwing a tantrum begging for more. I tried to ignore my urge to just turn around and take him by force.

He must not have been having the same problem. I was focused on not holding my breath too long or breathing too fast. How could I forget how to breathe when I was around him? No one ever made my hormones go this crazy. Every cell in my body was trying to overpower my mind and what I knew I needed to do. Be good. Legs together. Watch the game. Don't focus on his fingers barely touching my knee then gliding up my leg. Oh Jesus! His fingers were on the inside of my knee gliding…

I jumped up and grabbed the first pair of long pants I had in reach. Yoga pants. Whatever.

"I'm sorry, those aren't helping the situation," he said, licking his lips as he pulled his legs in. All I could think of was L. L. Cool J. "Really not helping," Oscar growled. *My sentiments exactly.* His breathing was as bad as mine. "Do you have baggy sweatpants? Really, really baggy." His eyes were traveling down my hips.

"Um…yeah… "

I dug in the bottom drawer of the dresser. Nothing. Oh yeah…closet. I snatched a pair of pants from the closet floor and pulled them on over the other pants. Okay. So it was September and I was in three layers. That was soooo normal.

“Better?”

“I think better is impossible with you,” he said, shaking his head. “You’re gonna fry.”

“Right,” I said trembling, then I took off my sweatshirt, crossed back to my dresser and snatched a t-shirt only to hear him breathe in deep. Holy crap. I had just taken off my shirt. In front of him! Again! *Put the t-shirt on, dumb ass!* Right, I can do this. My face had to be crimson.

I ran my fingers through my hair, trying to calm myself down, only to realize, *You have a ponytail in idiot.* I pulled out my binder, shook out my hair, then pulled it up again. Oscar’s jaw was dropped wide open.

“You have no clue, do you?”

Oh man now what’d I do?

“Are you sure you’ve never dated, hung out, performed Chinese water torture with any guy?”

“No. Jordan and I hang out, but nothing…ever…”

“I’ll cut the Tomato a little slack then.”

“What?”

“You’re amazing.”

He tilted his head and looked at me.

“You don’t even know what you’re doing do you? It’s just natural.”

“Being a clumsy, dumb ass. Yeah, I’m a professional.”

“I prefer your hair down, if you care.”

“Yeah, well I’m sure I’d prefer your shirt off, but you don’t see me asking…Oh God. I just said that out loud.”

I clasped my hands over my mouth. His laugh made me drop my hands.

“You’re right. You should keep the hair up. And not that I’m trying to get you to strip again, but the *little miss naughty* shirt…”

Looking down at my shirt, I couldn’t believe my luck. “I…I…you should just go. I told you I’m a freak. Not…that type of freak.”

I crashed down on my bed and buried my head in the covers.

“No really.” My voice was muffled.

He leaned over me, his lips were right by my ear.

“Your face lies, right?”

I nodded, not moving my head from its suffocating spot.

“So you’re having the same problem I am?”

I turned my head. So not a good idea. His lips were now a breath away from mine.

“Huh?”

“I just want to make sure we’re on the same page,” he licked his lips again and I used every ounce of my strength to suck mine in so I didn't latch onto his tongue. "I'm not the only one that's fighting the urge."

His fingers found a few stray hairs and brushed them behind my ear.

"Mmuhuh," I peeped.

"So the fact right now I want to kiss you so bad I can feel it in my toes…"

"That's all you want to do…Oh I...I…don't know where that came from," I said.

I rolled on my back and threw my hands over my face. Yeah. This wasn't gonna work. I was so gonna be pregnant by next month.

"You should just take me now. Get it over with and move on to the next girl."

"Take you?" He laughed. "I thought you wanted our first time together to be special. Memorable."

"Look, you can get it over with and be home by half time."

"Now, you're just insulting me."

"I don't mean to. It's just well…why me?"

"Ellie, I don't want the next girl. I want the girl I'm next too."

Damn, I'm in trouble.

"And waiting for you to really be ready for it is going to be worth it. I just didn't realize how much you effect me."

I closed my eyes, hoping I could calm myself down. I just wanted to cry from embarrassment.

He shifted and I realized he was looking around my room to distract himself from me. I wished I knew that trick. His hand reached to the ledge besides my window for a few CDs.

"Okay, so who're these guys?"

He shuffled the CDs like a deck of cards.

"Huh?" I said, rolling on my side to look at him.

He looked at me and smiled.

"Ya gotta work with me here. I want to spend the day with you, so distraction is the only way we'll both survive. Now I don't think I've heard of any of them. Oh, wait this one I know."

He held my *Idlewild* CD.

"You like this?"

"*Outkast*. Yeah, I have a brain."

"I didn't mean it that way. It's just…is that their first album?"

"Yeah," I scoffed, sitting up taking back *Southernplayalisticadillacmuzik*. "What?"

"Okay, who's this?"

"Lukas Rossi…are you kidding? He won *Rockstar Supernova*. I prefer his solo work, though. Kelly snuck me in a club he was playing at a few months ago."

"You…how did you pass to get in a club?"

"I don't know? Kelly's magic. She can always get in."

"You club hop?"

"I don't drink. I just like music. We only go to concerts, not clubbing."

"Okay, who's this?" Oscar asked.

"*Humbugs*. You know that movies and music thing?"

He nodded then shook his head no.

"You know the city does it every summer," I said. "Local bands play and then when the sun goes down, they play a movie. Kinda my two favorite things."

"And the *Thurabreds* played there?" he asked, holding another CD.

"No. Most of my stuff comes from garage sales. I can't see passing up a CD for fifty cents or dollar. There's always at least one good song on it. I looked them up. They broke up, but their album is amazing, I like almost every song."

"I know them," he replied. "Do you have a favorite type of music?"

"No. I like everything," I leaned in close and whispered. "Don't tell, but I have country songs on my iPod."

"You're doing it again." I pulled back and looked at him. His smile melted me.

I could feel the tingling again. Distraction, right. I needed to break the mood. I reached for my CDs, hoping to find something to stop the feelings running up and down my legs.

"What are you doing?" he asked, as his finger stroked the nape of my neck.

"Trying to find a Metallica CD," I replied.

"Why?"

"It's one of the few albums that won't have a song I can stupidly relate to you."

"You're gonna keep me on my toes, aren't you?"

He pulled me to him.

"I thought you were going to do that to me, gigantor. You know, the whole kissing standing up thing."

I could feel him laugh. He was holding me so close my body shook.

He put the CDs back as we turned our attention to the game.

"Why didn't he just run? No one was blocking him," I asked following a kickoff.

"Oh well, he was in the end zone," he said, as if that explained everything.

"Yeah?"

"If a kick returner catches it in the end zone, he has two options."

"Uh huh." I still didn't understanding the lunacy of not just running the ball back the way Oscar did on Friday. "No one was in his way."

"He waved and the defense knew he declared a fair catch so they stopped running. He put his knee down after catching the ball.

Since he was in the end zone, it's called a touchback. Now the receiving team gets to start from the twenty and the kick returner doesn't have to worry about being taken down under twenty yards."

His voice was slow and methodical like I was in a lecture at school.

"Really, he just has to look at the defenders and decide if he thinks he can get to the twenty-one. If he can, he'll run. If he isn't sure, he might as well take the…"

He looked at me to finish and see if I was paying attention.

"Touchback?" I said slowly, slightly unsure of myself.

"Exactly."

A kiss was my reward for paying attention. Much better than a gold star on the top of a test.

It took only a few questions for him to figure out that I wasn't a football expert and so he explained the game to me. I learned about downs, the pocket, encroachment, clipping, a spread offense and he even started to teach me some of the positions. He loved teaching me about the game. By half time, he asked, "Do you really care about this?"

"I want to know what I'm looking at when you're on the field. It's easy to cheer for you when you catch a ball, but there's so much more to the game than that. I don't know if I could remember all the rules. It seems like penalty flags are always flying."

It hit me I was supposed to be entertaining my guest, something I had no training in.

"You know, I've been a bad host. Would you like something to drink? I can go upstairs and get a couple of forks so we can eat the cake."

"I can't eat cake without milk."

I ran upstairs to grab forks and milk. On my way back down, I saw Grace packing the last of her things.

"Where in Uptown are you going to live?" I asked, trying to make nice.

"I'm not. I just told mom that so I didn't have to deal with her," she groaned, picking up the box she'd just sealed.

"So where are you going to live?"

"There's a guy in Minnetonka. He has a huge house and no one really living there, but him."

Minnetonka was one of the richest suburbs in the Twin Cities.

"He's going to let me move in rent free."

I knew my sister; it wouldn't be rent-free, her currency wouldn't be accepted at any bank branch.

"Sounds nice. Well, I've got to get back to my room," I said, thinking even if I told her she was stupid and that this decision would just end up having her being little less than a prostitute, I decided what would it matter. That's just the way she was.

It was then she noticed I was carrying two glasses of milk and two forks and I had a huge ring on my finger.

"Who's in your room?"

"Um…nobody."

My face felt hot and flushed and I got a little dizzy. She put down the box she was holding, crossed to my room and opened the door faster than I could say "Stop."

"Well hello, Oscar."

Rage filled within me. I'd seen that smile one too many times too not know it was one of seduction. A part of me wanted to jump up and down screaming he's mine, mine, mine.

"Hi, Grace, good to see you again. Are you home for the weekend?"

"I'm moving out today, but maybe I should stick around and go back to bunking with my sister. I didn't know we were allowed to entertain boys in our room."

It was all I could do to not throw the milk in her face, when I thought of all the nights the window had been opened and boys coming in and out of it. Having to cover my head with a pillow or leaving all together and falling asleep on the couch in the family room so I wouldn't have to hear the moans from whomever she had in the room.

I pulled myself together enough to say, "Well, geez, you're probably right. I thought the guys could only come over during the night. At least that seemed to be your rule."

She glared at me. She may have had first blood, but I think I won.

"It doesn't matter to me now anyway. I'll be leaving." She turned on her heels and left, bumping me just enough that some of the milk spilled on my foot.

"I'm sorry about that," I said, after I closed the door.

"It's okay, no big deal. I'm really not sure I'm comfortable being in your bedroom with your whole family in the house."

"You seemed comfortable last night," I reminded him, as I set down the milk. I wiped off my foot with a towel I had on the floor and curled up next to him, bringing my cake with me.

The third quarter started, but we really weren't paying attention. We started eating, only to find we had more fun feeding each other. Soon we had icing all over our faces and hands. I pushed the cake aside and straddled him. I slowly licked the icing off the outside of his lips. Before I knew what happened we were kissing, but not the passionate kisses from last night, instead the sweet gentle kisses that barely touch the skin. Waves coursed through my body with each touch.

"You know, we really should wash this off before we get stuck together," Oscar said.

The thought of being stuck together drove me crazy. I could feel he was having the same problem. I slid off him and went to the bathroom to give him some space to cool down.

I looked in the mirror and my face was flush from what just happened. I knew this was going to be harder than I originally thought. Maybe I'd judged my sisters too harshly. How easy is it to stop yourself when all you really want is to become one with someone?

After a few minutes, I brought the washcloth into my bedroom for him. He was drinking his milk and I couldn't help but stare. He was sitting on the edge of my bed, hunched over, his bicep was flexed as he brought the glass up to his lips. His lips were perfect, attached to a perfect jaw and his perfect...

"Thanks. Are you going to hand me that or am I going to have to come get it?''

His voice brought me out of my fantasy.

"Sorry."

I shook my head, trying to shake out the image. I handed him the washcloth, then pulled it away.

"I don't know how you wash yourself, but it tends to work better if the washcloth's in my hand. What? Did I say something funny?"

I brought the washcloth to his face and started to wipe off the icing. He looked bewildered for a moment and then he closed his eyes. After his face was done, I took his right hand and slowly washed it, followed by his left.

My door swung open, as I sat straight up in fear of being caught, even though I wasn't doing anything. Well, nothing too blatant. A young, but loud voice was yelling "Auntie El, Auntie El, Auntie...Who you?"

I knew this would happen. My sister's kids have no idea about boundaries, but Drew was only four.

"My name's Oscar. I'm a good friend of your Aunt Ellie. And who are you?"

"Andrew Matthew Chisholm," he said proudly. With his three-foot body and a blond buzz cut, he looked at Oscar unsure of why he was there.

"But if you not strange, then I's Drew."

Oscar laughed at the garbled English.

"Well nice to meet you Drew."

Oscar extended his hand and Drew obliged still a bit baffled by this giant in my bed.

"Drew, is there something you want?"

I didn't want to be rude, but I also wanted to get back to Oscar.

"I'm here!"

"I realize that."

"That all. Hug."

His little arms were out stretched, so I picked him up, gave him a big hug and carried him out the door.

"I come your room, Auntie El?"

"Not right now, maybe later. Oscar and I have some things to talk about first."

"You gonna kiss him?"

My face flushed red.

"Mommy says she's talkin', but she kissin'."

"No, I'm not going to kiss him. I really just need to talk to him."

The thought I was starting to act like my sister made me nervous, until I looked back at Oscar, who was smiling.

Drew took off up the steps and I could hear the rest of the family, milling around carrying boxes and causing a racket.

"I'm sorry," I said as I closed the door, my hand staying on the doorknob, afraid if I let go someone else might burst in.

"So am I."

He stood up and crossed the room to me.

"I was hoping we'd be kissing."

I let go of the doorknob and stood up high, placing a hand on each side of his face as I pulled him down, bringing my lips to his. He put his arms around me and picked me up, carrying me back to my bed.

The knock on my door, obviously wasn't a niece or nephew. I suppose I should've been happy with the small warning before my sister's head peeked around the door.

"Is there any chance you could help me get the stuff moved in? The kids are running everywhere and I guess Dad's mad about me moving in so he left."

My sister pleaded in her best victim's voice.

"Sure," an obliging voice came from behind me. "We'd love to."

We? We? What was this we he was talking about? I knew he couldn't mean we as in him and me. He stretched out his hand to me.

"Come on, it'll only take a minute. I'm Oscar by the way."

He reached his other hand to my sister. She took it, staring dumbfounded.

"Are you planning on staying for supper, Oscar?" my sister asked, lightly shaking his hand.

"We hadn't talked about it."

There was that damn we again.

He looked at me, "But if there's enough, I'd love to."

What just happened? I wasn't ready for the meet-the-family part of the relationship. My head was spinning.

If they don't know about him, they can't judge him, and if they can't judge him, then I don't have to worry about what they think. I can just be alone on an island with him. I don't want to share him! I want him all to myself!

It didn't take a minute. We missed the fourth quarter and the afternoon game. Oscar didn't seem to mind. He played with my nieces and nephew, and took orders from my mom. We rearranged furniture and packed up my mom's office. All that was her way of punishing me for wanting my own space. That probably wasn't originally on the menu, but then she saw Oscar and most likely realized why I wanted my own space.

"So, how long have you two been together?" Jennifer asked.

She'd be the one to act the most like a parent. She passed the tater tot hot dish to Oscar.

"Not long."

Oscar scooped a spoon full of the starchy mess onto his plate.

"Officially, only a day, but I've...We've been interested in each other for almost a month now."

He placed a hand on one of my legs. He seemed to be telling me he was okay.

I'd never had anyone who with a glance from me or touch from them could be a form of communication. Picking up on body language was never my specialty. I'd think someone was mad at me, or interested in me, or judging me and I always had it wrong. They weren't looking at me or even thinking about me. I was ceaselessly nervous and paranoid.

My mother was the exception that day. She glared across the table at me, telling me every hateful thought she was having. It made me feel as if she was using a cheese grater on my skin to expose my short comings. I held in the tears I wanted to cry, but the pressure was building in my forehead. Then she'd look away when Oscar would turn towards me wondering why I looked so upset. Mean while my father picked at his food. I assume upset he wasn't the point of attention for my mother. Jennifer became preoccupied with Taylor in her highchair, so I had to keep Drew and Adriana from throwing their food around the room.

We made it through dinner with little to no conversation. All the while I could feel Oscar's leg touching mine. It relaxed me just to have a part of him touch me. He was like a sedative, at least in social situations. When we were alone, his touch was anything but a sedative. The one good thing with Jennifer in the house was she tried to make my family appear normal.

"Isn't there one more game?" I asked, as Oscar and I cleared the dishes.

"Yeah, there's a night game, but don't you think I should leave?" he asks.

"I suppose, I have homework I was distracted from all day anyway."

Disappointment overwhelm me. I wanted every waking moment to be with him. I thought that seemed strange, like an unnatural draw. This wasn't who I was. I liked to be alone in my room watching a movie, listening to music and reading a book or doing my homework. So used to being alone, I didn't know how to act when I actually got attention. I had to tell myself I'd survive if he went home.

"I forgot about that," he said. "Football can be really distracting. I should've known you would've gotten into it."

"There was a game on today?" I joked, as I put a hand on his stomach. "I hadn't noticed."

I put my game face on as I walked him to the door.

"You know, I don't want to leave," he said, as he slid a hand down my back to what I now felt had become his spot on my body.

"You know, you don't have to leave." A glimmer of hope shot through my body.

"I should go, though. I think a little bit of distance would help strengthen my resolve."

Distance! Distance! One supper with my family and he's ready to break up with me. I could feel a vice tightening around my chest. How in one day had it all gone so wrong? What did I do? I was fighting to figure out what grievous error I'd committed when he suddenly pulled me close.

"Because I don't think I'll be able to control myself if I touch you much more today," he said as he kissed me lightly on the lips and the warm fleece blanket of security was back. "You know you're so hot! And every time I touch you shockwaves go through my body."

I wasn't sure how to respond. I wanted to tell him I felt the same. I wanted to tell him I never want to be without him. I wanted to let him know I want him to stay no matter what the cost. I turned it into a joke to avoid telling him how I really feel.

"Well, then we better separate before you electrocute yourself."

"I'm a relentless daredevil," he laughed and he kissed me, holding on for longer than I imagined he would, our lips sealed together.

When I got back to my room, Oscar had already texted me.

Thxs 4 shock.

Anytime:)

My wallpaper had changed from a picture of Edward Cullen to Oscar. He must've taken a picture of himself and put it on my phone.

Well, for now I'll keep it, but I'm not sure how much I like that. Memories of Jennifer's boyfriends made me question Oscar's motives. I shook my head and told myself Oscar would never hurt me. *God, please say I'm not deluding myself like my sister had.*

Chapter 9

The next morning, as usual, Jordan was at my door to walk me to school. This time, though, we walked in almost virtual silence. He usually was telling me about a game or a TV show. A block away from school, he finally broke the silence. Speaking faster than I thought a human could, he had his own moment of verbal vomiting.

"I'm sorry. It's just I thought eventually you'd end up liking me as more than a friend and I guess I never expected you to meet someone, especially as quickly…I mean, school's just started."

He looked down and kicked some acorns that were already starting to fall. Finally, calming down he asked, "Are you sure he isn't trying to use you?"

This time his tone wasn't one of mocking, but one of caring. This wasn't him trying to hurt me, but trying to protect me from some uncontrollable outside force.

"What did I say about that?" I asked, wanting to reinforce the boundaries. "If I'm being used, I'll be the one hurt by it. I'll learn and move on, but right now everything feels so right I don't want to over-think the situation. Can't I just have a few days of contentment? Is that too much to ask for?"

I wasn't going to address his attraction to me.

"I guess not, but please don't let your guard down too much, okay? No matter what, I'll be here for you when something happens."

"How about you be there for me, *if* something happens?"

We were at the school door. Even though the entire sophomore class had their lockers on the same long hallway, ours were at opposite ends, so I said goodbye and started to walk to my locker. I couldn't help but feel like all eyes, especially female, were on me. I kept telling myself it was my normal paranoia. Kelly had been working with me to try to stop that. I could hear her in my head right now: *You know for someone with such low self-esteem, you do seem to have a really high opinion of yourself.*

I don't understand what you mean.

Why would you be so important all those people would not only notice you, but form an opinion that matters? So what if they are talking about you? Are the opinions of these strangers, you will probably never see again, really that important?

I decided to fight with my inner voice.

These aren't strangers. Yes, I may only know half of them, but eventually after three years, I'll know them.

You do know you're the weird one here. Most people don't dwell or think about things for weeks or months on end. Most people get over things and don't remember who wet their pants in third grade...

Monica Dubbins, I see her on the right.

Okay, you're the only one that remembers that, or even thinks about it. Look at her face. Does she seem worried about the fact someone in the hallway remembers her bladder issues from seven years ago?

That did make me slow down and look at her. She turned toward me and smiled.

"Hi Ellie," she said, without a hint of caring I held this embarrassing secret locked in my head.

"Hi, Monica."

I passed, looking down, pulling my books tighter to my chest. Approaching my locker, I realized I might not be so paranoid. *Something foul was a foot in the sophomore hallway*, to attempt to quote the classic tale of Bill and Ted. Oscar was leaning up against the locker next to mine.

He backed off so I could enter my combination. He placed a hand on the small of my back and leaned in to kiss me on the cheek. I could feel my face flush as I stumbled to remember what my combination was. With my heart pounding, I tried twice to get it. Opening up my locker, I put my books away and grabbed what I needed for the next few classes.

"A little stalkerish to be at my locker, don't you think?"

His lips were still by my cheek. "You ashamed of me?"

"No," I scoffed.

"You're the first girlfriend I haven't been embarrassed to be seen with."

"Okay," I turned. Big mistake. Now we were nose-to-nose and my lips curled into a smile. "I just wasn't expecting..."

"You thought you were a secret?"

"Well, no...just... "

He kissed me and the hallway faded away.

"I saw you had a hole on your wall, so I thought you could use this," he said and passed me a poster. It was the football schedule. I'd seen it posted around school. Oscar was dead center with the rest of the varsity flanking him. Definitely a step up from HSM.

"Thanks," I said, putting the poster in my locker, being careful not to bend the edges. I smiled, thinking about how mean he looked in the picture, but right now he was so tender and caring for me, I couldn't imagine him ever being mean. That was, unless Sharyn pissed him off again.

"I'm sorry I couldn't pick you up this morning."

His statement caught me off guard. I scanned my memory, trying to figure out what would make him think I was to be picked up in the mornings. Or was this a test? Had he tried to pick me up and found out I'd walked to school with Jordan. *Oh, why can't I just shut my brain off sometimes?*

"Coach has us lifting weights on Mondays and Wednesdays for an hour. You know, you could use some weightlifting time too." He squeezed my upper arm. "I should be able to pick you up the rest of the week, though."

"Oh, that'd be nice," I said, flashing ahead to January when the temperatures dropped below freezing. The idea of a nice warm car waiting in my driveway sounded appealing. "But no to the lifting. I hate lifting weights."

"It helps prevent injuries and," his voice lowered to a whisper, "it gives me a chance to see you flex that amazing ass of yours."

I could feel his hand starting to move down.

"You're lucky there are witnesses here or you'd end up feelin' the few muscles I have," I said, pulling my body back, making his hand stop.

"What? I can't find you attractive? If that's the case, we'll just have to end this now."

"Look, you can admire all you want, I just don't like…Well, I don't like…Hearing things."

I remembered his comment from last night too. I couldn't think of a better way to say it. Being told I was special in any way I couldn't see myself made me uncomfortable; the kicker was I'd never felt special, like I had a stand-out body part, special skill or knowledge.

"I like putting things out there so we don't have any confusion. If I don't tell you what I like, then you'll think I don't like anything, then where will we be?"

He was right, but I didn't want to admit it. The first warning bell sounded, but he didn't seem fazed, where I started to get nervous. I hated being late. My stomach got tied up in knots when I didn't start moving right away.

"I want you to tell me things."

Another thing to make me nervous, he was batting a thousand today.

"Okay, I'll tell you something. I have History and I need to get there."

"Pierce or Craig?"

"Pierce."

He took my hand and we headed down the hall.

"Oh, I changed my lunch to A so can I meet you at your locker after third period."

"Why did you change your lunch?" I asked unsure of why in just a few days of being together he was ready to rearrange his schedule. I didn't even know if we'd make it to next week, how could he?

"Lil' Girl, there are very few times during the day we can be together. I just had a study hall, so I switched it."

I couldn't decide if that was a good thing or not. I did want to spend time with him, but hearing he changed his schedule I made me feel suffocated. *Great, now this was going to be my inner voice all through history.* When we got to the door, he kissed me on the top of my head and took off to his class.

History was my favorite subject. Something about *those who do not learn from their mistakes are doomed to repeat them* resonated within me. Mr. Pierce's room was decorated in Time and Newsweek covers. Anything he thought would be a historically significant cover ended up framed and on the wall. Nine-eleven, the fall of the Berlin Wall, evolution wars and hundreds of faces, Ronald Reagan, Hillary Clinton, Barak Obama, Richard Nixon. If nothing else, I could look at the magazines when the lecture got boring.

As I got to my seat, the whispers started. *I can't believe she's with him. She has to be givin' it up. Man, how good do you think she is that he's actually keeping her around?* I set my head down on the desk. Out of the corner of my eye. I saw two guys laughing. My mind was spinning, as I imagined what they were thinking about me, what everyone seemed to be thinking. I could understand it since I was still thinking it. *How could Oscar be with me?*

By the end of third period, I had had enough. I stormed to my locker. It was then I realized that all the talk wasn't just because Oscar was wonderful. Smashed up and down my locker were SnoBall cakes. Inside my locker, a few cakes oozed through the vents, destroying two of my pictures I'd decorated my locker with. I ripped down the pictures and threw them on the floor. Then I threw my books in, snatched some money for lunch and started towards the cafeteria. Suddenly I was no longer on the ground. From out of nowhere Oscar had come up behind me and picked me up. Out of reflex one of my elbows jabbed him in the ribs.

"Ouch! Okay, okay, you don't have to lift weights with me."

I saw Kelly coming down the hall at top speed.

"Ellie. Ellie, I need to talk to you right now. Oscar, put her down."

He obliged and I was on the floor just in time for her to grab me by the hand. She threw something at Oscar.

"Hey can you get us lunch? Meet us on the hill by the west side of the stadium. Thanks." Kelly commanded.

I was being pulled away at what seemed to be mach-one. All I could hear was a confused "Sure … No problem." Behind me.

Kelly burst out the side door, still pulling me, when I yanked my hand away.

"What the hell's your problem?" I snapped.

"I was trying to save you from yourself."

I couldn't tell if rage or confusion was my main emotion.

"Look, I've had a really bad morning, the last thing I need ---"

"The last thing you need is to act like a baby, throw a temper tantrum and end up losing him."

We slowed down, and she had an arm around me.

"I've been hearing the same things you have all morning. I guarantee he hasn't, because no one's stupid enough to make presumptions around him."

My rage started to subside and turn into a dull anger.

"If you want to be with the most popular guy in school, you're going to have to be stronger and get a thicker skin. I know how much you process everything, as if it was a judgment on you as a person. This is probably going to continue for the next few months."

How was that supposed to comfort me? I felt my tears welling up in my eyes.

"You can't let them see you cry. If you do, it will only make it last longer. Eventually, when you guys have been together for awhile they won't be able to keep saying it. You can beat this if you want to. Isn't he worth it?"

"I don't know."

The burning in my throat got worse, but I kept trying to hold in my tears. *I had to be strong. I wasn't going to break. Somewhere inside me was the resolve to be strong.*

Oscar was approaching us with our lunches.

"Did you not just have a great weekend? Weren't you happy?"

"Yes, but … "

"There's no but. You have to tell yourself you deserve to be happy. I know it goes against everything in your mind for your life. It's okay to be happy. You can be like the kids on TV if you want to be."

"Which ones? 90210?"

"No one's like 90210," she said and hugged me. "Remember, he's not hearing anything because people are too afraid to say it to him. Some people are seeing that he really likes you. Look at Mary."

She seemed excited for me on Friday when Oscar was talking to me. But Mary was sweet. She couldn't see the bad side of the Devil himself.

"Just remember whatever happens between you and him is between the two of you."

"So, what's the great girly crisis?" Oscar asked.

"Nothing I can't handle. What did you get me?" Kelly asked.

"A slice of pizza and Sprite. It'd have been helpful if you could have waited a few seconds to tell me what you wanted."

"Ah, but then where'd the mystery be in the world? I got to get going anyway. You two have a good lunch."

She squeezed my hand and then got her food from Oscar, skipping off towards the building.

"El, I'll take care of your locker."

"Thanks," I yelled back.

"What's wrong with your locker?"

"Someone put something through the vents."

"Excuse me?" Oscar snapped.

"It's nothing. They just destroyed a few pictures."

"Who's they?" He questioned.

"I don't know. What does it matter anyway?"

"It matters because you're my girl and no one disrespects my girl."

"What if I wasn't your girl? Then would it matter?"

"I told you I'd be looking out for you now. Tell me."

"See, I actually attend my classes, unlike the Klan member that used my locker as a political statement."

"Klan member?" Oscar's voice was solemn now.

"It was SnoBalls. I don't want to talk about it anymore. It's just a couple of pictures I'd cut out of a magazine, nothing worth getting my panties in bunch over."

"You know that's why I like you," he said, as he opened his pop. "You take things as they come. Right now I want to go beat the crap out of someone."

So did I, but that's what they wanted me to do. I was going to be the exception.

"If you need replacements, let me know," he said.

"What'd ya got?"

"Just a ton of my senior pictures. Dad went crazy."

"That's tempting."

"You got any pictures? My locker's empty."

"No. Not really. I don't exactly have the scrapbook-type family."

"Okay...So how was your morning?"

My mind ran through a dozen scenarios. Should I tell him or should I be strong? *Strong. The snoball thing was enough for one day.*

"I've had better, but now I'm with you I'm very glad you switched lunch periods."

He was the reprieve I needed in the middle of the day to get me through until practice.

We both sat on the ground under a tree, me between his legs, his arms wrapped around me, and I could finally process Kelly's words. She was right. What was between us was between us. Everything I heard that morning and would probably hear that afternoon melted away as I felt him hold me close, keeping me safe.

"Hey!" I said, to the sound of a snap. I opened my eyes to see him using his phone to take a picture of us.

"Not cool," I said reaching for his phone. "Where's your delete?"

"Nope."

He grabbed his phone back and held it out in front of us again. His lips caressed my neck and I squirmed, smiled and heard a snap.

"Perfect."

He smiled, looking at a picture of us.

"Now I got my Lil' Girl with me all the time."

The talking slowed down as Kelly predicted and by homecoming it was all but gone. People started to accept Oscar and I were together. We still had people who hated us. Sharyn was the president of the "I hate Ellie fan club." The jungle fever jokes came from all directions; it didn't matter if the student was black or white. In the cocoon of our relationship, the world melted away. I still had my friends Kelly, Jessie, Tia, a girl who seemed to be in half of my classes, and to a limited amount, Jordan. Life was starting to settle down. As afraid I was to admit it, I was happy and I was starting to allow myself to be.

The Friday before homecoming the school held a jersey auction. It was a tradition to raise money for the student council projects. The student council auctioned off the jerseys of the football players and the girls who won got to wear a home jersey all week. The girls usually gave them back reeking of perfume and smudged in lipstick. The players hated it because they didn't have time to wash the jerseys before the game. Oscar said he'd cover the cost if I got in a bidding war for his jersey. He'd given me three hundred dollars. I thought he highly overestimated the value and told him the bidding wouldn't get out of control.

"Lil' Girl," he'd said. *"I'm the President of the student council and I have things I want to accomplish this year. Either way, I'm going to be giving the money to the student council. I might as well get something out of it."*

It was customary that any attached player's jersey was supposed to go to his girlfriend. But Oscar and I had a feeling I might have some spiteful competition.

The sophomore jerseys were auctioned first, because few people wanted a sophomore's jersey and the auction wouldn't move forward until someone purchased a jersey, even if it only went for ten dollars.

It was fun watching the bidding wars, the anger from the loser, the excitement from the winner. As the auction got to the seniors jerseys I was feeling good. Except for Xavier Schultz's jersey that went for two-hundred and fifty dollars, the jerseys had been going for around fifty dollars apiece. I could cover that without any help from Oscar.

"Okay, who do we have here? Number eighteen, Oscar Jeffreys. Okay, girls, who will start the bidding at ten dollars."

Principal Oliva was starting to get tired, but was still trying to be enthusiastic. My hand shot up along with about sixteen other girls.

"Oh my, okay, twenty, thirty, forty dollars."

The hands were still flying.

From across the gym came "Two hundred."

Everyone's head turned. Sharyn was leaning against the wall, smiling, her hand clenched around a roll of bills.

My stomach dropped. I had the money to cover it, but I couldn't help but be mad.

"Do I hear two-ten?"

The other bidders who probably were members of student council dropped out. I slowly raised my hand. Principal Oliva turned to Sharyn.

"Two-twenty?"

"Two-fifty," she said with determination.

My hand started to shake.

Principal Oliva then turned to me, "Two-sixty?"

I just nodded. A burning from the bile rising in my throat made it so I couldn't even speak. I looked at Oscar, but he just winked. That didn't calm me as I saw Sharyn's temper rise at the gesture.

"Three hundred," Sharyn yelled.

The tension in the air was thick as everyone could feel this was a battle a long time in the making. The whole room was quiet as our bidding turned into a tennis match with Sharyn and I volleying for control.

"Three-ten," I squeaked.

"Three-twenty," she yelled. *Maybe she's reaching her threshold,* I hoped.

"Three-thirty," I said, with more resolve and feeling as if Principal Oliva had been removed from the equation.

"Three-forty."

Sharyn stepped forward.

"Three-fifty."

I stood up and stared her down. My entire body shook.

"Four-hundred."

She had me. That was my limit. My eyes pleaded to Oscar in hopes he'd have some way out. His eyes were ablaze with anger as he stared down Sharyn.

“Five-hundred,” a girl’s voice comes from behind.

I’d lost the jersey. The bitter taste reached my mouth. I tried to not cry. *At least Sharyn wouldn’t have it,* I told myself. I lowered my head because I knew if I turned around and saw who won the jersey, the tears would flow. I saw Oscar nudge the dumbfounded principal to end the bidding.

“Five-hundred it is.”

Oscar told me that one year a bidding war ended in one girl charging fifteen-hundred dollars to her parent’s credit card. After that, the student council enacted a cap of five-hundred dollars.

“Come claim your jersey, young lady.”

Kelly put her hand on my shoulder. Max’s jersey had only gone for sixty dollars, she wouldn’t understand the pain I felt right then. I kept my head down in shame. I saw her hand slide in front of me holding a hundred dollars as she nudged me forward. Shaking, I stumbled up to the podium and passed the five-hundred dollars to the treasurer as Oscar passed me his jersey. He kissed my cheek. His eyes still looked enraged and were staring directly at Sharyn. He went back to his spot on the bleachers with the team.

I slipped the jersey over my head. It dropped stopping right above my knees. It smelled like Oscar and helped me calm down. My head throbbed. I took my place next to Kelly, who held one of my hands as the rest of the senior’s jerseys went up on the block.

After the next jersey was sold, I was calm enough to turn to her and I whispered, “Thank you.” My voice still shaking.

“Not a problem. I’m here to look out for you.”

Chapter 10

"Well, so much for me buying an outfit for the dance," I said as Kelly and I changed for practice. "I guess I could wear his jersey with a belt around it and some leggings. Wouldn't I just be so formal?" I struck a pose.

"Don't worry about it. We'll go hit the thrift stores this weekend. You always have amazing luck there."

That was true, and it gave me a good reason to get out of the house. Oscar started me watching college football with him every Saturday I didn't have a tournament. I needed a good girl day without football, especially college football. That just reminded me the next year he'd be playing at USC, Virginia Tech or Florida. He hadn't actually talked about where he was going to play, but he seemed to like watching those teams the best.

Practice flew by and before I knew it, the football team was shuffling through the gym on their way a game way in Mahtomedi. I knew the school was north, but I had no idea where. Thankfully, Kelly would be driving us.

I ran to Oscar when I saw him come in. The good luck kisses were no longer just for volleyball games. Since the football team was undefeated, I'd have hated to have had the blame placed on me for a loss. So I suffered through the pain and agony of kissing Oscar before every game.

"You're a martyr, you know that," Kelly teased when I came back over.

"Yes, I know, it's the cross I must bear."

The game was a success, as usual. Afterwards, before the boys jumped on the bus to ride home, I caught Oscar.

"Is it okay if I skip tomorrow's games? Kelly wants to take me shopping for an outfit for the dance."

"Only if you promise me it will be a dress."

"Oh, I'm not promising anything."

"Well, then no. Sorry, college football game day is a must. I just can't give you up."

He wrapped me up against his body.

"Okay. Okay, I'll try on a dress. No guarantees it'll stay on."

"It's amazing how much we think alike."

He picked me up, kissed me and carried me to Kelly and Max.

"Now, Kelly, I want to see her in a dress at the dance."

Kelly laughed, "Yes, sir, I'll do my best."

The coach was yelling at the boys to get on the bus.

"Are you coming over tonight?"

"Only if you're wearing my jersey."

"I'm wearing your jersey."

I was confused because Kelly and I'd both worn our auction jerseys to the game.

"Just my jersey," he whispered as he kissed me one more time. His hand glided down from my back as he lightly squeezed my butt and then ran off to the bus.

"What was that about?" Kelly asked.

"Nothing," I smiled. I glanced at Oscar and saw him talking to his coach. I'd only seen Oscar get mad when someone attacked me. The coach must have said something because Oscar's body language was no longer a happy camper.

I knew I'd have at least an hour before Oscar would be knocking at my door, so I asked Kelly if we could stop at a Dairy Queen on our way home. After getting our orders, we sat on the patio. The nights were coming sooner and getting colder, but it felt good to sit outside and shiver.

"Kelly?"

"Yeah."

"Do you love Max?"

"Of course I do."

"No, I mean love him, like you see yourself with him forever. You know, marriage, kids the whole thing. Or do you love him now and don't think about the future?"

"I'm not going to marry him in the next few months, but I can't really imagine my life without him. It seems like he and I've been together forever. Almost like, I can't remember my life without him."

A sly smile crossed her face.

"Why? Are you finally letting yourself fall out of lust with Oscar and into love with him?"

"I just don't know if I could love him. I hate every minute we're apart, but I hate myself for feeling so dependent on him at the same time. I don't want to resent him, but I want to feel whole with and without him."

"I don't think it works that way," she said, licking her spoon.

"What do you mean?"

"Don't get me wrong. You can be a whole person without him. Go about your day-to-day routine. Achieve greatness, cure cancer, the whole thing, but as humans we need someone to share life with. A life mate or partner. It doesn't mean you're losing yourself, you're just gaining a partner to enhance the world you live in. You can only catch so much beauty in the world, sometimes you need a little help seeing the rest of it. That's what you do for him and what he does for you."

She leaned over and nudged me.

"It's okay to love someone, to feel dependent on him or her. It's only unhealthy when you can't complete simple tasks without their approval."

She put an arm around me.

“One of these days you’ll believe me when I tell you it’s okay to be loved and to give love in return. I promise you, he loves you as much as you love him, if not more.”

When Kelly imparted her words of wisdom on me, she always seemed as if she had centuries of knowledge to pull from.

“Love, really, I…I don’t know about that. Lust, on the other hand, I’ve got covered.”

When we got home, Oscar’s car was already in front. Inside, he was talking with my dad.

“Hello?”

“Oh, hey Honey, Oscar and I were just talking about the game. It was a good one, huh?”

My dad was acting…well, normal, not normal for me, but normal for the rest of the world.

“I looked up through the spindles on the landing at Oscar.

“How did you beat me here?”

“I was going to ask the same thing,” he said.

“Kelly and I stopped for ice cream.”

My father excused himself and Oscar and I went to my room.

“Sorry I didn’t shower,” he said when we were alone. “The thought of you in just my jersey had me a little bit jumpy.”

“Oh, that explains why you beat me here. I guess I can put up with the smell.”

Actually something about the way he smelled after a game always drove me crazy.

"Wait here," I said, putting my hand on his chest to stop him. I went into my room and closed the door. I slipped off the shirt I had on under the jersey and threw it in a pile in the corner. I pulled off my pants and opened a drawer I tried to decide if I should put on shorts. I chose the small pair that were a favorite of his. The length of his jersey hid them anyway. I slowly opened the door to find him leaning against the doorjamb.

He looked me over and slowly walked in, closing the door behind him. He picked me up, kissing me as he walked and I wrapped my legs around him. His hands slowly worked their way down my back until they reached the top of my hip.

"I thought, I said, only my jersey?"

"I thought it'd be easier if kept a small barrier," I said, knowing as much as he drove my body crazy, I felt it had to be harder for him.

"I could think of a smaller one."

He placed me on my bed and his hands glided up my thighs. He tugged on my shorts, pulling them off and leaving only my underwear -- definitely a smaller barrier. He was on top of me, his hand continuing up my leg to my hip, then my stomach. His lips were on my throat and I smelled the dried spicy sweat on his skin.

He returned his lips to mine and his hands continued to explore my upper body. My legs spread and he slid in between them, with only my small barrier and his light jersey shorts separating us. He rocked slightly in between my legs. His excitement built as his hand brushed against my bra.

All the blood in my body seemed to rush in between my legs and I started to burn. I wanted him inside me more than I ever had. My hands explored his body causing me to shiver in response. His lips caressed my neck and he worked his way up to my ear.

"Do you see…why I want…you in a dress?" he whispered.

My body shook, goose bumps ran up and down my arms, legs and neck. Breathing heavily, I was willing to do anything if he'd only continue.

"I'll get a dress."

My arms wrapped around his neck and pulled his body closer.

He abruptly stopped kissing me. His hands were out from under the jersey and on either side of me. He pushed himself up as he walked to the other side of my room.

"Good. I'm glad I won."

His voice was too under control.

I laid there flushed, my body aching for his touch. How could he do that! Stop. My legs were still covered in goose bumps. I could feel myself burning inside to be touched and he just stopped! I pulled my legs up to my chest, under his jersey and tried to return my blood to my extremities.

"Don't look at me like that. Just because I stopped doesn't mean I didn't want to keep going."

"I beg to differ."

"Please, don't beg," he growled, desire burning in his eyes.

"Why?"

I sat up on my knees and tried to stare him down.

"Because…"

He returned to my side. He buried his face in my hair, breathing me in, making me fall back on my pillow. His arms were at my sides.

"Trust me, I always want to keep going, but there's only so much I can take before I'll explode. Physically, I'm stronger than you. If I go past a certain point, I don't know if I could stop myself. You wouldn't say no, but you wouldn't say yes either. I love you too much to do anything to hurt you."

Did he just say he loved me? No. I heard him wrong. I must have. The hormones had me going crazy.

"You what?"

My mind was no longer focused on his body.

He pulled back and looked in my eyes. I could see him rewinding what he'd just said. His face changed as he hit the part of the conversation that stopped my heart.

"I love you."

He said it softer than before, but with the same result, my heart skipped. His hands held my arms.

"I do. I can't imagine a day when I didn't see you."

"I love you, too," I blurted out, not realizing what I was saying.

I did love him, he wasn't taking over my life, he was enhancing it, showing me things I never knew existed. When I shared them with him, it heightened the experience. The few things I'd done without him seemed empty. Even, eating ice cream at DQ, I wished he were there. Not so I could be with him, but so he could share in the sweet taste I in my mouth.

I put in a DVD and we took our regular positions on my bed. Oscar against the wall and I was lying in between his legs. On nights when I was really tired, I used his leg as a body pillow, my head finding a nook between his thigh and hip and my leg wrapping around his. All the while his hands had been gently stroking my back.

I woke up the next morning alone, searching my pillow for any traces of him. In addition to his fragrance I found a note.

Ellie,

Since you came into my life I've felt as if my world was complete. Before you, I was just going through the motions. Doing what was expected and thinking that was enough. Now I'm living life, experiencing it, swallowing it whole. I'll wait forever for you and I hope you can understand I don't feel a loss by not

being with you in every way. To me, it's a build up to something that will change our lives, but I need to know you're truly ready for the change. I love you, and feel blessed to have you in my life. Please never doubt that.

Yours forever, Oscar

P.S. don't forget the advantages to wearing a dress!!!

I rolled over and grabbed my cell phone. I pressed speed dial and hoped I wouldn't get voicemail. Luckily, it only took two rings.

"Kelly, I need to get a dress!"

Chapter 11

The bonfire on Thursday night, the week of homecoming, was especially warm for me. Oscar gave me his letterman's coat. It covered me to my mid-thigh. It seemed as though a hundred hash marks went up the arm, and patches from state tournaments covered the back of the jacket.

But now I was in volleyball practice, not that anyone was focused. Everyone was talking about what they'd wear and how would they be able to change in enough time after the game to get to the dance. Other schools averted this problem by having the dance on Saturday instead of after the game. Some school administrator had the misguided notion students would drink only one night instead of two if the dance was after the game.

Our coach was on her last straw when Oscar came in, flipped me over his shoulder like a sack of potatoes and carried me off the court.

"Sorry, Coach Marks, if this wasn't an emergency, I'd never interrupt practice."

I could see Coach wanted to demand to know what emergency, but knew better. Usually, Oscar would wait until I was free or practice was over before he'd steal me for a good luck kiss, but this *was* homecoming. She just shook her head.

"Sharyn, take her place."

I giggled, thinking Sharyn wishes she could take my place, being carried off by Oscar to make out for five minutes. A few of the girls laughed as I laid there, the blood rushing to my face because I was upside down. I knew their laughter wasn't one of jealousy, but envy.

The girls in the school were finally over the initial shock of Oscar and I together and all seemed to wish they had a boyfriend just like him. He was always bringing me flowers or stealing me at the end of practice. Whenever we were together, his hand was somewhere on my body. I joked with him that he was marking his territory, but he pointed out I wasn't much better. All it would take was a girl to look at him and no matter how close I already was to him, I found a way to be just a little bit closer.

In the hallway he finally put me down, causing a head rush.

"Now it's homecoming so you need to wear my away jersey."

I returned the five-hundred-dollar home jersey to him that morning. At first he was mad I washed it, but then he said he wouldn't be able to concentrate if he could smell me during the game.

I threw the other jersey over my shoulder. Then Oscar sat down on a table that had been set out for the dance. He pulled my ponytail out so he could play with my hair. We were face-to-face when he put his hands on the back of my neck and brought my face to his. Our mouths opened, inviting each other in. Before I knew it, he was pulling away.

"I've got to get my head in the game, so I better go."

I kissed him on the forehead.

"Then I shouldn't tell you about the dress I found!"

"That wouldn't be helpful," he said, sliding off the table. Hand in hand we walked back into the gym. It was empty. I guess coach gave up and let everyone go. We parted, me to my locker room, him to his.

As I reached the door, I yelled over to him, "It's red!"

"Reallllllly not helping," he yelled back.

I giggled and went in. Kelly already showered. How long had we been kissing?

"Crisis averted, I see."

"Yes, I saved the world once again," I said, taking a bow.

I hopped in the shower. The more I was with Oscar, the more comfortable I was with my own body. I guess it was another way he showed me beauty I couldn't see. Kelly was waiting for me. I had everything I needed to get to the game. My dress was laid out at home for a quick change after the game. As I dressed, I laughed thinking about the marking-his-territory theory.

"What?" Kelly asked.

"Remember the marking the territory thing?"

I pointed to the jersey, ring and coat.

"Well, I'm just as bad."

Kelly and I could've been twins. The crowd for pregame activities seemed three times larger than the usual crowd. I was nervous we'd lose our spots in the stands. There was a dunk tank, pie throwing booth and quarterback toss-- all with the teachers and administrators as victims. Across the homecoming midway in the alumni stand I saw Sharyn, talking to the most beautiful woman I'd ever seen.

"Who's that?"

The woman looked familiar, but I couldn't place the face.

"Mya," Kelly said flatly.

Mya! My chest felt as if a vice had a hold on me. She wasn't the person I'd sneaked peeks at in the trophy case. She was a woman. Her hair was an adorable pixie cut, her skin was the color of an iced mocha and her brown eyes resembled a baby deer. Then there was her body. A woman's body! I never felt more like an inadequate child. All the positive words from Oscar were suddenly null and void. My A-cup chest was nothing compared to her C or D's. Her body cut in and back out like a woman's should, and she was at least five-foot-nine. She could've easily been a model. I started to wheeze and got so dizzy I could've been on a tilt-a-whirl. I reached a hand out for Kelly.

"Hey, hey, it's okay, calm down. He's yours now."

“How?” was all I could eek out. I saw Sharyn pointing to me. Mya’s eyes met mine and she laughed. They walked towards us. My hands felt like blocks of ice frozen in fear. Kelly moved her body slightly in front of me in a protective stance.

“So, you’re the one getting my throwaways.”

Her voice was shrill, and I started to see what Oscar meant by her beauty being only on the outside.

“You have a weird idea of trash,” I said, my voice steady.

Kelly turned to me, as surprised as I was I had stood up for myself. Maybe I still had Oscar’s strength inside me somewhere; it was like the weight of his coat made me strong and his arms were around me. My inner voice was actually working with me and not against me. I could hear Oscar telling me how much he hated her, how she was an empty person that needed others to validate her.

“But then again, those who are trash tend to treat others as if they were too.”

I said that out loud! I usually only said those types of things in my head. “I’m trash? You’re a frickin’ novelty. I’m sure he had some fantasy of doin’ a midget and that’s why he picked you. You’re short, ugly and flat-chested. If you weren’t easy, he wouldn’t even be talkin’ to you.”

Her words cut through me like a knife. It’d been at least a week since I’d been called a slut. The rest of the school stopped when they realized Oscar wasn’t leaving me.

Sharyn laughed, "Ohhh, she has you there, Soft Meat."

"Really, we're back there again, Sharyn."

My inner voice had gotten out of control and I couldn't shut it up.

"I thought Oscar made it more than clear to you that if he wanted a slut, he'd have returned your call."

Sharyn's eyes burned with hate.

"Hey, Ellie, how are you doing?"

A voice, deep and strong, came from behind me. I turned and saw Oscar's father smiling. Oscar and I'd watched football on Saturdays and Sundays at his house the past few weeks. We were both more comfortable sitting on his couch than my bed, having his dad two feet away in his recliner also helped us from going too far.

Mr. Jeffreys, a firefighter, was tall, but only six-foot-three. His hair was cut short in a fade, his skin the same chocolate shade as Oscar's and he was as fit as his son from the way his t-shirts hugged snuggly. He said he has a spare tire not a washboard. I could see Oscar in his smile, but a lost Oscar. He had a flat look, which never matched the face he tried to show the world. Oscar said his dad never got over the loss of his wife, which seemed to be the loss you could hear in his voice. Usually, he worked on the field as one of the paramedics for the game, but today he was in street clothes.

"I'm fine and you?" I replied, as my heart rate slowed.

"Oh, you know everyday above dirt's a good one." His voice changed when he said, "Mya." He barely acknowledged her. I could tell by the look on her face she didn't appreciate that.

"Mr. Jeffreys, anything new in your wood shop?" Wood shop? I didn't know about that and she knew I wouldn't. She looked at me and smiled as if she had just one-upped me.

"It's fine. Oscar and I've been working on some Christmas presents, but I better not talk 'bout in front of mixed company."

Was he talking about me? What was wrong with me?

Kelly nudged me, "You're getting a homemade gift for Christmas."

It was bad I needed someone to point that out to me. Mya's really effecting me.

"I need to steal Ellie. There're some people she needs to meet."

He clutched my elbow, pulling Kelly and me away.

"I saw the attack. You did good," he said. "I've always hated that girl."

I breathed in deep thinking at least I had an ally.

"I really do need you to meet some people. I hate doin' this stuff."

We crossed the midway and came up on three men eating popcorn. They all looked to be in their mid-to late forties. Each wore a pullover and a ball cap from a different college, University of Florida, Kansas University and the University of Southern

California. It suddenly struck me -- they were recruiters coming to talk Oscar into moving away.

"Hey, gentlemen, this is Ellie, Oscar's girlfriend, and star of the volleyball team."

They looked at my small stature and turned questioningly.

"She's one of those set things."

"A setter," Kelly corrected. "She's become invaluable on the team. I'm Kelly."

She extended her hand and nudged me to do the same.

"Nice to meet you," the man from Kansas finally said. "We have a great tradition for volleyball in Kansas."

"Okay, I'll keep that in mind. I still have a few years left before I have to make a decision."

"You're a junior?"

"Um…No, sophomore."

Nervously, I pulled Oscar's coat closer, trying to play off my shaking voice was from the cold, not my inability to create a full sentence.

The other two coaches looked away, not really interested in a sophomore. If anything I was a liability to them.

"But you're the star of the team already. That's impressive," the Kansas coach said. Obviously, he thought I could still be of some help to him.

"I don't know if I'd say I was the star…" I replied, nervous about the way this was going. "So it looks like you came a long way. I wouldn't think that you would be up on Minnesota football."

"Normally, we aren't," USC answered, "but when we got information on Oscar, we suddenly became interested. It's amazing what you can catch online. We saw his game against North St. Paul a few weeks ago. He's got some great raw talent."

"He's a great guy, volunteering and helping out others. I'm sure he could adjust to any offensive scheme you run."

It was killing me to say that. I know that USC runs a pro-style offense and Florida a spread. I'd heard Oscar talk about it enough. The thought of him going three thousand miles away made my stomach hurt.

I could see that I'd impressed the coaches with my small knowledge, that they each ran a different offense and that was my job to help sell Oscar no matter how much it killed me inside.

"We need to get to our seats. I can't miss this one," I said, shaking their hands. "Goodbye, Mr. Jeffreys, I'll see you later."

I grasped one of Kelly's hands as we headed in. "Oh my God, that was hard," I said as I tried to catch my breath.

"You did great, but what was so hard about that?"

"Did you see where they're from?" My voice was almost a whine. "The closest one's over five hundred miles away. The other two are over three thousand. How am I going to live without him?"

"Slow down. They're looking at him. You don't know if he's looking at them."

"He must be. He requested information from them."

"That could've been before he met you and you have no idea what he's thinking. Don't do this to yourself."

She knew me well enough if she didn't stop my inner tormentor it would consume me.

We found our regular spots and somehow they were open. The stands filled up. On the field Oscar led the stretching. We had at least fifteen minutes before the game was to start. Rescanning the stands, I saw Mya sitting with a few other alumni and some of the girls that still were talking about me behind my back.

The first half went by really fast. The games were more exciting now that I understood what was going on. At halftime, we led 14-0. The band went crazy doing all the tricks they could. The dance line followed them. With five minutes left in halftime the Homecoming court was introduced. Oscar was one of the five seniors up for homecoming king. It was then I realized Mya won both homecoming and prom queen last year. She stood behind Oscar. His arm was linked with Steph, one of the few seniors on the volleyball team. The rest of the players were walking with cheerleaders. Even though this was a tradition, it was hard for me to see him with Steph. They were laughing about something. I breathed in deeply. I knew I should be more worried about Mya.

The emcees slowly announced the princes and princesses. The choice of king was now between Oscar and Trey, a defensive end. Mya played up the crowd, holding the crown above everyone, even a ref who accidentally stood too close. She walked in front of Oscar and placed the crown on his head and a hand on his chest. The crowd erupted with cheers. Oscar step back to get her hand off him and I smiled. After waving to the crowd, he motion to me, wanting me to come to the bottom of the stands. I ran down, stopping at the railing. He came over holding the crown and with his finger motioned me to lean over. I did, my reward a kiss, as he put the crown on my head and he ran back to the sidelines, ready for the second half.

Back at my seat holding his crown I felt as if I'd won first prize. On the sidelines one of the coaches was talking to Oscar again. But he just looked at the coach, then me, and turned back to the game. I didn't know what was going on, but that coach was really getting under Oscar's skin.

The game took a turn for the worse. A fumble on the twenty-yard line led to a touchdown by the opposing team. Five plays later, they ran back a punt sixty-five yards for another touchdown. The score remained tied for the rest of the third quarter. I could see Oscar was getting frustrated. The defense wasn't doing their job and the opposing offense was staying on the field. Out of nowhere Max burst through the line of scrimmage causing the quarterback to second-guess his plan. Max had him on the ground before he knew what hit him. The loss of seven yards was enough to get the team pumped back up. On the next play Max broke through the left guard and headed straight for the running back hitting him so hard he fumbled the ball. Trey was there landing on it and we regained possession on their thirty-four yard line.

Finally our offense could take the field with less than two minutes left on the clock. I was on the edge of my seat, screaming.

After the hike to the quarterback Oscar was in motion cutting across the middle for a slant play. He caught the ball, but was tackled immediately. It was just enough for a first down, but the clock still ran. The quarterback called them all to the huddle as fast as they could. The clock still ticked down 1:40, 1:39, 1:38. The huddle broke and they're all on the line again. A run play got us three yards, but cost us fifteen seconds. Again they ran to the huddle 1:14, 1:13. Break. They were lined up with three receivers just off the line. Oscar was to the right. The ball was snapped. Oscar ran to about our 40 again, the quarterback threw to him, but it was high. Oscar jumped and caught it right above the cornerback. He landed and turned to run, but saw he was trapped so he ran out of bounds to stop the clock.

Finally, we were down to forty-five seconds on our forty-yard line. Another run play ate up ten seconds and the team didn't even huddle. They must've been doing the hurry-up offense. I couldn't tell if it was just good clock management or their way of trying to kill me slowly. We were down to twenty seconds. The line was set :19, :18 the quarterback called the play "Blue 22, Right 45" :17, :16, "Hut, hut, hut" :15, :14, the ball is hiked. The quarterback fell back into the pocket. :13, :12. The left tackle missed his assignment and a defensive end barreled towards the quarterback. :11, :10, :09. The quarterback scrambled to the right looking down field. :08, :07 :06. Oscar was in the end zone. The quarterback dodged the end one more time and threw to the back corner of the end zone. :05, :04, :03. Again the quarterback threw high. Oscar adjusted, moving slightly over. :02 :01. He jumped and caught the ball with one hand behind his head. He pulled the ball into his stomach with all his might. I knew this was an attempt to pull his body forward so he could land inbounds. His feet touched down as he fell forward holding the ball. The buzzer sounded. We won! They kicked the extra point as the crowd erupted with applause. Up in the stands, Mr. Jeffreys and the three scouts are all shaking his hands and nodding in unison. I knew Oscar earned a free ride to whatever college he wanted to go to.

The adrenaline from the game was overwhelming. It overwhelmed my thought of Oscar leaving for college. It was a drug that had me happier than I'd ever been in my life. Kelly and I ran to our normal place at the end of the tunnel and waited for our heroes to come running through. The screams were louder than ever.

Defensively I used my arms to cover my face as the players ran around me. Someone picked me up. I threw my arms around Oscar, my lips meeting his. Sweat was dripping off him, making his kiss salty, but I didn't care. He was mine for now and that's all that mattered.

I pulled my face away and said, "That. Was. Awesome!"

Our eyes were locked and noses were touching as we kissed. I'd been wearing his crown and it fell down over my eyes. I let go of his neck as he laughed at me being blinded. I placed the crown on his head.

"That's better."

"I don't think so."

But between his helmet and me, his hands were full so he had to wear the crown. His father called for him, Oscar turned and his face fell. He let my body go, moving his free hand to mine as we walked over to his father. I couldn't understand his change in mood.

"Oscar, this is Coach Marvin, Coach Kane and Coach Tomlin."

Oscar extended his hand, shaking hands with each one, then returning his hand to mine.

"Hell of a game you had tonight, son," Coach Marvin said.

"We understand you have some activities planned tonight, but I know I'd really like to talk to you about what USC can offer you at this time," Coach Kane said.

"It was nice to meet all of you. Maybe you could set up sometimes for me to talk to you tomorrow. I really need to get showered and changed. I'd hate to disappoint my Lil' Girl here."

His eyes cut to his father as he said, "Dad, can you please set up some times. I have to go to the garden at one and meet with my scoutmaster at three."

The garden was his eagle project. He had taken me there one day. He convinced the city to turn a lot into a community garden at no cost for the first five years. Area nurseries donated vegetables, seeds and small pots. It was amazing. It was in a poor neighborhood, and now at least during the summer the residents would have fresh vegetables to eat. He needed to finish the paperwork and his project would go before the Eagle Board of Review. I was amazed at all he had done; I only wished I could've seen it from the beginning.

"I really have to run, but I look forward to seeing you tomorrow."

He squeezed my hand to let me know we were leaving.

"It was nice to meet you. Goodbye," I said as we walked away.

"I don't know why he did that. I told him I want to go to the U," Oscar said when we were out of earshot of his father.

"You're going to the U?" I asked, trying not to sound too excited.

"That's what I was planning. I don't want to go away to school. I have too much here to lose."

He squeezed my hand and pulled me closer. "You're staying here because of me?" I asked, not wanting to have him sell himself short because of me.

"Not just you, but I've got my garden and scout camp. This is my home. Minnesota has a D-one school with great academics. I'd be getting in-state tuition. I'm not ruling the other school out," he said, looking over his shoulder, "that's why I said I'd meet with them. No reason to burn a bridge, but I really don't see any reason to go away to school. Look, there'll be at least five other big schools coming over the next few weeks. I have no idea how many during basketball season. My dad decided to send out information on me to a ton of schools, hoping I'd get a full ride."

"He seems to be doing that for everyone," I said, remembering his introduction of me.

"What'da you mean?"

"He was tryin' to sell me as part of the package. The volleyball player their school was missing."

"He likes you," Oscar teased, a small smile returned to his face.

"I gathered that, but I have a red dress to put on and I see a very impatient friend waiting for me."

Kelly stood by her car with her arms crossed, tapping her foot.

"Uhhhg, look at the line of cars. Do you think it'd be okay if you came and picked Kelly and me up at my house? We we're just going to change and I bet I could walk there faster."

"I guess, just be safe."

"Kelly has killed before, you know?"

"I heard she just maimed."

Kelly and I walked to my house with me gushing all the way. I felt happy. Kelly reminded me it was not against the law for me to be happy.

As we were dressing my nerves started up again. I looked in the mirror and didn't recognize myself. Kelly worked with me all week so I could walk in heels, but I was still wobbly. My hair was pulled up with loose curls around my face and in a very loose ponytail, my lips and eyes were now defined thanks to makeup, and my dress was red. The three-quarter length dress I'd found in the back at the ARC animal thrift store had three spaghetti straps attached to a tight upper bodice with a flowing skirt that fanned out. The shoes were also red, a Mary Jane with a medium heel. Red made me look paler than usual, but Kelly grabbed me by my shoulders and said, "You look beautiful."

Chapter 12

The doorbell rang and I walked slowly to the door, steadying myself as I maneuvered in heels. I slowly opened the door, Max and Oscar both wore khaki pants. Max had a yellow button up shirt, Oscar a French blue shirt and a sweater vest with a diamond pattern down the front. The vest fit snuggly. Oscar's look was all I needed to lose any doubt about how I looked.

I put a black shawl around by shoulders, but as I walked out I realized Oscar was all I needed. With his arm around me pulling me close, the sweet smell of his fresh cologne filling my lungs my whole body was warm. As we drove to the dance, he placed a hand on my thigh. The sheer size of it amazed me; his hand was as big as my leg. I had gotten used to how big he was. To me, he was just the right size and didn't seem strange, but then I'd see someone look at him or he'd touch me and his size came to the forefront of my mind.

We arrived just before the royalty dance. Oscar had to dance with the queen; who was one of the cheerleaders. They were all the same to me. I stood to the side waiting. Halfway through the song, the DJ told the royalty they could dance with their dates. Oscar immediately walked over to me and escorted me to the dance floor.

He was more graceful than I'd imagined he'd be, exceptionally so. As we glided around the dance floor, I noticed Mya. Someone must've brought her. I breathed in deeply to try to control my jealousy. As the song ended, Oscar walked me to a table.

"So what's wrong?" Oscar asked catching me off guard.

"What do you mean?"

"I heard you sigh," he said, putting an arm around me.

"Mya's here. I'm just a little intimidated, that's all."

I placed my hands on his leg.

"No one in that dress should ever be intimidated," he said, kissing my cheek.

We sat in silence for a few minutes. He nuzzled my neck. *Lady in Red* started to play and he led me back to the dance floor. This time his hands stroked up and down my back. Every time his bare skin touched mine, I shivered. I couldn't wrap my arms around his neck like the other girls were doing with their partners, so I had one arm around his waist and rubbed his chest with the other.

"Did you request this?" I asked, thinking it was the perfect song, but it was from the 80s and there's no way it's in the regular rotation.

"No, but now that you mention it…"

He listened to the words.

"It does seem appropriate. You've stolen my breath away more than once tonight."

"Maybe I'll have to give some back," I said, bringing his head down so I could kiss him.

We danced in a group for fast songs, with Kelly, Max, Jessie and her date Brent, and got tighter and closer with each slow song. About an hour into the dance, I excused myself and walked to the bathroom. Mya was there checking her make-up.

"Having fun?"

She was talking to me, but not taking her eyes off herself. "Wow, you're so young. This must be your first dance, huh? I remember when Oscar and I came last year. It was great. I wore this short skirt and I stole my parent's credit card so we could get a motel room. I didn't get any sleep that night, but I'm sure you know all about that, don't you?"

"Not really."

The thought of her with Oscar all night was making my head ache. I began replaying every movie sex scene I'd ever watched, but with the leads replaced.

"Don't tell me you're not doing him," she said. Finally turning to look at me. "I thought for sure you would be. He has to be getting it somewhere.

"I guess you're his little Madonna virgin he parades out for show," she scoffed, turning back to look at herself. "But trust me, he's getting it somewhere. He's got quite the stable. Girl or not, Oscar's gotta get his dick wet a couple times a day."

I didn't know if she was being spiteful or not. It's not like it wasn't something I hadn't thought about. *If I can't give him what he needs physically, would he? Is he?* Every time he touched me it sent surges through my body I loved him and he loved me. Why shouldn't I just get it over with? It's not that big of a deal. But then I looked at my sisters and knew it was.

If he wasn't with me, he could go away for college, he could be satisfied physically. Why would he be with me? All the work Oscar had done to make me start believing in who I was crumbled in one sentence. *Trust me, he's getting it somewhere.*

Leaving the bathroom, I brought a hand at my eyes trying to keep any tears at bay. I turned left and saw Sharyn kissing Oscar in a dark corner, a hand groped one of her thighs sliding her dress up as a leg started to wrap around his body. My heart was in my throat. I couldn't breathe. I gasped for words when from out of nowhere, Kelly yanked me into a classroom.

"It's not what you think," she said, trying to calm me down, the vision of Oscar's mouth open, accepting Sharyn's, was seared in my mind. My heart felt as if it was being burned and the flames were licking my throat.

"He's sleeping with Sharyn!" I screeched.

"No, he's not."

She made me sit down. I wanted to stand, but I lost all power in my legs..

“I knew this was going to happen,” Kelly babbled, more to herself than to me. “I just don’t know how much I’m allowed to tell you.”

“You knew this would happen?” I shrieked, thinking of all the times she told me to allow myself to be happy. “How are you my friend? Why’d you let me be around him? You encouraged me to let myself love him!”

My hand was at my chest, my eyes burned and tears flowed.

“He’s not kissing her.”

“I saw him kissing her!” I screamed, slamming my fist onto the desk.

“No, you saw the illusion of him kissing her. She’s making out with Spencer, she just wishes it was Oscar and…” Kelly breathed in deeply. “I’m getting ahead of myself.”

I couldn’t understand what she was saying. I just knew I wanted out of there, but I couldn’t move. Kelly seemed extraordinarily strong, only she wasn’t touching me, just holding out her hand, but it felt like I was tied down.

“I need you to understand something. I’m not who you think I am. Do you remember me from before Caleb’s accident?”

Nausea surged from my stomach to my throat. Why was she asking me this? What did that have to do with Oscar cheating on me; crushing my heart into a million pieces?

“Focus!” she said, seizing the desk and looking me in the eyes. “Do you remember me?”

"No," I blurted, wanting her to end the asinine questioning.

"You don't remember me because I wasn't there before Caleb died. His death is what brought me into your life."

I wasn't sure what she meant and really didn't care.

"There's...well, the best way to describe it is a curse. Sometime ago someone in your family upset a demon. 'Upset' is too light of word, but it's the best I have now. He's been integrating himself into your family in hopes of making your lives miserable. After Caleb I was sent to protect you, since you were next in line."

"Caleb was killed by a train."

"No, he wasn't. There's a demon after your family."

I shook my head, not understanding.

"A demon, pitchfork, horns, Lake of Fire, demon. Lucifer? You're trying to tell me demons are real?"

"Very real," she said. Her eyes, the ancient old soul eyes always been there imparting wisdom on me now pleaded with me to believe her.

"So, you're telling me Caleb was killed by a demon?"

I forgot the hallway and the vision of Oscar with Sharyn. Now I was caught in some parallel universe where nothing made sense.

"Not really killed. As humans you have free will. The demon twists reality to make you or your family members do things you wouldn't normally do, but you have the ability to stop it."

Her voice finally slowed, knowing I was at least listening to her.

"When Caleb died, God as you would choose to call him, had had enough. It pained him to see Jennifer, Levi and Grace do what they did, but they were older. Caleb was just a small child. The demon possessed a young boy and taunted Caleb to ride his bike on railroad tracks. Think about it Ellie, how far away are the tracks from your house? Over a mile. The little boy had been goading Caleb for months and he finally broke, but then the demon used an illusion to cover the train noise, so Caleb hadn't really made a choice of his own free will. He attacked because Caleb was happy. Remember he'd just gotten a new bike, he loved his fourth grade teacher and he'd just started to play tackle football. The demon can't stand when anyone in your family's happy. Your older brother and sisters were easy. He just steered them down the wrong path and now they're stuck in a miserable life with no hope of escape."

"But Caleb wasn't easy?"

"No, not with you as his sister. Remember how much Dawson hated you?"

I nodded.

"He hadn't hated you until the demon was with him. But Caleb…Caleb and he would fight because he felt bad about being mean to you."

"Why? Why us?"

The years of paranoia no longer seemed so absurd.

"We don't know exactly what happened. We just know something changed around ten years ago."

"What are you?"

I hoped I was in a dream, but something about her voice made me believe what she said. It could've been real. I'd seen chances for my family to be happy a hundred times, but they always went the other direction.

Even now Grace had chosen to move in with a guy she had to be selling herself too instead of just staying in the house or getting her own apartment. And Levi, he always said he was going to stop but then he kept hanging out with the same people, making the same mistakes.

"For lack of a better word, I'm a guardian angel. I'd have been classified as a goddess in other cultures. You humans have always amused me with your need to explain the world around you. In Norse tradition I was Sif, in Roman, I was Juno, Athenia in Greek, Isis is Egyptian, Matronit in Spanish…"

I could tell she wanted me to acknowledge one of these names.

"None of them truly got it right. I've always been the protector of women. Some had me as a goddess of fertility and a thousand other things. But I digress. When you as humans moved to a monotheistic philosophy, all of the 'gods' became angels, still protecting the humans.

"This is a lot to absorb, but I need you to listen to me. Oscar's in love with you. He wasn't the one in the hall. The demon was using Sharyn's imagination to change Spencer into Oscar *in your mind.* She's telling herself that he's Oscar and that's why she's letting Spencer do what he's doing."

"Who's the demon?"

"We have ideas, but we can't know for sure. We aren't omnipresent like we've been described. I can't see the future or the past, for that matter. There are just too many people to watch. You humans really like to procreate."

There it was again, *you humans.* She spoke as if I was a second-class being.

"I have a few powers, but the one that's important to you is that I can see auras. You know what those are, right?"

I nodded, thinking of a *Sci-Fi* show on aura cameras. Outside every person's supposedly layers of color that determine things about you. Your health, love, happiness.

"Humans have one, immortals don't."

Immortal? Thoughts of vampires and werewolves crossed my mind as I replayed all of the *Underworld* movies in my head.

"The demon may be able to disguise himself as a human, but I should be able to pick him out. I wasn't sure how he was going to attack you, but I knew it was going to be soon. Your aura has been almost blinding, it's been so bright. For years it's been a dark brown. We knew eventually your love would come and change your aura and the demon would attack. After Caleb we couldn't stand by anymore."

"My love?" I asked, forgetting my thoughts of her drinking my blood.

"Everyone has a love, Ellie. When they connect for the first time, there's a flash that shoots off them placing a hook in their hearts. If they ever break apart, it causes a hole that leaks forever and can never be resealed. The reason I didn't see you when you set the ball was because there was a blinding flash when Oscar touched you."

Oscar was my true love? How could that be? We were so young. As much as I couldn't imagine my life without him, I wasn't about to delude myself he was the one I should be with forever. The mere thought was more overwhelming to me than the thought Kelly was going to sprout wings and a halo.

"That's why I've been trying to keep you together," she continued, "he's your love. Many people pass theirs by or rush to get married and just settle for the first person to say yes because that's what was expected. They didn't wait for their flash and they ended up living a life of sorrow. Oh, they may've been content, but neither was ever truly happy. Deep down inside they knew they were with the wrong person. When you touched Oscar, he felt as if his whole world suddenly made sense. He can't even explain to himself how he has an unconditional love for you from the start. If you walk away from Oscar, you'll never be happy and then the demon will win. Men will come into your life, but you'll never be able to love or care for them. With your heart closed off forever, you'll never feel fulfilled and eventually you'll start to take risks that could be detrimental to your soul."

"Who's the demon?"

The only demon I knew was Lucifer and no matter how paranoid I was, I could never believe the Devil himself was after me.

She sighed in annoyance.

"We believe it's Gaap, a prince of hell. There are so many of them, it's hard to pick out which one's tormenting your family, but he's our top suspect. We'll help you try to reason with him, but we can't kill him. Only a human can do that. As far as who he's posing as, I have no idea. It'd have to be someone that knows you, but isn't too close. I'd have felt him if he was close to you."

My mind reeled as I tried to think of all the people that make my life miserable. Sharyn, Mya, Jordan, my mother. No, I think I'd know if my mother was a…I couldn't even fathom what she was saying.

"Why can't you just go after Gaap?"

"We need proof. The damnation of a celestial that accuses without cause is unthinkable. Don't worry. We'll be looking out for you."

"Wasn't Caleb proof enough?"

"No, we weren't watching as closely as we are now. We never thought he'd have gone as far as killing one of you. Let you live a life a misery, try to steal your soul, yes, but not take a life."

Was that supposed to be a comfort to me? That my life was destined to be one of misery?

It was then I realized she kept saying the word 'we.'

"Who's we?"

"Oh, Max you may know as Thor, Mars, etcetera. I got bored after a few years here living with you," she said nonchalantly. "He's been my love for many millennia."

I wasn't sure if I believed what I'd heard or if I wanted to. I always wanted an excuse for my paranoia. Kelly had just given me one; someone was out to get me. A magazine cover caught my eye and I suddenly realized I was in Mr. Pierce's room.

"Was Jesus black or white?" I read the cover out loud.

"What?" Kelly asked.

"Was Jesus black or white?"

I needed something to take my mind off the thought of my doomed fate.

"What does that matter? Jesus, Mohammed, Buddha, they were men that embodied love. Only humans who don't love put a value on color. When you look at Oscar, do you see a black man or man?"

I closed my eyes and pictured Oscar, the smell of his cologne, the softness of his skin, his body, his eyes, his mouth, but I couldn't picture his skin, it was just him, a man. A man I loved, a man who was black, but that wasn't what he was.

"I never thought about that."

"Neither does he. When people start seeing other's outside more than their inside it darkens their aura. It eats at their soul, if you will. If Oscar had been born white, short and chubby, you'd still find him attractive because you see him, not his color. His aura's as bright as yours. When the two of you are together, it's really hard to keep my eyes open," she sighed. "He puts up with a lot to be with you because when he thinks of leaving you, he can feel the pain in his heart."

"Am I that bad?" I said, thinking we rarely fight, everything seemed wonderful when he was around. "Is it because we're not sleeping together? Mya said—"

"Mya's a dumb ass who only knew one part of Oscar. Oscar only wants you. He's done settling."

"Then why does he think about leaving?"

"His friends and coaches," she said, looking at her hands. "They don't want you two together because of your race. And they aren't always diplomatic in their comments to him. We need to get you back to him, by the way. Max can only talk for so long. I want you to look down the hallway and tell me what you see. Remember, you have to focus to see the truth. Mya weakened your aura, making you susceptible to Gaap's tricks. You must clear your head. Think about those magic eye posters you have to relax your eyes to see the real picture underneath."

"Like in *Mallrats*."

"Yes. It's a schooner."

I'd forgotten about Mya and I tried to force the image of her out again. I opened the door and peered down the hall. Sharyn was still pinned up against the wall. I made my eyes relax and then adjusting my point of focus until I saw Spencer trying to get Sharyn to leave with him. Then closed my eyes to refocus to make sure what I'd seen this time was real, I reopened my eyes and immediately saw Spencer and Sharyn. I went back in the classroom looking at Kelly or whatever her name was.

"Ellie, you knew it'd be hard to date Oscar. You just didn't know the real reason why. We will be helping you until the demon's gone. You have the right to be happy. This was just the demon's first subtle attack meant to get you so mad you'd never believe anything Oscar said in his defense. There will be more, they will start getting physical, but I know you're strong enough to handle it."

Strong. That's a word never used to describe me.

"You can't tell Oscar. He just wouldn't understand. He has enough to deal with already."

"I was about to send out a search party for you," Oscar teased, not fazed by my extended absence. "You okay, Lil' Girl?"

When we saw Oscar and Max, Kelly knew she had to explain my demeanor

"Sorry, it was a girl thing. Mya was runnin' her mouth, so I had to calm Ellie down. It's okay. The crisis averted."

I could see the anger in Oscar's eyes. My arms went around his neck as I sat down on his lap.

"Just hold me and tell me you love me," I said in a low tone.

His arms surrounded me.

"Lil' Girl, you know I love you more than peanut butter and chocolate."

I giggled with my face buried in the crook of his neck, but I peeked to see Kelly and Max turn their heads like a flashlight was just shone in their eyes. I felt warm as tears escaped my eyes.

"Hey now." His hand came to my head, gently petting my hair. "It's okay. It's over now."

His words reminded me of Kelly's warning. *That was just the first attack.*

Chapter 13

My inner voice wouldn't shut up. All night long it was harassing me, throwing images and scenes through my head, yelling at me in a thousand voices, telling me I was damned. By four a.m. I knew I needed help. I got up to find anything with a p.m. in its name. My closet was always stuffed with junk because I just couldn't let anything go. If I did, it'd be something I needed the next day. After Levi started taking drugs, our family removed everything but straight Tylenol and ibuprofen from the house. I always kept a small bottle of Advil or Tylenol P.M. in my closet.

I shook the bottles contents into my hand and six pills tumbled out. I ran my fingers over them and thought about that night. Kelly's words boomed in my ears. Gaap wanted to torture my family and me; his mission was to make my life horrible, a living hell on earth. He would keep attacking me until I not only lost Oscar, but lost myself and becoming a shell of a person. Was my life worth fighting for? It would be easy to empty the rest of this bottle. No one would stop me, not even Kelly. I had free will. She said that. I could make the choice to end this fight here. I didn't have to fight. If I was doomed to a life of pain and disappointment, why not just end it now?

The bottle felt light in my hand, as I dumped the rest of its contents into my palm. They tempted me, a handful of sweet candy made a light clack when they touched each other. I rolled them around in my left hand, examining them in the light. There had to be at least twenty. I touched each one, counting them as my brain tried to calculate if I had enough to complete the task.

In this house no one would check on me for a least a week, unless the smell got bad. I turned to my pillow, imagining my face cold and empty. They would feign grief in an effort to illicit sympathy.

I could see my sister Grace holding the hand of some random stranger, telling him how she just couldn't go to work because of my death and she was afraid she'd lose her car. She wouldn't care about me; she'd just want the car.

Levi would be mad I beat him to the punch. Ironically, he thought the drugs and alcohol could chase away his demons. He had no idea they pleased the demon that was hunting all of us.

Jennifer, she wouldn't understand, no matter what was thrown at her. She accepted it as her cross to bear, the consummate victim, she adored the role. It amazed me she hadn't started to hurt her kids in an attempt to get attention. Oh well, only time would tell.

I dropped the pills like an hourglass between my hands, slowly counting down the minutes to the end of my life, my left hand created a cup, slowly dripping them into the right like a leaky faucet. My hand turned slightly and the stone in Oscar's ring and the light from small lamp on my nightstand created a flash that blinded me for a minute.

A blinding light. I hadn't thought about him, how it would affect him. His heart would leak forever. Would that be as bad as the torment I'd put him through? I got up and crossed the room to where his coat laid. As I put it on a couple of pills dropped to the floor. I picked them up, but they didn't hold the same allure as they had a minute ago. I put them away, but kept one for if I still couldn't sleep.

With Oscar's coat around me, I could feel his arms encircle me keeping me safe, his cologne still strong, and I breathed in as much of it as I could. It filled my body up as if he was in the room with me. I could feel his hand stroking my hair and whispering, *it will be alright as long as we're together*. I felt as if I was being rocked to sleep. The pill fell from my hand, landing on the pillow next to me, as my eyelids became heavy. My inner voice finally helped me to fall asleep as his voice echoed all the wonderful things he'd ever said to me, or I wished he had, until I was asleep.

The morning broke too early for me as Drew ran into my room and crashed with a thud on my stomach.

"Ouch, Oh my god, that hurt."

"Up, Auntie El, momma made pannycakes."

He jumped off me as quickly has he jumped on and ran out the door.

With my eyes not wanting to adjust to the light, I looked at my clock only to read the red digital numbers 8:30. I rolled over, knowing all too well if I didn't get up soon I'd be the victim of another drive by jumping.

I hit me I hadn't taken my pill the night before. Frantically, I dug around my pillow and hoped Drew, *the boy who could eat anything as long as he thought it contained sugar*, hadn't found it. My hand reached under, over and in my pillow. Nothing. I jumped out of bed and felt something hard under my foot. I quickly put the pill back in the bottle and hid it in my closet. I didn't know if Gaap would be attacking my nieces and nephew. It made sense. It'd be free will for a small child to eat a sleeping pill. The thought sent shivers down my spine. I'd never think of suicide again. With me out of the picture, Drew, Adriana and Taylor would be at too much risk. I could do this. I could be the one to save my family, if from nothing else but itself.

It was cold in the house and I wasn't ready to lose Oscar's jacket yet so I walked upstairs with it on. The ruff wool on the outside was scratching against my neck, but somehow it still made everything all right. I sat at the table, wrapped in his coat, and eating slowly. The kids were making a mess as usual and Jennifer just kept cooking pancakes to add to the stack in the center of the table.

"Sorry about Drew waking you up," she said, not turning away from the stove. "I hope it wasn't too early for you."

Knowing I had had only four hours of sleep, I decided to take Jennifer's role in the family and bear the cross. "No, I got in early, so it wasn't too bad."

"That's good. How was the game and the dance? We could hear people yelling last night. Did they win?"

"Yeah, Oscar caught a pass in the end zone right as time ran out."

"Oh, isn't that exciting. I don't remember going to too many games when I was in school."

I could tell she was trying to think back to when she had freedom to go places.

"I guess I just hung with the wrong people. I do remember wanting to go to homecoming one year, but Jeri talked me out of it. She said it would be boring and we could find something better to do with our time than watching a bunch of jocks pummel each other. I guess she was right. That was the night I met Marcus." Her hand instinctively reached for her right forearm, the one he'd broken because she couldn't get Adriana to be quiet one night.

Then it clicked.

"Jerry?"

I didn't remember Jerry, but Jennifer was very popular. At least she was before Marcus.

"Oh, you remember Jeri she…"

She? I thought Kelly said Gaap was a man?

"…had these really cool eyes, the truest green I'd ever seen."

She looked at me like this one trait would make me instantly remember who she was talking about.

"Well anyway, she transferred, I think from Harding mid-sophomore year. I don't know where she's now. I kind of lost track of her once I started dating Marcus…"

She caught herself, not wanting to let the kids in on the tale of abuse.

"Anyway that was a long time ago. So how was the dance?"

My mind was processing what she just said. A female tricked her into dating someone who set her down the wrong path. I did know most of Jennifer's friends. It was weird I hadn't known that one. Jennifer was looking at me for an answer.

"Oh, it was great. He's a really good dancer."

I ran downstairs to call Kelly.

"Is this the story of my sister making her own choice that ruined her life?"

"I think it may be part of the story," Kelly said.

"You told me Gaap was male."

"I also told you he'd disguise himself."

"How am I going to do this?" I asked, hope fading from my voice.

"In a word, Oscar. He's repaired so many years of damage, faster than anyone I've ever seen in my life, and that's saying something.

Haven't you noticed how you've been standing up for yourself lately? You haven't been running away from fights, but embracing the challenge."

"I have not," I said defensively.

"Think about it. You shower after practice in the locker room. You wore a dress, a red dress to the dance! You've snapped on Sharyn more than once." Kelly paused to help me consider her theory. "You haven't been winning too many, but you've been testing the water. You're like a baby pulling itself up and walking around a table. For every negative thing said to you, it takes ten positive to counteract them. Oscar's been doing that for you."

She had me there. I never wore red even under another shirt.

"I'm still not sure if I'm ready for this."

"I'd be surprised if you were," Kelly said, in an understanding voice. "I'm asking you to not only defend yourself against something that's immortal and extremely powerful, but to fight it and try to defeat it."

"How am I supposed to defeat something that's immortal?"

"Immortal's your term for it. Everything can die. Sometimes things are harder to kill. In your world you've had some of those. Look at Rasputin."

Rasputin. Images of the cartoon *Anastasia* ran though my head. The girl who never knew the man who initially befriended her had hunted her. That cartoon no longer seemed as cute and adorable as it once had.

"You sound like you had a hard night and are still tired?"

How much did she know? Had she been watching me as I had been playing with the pills?

"Take a nap. When you have your strength again, we can talk about defending yourself."

She hung up and I turned on the TV. *ESPN.* I guess I hadn't been watching TV lately if this was the channel it was on. I looked for the remote by my bed, but gave up. *College Game Day* had already started. Predictions and theories about the games abounded. It amazed me commentators could take up almost three hours with predictions, then that night there would be another three hours of recap. I turned the volume down low and started to fall asleep. Although I appreciated the games more, I was glad I wouldn't be stuck watching these games all day since Oscar would be interviewing with the coaches.

I curled up on my side and fell asleep, too exhausted to worry about the world that was starting to surround me. It felt like I'd only been asleep for a minute when I felt someone kissing my neck and working his way up to my cheek. I rolled over, not knowing who it was, but having a pretty good idea. The now familiar lips moved to mine and I tasted something sweet in my mouth. My tongue automatically accepted it and I felt him tease me. I could barely move, I was so exhausted from lack of sleep. A familiar hand swept up my body, as I shivered.

His body was on top of mine, our skin touching, his perfect bare chest weighing on my now naked chest. His body slid between my legs, as his hands slowly pulled down my underwear. His lips never leaving mine, my eyes still not open, I shivered, realizing there were no longer barriers between him and me. He'd lost control and I wasn't going to stop him. He no longer hovered above me, but let his sheer body weight press against mine. His lips were moving to my neck. My hands explored his body. I could feel something wet and warm as if we were sweating, but it was thicker.

I started to gasp for air and knew something was wrong. I pushed against him, but he wouldn't move. I tried to scream. I opened my eyes to see Oscar, lifeless on top of me. His eyes empty. I was no longer in my room, but on a cliff with fire shooting up all around me. I struggled to breathe, as I started to push Oscar off me. I felt warm blood flowing down from his back, dripping on me. My whole body was warm as heat from the fires surrounded me. Freeing myself, I saw a pitchfork, red and smoldering, stuck in his back. I took his face in my hands, his blood still covered them, and I apologized for loving him. If I hadn't cared about Oscar, he'd be alive now.

"He would be, you know." A high-pitched male voice said from a few feet away. "You killed him."

I turned and looked at this creature with tight red skin and jet-black hair. He wore a black suit and tie and was the culmination of all the cheesy horror movies I had ever seen, except for his eyes. The eyes were green, the greenest eyes I'd ever seen.

"Everything you touch will die," he continued, as I cowered, balled up next to Oscar. "No good will ever come of your life."

"Why are you doing this to me?" I yelled.

There was a loud pounding and the walls started to shake. Rocks came tumbling down. "Ellie, Ellie," a voice called to me as something hot burned my skin. I defensively swung to hit it away and the walls shook even more.

"Hey, Lennox Lewis, wake up."

I opened my eyes. I was still in my room and Oscar was there, alive. I flung my arms around him, holding him so tight he started to choke.

"Hey, calm down," he said, trying to breathe.

Tears flowed from my eyes.

"I thought he got you," I sobbed.

"You thought who got me?"

"He killed you, I saw you lying there," I said, as my body shook with fear.

"It was just a dream."

He pulled my arms from around his neck.

"I'm here," he continued, "but if you keep hitting me and trying to strangle me, I don't know how long I'll survive. I'll have to keep this in mind if I ever get to spend the night with you. Has violent dreams that'll be taken out on others."

I wiped the tears away as I held my breath trying to get myself under control. He lifted my chin. His face was darkening around his eye. My hand touched his cheekbone slightly and he winced.

"Did I do that?"

My hours of *TV Land* threw a picture of Steve Eurkle into my head.

"I've had worse. Although, I might have to get a restraining order and go to a shelter to protect myself from you."

"Don't joke. I feel bad enough already."

I laughed lightly, thinking I was actually strong enough to hurt him. "Do you want me to get you some ice?"

"No, it's my own fault for waking you up," he said.

"Maybe you do need the shelter. You're making excuses for me attacking you."

"I was wondering where you were. It's almost game time. Have I gotten you addicted?" he asked, glancing toward my TV.

Not wanting to disappoint him by telling him I was just too lazy to look for my remote, I changed the subject.

"I thought you had meetings today?"

"I do, but there's no reason you can't be there. I can't explain it and I don't want to, but I just can't see making a decision that effects us without getting your input. So get dressed. I need you to help me be the perfect package."

He got up to leave the room.

"Don't you want to pick out my outfit? Lord knows, I don't know how to be perfect," I said, thinking of how he was always put together.

Oscar rolled his eyes and walked over to my closet. He pushed aside my clothes. I walked over to him, took off his letter jacket, wrapped my arms around him and laid my head on his back.

"Now how am I supposed to focus on this?" he asked.

"I don't care," I said, acting like a little kid.

My hands were at his waist and then I rubbed his stomach, but when they slid under his shirt, his muscles tensed. Stroking his washboard stomach was probably not the best way to get him to focus, but I didn't care. He sighed and turned around to face me.

"I promise I'm not going anywhere and no one's after me."

Oh, how I wished that was true.

"How bad was that dream?"

"The beginning wasn't so bad."

I brought a hand to my lips as my mind returned to the feeling of his skin against mine.

“Really, anything you want to talk about?” he asked with a slight lilt in his voice as he raised an eyebrow.

I became embarrassed, pulled away and sat back on my bed with my legs crossed underneath me.

“That good, huh? If your face get’s any redder, I’d think you fell asleep in a tanning bed.”

He turned back to the closet and resumed to looking through it.

“My dad said you handled yourself really well yesterday,” he said as he pulled out a thin, blue v-neck cable knit sweater. “Now where are your skirts?”

“Um, last time I looked they were at the store,” I said with a tone of authority.

“You have no skirts?” he asked, shocked.

“How many do you have?”

“More than you obviously.”

“Please note, the dress you saw last night is the only one I have. Just because I’m a girl doesn’t mean I dress like one. Haven’t you noticed I’m not a ‘girly girl’?” I teased and used air quotes.

“Yes, I noticed, but I figured you were just holding out on me.”

“Nope, sorry, I think I hold out on you enough as it is,” I said, recalling what Mya said.

“What does that mean?”

“Nothing.”

I turned to my dresser for a pair of pants. I held up two pairs and asked, "Jeans or khakis?"

"What did you mean?"

I threw the jeans back in the drawer and snatched a white tank top to wear under my sweater.

"Are you going to stay while I change or are you going to step out?"

"I'm going to have my question answered, that's what I'm going to do," he said with a voice firm like I'd forgot to turn in an assignment.

Assuming he'd leave I dropped my pajama bottoms, but he just stared at me, not even looking at my bare legs. I turned to the side as I slid on the khakis. As I pulled them up, I stuck out my butt. Nothing! Placing my hands at the bottom of my shirt, I challenged, "You really want to do this?"

He didn't move, so I took off my shirt and stood there in just khakis and my bra. His face twitched, but returned to a firm glare. I crossed the room to grab my sweater, hoping he'd give up; instead he held it up and hit the ceiling with his hand.

"How…are…*you*…holding…out…on…me?" he asked slowly.

I turned around and put my tank top on.

"Can I have my sweater?"

"No!"

Okay, now he was really mad.

I bit my lower lip and breathed in deeply. Keeping my back to him, I said, "Mya just implied you weren't one to not have sex, a lot, so if I'm not giving it to you, then you're getting it from someone else."

I turned around as his arm dropped.

"She said what to you?"

His face filled with disgust.

"It started with her telling me the only reason you were with me was because you had a fantasy about sleeping with a midget and then it turned into a retelling of your escapades last year…" I said, my voice trailing off, because I didn't want to finish the thought.

He took my hands in his and led me to the bed and we sat down. "I have had a lot of relationships based on what I was, not who I am. This summer I was set down and given a talk about what I was doing and given a perspective I never thought about. I thought about the meaninglessness of sex without feelings. There were and are girls who will do anything for me because of what they see me as. The next big thing, the one whose gonna make it." He began massaging my upper arms. "They think if they can do something for me I'll do something for them. I was immature and doing what any other guy would or does do. I didn't care about what it may have done to them in the long run. What they were turning themselves into. Giving their body away like free samples in the grocery store. I never thought about how they must be feeling inside. Look at your sister Grace."

She was never happy but was always trying to make us think she was.

"You didn't sleep with Grace?" I whispered, as I could feel vomit rising in my throat.

"No!" he said. "But she's the easiest example of what I saw. I never thought they even cared about me as a person, then I thought about the fact I was giving myself away too."

He sighed deeply.

"There was an emptiness I felt inside me and I was tired of that feeling. I wasn't going to date anyone this year because I was just going to take this year to change into who I wanted to be and start fresh in college." Then he laughed. "But then you had to come along. You frustrate me and break my resolve, but I promised myself I was going to be good."

He paused and looked me in the eyes to make sure I heard what he was about to say.

"If you undress in front of me again, we're going to have words."

He kissed me and lowered me back on the bed. "Now, we've had our emotional talk for the day, can we have the rest of the day off?"

"I might just give you the week, if you play nice," I offered and kissed him again.

Chapter 14

The coaches made me want to gag. They promised Oscar the world on a platter if only he'd choose their school. Statistics spewed out of their mouths at a record pace. Wins, losses, graduation rates, and NFL draft levels of the past five years. I sat quietly with a hand on Oscar's leg under the table. Oscar was obliging to all of them, asking all of the appropriate questions. The coach from Florida actually engaged me in the conversation, questioning what I planned for my future.

"Are you a good student as well as a good athlete?"

I actually was a good student. School was interesting, but I got bored easily since the classes didn't seem to challenge me. I was hoping that being in high school I could try some harder classes.

"School's pretty easy to me so I'd say I'm above average," I answered.

I had a 4.0, but midterms could change my average.

"You know, my daughter was in a similar situation as you…bored with school."

I thought he hesitated a little too long and as if he really meant to say she fell in love with an older guy.

"So she started not taking study halls, then she took summer school classes. She ended up graduating a year and half early. Anymore now, senior year, half the classes are for college credit. She found out college was more about being mentally able to push yourself, since professors aren't your parents and won't push you. After maxing out on hours and staying during the summer and graduated with a bachelor's by nineteen. It's not always about being a genius, it's about hard work," he said, then redirected the conversation. "And speaking of hard work. You'll never work as hard as we work during two-a-days…"

I checked out on the rest of the conversation. The school handbook we received at the beginning of the year had a table based on credits separating the grades. If I could gain even one year, that would be huge. I started to figure out how to graduate early. I knew I didn't want a GED, but if I set up a meeting with the guidance councilor Monday to formulate a plan I could push myself to finish early.

We said goodbye to the last coach and drove to the garden to finish the last of Oscar's project.

"What do you think about me doing that?"

"Doing what?"

I assumed he read my mind over the last hour.

"The summer-school-graduate-early thing. I'm the oldest in my class as it is."

"It could give me a reason to help you with your homework. Are you sure you could handle it?"

"I don't know, but getting out of high school sooner would be nice."

"As long as you feel you can handle it, I don't see the harm."

At his garden, a small sign designated it as "*A community garden bringing the country to the city. Brought to you by Troop 453 and the City of St Paul.*" Oscar told me his dad carved the sign in his wood shop when we pulled up. A few families were harvesting the last of their tomatoes. Others were starting to till the ground, getting ready for the winter.

"Hi, Oscar, I have your final paperwork."

Trahn was in charge of the garden. He was as short as I was and wore his black hair in a bowl cut. He was part of the Hmong community that had immigrated to Minnesota after the Vietnam War. I don't know how Oscar broke into this community, they really close ranks and keep to themselves, but somehow he met Trahn and created a friendship.

"Thanks, I have to take it to my scoutmaster in a few hours."

"We really appreciate all you've done for us. Did you know a few families were able to sell their vegetables to make money? You've helped more than you may ever know. We'll miss you."

"I'll be back to check on you next summer."

"I hope so." They shook hands and we were off again.

We made another stop to drop off all his paperwork. It was a nice day, listening to how wonderful Oscar was. He was a good man. It was then it hit me. I was just a girl, he was a man. Although only a year separated us, it seemed as if a lifetime was between us. Would a year turn me into a woman, strong and courageous? Sure of myself and ready to take on the world? Would I even be alive or would I've taken the wrong path? According to Kelly, as long as I was with Oscar I'd be taking the right path. But would I corrupt the path he was on? Would I be the downfall for this wonderful man?

Chapter 15

"Hey, this whole day was about me. Why don't we spend the evening focusing on you? Tell me something you want to do," Oscar asked.

"I don't know. I really enjoyed just watching you today."

"There has to be something besides volleyball you like. What's your favorite subject?"

"Um, well, I like history."

I tried to think of anything else I liked to do. In art we had started a photography unit.

"And I like pictures, you know, photographs and stuff."

"Hmmm, let's see. I got a great idea."

He turned off Marshall toward the highway and suddenly he was speeding down I-94 towards Minneapolis. Although we share many things in the Twin Cities, The cities are very divided. We just don't go to the other side of town. Minneapolis people see no need because nothing's in St. Paul, and the St. Paul people are afraid of the violence in Minneapolis. Both sides are wrong, but I was a St. Paul girl. I was always nervous crossing into Minneapolis.

Chrysalis

A few turns off the highway was the Minneapolis Institute of Art. I'd never been there. The first thing to greet me was a massive yellow, glass ball with tendrils shooting off. The quiet in the museum was calming instead of unnerving, like it usually was. Oscar took my hand and guided me to the third floor. About halfway down the hall, I could see a huge picture of a face staring at us. Turning left was a gallery with hundreds of black-and-white photos.

I stepped forward, releasing his hand to view a picture of someone jumping into a pool, their body cut through the smooth surface. The photographer's technique made it impossible to tell if the subject was a man or woman. The next photo was of a family during the dust bowl. They were losing their house and they just stared as if they'd lost their lives and were the walking dead. I sat on a long bench in front of the display and just stared, absorbing the lines, lighting style and imperfections running though the pictures, somehow creating depth. Oscar sat beside me in silence and put an arm around me. I breathed low as if I was in church. The next room had older photos, but they were color, bright and bold reds, blues, yellows and greens popping out of the pictures from all over the world.

I walked around, looking at each picture, reading the cards attached and breathing in the information. Oscar just walked beside me, not commenting, just enjoying the moment of newness and learning I was experiencing. His finger twisted in my belt loop, keeping me close to his body. We walked in unison as if we were one continuous unit, curling around the museum. The modern art, early American and African sections. We turned into the Renaissance and I stared at the biggest painting I'd ever seen, God in all his greatness with angels surrounding him. The next rooms had dozen of paintings of angels and Jesus with Mary. I stopped in front of the demons and tried to figure out who was after me.

My body was warm and relaxed. Leaning against Oscar made me feel safe, like nothing could hurt me. I snuggled myself closer and rested my head on his chest. His hands ran up my back, locking me to him.

A bell rang announcing the museum was preparing to close.

I looked up at Oscar.

"Can we come back?" I asked excitedly.

"Of course we can, Lil' Girl," he smiled.

"Thank you, this was wonderful. I'll never forget today."

We walked out, still in silence. Driving home, I held his hand and leaned my head against him.

"Is this what dating's supposed to be?"

He laughed.

"Yes, if you want to know about the person."

"I can't think of a more perfect day."

I could feel him smiling as we drove down the highway crossing back to our side of town.

"Can I share one more thing with you?" I asked, as we finished crossing the river.

"Of course, anything," he said as his hand slid along my thigh.

"You've got to promise not to laugh."

"Is it something about you?"

"Yes, it's my favorite song."

Suddenly, I was regretting bringing this up to him. Butterflies started to flutter at hyper-speed in my stomach.

"You're not a secret Hannah Montana fan, are you?"

"No," I said, scanning my iPod for a song. "I don't know why I love this song but I can't hear it without smiling."

The words were a jumble of silliness but they had a good message. One line was about being open to new ideas and not closing yourself off. I was afraid if I shared that with him, he'd see a part of me I always tried to keep hidden.

I realized his stereo system was definitely not original to his car. As the song started to blare, I turned down the volume.

"You like *Starfish and Coffee*?" I was amazed, because most people never even heard of this song. "My mother was the biggest *Prince* fan ever. She said she practically lived at First Avenue before she had me. This was one of the few songs she'd let me listen to even when I was little."

A huge smile crossed his face as I said, “See, you can’t listen to this without smiling, can you?”

The butterflies went away as I found yet another thing he didn’t judge me for.

He walked me to my door.

“So, tomorrow, I’ll pick you up at eleven thirty.”

I knew I had to meet with Kelly to learn how to defend myself, especially after a day like today.

“Um, actually, I needed to do some things with Kelly tomorrow. Could I just do the seven o’clock game instead of the whole day?”

At first he looked disappointed, but his smile returned.

“Only if you help me cook for it! My dad’s going to be really disappointed. He’s gotten used to you being there for a new view on the game.”

I actually was starting to understand some of the pregame commentary. Mr. Jeffreys and Oscar thought it was great I was finally getting Terry Bradshaw and Jimmy Johnson’s jokes, Oscar and his father had such reverence for the older coaches’ wisdom. *College Game Day* wasn’t much better. It was scary how much Oscar worshiped at the altar of Lou Holtz. Sometimes he would load his pregame speeches to his iPod to get pumped up for a game.

“Well, I hope your dad isn’t the only one being disappointed. Sometimes I feel like I’m the only one missing someone.”

I stood on my tiptoes, brought a hand to his cheek and kissed him gently on the lips, his arms quickly wrapped around me as he picked me off the ground so I no longer had to stretch.

Pulling away, but not letting go, he looked me in the eyes.

"You will never be the only one missing someone."

He set me down and I opened the door to my house.

"Five-thirty. Is that enough time to get your girly stuff done?"

"It will have to be. I'd hate to be late, for your dad's sake."

"I'm not going to tell him that. It would only encourage his bad behavior."

He leaned in for one more kiss good night and whispered, "Goodnight. I love you."

"I love you, too," I said, happy and content, something that should've made me feel safe and warm, but instead slowly a chill traveled down my back as the fear of how dangerous my joy could be.

Chapter 16

I called Kelly as soon as I got up on Sunday morning. The irony of calling a god on Sunday wasn't lost on me.

"Kelly, can you teach me what I need to protect myself and Oscar?"

The thought of me being Oscar's protector made me laugh. "Or is this your day of rest?"

I had to joke. It was becoming my defensive mechanism of choice, because the thought of having to face someone who'd already killed one of my family members truly scared me.

"Yeah, I can. I'll come pick you up," she yawned, although it seemed to be more from boredom than lack of sleep.

I had no idea where she was going to take me. The less I knew the more I could delude myself into thinking I was just having a girls day. We'd just have lunch and go shopping to pick out a new sweater for winter. I kept telling myself this idea as I looked for a tight t-shirt I could easily put the sweater over and still be able to judge if it looked good on me. When Kelly drove me to the Mall of America in Bloomington, *because it'd be the easiest place to start*, she said, I just kept the illusion going.

We parked on the third level and walked across the skyway. The mall was busier than I expected. A model search was happening in the rotunda. We looked down at the craziness below.

"The first thing I need to teach you is to read people's auras," she said.

"Don't you have to be born with some psychic ability to do that?"

"No, you just have to focus. The reason we as immortals can do it so easily is because we've been doing it for millenniums. Although I do have great strength and abilities, almost all of it's because I've had years to practice. There're higher angels or gods that do have more powers and they were our creators." She breathed deeply.

"You must understand we limit the knowledge of who we are, our skills and our role in protecting humans."

She looked across the space above the rotunda. I tried to see what was catching her attention, but all I saw were people riding the escalators.

Returning her attention to me, she said, "In the past we learned humans couldn't always handle the information. The pain of losing them was too much for us to bear."

With a pained look on her face, she asked, "How much do you want to know? I'm not bound by any law or dictate from on high as to what I can and can't say. We limit what we say because of the damage it may cause the person."

"I don't know?"

My whole life seemed full of questions. Why was I here? What did I do to deserve this or that? What's the plan for me or if there even was one? Why does bad happen? I look down at the hundreds of people below us.

"I want to know about you and your kind, but I need to know about how to protect myself. What happens if I can't understand?"

"Remember, I told you we learned to limit what we say a long time ago. Sometimes we've had an occasion to discuss things with people. Some go into a deep depression, becoming hermits or eccentrics. Others try to tell what they've learned. They sometimes become violent and end up in psychiatric units because their mind never gets off the track of spreading the word. Lastly, some find it's all too much and take their lives. This doesn't always happen. It depends on the person's inner strength."

I sighed. My hands gripped the railing I was full of doubt.

"Stop that. You're young, and although there has been quite a bit of damage done to you, I'm glad it didn't take another five to ten years for Oscar to find you. I may've never been able to help you if it had."

"How did you come to be?" I asked.

"Let's walk."

We headed towards Bloomingdales and as we walked, Kelly would point to an item and not comment on it, but it appear as if she had.

"I'll try to break this down to you as if you were a five-year-old. As you know, there's God, Allah, Zeus, Apollo, Ra, and etcetera. He wanted to create something that was his contemporary."

"Adam and Eve," I said with a tone of authority.

"No, Adam and Eve were human, and created in the image of the gods. He was creating Gods like him. Immortals. Unfortunately, upon creating Gods, you have some that thought they were more suited to rule. They attempted to kill him and take over. The demons, titans, Satan."

"Got it."

"There was a great war. It's depicted in all of your human stories. Sides were chosen. I went with my creator."

Kelly sighed.

"I know it's hard for you to understand, but for right now we need to focus on strengthening you. I'm not sure how he will attack, but there's little chance that he won't. For some reason the souls in your family seem delectable to him."

We walked without stopping because Kelly was afraid we might be overheard.

"You first need to be able to find a person's light. If you can do that, you can know who's human and who's not. In addition, you'll need to know who has been manipulated by Gaap or any other demon."

"You can tell all that by just looking at a person?"

"Yes, usually they mask themselves…I'm getting ahead of myself now."

We stopped again above the rotunda. The numbers swelled and I didn't know how the security was keeping these people under control.

"Okay, I need you to choose someone, anyone in the crowd down there and focus. Look at them and try to see…well, anything."

I now realized why we were at the mall. Thousands of people were in a competition. It was great people watching without being too conspicuous. I zeroed in on a young girl in a chair with a number on her shirt. She was probably only twelve years old. Her strawberry blond hair was swept back with a few barrettes and she was wearing a trendy outfit that looked too old for her. She had a few freckles on her pale skin and her eyes were crystal blue. I wasn't sure what I was supposed to be doing, but I stared at her as she fidgeted in her seat. Her hands held some sort of paper rolled up into a tube that she kept twisting to make it tighter and tighter. After a few minutes, I was about to turn away when Kelly said softly, "Relax yourself, you're trying too hard. Remember the hallway."

I closed my eyes, breathed deeply and then slightly lifted my eyelids. Adjusting my point of focus, my eyes started at her shoes and moved up her legs to her body then face. Something was different about her this time. It was as if my eyesight was blurred, but she was in focus except the outline of body was softened. I concentrated harder a light encircled her body, dull but definitely something there, as if she had walked into a dark room from one with a few lights turned on.

I couldn't tear myself away from her, but I needed to ask Kelly a question. It was as if I was mesmerized.

"Um…ah…that girl."

"She's nervous. That's why it's so dull."

"What?"

"Your aura's like a defensive shield. Your health, your fears, anything that lowers your immune system will lower its color. Right now she's afraid and nervous. You'll see when she get's pulled up on stage it'll brighten, but there will be ooze seeping from it. She'll be putting up a mask. Cracks mean guilt or lies. Ooze means they're focusing on the lies and they're trying to make people truly believe it. You may not be able to see these yet, but the cracks and ooze will be there. You can turn away and look back and will still be able to see it. You've linked with her. Although you may never see that girl again, if you were to, she'd instantly have a light around her for you. After awhile, you'll learn to turn this sense off. It gets annoying to be in a room full of hundred-watt bulbs. Learning to turn it off and on is a whole other thing that may take a long time to learn."

The more I heard how long this would take, the more I worried I'd never be able to protect myself. The girl walked on to the stage.

With each step her light got brighter and brighter, until it was almost like looking at an uncovered light bulb. I turned back to Kelly.

"Besides figuring out my enemies, I don't see how this will be useful because by the time I figure out they don't have light, I'll already be dead."

"It'll take time, but I think we have some. Eventually, it will take you a few seconds not twenty minutes."

I hadn't even realized I'd taken that long.

"After you can master this, I can start teaching you how to defend yourself. There will be no offense in this war, only defense. As strong as you are, you couldn't handle on offensive attack."

Strong was never a word used to describe me. Weak and cowering was more precise. Although I'd been gaining some resolve as of late, I'd never considered myself strong.

"What about Oscar?"

"What about him?"

"Could he be in danger, physical or otherwise? Would it be safer for him to not be with me?"

Kelly took my hands in hers.

"Losing you would send him on a worse path than being with you. He'd be happier living in a one-room shack with you, working double shifts at SuperAmerica, than without you in a lake house in Minnetonka and playing for the Vikings. Trust me, his love for you amazes me. You hit him like a Mac truck. From the first time he saw you, something inside him clicked, like it all suddenly made sense. He doesn't even understand how his feelings could be so strong for you so quickly. Every step he takes he calculates how it effects you so he can make sure that you and him are never apart."

As much as I wanted to believe Kelly, the thought Oscar loved me that much was overwhelming. He did seem genuine when he spoke to me, but how could anyone love someone that way? Let alone love me that way. And how could I ever return his love to him when I couldn't even grasp the concept?

We continued walking around the third floor and went into a few stores. Kelly would engage the sales staff so I could look at them. The women were less likely to give her the time it took me to see their auras. The men seemed infatuated by her. Most of them had bright lights, but by the third one I saw the cracks and a few drops of black ooze escape. He was lying to her to get her phone number. I finally realized what she meant. It was like when an actor put on a bald cap for a roll instead of shaving their heads. Just the subtlest turn of the head and there was a line that you just wanted to pick at and scratch to see underneath.

At Macy's, Kelly picked up tops and skirts to coordinate them. Then she held them up to me.

"What are you doing? I don't see how this is going help me."

"I'm building your self-confidence."

"Putting me in a skirt is the last way to do that. Besides, I didn't bring any money."

I took the items from her and put them back on the rack.

"You didn't, but Oscar gave me two-hundred dollars and told me I needed to help you dress like a girl."

"He did what?"

She just smiled and went back to sorting through items on the rack.

"How's this going to help me?"

"Next time, you might want to give me some warning when you make plans with me. Oscar tends to not want to share you."

I realized I hadn't asked Kelly until this morning if we could work on protecting me.

"Look, Oscar likes you. He *really* likes your body and wants to see it," she said. "I made him promise to only expect it when it was just the two of you. I can't work miracles."

She drugged me to the dressing rooms.

"No complaining. Get girly. You don't want to have lied to him about what you were doing today, do you?"

"Just tell me you didn't promise him hair and makeup, too."

"No, he hates that stuff. He doesn't think your face could be any more beautiful," she said, smiling then slightly gagging.

I tried on a few outfits and agreed to three of them. That should appease him. But then the idea of him giving someone money to dress me started to upset me. I could pay my own way. Just because it was the thrift-store way didn't make it bad.

Kelly picked her favorite top. It was lilac colored and tight against my skin, with long bell sleeves. The shirt was long, it ending at the top of my thigh. She matched that with a steel grey skirt that came to just above my mid-thigh. She then found some cute grey ballet slippers and a purple, grey, pink and blue scarf to use as a belt to pull the ensemble together. I looked older. I looked pulled together instead of my usual hodgepodge outfits. I looked like a young lady, as my grandfather would've said. Then I looked at the length of the skirt. It would only be for Oscar.

"Come on, I promised him I'd get you to his house by five thirty," Kelly said, tearing me away from the reflection of myself I was still trying to comprehend.

On the ride home I told Kelly about my dream from the day before.

"It was just a dream, Ellie."

"It seemed so real. And that demon…"

"From your description, I'd say it wasn't Gaap. He's a vision. His pale skin is smooth. Curly blond hair…and like most celestials he has a strong, firm body. But that's when he's in his real form."

"Real form?"

"He can turn himself into whatever a human desires. Black, white, tall, short. He becomes what the woman or man would want."

"Man?"

"Don't be naïve. He torments who he wants."

"So he'd turn into a woman for a man?"

"No. He'd send one of his wives for that..."

"Oh...got it...is that a sin?"

"Sin? That's your word for a damnation, not ours. We don't judge the way you do."

"I don't judge."

"You judge every day. Every human does."

We pulled up outside Oscar's house.

"Just promise me I won't be the cause of any pain or suffering to Oscar."

"I can see my job won't be done until I can turn off your inner voice. Now, get out of my car."

I got out of the car with my shopping bags and smiled at Kelly.

"I'm sorry," I said.

"Don't apologize. You've done nothing wrong. Just go see your man."

Chapter 17

The sidewalk to Oscar's house seemed way too long. I was pulling down my skirt as I walked scared someone would see me in the short-assed skirt Kelly picked. Oscar's house was an older, two-story. It looked like Oscar and his dad spent the day removing the air conditioners from the windows. The windows were now covered in plastic, a Minnesota tradition for keeping a house warm in the winter. It was still a fall warm today only fifty-five. The front porch stretched the front length of the home. Oscar's car was parked in the driveway in front of the one-car garage. I nervously fidgeted with the bags and my skirt as Oscar opened the door. He obviously had been waiting for me.

"Keep dressing like that and I'll have to stop calling you Lil' Girl. I'm gonna have to let you go with Kelly more often."

I looked up at the biggest smile I'd seen in long time. Oscar helped me with the shopping bags.

"That's twice she's worked a miracle," he said.

I laughed thinking about the conversation I'd just had with Kelly *I can't work miracles.*

"Am I that bad?"

"You're so hot."

I now understood how Oscar was strengthening to me. I felt like I just had a shot of steroids. He took my hand and led me down the hallway past the living room and into the kitchen. I could hear the end of the last afternoon game.

"Is that Ellie?" Oscar's dad was yelling.

"Yes, we're about to start supper."

"Hi, Mr. Jeffreys," I muttered, confused why Oscar was almost yanking my arm out of the socket to get me into the kitchen.

"You don't have to hog her," his dad bellowed. "You're the one who lost the bet. She can take it easy in here with me, you know."

"She'll be in there in a little bit," Oscar yelled.

He turned to me and in a low voice said, "I'm not sharing you until I have to."

His lips caressed mine and his hands were at my hips, lifting me and setting me on the counter. My legs spread, as he pulled himself between them. He held me closer as my legs locked behind him. My hands explored his body, going under his shirt to feel his perfectly chiseled body. Oscar's tongue was now explored my mouth and the world fell away. I floated in a place where only Oscar and I existed. Sounds all became white noise and not something to respond too. The only thing that mattered was the rush of love Oscar showed to me.

Heat coursed through my body when Oscar's hands glided up my back, causing me to tremble.

"Well, excuse me."

Oscar's dad stood in the kitchen. The white noise had been his footsteps on the hardwood floors. Oscar pulled back as my legs automatically released and closed, crossing at the ankles. My hands landed on the edge of the counter.

"Ellie, don't you look nice today."

I could feel my face flushed more from wanting Oscar's body next to mine again than from being embarrassed being caught by his dad.

"Thank you, Mr. Jeffreys. I had a girls day, Kelly thought Oscar would want to see me in my new outfit."

I wanted to add Oscar should've really wanted to see what his investment bought him, but I had to talk to Oscar about the money before going there.

"Well, that appears to be the case. Now Ellie, Oscar lost a bet to me so he has to make supper tonight. I see he's tryin' his best to pull you in. Don't fall for it."

"I'm not really a Becky-Homecky, so I won't be much use to him anyway. I'll make sure he holds up his end of the bargain."

"Are you sure you wouldn't rather come sit with me? Sometimes it's better to not see how food is prepared."

"I'll risk it, but save me a seat for the game. I might need to sit next to someone who can recognize the symptoms of food poisoning."

He laughed and left the kitchen. Oscar gave me one more kiss, releasing the pressure that had been building in my lips. The other Sundays we had just ordered pizza so I wondered what was going on. And I really did want to watch Oscar cook because it seemed really sensual. Maybe I should go sit with his dad.

I hopped off the counter and adjusted my skirt again.

"Stop doing that."

"What?"

"Adjusting your skirt. I swear you've done that twenty times since you got out of Kelly's car."

He was watching me.

"Sorr---" I started to apologize, but decided to take Kelly's advice. "Fine."

Oscar was making meatloaf with spinach and mashed potatoes. He handed me a bag of potatoes and a peeler. Smiling at me, he leaned down, kissed the crook of my neck and worked up to my ear.

"Would you please peel the potatoes?" he asked sweetly, his voice almost musical. My body quaked as I took the bag and peeler.

"That's not fair."

My face was flush again and my legs were covered in goose bumps.

"I promise, I'll make it up to you."

"So what are these for?"

I held up the bag.

"Well, most people eat them," he said, looking at me as if I were crazy.

I rolled my eyes.

"What are you making out of these?"

"Mashed potatoes. What do you make those from?"

"Flakes in a box," I said, as I sat down to start peeling.

"You'll never make it as a Jeffreys with flakes from a box," he said and laughed.

I liked feeling he already saw me a potential part of his family. I loved his dad, and from how Oscar talked about the rest of his family, I knew I'd love them too.

Oscar washed his hands and started to throw together the meatloaf. The muscles in his hands and arms flexed mixing the breadcrumbs, eggs, seasonings and meat. I was mesmerized watching his hands. Suddenly, I noticed a light all around his body. I was amazed at the glow emanating off him. He looked up at me smiled. "Tell me you love me," I said.

The light around him brightened.

"I love you, Lil' Girl."

There wasn't a crack anywhere around him.

I smiled and turned away so I could keep myself under control. I finally started peeling the potatoes and dropping the peels into the trash. When I had about half the bag done, I turned to him. He was just finishing pressing the meatloaf in a pan. Knowing he couldn't touch me with his hands, I put my arms around his waist.

"Hey, now let me work."

"No."

My hands were going back under his shirt.

"Come on now. If I mess this up, I'll never live it down."

My body tight against his, I started kissing his back.

"I don't want to ruin your new outfit."

I still didn't stop.

"If you let go, I can wash my hands."

I finally let go. He crossed to the sink and looked at me as he washed and dried his hands.

"You're not done."

A smile crossed my face as I went to him.

"No," he said leaning his face back, "if you haven't noticed, I'm an abnormally large person. You need to do the whole bag."

I crossed my arms.

"What was the bet I'm helping you pay off?"

"Oh, nothing."

I picked up another potato, "if I'm doing slave labor here, I should at least know why."

"That's fair. He bet me I wouldn't be able to talk to the coaches without you by my side."

"Um, that seems like something that'd be pretty easy to win."

"You'd think so, wouldn't you?"

He didn't look at me, but went back to digging in the freezer for something.

By the time I'd peeled the potatoes, Oscar had started cutting them and setting the pieces in some boiling water. I washed my hands and turned to him.

"Anything else I can do?"

"No, you've done plenty. I better let you go in with my dad or I'll never hear the end of it."

"Are you sure, because I really don't know how you're going to turn those into mashed potatoes. It still boggles the mind," I said, as I put my arms around him one more time before I left.

"You really come from a family with no cooks, don't you?" he smiled and kissed my forehead holding his hands away from me so he wouldn't get me dirty.

The game wrap up was still on when I sat down on the couch closest to Mr. Jeffreys' chair.

"Oh, so he finally let you go," he said as he stretched. I must've woke him up when I came in the room.

"Yep, I guess I've served my sentence."

"What did you do?"

"I don't know, but I'm sure I'll find out."

"Sorry about earlier," he said with an embarrassed tone. "I'm just not used to seeing my son kissing anyone, let alone well…"

"No. I'm sorry. It was inappropriate," I said.

"It wasn't. That's what you two are supposed to be doing. He just started to bring girls home last year with Mya, but it's not like he ever seemed to want to touch her. That never seemed right to me. Why waste your time with someone that disgusted you? I mean she's easy on the eyes, but I could just see his skin crawl when she touched him, especially at the end. You two on the other hand…why he'd kill a stick or put a brick in the hospital for you."

Oscar's dad was from the south and he had a crazy saying for everything.

I thought about how Oscar couldn't keep his hands off me, never wanting to let me go. Then I thought about Kelly telling me he doesn't even understand why, but he has to be with me.

"Anyway, it let me win the bet so, hey, that's all that matters," he said, turning back to the game.

Oscar walked into the room bringing a wonderful smell from the kitchen with him. He looked at me, then his dad, and turned and walked out without saying a word. His dad looked at me and just shrugged.

I heard a loud noise, as Oscar seemed to be climbing the stairs and then tumbling back down. He came back into the room with a blanket and a bottle of something. He laid the blanket over my legs, caught hold of my feet, and turned me sideways on the couch. Taking off my shoes he reached for a bottle of lotion.

"Boy, are you still cooking?" His father shot him a look.

"Yes, sir."

"What are you thinking? Save that stuff for later." Mr. Jeffreys then started to mumble, "Touchin' feet then touchin' food that's 'sposed be goin' in my mouth. Boy, done lost his mind."

"Yes, sir," Oscar said and placed his hands above the blanket, rubbing my legs through the cloth instead.

After about a half hour his father said, "I'm starving. Any chance this dinner will be done before the game? I don't know if I'm gonna be betting you anymore if you can't even get dinner done at a decent time."

"So you want next week back, too?"

"No, no just plan better next week."

"You lost another bet?" I smiled, thinking he'd be cooking again next week. "You're a lousy gambler."

"Yep, I guess I am."

He stood up and reached his hand out to me.

"Would you mind helping me finish up?"

"I suppose, but you might want to consult me from now on before you make any bets, if I'm going to be having to pay for them."

His dad laughed as Oscar and I walked back to the kitchen.

"Hey, look at that. I got you barefoot in the kitchen," he mused as we walked through the door.

"I'm so glad I could fulfill your fantasies. So how did you lose next week?"

"I bet against Florida."

"Didn't they have a bye week?" I asked. He knew their schedule better than his own.

"What's your point?"

I looked quizzically at him.

"My dad's a bad cook, okay? No flavor, just starch. He's a firefighter, shouldn't he be able to cook chili at least? It astounds the mind."

He spooned a bit of the mashed potatoes in my mouth. They were hot and creamy with just the right amount of butter.

"I was getting tired of feeding you pizza."

After letting the sweetness slide down my throat, I asked, "So how come you're such a good cook?"

"Well," he said, taking the plates down from the cabinet and spoon out the food, "my mom was a great cook and taught me a few things. Also, I learned from some adult leaders in scouts, since I liked being in charge of cooking on campouts. Because if I'm in control of the food, then I at least know it'll be good."

We spooned up the rest of the food and we walked it back to the living room, where his father set out some trays. Kick off was just five minutes away. Oscar cleared the dishes after we had all finished eating. I'd never had such a good dinner. He put Jennifer's cooking to shame.

Then I got my foot rub as payment for my kitchen duty. Halfway through the third quarter, a light snoring came from the chair across the room. Oscar and I faced each other and smiled as he leaned over and kissed me pulling me on his lap wrapping us both up under the blanket. My head rested against his chest as he wrapped an arm around me, landing at my hip. We both fell asleep watching the game.

Chapter 18

Over next few weeks Kelly worked with me on seeing auras. I surprised myself by catching on pretty quick. By the Monday before Halloween, I had it down pat. Around Sharyn, I saw the slightest light of all people. She really was a very dark person.

I was dropping off my books at my locker before lunch, Oscar was waiting with a smile on his face like the cat that ate the canary.

"You know what we're doing for Halloween?" he asked.

"Trick or treating with my nieces and nephew?" I asked, since that was my plan.

His face dropped.

"Um…I forgot you said you had to do that."

"Well, Jen wont in her condition."

"Yeah, yeah, I know. What time are you doing that?"

"Um, five o'clock. I'd be surprised if they lasted more than an hour anyway."

"Hey, Oscar," Zachary Schultz, a blond senior who was the second string receiver behind Oscar, interrupted our discussion. "There was a guy from USC that called me last night. He was asking all sorts of questions about you."

"Really? Like what?"

"What kind of player you are, how you act in school, you know the usual stuff."

I could see blackness oozing from his aura.

"What'd you tell him? Hopefully not the truth."

"Oh you know me, nothing but good words."

The blackness was now almost a gusher. He was lying! I didn't know if it was that a coach called or that he had said good things, but he was lying. Maybe he was just trying to be friends with Oscar. He took off down the hall and waved.

"He's lying," I said out loud, not realizing I had until the words were out of my mouth.

"What? Why would he lie about that? We get along great."

"No, you don't. He's jealous of you all the time and is always fake with you," I said, still not able to stop myself from speaking out loud.

"I think someone's paranoid," he said, kissing me on the top of my head. "So, can I come with?"

"Come where? Oh! Well, let me see…well it'll cost you."

He leaned down and gently kissed me while holding my head in his hands.

"Okay. So what is it you wanted to do?" I asked.

"Oh, I wanted to take you to Fright Farm."

The sheriff's department sponsored the haunted barn on the east side of town. I'd always been afraid to go, but the thought of going with Oscar made me feel like nothing could hurt me.

"Sounds great, but I'm going to warn you, I might be a little girly and have to grab on to you for protection."

"I hope you do."

He kissed me again softly and took a step towards the cafeteria.

I didn't move, but held on hand.

"I have my meeting today. I can't go to lunch."

"Oh yeah, I forgot. It took long enough."

"Tell me about it. I was going crazy."

I had been trying to meet with the school guidance counselor for a few weeks.

As I walked to her office, I tried to figure out what to say to get moving on this new plan for my life. Mrs. Stafford was an older, heavy-set woman. Her hair was always in a bun and her clothes always looked like they were dragged out of the back of her closet. She had bags under her eyes and smiled out of reflex. Her light was dim. She must not have liked her job or felt good that day.

"Ms. Chisholm, how can I help you?"

"I was wondering about increasing my class load and working during the summer to try to graduate early."

"What's your motivation to skip a year of school?"

I'd practiced this since I had decided I wanted to get out early. *I can do this.*

"I'm the oldest in my class and have always felt I wasn't being challenged enough. I feel I really relate to the class above me more."

"This isn't for any personal reasons? *Like the fact that you're sleeping with the star football player that's graduating and leaving you in the spring"*

"Excuse me?"

"I said, is this for a personal reason?"

I swore she had just said my reason was because I was having sex with Oscar. Where had she gotten that idea? But she acted as if she hadn't said it.

"Um, no, I really would just like to move forward as fast as I could."

Remembering what the Florida coach said, I added, "senior year is really just taking college credits so I might as well just go to college."

"So you are planning on attending college? *Deluded girl, she actually thinks he's going to stay with her. She's probably imagining a love nest just off of the campus."*

"What…um, yes, I am. I've already talked to some college coaches about it."

What was I hearing?

"Well, looking at your schedule for this semester, you seem to be doing well in your classes. Also, aren't you in a sport? That can count for your physical education requirement. I wouldn't waste time with any study halls next semester and I'll note your file to get you into summer school," she said. "*Oh well, it's not like I'm going to have to do anything. He'll have his fun and leave her before summer.*"

The light around her was still dim, but now had cracks everywhere. Was she Gaap? Why was I hearing these things? Is this an illusion? My mind flooded with the feeling I was being attacked. I shook, afraid I wasn't going to make it out of the office alive. Mrs. Stafford turned and rummaged through her files.

"*Where the hell is the catalog? I can't believe I have to do this. I figured she'd be coming in here to get the info for pregnancy and GED. If I were her age, I'd be riding that boy like Roy Rodgers rode Trigger. That's so wrong, but oh it'd feel so right. Oh there it is.*"

She turned back to me, slightly flushed, her light was brightened and she handed me some papers. This wasn't right. I needed to find Kelly as soon as possible. I took the papers and got up, almost running, afraid of another attack. Kelly should be coming soon. She always came when something bad was happening.

In the hall, a few guys from the football team saw me. I'd figured out a week ago they were safe. Their auras weren't as bright as Oscar's, but I'd found few that were.

"She doesn't walk like she'd be good in bed."

One smiled at me as I walked by hugging my papers.

"She's stick thin. How does he not break her in two? But her face's round like a little kid, weird."

I kept my head down, if I could've walked with my eyes closed I would've. For some reason I could see everyone's aura in the hallway. Deer in the headlights was an understatement. Only I couldn't really think because of all the noise. It seemed as if everyone was talking gibberish. I bumped into Sharyn.

"Watch out Soft Meat. *She just thinks she can do whatever she wants because she's so damn special.*"

I heard Oscar yelling for me.

"Lil' Girl! Ellie!"

"Oh, his precious Ellie. He sleeps with all the black girls in the school, but no, not the precious white girl. She's too fragile. He just thinks he's the big black man protecting his delicate white flower. I hate that bitch!"

I was shocked at what Sharyn said out loud with me right there. But she just looked at me.

"What do you want?"

"Um…nothing."

"Lil' Girl," Oscar said. "How did it go?"

He pulled me down the hallway.

"God I hope she can get out of here sooner. I'm getting sick and tired of coach's crap about me dating her. I love her. Why can't that be enough? God, I love her body! Her hips are so perfect and her eyes are like big pools of water I just want to dive into. Is there something on my face? Why's she staring at me?"

"Um, she gave me this catalog. She said I shouldn't take study halls…" My head was reeling. Whose thoughts were running through my head?

"God, it's so wrong what I want to do to her right now. Stop it Oscar, don't rush her. Touch, don't break, she's worth it. Those lips are going to feel so good wrapped around..." I heard Oscar's voice again.

"…And that…I could graduate a year early. I really need to see Kelly about something."

I quickly kissed his cheek goodbye and ran down the hall. Pushing through the pain, I kept my head up and ran to the edge of the lunchroom because I knew Kelly would be waiting for Max there.

I saw Kelly across the cafeteria. My head was pounding and a hundred voices boomed inside. I waved to get her attention. She finally saw me as I crumpled on a bench waiting for her to rescue me.

Kelly was at my side within a second.

"Breathe," she said, her voice soft and mothering.

I took a deep breath, but I stopped short as my head started to have a stabbing pain and my left eye suddenly burned. I closed that eye and everything went white. Visually nothingness surrounded me. I could feel the bench beneath Kelly and me besides me, but I was blind.

"Breathe."

She gathered me up and tried to walk me to the hall. Pain ripped apart every part of me, my stomach the worst.

"He's attacking me, please help." Was all I could eek out.

"He's not attacking you. I was afraid this might happen."

Kelly walked me down the hall. I heard a door open and felt a gust of wind. Outside the sleet burned the skin my face.

"I've got to get you cooled down."

My body wasn't reacting to the cold like it should've been. It could've been eighty degrees outside the way I felt.

After five minutes my stomach started to ease and I could finally stand up straight. Breathing in, my lungs filled up with the wet, cool air. My head still pounded, but my vision returned. I looked out across the parking lot and tried to focus on anything. Sharp pains still shot through my skull. Every noise was like a jackhammer.

"Breathe, Ellie."

I pressed my palms against the brick of the building, every groove felt as if it was a knife, but it took the pain from my head so I pressed harder. I tried to focus on what Kelly was saying.

“What’s…happening…to me?”

The nausea abruptly came back like a tidal wave roaring and I vomited on the front steps. The pain ceased as if I’d thrown it out of my body. My muscles ached like it was August and I’d just finished my first practice. The cold now found me and I shivered uncontrollably as Kelly put a coat around me and handed me a water bottle from her bag. My eyes still burned with pain, Kelly was finally in focus.

“What was that?” I asked. I swished the water in my mouth to rinse the taste.

“You may be more powerful than I imagined. Sit here…”

She glanced at the pile on the bottom of the step. “Come with me, but walk slow. I’m going to take you home.”

She walked me to her car then turned to go.

“Wait! You can’t leave me alone.”

“You’ll be fine. I just need to get you checked out and let Max know what’s happening.”

She walked back into the school. My cheek felt good against the cool window. My mind was clearer than it had ever been. I’d never had a migraine, but that must’ve been what happened. Strangely everything seemed crisper and cleaner. It was as if the pain opened a window showing me a world I hadn’t known existed.

Chapter 19

Outside of my house I could hear *Dora the Explorer*, my sister's babysitter, blaring on the TV.

Kelly carried me inside and got me into bed. It was weird she could literally carry me. Sure, Oscar was strong and seemed to love holding me, but Kelly's strength was still obscure and strange to me. She said she was about to leave when the TV was no longer blared and my sister was at my door.

"Are you okay sweetie?"

"Yeah, she'll be fine. A lot of kids are getting this flu 'cause of the quick weather change," Kelly explained. "I'll take care of her. I'd hate for you to get sick with the baby and all."

My sister softened since she had her own kids. It used to be that her mother role was just to boss us around, but it changed to taking care of us when we were sick. Every time Levi tried to quit using, she was there with a cold compress and bucket trying to get him through. Her love for her own children made her see none of us had had a mother.

Kelly closed the door and brought me some Tylenol and water.

"Well, look at you. I think you should skip school for a few days."

Although my body felt as if it had gone ten rounds with a MMA fighter, I still needed questions answered, so I boosted myself up on my elbow.

"What happened to me? Kelly I was hearing voices. Gaap was in my head, trying to control my inner voice."

"Do you remember, I told you some people end up in psych facilities? Those who are good at aura reading can sometimes, not often, but sometimes hear what the person is thinking. You were hearing other people's inner voices."

"Those couldn't be their real thoughts?" I asked.

"Why'd you think they weren't? I don't have this power, but for some reason when God created humans, a few were granted this ability. Most can't deal with it, so they end up institutionalized."

"So what, schizophrenia isn't real?" I asked, thinking of the only thing I knew that would get you locked away.

"'Oh, it's real, but some people are misdiagnosed. Mostly by doctors that are insecure when they tell them what their real thoughts are."

Her eyes looked at me as if she pitied me.

"Why did I get sick?"

"You fried your brain. That caused the migraine, which triggered the nausea and the fever was only natural. Really, that's about the only natural thing your body just did."

Her hand brushed the hair back on my head.

"I don't know how to deal with this," she continued. "I was just about to teach you how to turn off the aura lights and only get them when you needed them. It may be the same method, but I'm going to need to go away to find out. In your weakened state, I'm too afraid to leave you alone. Max said he'd try to look out for you, but he's not really good at seeing things coming, he's better at dealing with the problem once it's there."

"I did this to myself?"

"If blaming someone will make it better, then yes. But, truly, you opened yourself up more than you were ready for. I don't know what this'll mean against Gaap."

I was shivering under the blankets, even though I could feel sweat on my head.

"What haaapppens now?"

"I'll stay with you for a few hours. Hopefully, this fever will break. Right now you need rest. I'm going to try to figure out what my next move is."

She pulled the covers up to my chin and smoothed my hair. I quickly fell asleep, my exhausted body overpowered my mind and shut it down.

It was dark outside, and only the faint glow of Kelly's cell phone in the corner lit my room. My body ached and I felt as if I was sitting on a giant ice cube. My clock showed it was only six-thirty at night. Stretching caused my muscles to cramp and I let out a yelp.

"Oh, Ellie, you're up," Kelly said. "Don't move too quickly."

"Okay." My voice was hoarse and my throat felt as if I'd swallowed a thousand razor blades. Slowly I pulled back the covers and felt a blast of cold air hit me. Goosebumps abounded on my legs.

"Can you please pass me my flannel pajama pants and heavy socks?"

I still had my sweatshirt on.

"I need to take your temperature again," she said.

Again? How out of it was I? I don't remember taking my temperature…Kelly placed her hand on my head.

"104.6. You're just not going down. Let me get you some ibuprofen. I feel so helpless."

An angel felt helpless. How bad off was I? She passed me my pants and socks just in time. There was a light tap on my door and it opened a crack. A bright light shone through the door. I covered my eyes.

"Hey, sickly, you scared me just taking off like…*oh my God. My Lil' Girl. She looks so sick. What happened? She looked so good this morning.*" Oscar said.

My brain started to scream again. Kelly could sense my pain.

"Maybe you should go. I'd hate to have both of you sick."

"I don't think so. She could be Typhoid Mary, I'm not leavin'. Lil' Girl, tell me what I can do."

He placed a hand on my back, his gentle massage finally brought me warmth. He sat at the edge of my bed and my legs curled up to enclose him. His hands magically relaxed my muscles, which had been rock hard.

"That helps, thank you."

"You're burning up. What've you taken?"

"I was about to get her some ibuprofen. The Tylenol didn't help. I'll give you and Ellie some time alone. You'll need to eat something with the ibuprofen. What do you want?"

"Just some crackers."

Oscar's aura seemed to dim. I assumed it was because he was worried.

He leaned in to kiss my forehead. His lips were warm on my freezing head.

"I think you just gave me a second-degree burn."

"I was thinking the same thing. I'm freezing, but you feel like you're on fire."

"Do you want me under the covers with you? I'll keep you warm. I'd make that sacrifice for you. Throwing myself under a bus to save you."

I knew I didn't really have the flu so I couldn't give it to him, and he was the only thing that didn't hurt me. Even my clothes and blanket were scratching me. Every small fiber seemed to stick up like a briar.

"How did I get so lucky to have you?"

"Somebody up there must like you," I laughed thinking about God sending me Kelly.

Oscar crawled under the covers putting me between his legs and sitting his back against the wall.

Kelly came back with ibuprofen, crackers and juice. I drank the juice and swallowed the pills while my throat still burned. Drew burst through the door hitting the overhead light and jumped on me in the bed, spilling the rest of my juice everywhere. I howled in pain.

"Auntie El, I made you a picture."

My stomach was stabbing with pain. Oscar jumped up snagging Drew.

"Hey little buddy, Auntie's really sick. You need to stay out."

I curled up in a ball and could taste the vomit coming up my throat.

"Bathroom."

Oscar dealt with Drew, who was throwing a tantrum. Kelly had me in the bathroom faster than I could've ever imagined, my head in the toilet bowl.

"Is this just from Drew or is your head screaming again?"

"No," I said, heaving in the bowl again. "Just Drew."

I rested my head against the cabinet.

"I heard Oscar's voice in my head when he first came in, but nothing since, and his light's really dim."

"Was he dim to you when he first came in?"

"No, he almost blinded me. Why?"

"His light hasn't dimmed. You dimmed it to be around him."

"What?" I asked.

"You controlled his light to get it at a level you could handle. I can't imagine his mind is quiet either. It's probably because of your feelings for him that you're able to do that. Interesting…"

"Why does everything hurt but him? Everything feels like sandpaper, but his hand doesn't hurt like yours does."

"I'm hurting you when I touch you?"

"My shirt hurts me, everything, even the bricks at the school. The grooves felt like razor blades."

She helped me up gently as she could and handed me a toothbrush.

"Do you think you could be safe here until Oscar leaves?"

Spitting out the toothpaste, I looked up at her and said, "I think so. I always feel safe around him."

Her hand was on my forehead again.

"104.9. Did you throw up the pills?"

"I forgot to take inventory."

She walked me back to my room. Oscar was stripping my bed and a bag was in front of the dresser.

"You're coming to my house until you're better," he ordered.

"Excuse me?"

"I already talked to Jennifer and she'll handle your parents. I assured her my dad was a firefighter so he's got medical training and you'd be in our guest room."

He was talking fast as he threw my sheets in a pile.

Shaking his head, he said, "You can't stay here. It's just too disruptive."

"I don't think she needs to go to that extreme," Kelly said, stepping in front of me in a protective stance. "If she's going anywhere, it'd be to my house."

"I can take care of her better and she's my responsibility."

His responsibility? I wasn't a damn puppy. What were these two fighting about? My head started to spin, probably from me over thinking the issue. I steadied myself on the dresser.

"I've been here since she first got sick and I know what she needs."

Oscar's hand reached around Kelly to take my hand and Oscar's light shot through Kelly.

"She's going to my house and that's final!"

Kelly turned to me and smiled, knowing there was no way I missed that.

Raising an eyebrow, she said, "Fine, but she threw up her pills, so she'll need more."

Taking me gently aside she said, "Your body's as sensitive as your mind is right now. Everything you touch is going to be intensified."

I nodded now understanding why everything hurt.

"It's too bad you're sick, Oscar's kisses would be amazing right now."

When Oscar wrapped his coat around me, the wool cut through my skin, but I didn't want to show him it hurt. I swallowed my pills and Kelly helped walk me out to his car.

"Sorry about before," she whispered, "but I had to make sure he could protect you."

Chapter 20

"I didn't tell your sister, my dad's on a tour. He won't be home until morning. I hope that was okay. If it makes you nervous I can get Kelly back here."

"I'm not nervous. I doubt I could take advantage of you in my condition anyway."

He laughed. At least I still had my sense of humor.

At his house, Oscar took my temperature and then wrapped me up in blankets because I was shivering. It was one-oh-five point two.

"What was your temperature the last time Kelly took it?"

"One-oh-four something."

"I know you're freezing, but I need you take off the blanket and sweatshirt."

My body shook as I sat there in just my cotton camisole and pajama bottoms.

"Are you sure this is better?" I asked, my teeth chattering.

"Maybe not," he said and wrapped the blanket back around me. "Do you want some soup?"

My stomach flipped at the thought of food. I ran towards the bathroom that was thankfully attached to the guest room. Oscar turned on the water, swept back my hair and placed a cold washcloth on the back of my neck, then massaged back.

"Why did you want to see me like this? Aren't we still in the girls-don't-use-the-bathroom stage of our relationship?"

"We were never in that stage. If you haven't noticed we went from 'hi my name is' to 'I can't live without you.'"

He was right. We were like an old married couple now. We had a schedule that we stuck to and we never had sex. Sounded right. Back in the room, he helped me into the bed. My skin itched even more than before. I scratched violently.

"Are you okay?"

"No."

I pulled off my pants before they burned my skin off and threw them in a corner. I decided how to word my request, but became because my bare legs were freezing.

"Everything itches. How strong do you think you can be?"

"Why?"

"This is totally an experiment, but you feel warm to me …"

He raised his right eyebrow.

"And you don't make me itch." He smiled. "Do you think we could lay together with minimal clothing since everything's making me itch?"

He stripped off his shirt and I caught my breath. His perfectly formed chest and abdomen were shining in the light from the bathroom. As he crossed the room to the light switch, he slowly dropped his pants. *Damn.* He was wearing boxers.

"I'm here to heal you."

He slid into the bed and wrapped his body around me. My skin finally relaxed as his hands swept up and down my arms. I always thought his body had special abilities; I never thought healing the sick was one of them. He used a remote to put the TV on low. He found *Roman Holiday*, a good Audrey movie about escaping yourself. That's what I hoped Oscar saw, or maybe he just picked that movie because I had a poster of Hepburn in my room, so he knew I liked her.

Princess Ann's secret and Joe Bradley knowing it all along did made me look at Oscar and wish he knew what was going on with me. I hated I was lying to him.

We fell asleep intertwined. I woke up a few hours later to *ESPN* and a discussion of the start of basketball season. Something was just not right. I was still itchy. I sat up, put my hands on my hips and pulled my cami off. Laying my bare upper body next to Oscar, I felt his body shift.

"Your fever's down," he said groggily.

His fingers gently moved up and down my back and he started to wake enough to figure out I was only wearing my panties. The chills coming off my body were now because of him. Kelly was right, everything was intensified, his very touch set me ablaze. I looked up to face him.

There were no voices and no aura, just him, his smooth chest warm against mine. The blanket fell from around my shoulders as he continued to stroke my back. I kissed his chest, lightly touching his nipple and working my way down to his abs. My tongue traced each muscle up to his neck. I couldn't get enough. My body was raging with desire.

"You're definitely feeling better."

"Mmmm" was all I could say as I started to suck on his neck. "Thanks to you. You're a great doctor."

"Why do I have the feeling that you want to play doctor?"

My head was clear like it had been earlier that afternoon, only now my whole body felt as if I'd slept for three days and I was refreshed and awake, alive with the idea I could spend the night with him alone.

"Well, I'm taking biology and you promised to help me study."

"I'd hate to go back on my word."

"That's why I love you."

My mouth met his, as my legs spread and straddled him. His hands explored my naked back, moving down but staying outside my underwear, gently cupping my butt. My body quivered. His hands moved back up to my head and he ran his fingers through my tangled hair. I suddenly became aware and pulled back, catching him off guard and he reached trying to continue the kiss.

"I probably need a shower. I'm sure I smell."

"You smell wonderful," he said and he kissed me quickly on my neck. "Beautiful," He kissed me on the other side. "Desirable." He kissed my lips.

With our lips we explored each other's bodies. He kissed me down my spine, around my hips and onto my stomach. A hand was on the inside of my right thigh as his mouth caressed its way back to mine. My breath quickened in anticipation. He pulled away and pushed me away as I struggled to get closer.

"Stop, please," he pleaded.

Oscar pushed us apart. He fought me by crossing my arms in front of my chest, holding them one hand and snatched his shirt with the other. He passed it to me. I obliged, but made my disproval apparent on my face.

"We have to stop. I can only handle so much and I don't want this to go any further," he said, looking straight in the eyes.

"I'm not saying no," I insisted. "I'm saying yes. There's no second guessing here. There's no regret."

My eyes pleaded with him. Although my body was intensifying every sensation, I knew my mind was clear in my request.

"You said I would say yes just because it's you. That's not the case here. I want you. I want to be with you. I want to give myself to you."

"No, you don't. You want to use your body as a replacement for your heart. I can tell by how you act and what you say you haven't given me your heart yet. I will not accept a substitute."

I was confused by what he was saying. I loved him. I told him so a million times.

"I love you. How many times do I have to tell you I love you for you to believe it?"

"You said the words. You've heard them said and you repeated. It's a learned behavior. That isn't how you really feel. It's what you think I need to hear. You may have deluded yourself into believing it's real, but we both know deep down inside, you haven't given an inch of yourself to me."

That pissed me off. How he could even think that way about me? I'd opened myself up to him more than anyone.

"You do it to everyone. I'm not offended. I've talked to Kelly, your best friend. She can only tell me surface details about you and not because she's holding back. The way you look at me, talk to me, even the way you touch me, tells me you care for me, but you don't love me."

He sighed and got up to grab his jeans off the floor. His body had a halo of light around it, but I knew it was just from the TV.

"I don't want to have sex without love, not with someone I truly care for, that I truly love. Look, I've had sex without love. I've done that, I wasted my time and my life. I have so many regrets you have no idea. I've hurt people and I've hurt myself."

I was angered that he dared to say he loved me more than I loved him.

"Are you sure that's the reason?" I snapped at him. I remembered Sharyn's inner voice. Was he making up this whole oh-you-don't-really-love-me thing as way to keep me this vestal virgin trophy? He looked confused.

"You can sleep with any black girl that comes along, but the white girl you keep on a shelf like some Goddamn trophy."

I knew trophy would hurt him since that's how he felt Mya treated him.

"What the hell would ever make you say that!" He snapped.

I knew I crossed a line.

"You think I'm not sleeping with you because you're white? How dare you say that to me? Race has never been a factor in our relationship until now."

I'd never seen him so mad. Every muscle in his body was tensed, and his fists were balled.

"If race isn't a factor then why I'm I always getting called a mud shark or a SnoBall you're always getting called a hoho or coconut?

And why do I know all the words to *Jungle Fever*? I get serenaded in the halls almost every day."

My voice was raised, too, as I sat up on my knees in a vain attempt to stand up to him.

"That's not me. That's the jackasses at school. But if that's who you're living for then I think you've been around me long enough to piss off your daddy and isn't that the only reason white girls go after black guys?"

His words cut through me.

"'Cause you know black guys only go after white girls because they go down on them three times a day. By the way, you owe me a few by now, don't you think?"

He face came within an inch of mine. My jaw dropped open. I couldn't believe he was being so hurtful.

"You're going to need to widen that," he sneered.

I snapped my jaw shut and glared at him. Through gritted teeth, he asked, "Now, are we done with the childish B.S? Can we go back to the issue at hand or are we just done?"

I fought back the tears. He wasn't going to make me cry, I refused.

"I'm sorry, I just don't understand what you want from me. I was wrong to bring up what I heard. I…I…I…I'm sorry, I didn't mean it. It's just I don't understand what I've done or haven't done to make you…Not want me."

"Believe it or not, Ellie, this isn't just about you. You want to know the truth? I've slept with white girls before, I've slept with Asian, Hispanic and black girls. My sex life was like a frickin' United Colors of Benetton ad. I don't want just any girl. If I wanted just any girl, I'd have just any girl. I want you, but I want all of you, not just what's between your legs. And that's what you don't understand. You've never thought you anything else to offer. Trust me, I wouldn't go through what I've had to go through dating you just to get a little piece."

What had I put him through that was so horrible?

"What did I do?" I asked softly.

"You? You didn't do anything, but do you have any idea what I go through because you're white?"

My face contorted as I tried to think of what he went through. He never said a thing. But Kelly said the other guys wouldn't say anything to Oscar. He was the guy everyone wanted to be. They wouldn't question his choice to his face. I was the one that had people coming at me from every direction.

"My coach sat me down and told me I really needed to think about what I was doing with you," he said. "The guys on the team are constantly at me about you, because they think I couldn't possibly actually like you, let alone love you. And really, I should leave you so one of them could have a turn with you. Max's the only one that doesn't make comments to me."

I thought about when we went to Pizza Luce', we usually sat in a booth with Max and Kelly, while the rest of the team pulled tables together. I thought we sat with Max and Kelly was because they were our friends and we were both a couple. Oscar had been more and more withdrawn into our booth as the weeks passed, instead of hanging out with everyone.

"I made a choice that I wasn't going to be that person anymore. I wasn't going to go out drinking and having sex with some random girl wherever I happened to be at. I've sown my wild oats. Maybe you need to go sow yours," he said flippantly. "But there are no condoms in this house, in my car or in my locker at school. I—"

"You had sex at school?" I interrupted him, catching him off guard. That thought even stopped me from thinking about the fights I'd see on the sidelines with his coach.

"That's not the point."

"You had sex at school?"

Oscar was no longer the clean-cut Boy Scout with the perfect image. He was a daredevil and, even though I felt I was losing him, the thought of him skipping study hall to sneak off to a back corner of the school was driving me wild and made me want him even more.

"I'm not proud of what I've done. But there are a lot of girls who have wanted a lot of things from me. They've been throwing themselves at me since I was fourteen. But they never wanted me as a person, they wanted me as an idea. They were willing to do anything and everything with me."

"How many girls have you been with?"

"Quit trying to change the subject."

"You're the one talking about how much sex you've had. How am I changing the subject? How many?"

"We aren't having that conversation right now. We're talking about you."

"You had sex at school?"

"Quit trying to throw this back on me. This is your issue. I told you, I refuse to do this until I feel I'm ready and you're ready and you're not ready for this."

How dare he tell me what I'm ready for, treating me as if I was a child. No wonder he didn't want me; he saw me as his Lil' Girl, 'girl' being the operative word here.

"You need to break down the walls around your heart and let me in," he continued to lecture me. "I refuse to accept your body as a consolation prize for your heart. I'm willing to put in the time and deal with all the jerks telling me we shouldn't be together because you're white. Somewhere I feel deep down inside me, you're worth it. You need to get rid of these crazy ideas of what love is. Some convoluted mess between movie love, which never seems real, and what's modeled for you at home."

He stepped closer to me, calmed himself and sat down on the edge of the bed.

"Look at your sisters. You have one who gives herself fully and completely all the time to people who don't deserve it and ends up crumpled in a ball in the corner crying. The other sister, who you seem to be taking after, will give her body, but no other part of her. She uses men and throws them away. You want to be like her, never allowing anyone to love you? What would that say about you if you became like her?"

He paused.

"And what would it say about me if I let you become her?"

I realized I was wrong about him. I knew he was wonderful, but he wasn't just a boyfriend. He wanted more out of life than to play ball and go camping. He wanted me, all of me. I had no idea how I could give him that. He was right. I only knew how to give him my body. Everything else was just a theory. I was still figuring myself out. How could I share what I didn't have with him? He didn't want what everyone else wanted. What was expected of me to do? I knew how to do that. Please the person in front of me. Lie to them and myself that what I was saying was truly how I felt. He could never understand the thoughts running through my head. They scared me most of all.

"If you think you can't handle giving me all of you, then let's just end this now. I'm willing to wait, put up with a constant barrage of insults and innuendo and be patient, but I refuse to play games and I refuse to accept less than everything."

A vice tightened around my heart as the fear of losing him swept over me.

"I want someone to be with and I knew at sixteen that may be too intense for you, and I can appreciate that, but I've done it the other way and I have to live with that. If you're willing to try, I'll protect you from the mistakes I made and I'll stay with you. But if you can't meet me even half way…I need someone who can keep me grounded and help me become the man I want to be. I see that in you and that's what I want. If you know you won't be able to work through your issues, please let me know."

The tears welled up again but I composed myself, not willing to let him see he was destroying me. I knew what he wanted. He wanted to know I had feelings, not that he'd hurt me, but that I actually cared. Maybe he was right. My urge to fight the tears for fear of embarrassment overpowered his desire for me to be vulnerable enough to love him. I didn't want to be the one crying and crumpled up in a little ball because he left me. If I never gave him my heart, I'd never have to worry about that. He was right. I was trying to substitute my body for my heart. But that was the only part of me I could give away. That was all I'd ever expected to give someone. And as much as I tried to not fall into the trap of what was expected of me, it was the only road I knew to take.

“I’m going upstairs and going to bed.”

He put a hand on my forehead.

“Your fever’s coming back. I’ll get some medicine and be right back. I’ll tuck you in, but I think I should be sleeping upstairs tonight.”

I wanted to say no, please stay, not wanting to have him away from me, needing his arms around me to let me know everything would be okay. But I was too afraid I might cry and he would see.

Before he dropped the medicine in my hand, he said, “If you ever question my motives again and say it’s because you’re white. If you ever bring race into our relationship again, it’s over. I get enough of that at school.”

I knew from the inflection in his voice, he meant what he said.

“We have enough issues coming at us from every direction. What happens in this relationship is between you and me. Race isn’t an issue and never has been. I only saw you, not the ‘lily-white girl.’ I only hope you fell for me, not the ‘big black guy.’”

The words cut me. How could he think that? And then I recognized I put the thoughts there myself. I’d brought this nastiness into our relationship. Kelly said when I think of him I don’t see color, I just see him. Maybe I was capable of love.

****

That morning I heard Oscar in kitchen and then I heard his dad come through the front door.

"Oscar?" Mr. Jeffreys called.

"Dad, please be quiet. Ellie's sleeping in the guest room."

"Why?" he said with a low and judgmental tone.

"She got really sick at school, and at her house there are too many little kids and her sister's pregnant."

There was a long pause.

"Don't worry. I slept in my bed last night."

He wasn't lying, but I knew that hadn't been his first idea.

"Okay, but you should've called me. Is she better now?"

"No, the fever just won't break. I've been giving her fluids. Is it okay she's here with you all day? She'll probably just sleep."

"I guess so, but, Oscar, promise me you will not destroy this girl's life. You've been bullrushin' her from the moment you met her. I like her. She's a good girl."

He probably wouldn't think that if he'd seen me last night.

"Just assure me you're not trying to replace what you lost."

"No!" Oscar's voice was firm. "That's not my intention with her."

"Okay, I just don't want any repeats. A man should never have to live through that, but if they must, it should never repeat itself."

What was he talking about?

"It won't. I promise you," Oscar said, his voice now solemn. "She's different. I love her."

I breathed in deeply at hearing he still did love me, loving me enough to tell his father.

"I won't screw up again. I promise. I've already learned the hard way."

"Okay, son, just please try to reign yourself in. You're going to overwhelm her. I'm going to go to bed, just let her know where I'm at if she needs anything."

I heard his footsteps going up the stairs.

The doorknob turned, so I closed my eyes to appear as if I were asleep. As the door slowly squeaked, I tried to slow my breathing. Oscar sat down on the bed next to me. I didn't move. I was afraid to let him know I heard the conversation with his father and afraid he wouldn't stay if he thought I was awake. He gently brushed my hair back. Then he laid a hand flat against my forehead to check my temperature for the last time before he left for school.

I still tried to decide if I should pretend to wake up. His lips gently caressed my forehead as he said softly "I love you Lil' Girl." And then he was gone.

My fever finally broke that afternoon. By the time Oscar got home from practice, I was feeling better. He took me home. And suddenly I was scared I'd be alone with only the wall I put up around my heart to comfort me.

Chapter 21

We didn't go trick-or-treating together or to Fright Farm. For the next two weeks, I lived my father's life. Oscar would be outgoing and loving just enough in public as to not raise any red flags, but in private he would either find an excuse to not touch me or not be around. I now had sympathy for my father. He loved my mother, but she wouldn't go near him in private. She'd only touch him if someone else were around to witness it.

Oscar would hold my hand as we entered school in the morning. But I was facing a winter of walking home alone and was mad at my parents for not letting me at least try for a license. Volleyball was over and basketball began. Oscar and I would only go out in groups, and with football season over, that was more infrequent.

I'd lost my ability to see lights and hear people. Kelly said it was because I was depressed. She was worried about me, but in a way she was relieved. She didn't know how she'd be able to protect me from myself. At least while I was unhappy, I was safe.

Oscar kissed me but didn't really kiss me; there was no longer a passion to his kisses. He had thrown up his own wall. Maybe to teach me a lesson, maybe to protect himself from me. Maybe he was ready to leave me, this shell of person who wasn't whole as he'd envisioned. Whatever the reason, my inner voice tormented me daily. I was questioning who I was, what I was, could I ever be enough for him. Could I ever be a whole person even for myself?

Here I thought I'd been telling him so much more than I'd told anyone ever before. But as I replayed our conversations in my head, I realized he was right. My fear of knowing who I am was enough to block even me from my true feelings. What was buried deep inside my heart? Could I trust him enough to let him be the one to help me find the answers?

Every night I sat in my room crying as I tried to turn my attention away from the pain of no longer having Oscar's arms around me. Thoughts of how I could fix this problem filled my head. I felt as if I was falling in hole with no bottom. Darkness was all around me and I was grasping at any glimmer of hope.

Watching movies, I wondered, was that me? Could I make it be me? Who was I? I knew there was more to me, but I could only see Oscar, his love consumed me so fully, then left me to rot in the gutter.

I sat in English class, the worst class to have at the end of the day. Tia turned around to talk to me.

"So how far along are you?"

"I've only read four of the poems, why?"

"Not the book. You know."

She looked at my stomach.

"I'm not pregnant."

"You're not?"

"Why'd you think I was pregnant?"

I had been losing weight, not gaining it.

"Well, you and Oscar have been together for –"

"Two months," I said, cutting her off. "We've been together two months. Why'd you think I was pregnant?"

"I don't know?" She said, suddenly embarrassed. "Well, he's still with you…"

"And he couldn't possibly be with me because he likes me. Got it, thanks."

I knew if she thought this, most of the school did, too. I flipped open my notebook to scribble my frustrations out. Why else would he be with me? Heaven forbid that he liked me. Right now, he probably doesn't.

"Well, he's, you know?"

"I know what? He's wonderful and that's why he couldn't stay with me?" I asked angrily.

"No, he's –"

There it was, laid out in front of me. She was going to say it. What Oscar been going through, *guess it's my turn.*

"Black."

I wanted to yell at her, to tell her she was a racist bitch who didn't know what she was talking about. Her stupid stereotype was just ignorant. But I didn't. I wasn't strong enough. Two weeks without Oscar holding me, telling me I was wonderful, beautiful and someone he loved above all had weakened my resolve. I rolled my eyes and laid my head on my desk.

Mr. Bjornquist finally entered and set down a stack of books. He shared this classroom with two other teachers and was always lost when he came in.

We were going over great American poets. Robert Frost was a perfect choice as winter was now upon us. I already studied Frost in third grade. Mr. Bjornquist was trying to make *The Road Not Taken* into some huge, deep poem. I couldn't see it, until he started to talk about how the choices we make today would determine the rest of our lives. *Two roads diverged in a wood. I took the one less traveled by and that had made all the difference.*

It made me think about where I was in my life. A crossroads. I could let Oscar go and protect myself from the possibility of pain. Or I could open myself up to Oscar and risk the pain of rejection, but also give myself the chance for true happiness. According to Kelly, it was my only true chance for happiness. I had someone chasing me, trying to make my life miserable. I was doing what Gaap wanted. I was letting Oscar slip away. Each day I could feel the hook ripping from my heart as the blood pooled in my chest, causing a pressure that was more painful than anything I'd ever experienced.

My own free will was destroying my happiness, I was fulfilling my family's legacy. It was then I decided I would take the road less traveled by. I'd put myself out there and allow myself to love and be loved. I was going to fight. It seemed strange that my fear of fighting with Gaap was less than the thought of allowing myself to truly love Oscar.

****

I walked home with Jordan. He had been so elated to have me back to catch me up on everything he felt I'd missed by spending too much time with Oscar. Mostly, I just nodded or 'mmm'ed' at the right places in conversation, but I was really figuring out my plan. I had to let Oscar in. As much as I didn't want to let him in, the pain of the last two weeks was too much for me. The fear of him continuing to push me away until I was a distant memory was unbearable. Living on the fringe of his love knowing any minute he may cut me loose was excruciating. How had my father done it for so long? Was his love for my mother that great? So great he lived for the moment when she'd turn and put her arms around him? Letting him know he was loved in return. Could I go on living like that as long as there was the hope that someday Oscar would turn to me, take me in his arms again and tell me he still loved me?

I walked back to school around six-thirty. Oscar should've been out of practice. His coat wasn't helping keep the cold out. My fingers were freezing through the thin gloves. Why did my mother keep buying the knit one-size-fits-all gloves? The wind whipped up the light snow that had fallen that afternoon and the last of the fall leaves.

I stood by Oscar's car in the parking lot. I could feel my cheeks chapping. I put my head down to try to reduce the damage. After about ten minutes, the chill hit my bones and my body was numb. I heard Oscar say goodbye to someone. My breath released a cool, white mist.

"What are you doing here?" he scolded me like a child. "You need to be inside. It's too cold out. You'll get pneumonia."

I didn't look up, because tears were streaming down my cheeks and burning my wind-blown skin.

"What do you want to know?" I asked in a low voice.

"Excuse me? What did you say?"

I tried to raise my head. Blood rushed to my forehead, caused it to ache and feel as if it weighed a thousand pounds. Breathing deeply, I looked at his hand flipping his keys in irritation. I was now a burden to him. He hated me. I knew it, but I loved him so I gathered all my courage.

"What do you want to know?"

"What do you mean, what do I want to know?"

"You said you wanted me…You wanted all of me. I have no model to show me how to give you everything."

Once again, I tried to lift my head, but couldn't.

"I can't lose you. You're too important to me." My hot tears froze as they streaked down my face to my chin.

"I can't not have you in my life."

I could feel him looking at me as he stilled his keys. He placed a hand under my chin and forced me to look at him in the eyes. I batted away the tears, which flowed faster when I saw his deep brown eyes, which seemed to show he was in as much pain as I was. I faced my fear.

"Get in."

Cold air blasted out of the vents, and he turned down the heater to let the car warm up. My face was burning from my tears. Suddenly he held my face and he wiped away my tears.

"What'd I tell you about wet-eyein' me?"

"I'm sorry. I…I…I'm tryin' to stop," I said, only to cry harder.

"You mean it? You're ready to open yourself up to me. I'll be here. But no games, please."

I nodded, as he captured my lips, finally truly kissing me.

Chapter 22

As we drove to his house, I held my hands together to warm them up. The house was dark as we walked up to his house, I could feel his hesitation as he put a hand in mine. I squeezed tight, not wanting to let go.

His house was warm and my body was stinging as it started to thaw.

"I need to take a quick shower. I hate taking them at school in the winter." His cool tone sent waves of fear through my body that he was trying to get away from me.

"Would you mind heating us up some soup? It should be in the fridge. I'll only be a minute."

I poured a bowl of soup for him. My appetite had been gone for the past week and a half, partially due to finishing volleyball, but mostly due to my lack of wanting to do anything. I was shutting down one part of me at a time. I heard the shower turn off, as I sat at the table and waited for Oscar.

My body shook in fear of what was about to happen. To distract myself I sorted through some ads and bulk mail on the table. Among them was a letter congratulating Oscar on getting into Howard

University. The letterhead said Washington, D.C. He hadn't told me about this school. Was he really going away to Washington, D.C.? He promised me he was going to stay here at the U. But after the last two weeks maybe he really was done with me. He'd keep me around for the rest of the year and be gone in the fall, starting over on the other side of the country.

I heard Oscar come down the steps, so I slipped the letter back under the other mail. I got up, took the soup from the microwave and set it on the table.

"Oh thank you, Lil' Girl," he said, as if the silence of the past two weeks hadn't happened. "Couldn't you find the bread?"

"What bread? You said you wanted soup."

"Soup and sandwiches, just plain peanut butter, nothing special."

He looked at me as if I was supposed to jump up and make him sandwiches.

"You want me to make you some sandwiches?" I said, infuriated at the request.

"Yeah, if you wouldn't mind."

Did he wash his brain while he was in the shower? What was going on? Was he testing me? I sat there confused for a moment, but then I made him some sandwiches. I set them on a plate in front of him.

"Didn't you want any? There was enough right?"

"I haven't been eating," I said under my breath.

"Oh, why's that?"

Damn it, he heard me.

I was so confused. This wasn't Oscar it was some strange guy who wasn't who I had been missing.

"What's going on?" I asked, my hands still shaking. My stomach hurt, not from lack of food, but from his behavior.

"I'm asking you a question. You haven't really been around, so I was wondering why you haven't been eating," he said, slurping a large spoonful of soup.

"I haven't been around because you haven't let me," I snipped, as I tried to control my temper. "You won't deal with me. You pushed me away from you."

"If that's how you see it," he said, taking a bite.

"What other way is there to see it?" I was trying not to walk out the door, considering it was probably only ten degrees out and my house was fifteen blocks away.

"You said you wanted to tell me what I wanted to hear. I want to know why you haven't been eating. You brought it up. I'm just asking for you to clarify."

So that was the way he wanted to play this. He told me I couldn't play any games and he pulls this. What did he want me to say? Did he want me to say it was all his fault? He ripped me apart inside and I no longer wanted to live, so I lost my desire to eat. Is that what he really wanted?

"So are you going to tell me or are you going to keep yelling in your head at me and never let your true feelings out?"

His voice was so placid, as if he didn't care what my answer was. It made me angrier.

My rage built as I looked at his face, his uncaring face, staring at me.

"You want to know why I haven't been eating," I screamed, "because of you. You made it so I didn't even want to move, let alone do anything to keep myself going."

I stood up and wanted to run out of the room, but still tell him he was a jerk and I never wanted to see him again.

How could he sit there eating his Goddamn sandwich, acting as if we were just friends and he was just catching up on the latest news?

"It was all I could do to get up in the morning, hoping you'd be outside to take me to school. That I'd get a few minutes with you and you might actually treat me like a human being. You told me to let you have all of me. I wanted to do that, but I don't even have all of me yet, so I guess it's over, because I have nothing to give. I'm an empty useless shell of a person that no one will ever love because there's nothing there too love."

Tears streamed down my face. I wanted to hit him and I wanted to run, but I couldn't move.

All my rage exploded in a plethora of screams as I didn't break down my wall. I ran straight through it.

"I hate my life, I hate myself, and I hate everything around me. You're the only light in my life and then you left me alone and destroyed."

He pulled me onto his lap and wrapped his arms around me, as I buried my head in his chest.

"I'm sorry, I just didn't know how to get across to you how I felt."

"Did I really treat you like that?" I said sobbing and thinking I'd have never been that cruel. By ignoring me Oscar hurt me so deeply.

"It doesn't matter, 'cause neither of us is going to treat each other badly again, right?"

He leaned back, lifted my chin and kissed me softly on the lips. I buried my head back in his chest. He stroked my back until my sobbing slowed down and I could breathe.

"Get up now. I really am hungry. I eat when I'm depressed. Look at my stomach. I must have gained ten pounds."

Oscar lifted his shirt. I saw the same perfect body and shook my head at him. He kept bouncing his leg until I got up and went to the other chair.

"Now," he said, taking another spoonful of soup. "What were you planning on telling me before the breakdown?"

"What do you mean?"

"You said that you were going to tell me what I wanted to know."

"I don't know, I was just going to answer your questions to the best of my ability. And how did you know about my inner voice?"

"You said something on our first date. I can usually see on your face when yours is fighting with you. You scrunch up your nose and your eyebrows go back and forth like the little devil and angel that are supposed to be on your shoulders."

He really did know me, probably better than I knew myself.

He finished his soup and we went into the living room. We left the TV off, but turned on a small table lamp. He wrapped me up in a blanket and sat across from me rubbing my feet.

"So, you'll answer any question honestly?"

"I said I'd try my best, but you need to be gentle. I'm new at this. You know, not giving the expected answer, but the real one."

"Okay, that's fair, but if I call you on it, are you going to get mad?"

"I don't know," I said and that was true. I never tried not giving what the expected answer was.

"What's your biggest fear?"

"Thanks for taking it easy on me."

He shrugged his shoulders and just smiled.

"Well … aside from losing you?"

"Naturally," he said and smiled.

"Pass me the lotion," I ordered, giving myself time to think.

"How's that a fear?"

"'Cause I was going to rub your feet, too!"

He passed me the lotion and scooted to the other end of the couch. I started to rub his feet to distract myself enough that I wouldn't over think what I would say.

"Truthfully, my biggest fear would be to be constantly hitting up against a wall of my own creation and never breaking through. Like I make a decision that sets forth a path that leads to my certain destruction and unhappiness."

"Don't you think that's a little overly dramatic?"

I sighed and knew I'd have to divulge more than I was comfortable saying. But I looked in his deep brown eyes and knew I wanted them in my life forever.

"My sister chose to skip a football game and ended up meeting Marcus who fathered one of her children and beat her regularly. When he finally went to jail on some stupid drinking charge, she started to date his friend, Matt, who got her pregnant. When Matt went to jail, she met Roger at a gas station on the way home from the courthouse and he got her pregnant, again, twice. He finds her useless and tells her every time he sees her, after they have sex, because she can't give him a son."

"Okay, so maybe that's not being overly dramatic."

"Next."

Feeling better about myself by really examining my thoughts we moved forward.

“What’s your favorite color?”

“Lilac why?”

“I just wanted to know and you’ve never said anything.”

We talked for almost an hour. He made me think about things I always shut away because no one cared before, so why should I? I was amazed how he could phrase a question and make me talk. As much as he learned about me that night, I learned more. I never knew I even had those feelings.

“Do I get to ask anything?” I finally asked.

I was emotionally drained. I felt like I’d been put through twenty rounds. I couldn’t stand up if I wanted to.

“As long as it doesn’t have to do with my past.”

“Wait a minute. Since when are we putting conditions on these questions?”

“You said I couldn’t ask anything hard.”

“Fine, not that you followed that rule,” I said, sighing. “How about the future? What’s up with the college search?”

“I’ve been accepted at a few schools, but I haven’t said yes to anyone.”

“What schools?”

“The U, KU, and Howard.”

“Where’s Howard?”

“It’s in Washington, D.C.”

“I’ve never heard of it.”

That was the first truth in this line of questions.

"You wouldn't have. You're white."

His lips curled into a smile.

"I thought we weren't bringing race into our relationship?" I teased, raising an eyebrow.

"It's a predominantly black school. My dad graduated from there. I think I'm done with question-and-answer time. We wasted two weeks of our life 'cause you're stubborn, and we need to make up for it."

"I'm not sleeping with you," I said, smiling.

He crawled across the couch and trapped me underneath him. "That's good, 'cause Lil' Girl, I wasn't planning on sleeping."

Chapter 23

With my life back on track, I started seeing auras again. Kelly found out more about how to turn off the voices in my head. But I no longer had that problem. Maybe I fried that part of my brain, killing it forever. I couldn't see Oscar's light anymore. That made me nervous, like he'd been taken over by Gaap and that's why we fought. Kelly assured me she could see his light and my feelings for him clouded my sight. With basketball in season I went to games two to three times a week. But I enjoyed it. Kelly saw it as a great training ground.

JV was playing, Oscar was sitting between my legs and I was lying with my arms wrapped around his chest and my chin on his shoulder. He would have to leave at halftime, so Kelly tried to be patient as Oscar's legs stretched across two and half rows of bleachers in front of us. Every once in awhile, he'd tap my knee and I'd lean close only to hear him caking me.

"I love you more than peanut butter." "I love you almost to the hate." Or "You know I only love you on days that end in Y." Then I received a light kiss on the cheek.

One of his fingers would play in the palm of my hand, tickling it, and letting me know even though his attention was on the floor and he was cheering on the JV team, he was always thinking about me.

My phone rang and, what do you know, it was Jordan.

"What's up, Jordan?" I asked, as Oscar's head fell back so he could look at me.

"Ellie, what's that cranial nerve thing?" Jordan asked.

"The good or the bad?"

"The bad, of course. Like I could remember the good one."

"Oh, oh, oh, to touch and feel a virgin girl's…vagus…" I said, counting each word on my fingers to make sure I hit twelve.

"Vagus?" Jordan asked.

"I'm not saying it. You can insert the correct word. Simply heavenly," I finished.

"Do the whole thing again...please."

I glanced at Oscar. He didn't seem to be happy with me so I kissed him.

"Where are you?" Jordan asked.

"Basketball. Oscar has a game."

"Yeah and your life revolves around him."

"Yes. It does. Do you want the mnemonic or not?"

"Fine."

"Oh, oh, oh to touch and feel a virgin girl's…vagus…simply heavenly."

"Thanks El. If you ever get a life outside of him…"

I hung up. His crap had to stop soon.

"Jordan?" Oscar asked.

"Yeah…cranial nerves."

"I know. Lester's gonna get fired someday from that one."

"Not the sweet and salty thing?" I asked.

"What sweet and salty thing?"

"He must only say it to girls. Never mind."

"No, what is it?"

"Let's just say it's a bodily fluid taste thing and leave it at that."

A look of recognition crossed Oscar's face.

"Where's Max?" he asked Kelly.

"Um…family thing."

Kelly's patience had worn thin.

"Oh…too bad."

The buzzer sounded for halftime and Oscar started to shift. He turned around and kissed me, then I kissed his forehead.

"Gotta go get ready."

"Love you."

"Love you, too," he said, heading off to the locker room.

"So where is Max really?" I asked.

"Trying to reign in a tsunami in the Pacific."

"Oh. Fun. What?"

"He can control the weather, but the crap you learned in fourth grade science is real. Max created the patterns and nature takes care of most of it. He just tries to reduce the damage."

"So what happened with Katrina?"

"We don't talk about Katrina," Kelly said, turning away.

****

The JV game ended and we moved to two rows up from the bench, close enough that for the few seconds Oscar actually sat on the bench, he could always turn and see me. I loved the time-outs when I could see the sweat running down from Oscar's head into his shirt but that made it hard for me to concentrate on the game.

"Focus," Kelly said, not referring to the game, but some kid on the other side of court. "Can you see the mask he's wearing?"

"Of course I can. It's really a bad fit."

It was, too. Darkness crept out of the edges of the hazy light that surrounded him. I looked at the girl next to him and could only assume what he was lying about.

"Can't I just enjoy watching Oscar?"

"He isn't even playing. It's a time-out."

"I don't care," I said, whining. "I feel great. I even found I can take two extra classes next semester, one Saturday and one Wednesday night. Isn't that great?"

"Yeah, yeah. I can forge the damn documents you need to be a high school graduate."

"Is that a good idea?"

"No! Ellie you're frustrating the crap out of me. Something's not right."

Her tone sent a shiver through my spine "What do you mean?"

"Haven't you noticed more and more masks showing up?" She sounded worried.

"It's high school, we're all hiding something."

"No, it's something more than that."

I didn't want to think about Gaap. He was a part of my life that I had to keep secret from Oscar and I hated that. We'd been talking more and more, which lead to kissing more and more. I had been letting him in, seeing me warts and all, as my grandpa would say. He hadn't run. In fact, we'd gotten closer. I just wished I knew more about his past, but I wasn't about to push that issue, at least, not when I still had a huge secret myself.

"Lil' Girl."

Half time was almost over when Oscar came to me.

"I have a problem. I'm out of gum. I thought I had enough. Can you run and get me some?"

"Your problem is you're superstitious. Come here." I curled my index finger to draw him closer. Kissing him, I slowly slid a piece of Juicyfruit from my mouth to his. His tongue licked mine in thanks.

"It's fresh, I promise. I just put it in."

"You really love me, don't you?"

"Yes."

He took off back to huddle with his team.

"What was that?" Kelly asked.

"It's a Friday game. Friday he has to chew Juicyfruit. Tuesday it's Doublemint. Thursday's Big Red. Saturday, bubblegum-flavored Extra."

"He's insane."

"He loves me. He'd have to be. I just try to keep a pack of whatever day it is in my pocket."

"So you have a whole pack?"

"Minus that piece." I smiled and Kelly looked at me shocked. "What? Can't I want a kiss?"

"Did you guys…"

Kelly's hands started to twirl.

"Join a sign language course," I joked then 'fessed up. "No, we haven't. But we're in a much better place."

"I'm glad, you're in a better place. It's none of my business about the other thing. I just didn't know you were in that good of a place."

"I love you, you know that but…But I think you're right. He's the one. Sharing with him is…"

"Lightening."

"You're the one married to Thor."

"He's the God of thunder, not lightening. I meant lightening on your soul."

"I guess so. But really, if he has a good quarter..."

Kelly laughed.

"How much of what's written about Gaap is true?" My question caught Kelly off guard. She hadn't been aware that I spent my final study halls on the internet trying to find out anything I could that could protect me.

"I mean is learning to conjure Byleth something I could do? Or would even want to do?"

It seemed fitting to me that Byleth was a higher demon than Gaap and could control him, but he also wrote one of the first books of mathematics. Something about math being helped by a king from hell played to my enjoyment of irony.

"Um, well, I haven't read about Gaap on the internet. What did you read?"

"He's the third son of the devil and the president of hell, but it also says…Yeah and one!"

I jumped up. Oscar had stolen the ball. He ran it down and scored, while drawing a foul. He chest bumped the wing Lincoln, then looked at me and smiled as he went to the line.

Oscar breathed deeply, tossed the ball up in the air, let the ball bounce once, then dribbled it four times. I had been trying to figure out what he said before he released the ball. With a light swish, his shot hit and he fell back into his zone defense.

"Sorry," I continued. "It says Gaap rules the southern part of hell and the southern part of the earth. Which is why I wondered why he'd be in Minnesota?"

"The internet's more accurate than I thought. We divide the earth up differently than you do but he's the third son of Lucifer. Did it tell you about his powers?"

"He causes strong feelings of love and hate. But one site said he commanded illusions."

I kept my face forward, afraid if I turned my attention I'd miss Oscar doing an amazing move. Everything about him captivated me lately. When he pivoted I could see every muscle tense in his lower body. I was impressed with his ability to palm a basketball or the way his bicep flexed as he dribbled. When he dribbled the ball in between his legs, it drove me insane. I kept that from him, simply because I thought he do it all the time just to get me to kiss him.

"They're one in the same," Kelly explained. "Gaap uses the illusions to intensify love and hate. He'll use an illusion, and you're going to have to be strong enough to understand it's not real. You'll be fighting your own mind. There's a chance you could end up like you did when your mind opened up and you were hearing thoughts."

My attention finally broke from the game as I remembered the pain that coursed through my body almost a month ago, followed by the pain of Oscar stepping away from me.

"How can I do that?"

"Remember the illusion with Sharyn?"

Now my thoughts were of Oscar kissing Sharyn in the hallway.

"You were able to overcome that illusion," Kelly continued.

"But you were telling me what I was seeing. What if you're not around?"

"I probably won't be. This is something you're going to have to do on your own."

Her eyes seemed all knowing, as if she really believed I could do that.

"But I can't let you invoke Byleth. Using one brother to defeat another has never had a good outcome."

"You still haven't told me if you think he'll attack Oscar."

My focus now was completely off the game and onto Oscar's well-being.

"I can't tell you what I don't know."

"Shouldn't we tell him? He has a right to defend himself."

In truth I wanted to know more about Oscar's past and that could be my in, revealing the final chapter in the book of Ellie.

"Not now," Kelly said, shaking her head.

The game ended and Oscar brought me home.

"Remember, I get a skirt tomorrow."

He finally was having his Eagle Court of Honor and I promised him I would dress in a skirt. Although when I made the promise I hadn't been thinking it would be zero degrees and December.

"Are you sure you want a skirt?" I asked, knowing the answer but my legs were hoping for a reprieve.

"Have you met me?"

Chapter 24

I'd gone to the Scout Shop on Marshall a few weeks before to find a gift. An overly jubilant clerk was happy to educate me on all the products and give me a brief history of everything so I wouldn't feel like an idiot at the ceremony. I decided, since I had Oscar's class ring, I would get him a Boy Scout ring. I'd been saving up and I had just enough money, but I had no idea what I'd get him for Christmas, which was just around the corner. I had gotten a phone call the day before saying his ring was in, so I was cutting it close.

I begged my dad to run me down the street. The Scout Shop was just too far to go by bike in this weather, so my dad agreed.

"So this Oscar thing's getting pretty serious, huh?" he questioned, as if he were a father who actually cared what happened to me.

"Yes," I answered shortly, not wanting to have the conversation.

"Well…um…I'm just wondering are you two…"

Being younger than my sisters, I knew what was coming, but I didn't feel like having that conversation with someone who rarely talked to me.

"Dad, we're not doing anything. If nothing else, Jen's kids are the best birth control in the world."

"Oh okay I…So have you figured out what to get your mom for Christmas yet?"

I hadn't even thought about her.

"Not really. I figured I might get her a sweater or something."

Ah generic clothing, a gift that showed I really had no idea what she wanted and I wasn't motivated enough to ask.

I ran in and out of the store in less than five minutes, and we headed home in silence.

I only had about thirty minutes until Oscar and his dad would be picking me up. I'd already set out my outfit on my bed. The black sweater had a high collar and the white skirt was adorned with black embroidered vines. My black shoes had a low heel, but they weren't as bad as the stilettos Kelly tried to talk me into.

Oscar's ceremony was at a camp he worked at about forty-five minutes away from the Twin Cities. He said it was the one place he found solace when the world became too much.

We pulled up a long, gravel driveway. I knew I was going to need help walking in heels. *Why did he have to push the skirt?*

The main dining hall was a large, brown building at the top of a hill. Oscar took my arm as I almost fell getting out of the car.

"Do you want me to carry you?"

If I weren't so stubborn I would have taken him up on it. As we got to the door he turned to me.

"Now remember, these aren't the football players. They're a little more..."

"Nerdy," I said, trying to be diplomatic.

"No, not nerdy. Reserved during ceremonies."

The football players at the football banquet were like a group of hyenas, hooting, hollering and yelling at every comment and award.

Inside, a few people were still decorating. Red, white and blue abounded amid a sea of khaki. Oscar took off his big coat to reveal his full dress uniform. He pulled two sashes out from his pocket and unfolded them. One was green and had about a hundred round patches on it. I'd seen them at the scout shop. The other sash was white with a red arrow on it. The way Oscar filled out the top of his uniform was quite nice, until he put on his kerchief. It was hard to look good wearing a kerchief.

"So what's this for?" I asked as he slipped the white sash it over his head.

"Order of the Arrow. It's a special group of scouts. It's based on how much you camp as well as some other things. It's kinda the national honor society for scouting. Remember that conclave thing I had to go to a month ago?"

That was when we were fighting so I thought it was just an excuse to be gone all weekend.

Mr. Jeffreys was across the room, unloading a box with all sorts of things from Oscar's years as a scout. Pinewood derby cars, other wood projects, scrapbooks, and two huge blankets covered in patches he'd earned over the years.

Crossing to the table I let my fingers run over the patches that told the story of this part of his life. Oscar was deep in conversation with a white guy with brown hair. He was probably six-feet tall, but next to Oscar he looked short. He looked like he was in his early twenties. Oscar's motioned me to come over.

"Michael, I want you to meet someone very special to me," Oscar said. "Ellie, this is Michael. Michael, Ellie."

I shook his hand as Oscar put his arm around me.

"Michael's the camp director during the summer here, and Ellie has graciously taken me on as her boyfriend."

"Well, you're a brave girl Ellie. I've known Grouchy for many years, but I've never seen him look so good. You must be doing something right."

"Thank you. He's a handful at times. Grouchy?"

"Oh, we all have nicknames. It makes it easier for the kids to remember us. Oscar's Grouchy."

"I get it. For Oscar the…right," I said, nodding and everyone laughed.

"Congratulations again," Michael said, "and I'm so happy to see you've been able to work everything out."

I had no idea what he meant, but Oscar's face became solemn. I guessed Michael might have been part of Oscar's transformation.

As the room filled up, I noticed Oscar and his father really did stand out in this group. Most people in the room were white. But Oscar was accepted and so was I. No comments. If anything, I think some people were surprised I was so plain.

Michael was the master of ceremonies. I heard how many people's lives Oscar had touched. The mayor of St. Paul was there as well as the leader of the Hmong Community Action Committee. Oscar even got a plaque from the governor. The ceremony was very moving.

An hour later we were eating and while we had cake, I slipped Oscar my present under the table. He opened it in front of everyone. The ring had the same stone as his class ring and was engraved inside. *To the eagle who taught me to fly.* I was glad his finger was so large the whole saying fit. He put it on immediately and kissed me in front of the whole room. There was thunderous applause and hooting. There was a little bit of football here. My face flushed and Oscar laughed at me.

"You know, I've got cake here. Don't forget what happened last time," I said, thinking back to the icing war from my birthday.

"Remind me to bring some home," he whispered in my ear. Across the room I Michael was smiling at us.

The night wound down. It was another day with Oscar being told how wonderful he was, and him being gracious. I didn't think I could've been that humble.

On the way home, Oscar and I sat in the backseat of his dad's older SUV. I was learning to cherish these perfect days, because Kelly said the more of these I had the sooner I would be attacked.

Chapter 25

Say Hey (I Love You) was on the radio and we danced around the kitchen. Oscar lifted me up to kiss him while spinning me in circles. He set me on the floor and I went in and out of his arms while he sung to me. Holding hands, we grooved together. I let go, brought my hands to my forehead and turned around and backed into his body. 'The white girl dance,' Oscar termed it. Moving and bouncing, he put a hand in between my hips on my abdomen and guided me back and forth while nuzzling my neck. His lips were right by my ear as he sung, *My momma told me don't lose you, cause the best luck I had was you.* He picked up the frying pan and I sat down at the table watching him dance.

Christmas was just a few days away. Oscar and I were preparing Sunday dinner, as had been our tradition for quite a few months. His dad had been called in. That wasn't odd, because his father liked the distraction of work, anything to keep his mind off of Oscar's mother.

Mr. Jeffreys aura seemed to change when he looked at Oscar. Kelly told me the droplets that are always on the outside of his aura were from his broken heart. When he looked at Oscar they increase to an almost solid state of running water. As much as he loved

Oscar, it hurt to be around him. I'd seen the photographs of his mother and I knew it had to be Oscar's eyes. They were warm and inviting, just like his mother's. I had been trying not to look into them at all, afraid I'd lose all control. When he looked directly in my eyes, I was entranced, unable to say no to him.

"Hey can you pass me the tortillas?"

We were having tacos. Oscar always warmed the tortillas up in a frying pan with a little bit of oil. It was funny, but I actually learned how to cook with him. He told me he couldn't always be the one cooking for us. I loved how he always made everything an 'us.'

"It'll cost you," I said, standing on my tiptoes to collect my due.

He kissed me quickly so I held the tortillas behind my back.

"Oh, I had to walk three whole steps after getting up from a chair. You're going to do better than that if you want to cover the shippin' and handlin' charges."

Trying not to smile, he picked me up holding me with one hand, as he kissed me and stole the tortillas from behind my back.

"Cheater."

"Yep and don't you forget it."

I went back to dicing up tomatoes when the doorbell rang.

"Can you get that? I don't want to leave the hot grease. It's probably just someone looking to sell us windows."

The doorbell rang again.

"I'm coming," I yelled, running down the hall.

I opened the door. The cold night air rushed in and sent a chill through my body. Mya stood in front of me.

"Can I help you?" I asked, swallowing hard.

"Oh, you're here," she said, annoyed as if I wasn't supposed to be in the house at all. "Anyways can you get Oscar for me?"

She looked me up and down and slightly snorted in disapproval.

I was frozen for a moment in my sweatshirt and jeans, as she stood there in her tight, short skirt and low-cut top beneath her open jacket. She pushed her way past me into the house.

"Stay here. I'll get him," I said, regaining my ability to move.

My hands were shaking as I walked back into the kitchen.

"Who was it?"

"Mya," I said trying not to sound too mad as jealously raged through me.

"Mya? What the hell's she doing here?"

His voice was firm as he turned off the stove and walked into the living room, where she was waiting.

"Stay here. This will only take a minute," he yelled back to me.

I turned off the fan above the stove and slipped down the hallway towards the living room. I could barely make out the two voices. Oscar was keeping his low.

"I told you to never come near me again."

Mya was talking louder than she needed to be.

"Are you still mad?" she said in a seductive tone. "I figured you'd be over all of that by now. You sure can hold a grudge. Look here, I'm only in town for a few more days. How 'bout you ditch the little one, and you and I can spend some quality time together? She doesn't need to know."

"Lower your voice. I wouldn't spend five minutes with you. I will never forgive you for what you did."

"Oh, come on. We had a great thing goin'. I'll be back all summer. Let's just get a little bit of playtime in first. I know you've to be missing it. According to Sharyn, little Miss has been holdin' out on you."

Mya's voice sounded coy.

Me holding out on him? What a laugh. It was all he could do to keep me off him.

"Oscar you know I'm the only one who could make your toes curl," Mya said.

"Curl? Or hurl? 'Cause when I think of you it's usually the latter that comes to mind."

"Play all you want, but we both know what I am to you."

"You were never anything more than a receptacle to me. In case you forgot what little we had you flushed down the toilet the day you went to that clinic."

Clinic, what clinic? Oscar never talked about his past relationships. From the little he talked about, Mya was the only repeater in his life. He never truly had a relationship, according to him, until me.

"And don't worry about me. I can handle myself."

"Well, if you ever get tired of handling yourself and you want someone else to do it…"

He cut her off sharply.

"Ellie will take care of me whenever I decide that I need help. She's my life now, something you never were or would be. You're a selfish, small human being."

"I was thinking of you. A child…"

A child? Was she calling him a child?

"…would've ruined your life and, God knows, it'd have ruined mine."

She was talking about their child.

"Yours, that's all you care about. That's all you've ever cared about. Your life, not my son's."

The cold air crept down the hallway from the front door still ajar. But wasn't what was giving me chills. Mya aborted their son. Was that what his father been talking about the day I spent in bed with a fever? Is that the big event that made Oscar rethink his life? I could hear him coming down the hallway, but I couldn't move. The thought of Oscar being a dad with a little boy had frozen me in place.

"I told you to wait in the kitchen," he scolded, as he passed me in the hall.

I walked back into the kitchen as he slammed the skillet down on the stove. He kept his back to me, but I put my arms around his waist anyway. A gulp shot down through his body as I felt a tear drop on my arm. He was crying, not sobbing like I usually do, but quiet, soft tears. The tears were for his son that she'd killed.

"I'm not hungry are you?" he finally asked.

"No," I said softly.

We stood motionless. He told me he had regrets, but he hid them so well I could've never thought it was this bad on him. My hands clasped around his stomach. He unlocked them and turned around.

"I guess it's my turn now, huh?"

I knew what he meant. It was his turn to open up to me, to talk to me about the one thing he didn't want to relive.

He sat me down at the table and composed himself.

"Last summer I was working down at camp."

I assumed he meant Phillippo, the camp he'd had his Eagle ceremony at a few weeks ago. He told me he worked there every summer for the past four years.

"I'd come back home on Wednesdays and go back on Fridays. That was my weekend. I went to Mya's around the end of June to see her. She was sick and laying in bed. I figured she had the flu or something. She had a pill bottle she asked me to grab. When I picked it up, I saw a pamphlet about what to expect following an abortion. I asked her what it was about."

I stroked his hand and as he wiped a tear with his other hand.

"She said it was nothing and not to worry about it."

His voice caught as he tried to continue.

"I asked her, did you have an abortion? She said yes, but it's no big deal. See, I'd gotten a little drunk at prom and I slept with her without protection. I woke up the next morning, not really realizing what had happened. I was still responsible for my actions.

"I asked her, did you ever think about asking me? She said it never even occurred to her and she really thought another man in the world was the last thing it needed. I threw the pills at her head and stormed off. I wanted to kill her."

Rage built inside him at the memory, like a wound had been reopened violently.

"I went back to camp and didn't come home on my days off. I just stayed by myself on the lake or hiking the trails all day, except when I ate. About three weeks later, Michael, came to me because he was worried after I blew up at Sara, the nature director."

"Oscar we need to talk," Michael said. "You've been staying here all week and being really short with everyone. I need to know what's going on because I'd hate to let you go because of your attitude. Can you please tell me what happened?"

"I didn't want to tell him," Oscar continued with his story, "But I also knew I couldn't go back home either. I needed the lake and trails to keep my mind off of what happened."

"'Did whatever happened with Sara warrant your actions or is there something else. Did you get into a fight with a girl when you went home? Is your dad okay?'" Michael asked intelligent questions."

"I told him about what happened. I can still feel the rage I had that day."

"'How far a long was she?' Michael asked the question I should've asked."

"I tried explaining myself but it all came out wrong then he said, 'Oscar, I've been watching you over the last few years. From the goofy kid coming down to be a CIT, to the councilor you are today. I noticed a change in you over the last year or two, is this a pattern of behavior?'"

"Not really. I mean I'm usually really good at protecting myself," I said not really understanding what he was getting at."

"He sighed and said, he meant how many times did I have to protect myself? For the first time I was embarrassed. I said, 'it just seemed like girls were throwing themselves at me left and right.' He told me, 'Just 'cause someone throws a ball at you, doesn't mean you have to catch it. The scout oath's a way of life. The ending, about being morally straight, isn't some item they tagged on. You took that oath, you can't just pick and choose what parts you want to abide by, and when you want to. Each rank you advance you're supposed to reflect and determine, are you living the twelve."

"So I started to ask if he and Beth had ever…and he stopped me. He said, 'This wasn't about him and his fiancé, who he had a commitment to, it was about me. Had I ever really thought about what I was saying and doing to the girls, and myself for that matter? It wasn't just their bodies they were throwing away, it was mine too."

I let Oscar keep talking about everything and I understood why he treated me the way he did, why he wanted me to be special, why I wasn't a throwaway. Tears were filling up in his eyes.

"It took me losing my son to get me on the right path. That's my biggest regret. Mya just saw him as a cancer that needed be removed, instead of seeing him as a part of me that was growing inside of her. She never asked me, Ellie."

"Did you want him?" I asked, thinking my sister never asked the guys anything, she just told them.

"I wanted to make the choice. Or at least be asked my opinion. I didn't love her, but the instant I knew I had a son, I loved him. If I'd have waited until I was with someone who loved me and I loved in return, I'd have my son right now."

I thought about the baby. It had to of been barely four months along. My sister learned that Taylor was a girl really early because she had been in the right position during the ultrasound. I didn't even know how to processes what he'd said, especially since math wise I questioned it was even his or her knowledge that it was a boy.

If she did know for sure, there was little chance she wasn't already pregnant at prom.

We sat silently for a few minutes, until I realized he needed me right then. I needed to be the one in control. There had been so many nights he held me, trying to make my problems go away. I wanted to help, but I never knew someone who needed me.

I stood up, taking his hands in mine and walked him to the living room. Even though he was so large, he felt light as I helped him up, his body drained from the story he had just told.

I dug in my bag for my iPod, finding my John Legend tracks. I selected *Take me Away* and loaded it into his docking station. Tugging Oscar up from the couch, I embraced him. John Legend's voice filled the room, singing to us about dancing between heaven and hell until he sang *Take me away from here, Take me somewhere where love is like breathing. I don't care where we go, 'long as I'm there with you.* Oscar held me tight, as we rocked back and forth in each other's arms. At the song's end, he recovered a bit, but he was still drained and started to sit down.

Knowing the next song was *Slow Dance,* I pulled him back up. Doing my best karaoke, I sang along *Can we wait just a minute*. I didn't know how to help him, but I knew as long as we were focused on just one another, we'd be fine. His body really moved against mine by the time John was singing, *We can argue and fuss all night, but I propose, that we go, to the floor, and we slow dance*. Oscar's hands were moving their way down my body in an attempt to pick me up. Jumping, I wrapped my legs around him. He then carried me upstairs.

He laid me on his bed. I'd never been upstairs. I was curious to see his room until he was on top of me and caressed my lips.

"Thank you, Lil' Girl," he said softly in my ear.

"For what?"

"For not judging me and still loving me."

"I'll never stop loving you," I whispered, as his mouth slowly moved back to mine. With his weight on top of me I felt as if I were in a cocoon, tightly wrapped up in his love. He clutched me tightly, as he rolled on his back. He removed my shirt when I was on top of him. Our lips found each other again and his tongue stroked mine. My hands held his head as he fumbled with my bra, finally unlatching it and throwing it to the ground. His hands cupped my breasts gently massaging them and then fondling my nipples until they hardened.

I tore at his shirt and he sat up holding my body to his as soon as his shirt was removed. His skin was warm and smooth against mine.

His lips brushed against my neck finding their way down to my breasts. One of his hands moved to my neck and his thumb was on my chin below my lip. My mouth moved down slightly nipping his thumb as my lips drew it in and I sucked lightly on the tip.

His lips slowly enveloped my right breast and I could feel a burning inside me. His tongue lightly licked my nipple and I held tight to his head not wanting him to move. My nipple tingled. My hips moved and rocked over him as he was got harder and harder. With him rubbing up against me, I moaned as electricity coursed through my body.

He sucked harder on my breast, while his fingers tugged at my hair. I'd never wanted anything more in my life, but I knew he would stop me, again. So I rode him harder and faster to free some of the pressure building between my legs. He released my breast, moaned and moved towards my lips.

Surrendering from our embrace he fell back on the bed. The moonlight cut across my body and Oscar stared at me. We were both breathing hard and my body was shaking lightly. As if possessed he came at me again, landing his face in between my breasts, exploring me again.

Oscar's mouth moved along my ribs, one hand held me above him, stopping me from laying down on him. My hands where on his chest as my hips rocked gently over his. His lips suddenly came back to mine as my legs locked around his body, and we rocked back and forth. From the center of me, waves of pleasure shot to every inch of my body. My hair rose all over. I tried to remove my jeans, which were too much of a barrier for me, but he stopped me by pulling my hands back to his chest.

"Do you love me?" he asked.

"Yes," I cried out in a low whisper. "More than anything."

His lips were back on mine as the rocking increased. I knew he was fighting with himself, not wanting to stop, but afraid of what would happen. I'd have to take control. This was my day to help him.

My hand slid down his chest and into the light sweatpants he wore. His hand grabbed my arm, as he softly said, "No."

"Trust me," I said and he slowly released my arm. My hand slid under the elastic waistband and found him. All of him. I had no idea what I was doing, but I understood the basic principal. I was going to bring him pleasure, without the pain of regret.

I tried in vain to wrap a hand around him. I understood why Mya wanted one more night with him. The delicate skin was so silky. As my hand moved, I kissed him. His hands were in my hair tugging it slightly. I slid my body off his, but kept my mouth and hand in place. His tongue moved into my mouth, as I sucked on it. I wanted to feel him, remember every bump and grove. The very shape of him.

At the top, I let my fingers separate and slide down, he gasped, so I repeated it, only faster. With every stroke, I imagined him inside me, gliding between my legs. I placed my head on his chest and licked and bit him, too. My hips were moving with the rhythm of my hand, and I locked my leg around his, so he could feel me against his thigh.

I squeezed a little as my hand went up and down, increasing its motion until I felt his body shiver and pulse, while his mouth released the most wonderful moan of pleasure. His lips told me what I already knew.

"I love you, El. I love you so much."

My body was covered with goose bumps, and I felt as if I was the one who had had the release. I sat at the edge of his bed and he wrapped an arm around my waist. Oscar butterfly kissed my back, which increased the shockwaves that were shooting up and down my body.

I finally took in his room. It was full of awards, but what surprised me was a poster on his closet door. It was my volleyball schedule. I was on the poster since I was on the varsity, but Sharyn had been blacked out. Then I noticed a few pictures he'd taken with his phone. I was everywhere in his room.

He pulled me down next to him and I curled into his chest.

"Thank you. But you didn't need--"

I cut him off by kissing him. I didn't want to hear what I did or didn't need to do. I knew it would be a long time before we would go all the way, but somehow we stepped into a new place and it was exactly where I wanted to be.

Chapter 26

The holidays passed with few surprises. Oscar gave me a small, handmade box he made with his father. Engraved on the top was a heart. Inside was an iPhone, and he prepaid my cell phone bill for the next six months.

"I hate not being able to get a hold of you because you run out of minutes. Plus your phone has a broken screen. I think you've dropped it about fifty times."

When I complained that he'd spent too much he gave me those reasons. Part of me wondered how he always had money, but he shut me down when I questioned him.

Thoughts of Oscar consumed me. Whenever I wasn't around him, I would feel him. During classes, as I did my homework, while waiting for him to finish practice, I'd feel him, his hands all over my body. A brush of my hand became his as I tried to bring myself back to that moment with him. My lips would ache, filling with blood as I waited for him to kiss me. Focusing on class was nearly impossible.

I felt like everyone around me could tell what was on my mind. Twisting my arm under my desk, I tried to jar the feeling of him from me. During the morning car rides, I tried to touch Oscar as much as possible just to have a trace of his cologne on my hands to carry me through until lunch, when I'd repeat the obsessive behavior.

I started to think about how much I shared with him. Could he be going as crazy about me as I was about him? Opening himself up to me burned his essence into my mind, unable to escape. Had I had the same effect on him? Was he sitting in his class daydreaming about me? Were phantom kisses running up and down his neck like they were mine? Was my voice telling him I loved him, whispering in his ear right now?

In class I tried to make it seem as though my hands were in front of my mouth because I was concentrating on the lesson. I actually was nibbling on my thumb, imagining his, and breathing in the smell off my fingers. I was lost in thought. Everyone was getting up, disorientated I copied and walked to the back of the classroom with everyone else. What class was I in? I had no idea? Oh yeah, art class. Ms. Finch promised to finally move away from theory and into practice. She handed out cameras and film that was hand-wound in reusable canisters.

"Now it's colder out, so you may want to use natural light from a window or attempt to use a lamp, but you must understand, either way you'll have open up your apertures and slow down your shutter speed to get the pictures you want," she instructed us. "I will be giving you two film speeds and you'll have to adjust accordingly.

By Friday we will start to develop your film and work in the darkroom."

The bell rang just as I got my old, beat-up camera. It'd been through hundreds of students in their attempt to pass their culture requirement. I didn't really care because it was lunchtime and that meant Oscar.

"Oh no, it's more paparazzi," Oscar joked as I approached my locker.

"Very funny. You're not gonna think it's so hilarious when I'm taking your pictures for an hour."

His arms encircled me.

"I don't do pictures."

"Yes, you do."

My hands wrapped around his waist and slid under his sweater, making sure I got enough of him on me.

"Oh no, I don't," he said stiffening. "Take Kelly's instead. She's a girl."

"And I'm your girl. I don't want to have a hundred pictures of Kelly."

"Now it's a hundred pictures."

"Practice makes perfect and if you want me to pass the tenth grade, I'm going to need motivation."

I reached for his face and kissed him deeply.

"You're the best motivation I can think of."

"That's blackmail, you know."

"Yep, I learned it from the master."

He had been getting me to try all sorts of new things by rewarding me with an embrace or run a guilt trip about how I'd be helping him in some obscure way.

"So after school today is the only time we have this week."

"Ugh--I'm getting tired of this," he complained repeating my sentiments exactly. "I never get anytime with you."

"At least you have basketball to distract you," I said with a pout. "I just have to sit at home by myself all alone."

"Okay, okay, after school. You're lucky my game's at home tonight or I'd have no time. Hey, why don't you just take pictures at my game?"

"Baby steps, Bob." I said, quoting the movie I watched the night before while waiting for him. "I need to learn how to shoot motionless objects before I try moving targets."

"What's with all the violence?" he said, joking.

"I'm just that kinda girl."

I was leaning in to kiss him just as the bell rang. My face twisted in disgust. I put my hands around his face getting the last of his scent on me. I brought my fingers to my mouth letting him think I just was picking with my nails, but really I was making sure I had enough to get me through the day.

****

After school I went home with Oscar to take photographs at his house. He was kissing me as he opened the door carried me into the entryway.

"Mmhum," Oscar's dad grunted, clearing his throat.

"Excuse us," I said. "Hey, maybe you'd want to help me, too."

"I don't think that would be very appropriate and it might cause a rift between my son and me."

"I need to take pictures for class," I said, holding up my camera.

"Good luck with that," Oscar scoffed. "He's worse than me when it comes to having his picture taken."

Oscar leaned in and whispered, "And I *will* have a problem if you kiss him to get him to do it."

"You need this for school?" Oscar's dad said, ignoring his son.

"Yes, it's for school," I said, backhanding Oscar in the gut.

"Ouch, again with the violence," he said, pulling back his body as if the smack really hurt.

****

I took a few pictures of Oscar and his dad. Then Oscar and I went into the kitchen, where the best afternoon light was. I took pictures of him next to the window, the light streamed across his face. I asked him to let me take a couple of focused shots; his hands, his neck as he arched to the left. Then I had him stand up and I unbuttoned his pants.

"Hey, there, Lil' Girl, Dad's in the other room."

"It's art, I have to push the limits," I said.

I tugged his shirt up to his chest for a good shot of his lower abs and upper hip. It was a perfect shot. I pressed the button on the camera snapping three shots. The camera rewound the film.

I didn't want to move my eyes from behind the lens, knowing I wouldn't be able to control myself. The camera was gently taken from my hands as the object in front of me moved closer.

"So are we done?" Oscar asked.

My eyes didn't move off his stomach as I nodded yes. My hands were hungry to feel the bumps his muscles created under his skin. Biting my upper lip, I imagined it was him and his body I was biting. I finally caught my breath.

"I'll use the other roll at the game."

I saved the 400-speed film for the action shots, sure I'd just get blur anyway. His hand was under my chin, turning my attention away from his body to his face. I was shaken from my trance, his lips were on mine and my hands slid around his waistband.

****

This had to stop. I was trying to focus on the game and take some good shots, but I always seemed to find myself waiting until Oscar was sitting on the bench. A shot of his shoulder coming out of his jersey. Or the cut of his muscle on his upper arm. I zoomed into the sweat sliding down his neck, disappearing into the jersey. At halftime he asked me if I got any good actions shots. I lied, but the second half I actually took action shots.

The next day, Ms. Fitch used my shots as an example of how to develop film because I was the only one who finished a whole roll. We learned how to transfer the rolls in the dark and mix the chemicals. As I hung the strips in the dryer I realized these shots were personal, something I wanted to save, but not necessarily for the masses. When they'd dried Ms. Fitch looked through the filmstrips, she breathed in deeply.

"Well, everyone" she said, wetting her lips. "Tomorrow I'll show you all how to turn these little squares into a picture. Hopefully, more of you'll be done with your pictures so Ellie won't have to share."

"Thank you," I said. I wanted to rip the filmstrips from her hands.

"Ellie, these are really good. A few appear to be blown out and some are too dark, but that can be fixed in the darkroom. A very good first effort. Please cut them into strips of five and put them in this sleeve."

She passed me my negatives and I started to cut them.

"You have a good eye." She continued. "I can see you became very attached to your subject."

She lowered her voice.

"Some can't be developed here with the class, but you could probably develop them on your own time."

I loved developing the pictures, seeing the forms floating in the developer. From the first day, I couldn't stop. When the bell rang, I told myself I'd just finish one more picture, then I'd go to lunch. Two pictures later, I heard the revolving door and saw the outline of Oscar coming through the darkness.

"So this is where you are," he said. "That is you, Lil' Girl, isn't it?"

His eyes hadn't adjusted to the low yellow safety lights.

"Yeah, I'm sorry. I just wanted to finish a couple of pictures."

I could see the photo of his hip and abdomen materializing in the developer. My heart quickened when I saw the V cutting down into his pants.

"That's awesome, but I have the real thing right here for you."

His arms were suddenly around me. I lifted the picture with a pair tongs and put it in the rinse.

"I know, but it's not always there," I said with too much whine. "Can I show you the other ones I did?"

I removed the picture from the rinse and brought it to the dryer.

The other photos were in a pile. I only had enough time to do five, but they were pretty good. I cleaned up my station, while I waited for my last picture to dry. Oscar wasn't being helpful, nuzzling me on the neck and holding me tight to his body.

"I like this darkroom stuff. I've never been in here before."

At least his in-school escapades weren't in the darkroom. His lips found mine, he picked me up and set me on the counter.

This time I had to stop him. I wanted to share what I had done.

"Okay, I want to show you what I did."

We could always come back here another time.

I laid out the black-and-white pictures on a table in the classroom. One was Oscar and his dad, another was just Oscar in the kitchen. His eyes really popped in that one. There was the one with his fingers intertwined. The next was the cut of his arm muscles and finally his abs.

"She's good, isn't she?" Ms. Finch said, coming back in from her lunch. "So you must be the inspiration. I thought you would do the sweat one. I'll love to see how the light catches in that one."

"The sweat one?" Oscar asked. "What were you taking pictures of?"

Embarrassed, I gathered my pictures together and placed them in my folder. "Okay, let's go. I think we have enough time to grab a cereal bar or something quick."

"That didn't answer my question," Oscar said.

Ms. Finch laughed as I drug Oscar out of the classroom. That was the start of my love of the darkroom. For the rest of the year, Oscar brought me lunch in the darkroom.

****

Inspired by my pictures, Oscar skipped practice and had me come to his house. Having not had a night alone in quite some time, we curled up on the couch and watched *Love Jones*. As the movie started, I nestled into his neck as his arms wrapped around me. I was enjoying the melody and words of the opening songs. Lorenz Tate's character Darrius, got up on stage and started to recite a poem. His voice was like velvet. As each word left his lips, my body started to twitch. By the time he got to *I'm the blues in your left thigh…trying to become the funk in your right*, I was sitting up holding my breath, my eyes filled with desire. I'd completely fallen into the movie, not caring if it was dangerous or not. Having Darrius speak to me that way was exhilarating.

"Should I be jealous?" Oscar said, as my hand went up to silence him. "Really, where's the remote? I'm turning this off."

My hand covered his mouth to shut him up.

I replayed the poem in my mind. The tone and tempo created a perfect delivery. I relaxed into Oscar's arms, but soon realized it was useless. My body was alive with desire.

"Eleanor, may I speak now? Should I be jealous?"

"No," I said, still breathless. "You should be thankful."

I turned and kissed him passionately. I'll have to remember to watch this movie without him. It looked like a good one. Unfortunately, by the time I released Oscar, the credits were rolling.

Chapter 27

Rose Week was homecoming for winter sports. It wasn't quite as big of a deal, but it was another reason to have a dance. Part of me dreaded the dance, considering how the last one ended. I'd started my extra classes'. Because Oscar was filling in on weekends at some winter camp, I wasn't missing him on Saturdays. Just Sundays. I missed our Sunday dinners. I tested recipes on my family on Sundays just so I could surprise Oscar by cooking a meal once the winter camping was over in March.

When we did get time together, we made sure we didn't waste it. We maintained our chastity. Handling him, as we came to call it, became our only sexual venture. I understood now his hesitation, and the fear of the sheer size of his package was making me nervous. Not that I'd ever let on or talk about it, I still hadn't given up all of the chapters of Ellie.

Meanwhile, Kelly's nerves were shot. Not being able to single anyone out in the school or neighborhood as Gaap was driving her crazy. Obviously, Gaap was stronger than her and that upset her. She felt she failed in her mission.

****

The week was just as crazy, going to games and having fun, as homecoming was, but I just couldn't enjoy anything. Oscar had taken me shopping for a dress because Kelly just wasn't up for it. It was weird having a guy help me. 'Helping' probably wasn't the right word. I had to pick out the dresses and try them on. It took forever because I still didn't have a sense of style. I started to realized I might not have the best of luck, instead Kelly might have made the right outfits appear. Finally, I found a blue-gray satin dress with a gossamer overlay. Oscar didn't like the length, but I convinced him covering my legs was a necessity in Minnesota, in February and not up for negotiation. The spaghetti straps and plunging neckline helped convince him. At least, I was getting a chest. Maybe it was all the hormones running through my system every time I was around him, but I was finally a B cup.

As I shopped for shoes, Oscar took off around the corner. A couple of guys browsed in the women's shoe department. They both wore jeans, t-shirts and heavy coats. They were attractive in a preppy white-guy way. I stood in front of a mirror and was checking the height of a pair of heels when one of the guys bumped into me and copped a feel of my butt.

I fell back as the other guy, who pretended to catch me, but he just started a ping-pong game with my body as the ball.

"Excuse me," I said, trying to get out from between them.

"My bad," the shorter one said. "We were just so awestruck by your body, we had to make sure it was real."

The hair on my neck stood up on end. I was trapped between them and the chairs.

"Well, now you know it's real and you really need to move on," I said.

I pretended I was tough, but I was petrified and wanted Oscar back right now. Where could he have gone?

"I don't think we want to," the taller one said. "I think we want to go somewhere a little more private. Don't you think that would be fun?"

"I think that'd be fun," the other one said. "There's a dressing room right over there."

Some girl at some time must have gone with them, based on their pathetic attempt to glorify her.

"No, I don't, and I really need you to back up."

I was becoming over come with claustrophobia. One of them started to play with my hair and I tried to pull away. Where was that damn sales lady?

"I think she's made it more than clear she wants you to back off."

Oscar's voice was tempered, but I could see the rage in his eyes. I hoped he could see the relief in mine.

The boys didn't turn around. The shorter one waved his hand.

"Hey, she isn't having any problems are you, Honey?" His eyes shot daggers at me.

"I don't think you heard me."

Oscar grabbed the short one around the scruff of his neck with one hand and lifted him off the ground.

"So let me make this perfectly clear," Oscar said, his face now at the shorter ones as his legs swung trying to find the floor and failing in his attempt. "Leave her alone. You have no chance in hell of anything with her. If you so much as look back at her when you leave, I'll rip your arms out of their sockets and beat you with them."

Oscar's voice was metered, making it seem as if he was calm, but I could see in his eyes that he meant it.

The taller guy started to talk, as Oscar grabbed his throat with his other hand. Methodically Oscar turned his head to him.

"Did I not make myself clear?"

The store clerks watched while talking on the phone, to security I assumed. I squeezed between the two guys being held by Oscar, I reached my arms around him.

"You can put them down now," I said. "They're ready to leave."

He slowly released them and they ran. A manager was on his way over to us.

"Excuse me, sir. I'll have to ask you to leave or I will be forced to call the police."

"Can I at least finish buying my girl's dress? Seeing as your clerks did nothing to stop her from being accosted in your store."

"No, sir, I will need you to leave now."

I could see the fear in the manager's eyes as he tried to not get Oscar too upset. Oscar passed his wallet to me.

"Use the cash to buy the clothes. I'll meet you outside."

Oscar was escorted out of the store and back into the mall.

When I opened his wallet to pay for the dress and shoes, our homecoming picture was tucked in with his cash. Still shaking, I walked out of the store. Oscar stood joking with a security guard.

"Are you okay, Lil' Girl?" Oscar asked, taking my head in his hands. The guard stepped back to give us space.

"I am now, thanks to you. I was so scared."

I handed Oscar back his wallet. The attack suddenly fleeing my mind I thought about how much money I'd just spent and Oscar was holding a garment bag, too.

"Okay, that's it," I said, knowing that he spent over two hundred dollars and I couldn't let him keep doing that.

"That is what?"

"How can you keep spending money on me? I know you don't make a lot of money at the camp. Where's it coming from? If it is from camp, then I really can't take it. You need to save for college..."

I thought of Grace trading herself for possessions turning herself into a possession.

"Stop." He snatched the bags and my hand. "Let's go grab a cookie, if it's okay with you that I spend five dollars on a snack."

I nodded, knowing he was annoyed. I wasn't sure if I'd said something or if it was because we were standing by the guard when I said it.

After buying a cookie and some hot cocoa, we sat down in the food court.

"It amazes me how little you know about me," he said. "I don't publicize my life, but you act as if you've never heard any of the rumors about me."

I hadn't.

"It's refreshing to me though. I've had girls come at me because of my money."

Money? What money? He lived in the same neighborhood I did. He actually lived on the bad end of it. His dad was a firefighter. The only thing I ever heard was his dad spoiled him. I assumed it was because he was an only child.

"My mom left me money that's in a trust for me to use for college. But just in case you haven't been paying attention, I'm going to be getting a full ride when I do choose a school. Also, and this has to stay just between us, if my dad found out that I told you..."

He blew a low whistle.

"...My dad's a financial genius. He loves the stock market and has been very successful. When everyone lost their shirt, he didn't. I don't know his exact worth and I'd never ask him, but I know that he's worth well over a million."

I stared at him in disbelief. His dad was a millionaire.

"So my camp money is mine to spend how I want. I really never spent money until you. There never was anything I really wanted, except my car. But ironically, my dad started to give me money to spend on you. I told you he likes you."

"So that's why you don't drive a flashy car and your dad doesn't live in a big house."

"We aren't scrooges. A scout is thrifty," Oscar said and smiled. "My dad and I just don't have many needs. And my car will be flashy when I find the time to finish fixing it up. My dad will never leave that house because my mom found it and loved it. Leaving there would mean leaving her."

"You Jeffreys' sure do get attached, don't you?"

I took his hand and smiled at him.

"If you only knew, you'd have run away screaming. Now you're stuck with me."

"Well, I guess that's the cross I'll have to bare. But I think I'm going to have to start listening to rumors."

"Really? Why?"

"You still haven't told me about your escapades in the school."

My interest was really only so I could pack my own nighttime fantasies.

"You really want to know about me in the school?"

"There's just something about it that intrigues me."

"It's not like it was during school hours…well, mostly not during school hours."

He shook his head.

"You know that opening that up is a Pandora's box. Nothing good could come from knowing my past."

"Fine. I'll drop it," I said, knowing I eventually was going to address this.

"Good."

"So, what's in the other bag?"

"Oh that," he said, pulling a garment bag off the chair. "It's a winter dress coat, so you won't be cold."

"Since you can afford it, I guess I won't be mad. Just remember, I'm broke and I only work in the summer."

"Deal."

Chapter 28

Three days later was the dance. Unlike homecoming, rose week didn't have a game before the dance. So I had all day to prepare and freak out. As I finished getting ready, the doorbell rang. With my new wool coat Oscar had bought me, I went to answer the door. The coat was black and three quarters length it was quite warm.

"Coming," I said as I tried to maneuver in my dress. I opened the door to see Jordan standing there.

"Where's your phone?" he asked frantically.

"In my pocket, why?"

"Check it. There was a video that just went viral. It looks like half the school's on the sent list."

Pulling my phone out I checked my email. I didn't know the email address it was sent from, but I opened the attachment. There he was, Oscar, his arms wrapped around someone I didn't know. They were taking off his shirt and I suddenly realized it was Mya stripping him down. His lips were on hers, the same lips that had been on my body just a night before. This had to be old. Oscar said he had regrets. Maybe he taped it before he started to date me and it was just now getting out. Her body arched as he entered her, her moaning blasting out of my phone.

This was old, it had to be, I convinced myself, but then his hand slid up her hip. His ring, the ring I bought him was on his finger. I felt as if my world was collapsing. Why'd he do this to me? The doorway started to spin around me, as I reached out to grasp the doorjamb. His voice was saying, "Oh, I needed this." He needed it? He needed it? I wanted to give it to him, begged even. My mind raced. Was this an attack? No, how could it be an attack? Jordan brought it to me. He'd seen it, too. He had seen Oscar's body intertwined with Mya's, his mouth now on her breasts. Her moaning was too much. I dropped the phone and started to walk.

"Wait," Jordan yelled, but I just held up my hand to tell him I wanted to be left alone.

I could see what I thought was the limo carrying Oscar, Kelly and Max coming down my street, but I didn't stop. My mind exploded with images of Oscar deep inside Mya. Why? Why'd he do this? He loved me, he told me so. I was stupid, stupid to believe he could've ever loved me. A nobody, a nothing. What joy did he get out of being with me?

My inner tormentor kept telling me how stupid I was. How could I've believed I deserved anyone like Oscar? I heard him and Mya laughing at me, lying in bed naked as his fingers circled her fully formed breasts, laughing about how stupid I was to ever think he would want a child like me when he could've a woman like her.

I'd been walking for over a mile. I didn't even know where I was headed. I crossed over I-94 and University Avenue. I was walking down Lexington Parkway, not the safest area. but I didn't care. I wanted something bad to happen to me. Maybe then he'd feel bad for treating me wrong, knowing he caused me to walk alone in the dark on an unsafe road. I opened my coat. The cold air cut through my dress. I wanted to freeze. Freeze my feelings. Freeze my heart. Every time I thought of Oscar and Mya, I let myself freeze, hoping the physical pain could block out the mental.

I walked until I reached Como Park. My heels dug into the back of my feet. I was sure I was getting blisters. I found our swing covered in snow. Walking up the hill, I slipped, falling. My hands left exposed turned red from the snow.

The swing, just like me, was lonely. I was alone. I picked the wrong path. I should've stayed on the one everyone traveled on. Why did I have to try to find love? Mya tried to warn me he'd satisfy his needs somewhere. Maybe he still loved me and just used Mya? What was I saying? I can't live like that. I won't live like that!

The wind helped push the swing for me. It creaked as it went forward and back. The metal chains seemed to cry out in pain from having been awakened by me. It almost felt as if someone's hand was on my back. I was numb, nothing was in focus, the world started to look hazy.

"Hey there, sexy lady."

The voice sounded as if it was in slow motion.

"Look at this, guys. Seems we have a little friend here tonight."

The second voice also was in slow motion.

I felt someone's hand on my frigid cheek, but I couldn't see anyone, I couldn't move. It was as if my body was now rooted on the swing. I had become a permanent monument frozen in time.

"Are you up for a party?"

The third voice had the same slowed-down manner.

"Come on here, little girl. Let's see what's going on under that dress."

Something warm reached up under my dress. I still couldn't see anything. Then something else warm pulled me off the swing and onto the snow-covered ground.

"Well, if she's not going to object, I don't see why we should stop."

I heard a zipper and started to come to mentally, but I couldn't move.

My dress was tight, down almost to my knees and I heard the sound of ripping fabric. I wanted to scream, but I couldn't even open my mouth.

"Don't even think of changing your mind," the first voice said. "You know you want this. And I'm going to give it to you."

My panties were pulled down, my bare skin screamed out in pain when it touched the snow. But still I couldn't move. I wasn't frozen in fear, although I should've been. I was just frozen, as if someone paralyzed me. The hot breath of the first man was on my face, but all I could see were the stars above me. His breath smelled of onions, rancid meat and alcohol. He leaned in and touched my face.

"Oh, your face maybe cold, but I have a feeling other parts of you are warm."

His hands spread my legs, but then I heard a crash the man was no longer on top of me.

Oscar was yanking me up. I could see him, but I couldn't see the three men that had just been there. Kelly and Max were running across the park. Max was throwing something that acted like a sonic boom. When the noise sounded, I could make out a figure falling backwards. Kelly had a sword and was wielding it quite well. I saw her turning, flipping and spinning around. The sword's blade reflected the glow of the streetlights that lined the park.

The sword cut through the air, then blood started to drip off the edge. The high-pitched, slicing sounds from the blade cutting the air pulled me into another reality.

Kelly lunged at least thirty feet, flying through the air, her sword came down hard into the ground. Under where it lay was a man, a dirty, overweight, older man. Blood gushed from a chest wound. I heard a gurgling from the man whose body contorted and arched, fighting the death that was soon to come to him.

She pulled out her sword, crouched, and swung the sword over her head like a helicopter blade. A head flew across the field. Landing with a thump, it bounced like a ball being tossed by a pitcher in a game of kickball. The cold, green eyes were blank from the death that had just come to them. The long, black hair around its face stuck and knotted from the blood that splattered following the decapitation. A headless body fell to the ground with a thud at Kelly's feet.

"Maravia, this is your last chance to surrender. I know he promised you something, but you need to come forward and give yourself up or I will be forced to kill you."

Kelly's voice was so forceful the swings rocked back and forth.

Maravia? Who was Maravia? From the shadows, a third man appeared. He was taller, not as large as Oscar, but large. His skin was pale white and smooth.

"Sharidan, my love. How can I be of service?" Maravia's voice was obliging.

"Now they call me 'Kelly.' Who sent you after this child?"

I realized Oscar had me cradled against his body.

"Why are you touching me?" I yelled, tearing myself away from him.

He looked confused.

"Be still, child," Kelly warned. "This isn't the time. I told you that you needed to see past the illusions."

My outburst gave Maravia an opportunity to try to slip away.

"Don't even think about it," Max growled. "Why'd he send you? Not enough of a man to do it himself?"

Max was closing ranks around Maravia.

"He? I wasn't sent by a man."

Maravia had a strange accent that seemed European, but I couldn't place it.

"Gaap didn't send you?" Kelly asked.

"Are you accusing him of something?"

I knew Kelly couldn't answer, because accusation carried a heavy burden if found to be false.

"Who sent you after this child?"

"No one sent me. I was told I might enjoy this park tonight and I should bring friends. But now my friends are no more and you have ruined my fun."

"So you were to take her virginity? Were you to kill her, too?" Kelly asked.

"We were to do what we do. Take what we want from those who are *willing*…and leave a little bit of ourselves behind."

A little of himself behind? He was going to get me pregnant and leave me to explain how it happened. Raped by a gang of men I hadn't even seen. Forced to carry a demon. My eyes were fixed on the scene playing out in front of me. The cold my body felt just a few moments ago left me as my mind couldn't process both the physical and mental.

Kelly's sword hadn't been lowered.

"Who told you to walk this park tonight?" she asked slowly and deliberately, as she brought the tip of her sword to his chest.

"Maria. Something about this little brat causing her pain and she wanted to return the favor," said Maravia, speaking quickly as he was trying to save his skin.

Maria? Who was Maria? I knew no one named Maria. How could I have caused her pain? What was going on?

"Does Maria plan on continuing this action?"

"Yes," a female voice boomed pushing Maravia into Kelly's sword and killing him. "She does."

Maria had long, straight black hair and raging dark green eyes. Her skin tone was olive and her black gown hugged her perfect body. The word *vixen* shot through my mind when I looked at her.

Kelly was the one frozen, as Maria pointed her finger towards me. Oscar held me again to protect me from this evil woman.

"You and your whoring family shall never have a moment's happiness."

She turned to Kelly.

"And you shall be powerless to stop it. Did you just kill three of my demons? And a grandson at that. You'll have to answer for that, you know."

"They were attacking a human. I had every right to do what I did."

"She looks unharmed. I bet she couldn't even testify as to what was going on. I never saw her move to stop the action. I think she even enjoyed it. Didn't you, Little One?"

She was instantly at my side and running a long nail along my cheek; my skin burned as the nail crossed my face.

"And you," she said, sneering as she looked behind me at Oscar.

Oscar who knew nothing of what was happening, because Kelly hadn't let me tell him. He needed me to protect him. I pulled away from his arms and I shoved her back.

"You think you can stop me from killing him Little One?" She cackled. "Even your guardian cannot protect him, she has no decree, same as her worthless mate. All the powers of the heavens, locked behind the creator's red-tape."

"You will not touch him."

My voice came back in full as I stuck my chest out, trying to tower over this woman. My adrenaline was pumping as I stepped forward.

"He's innocent and has committed no grievance against you. As long as I breathe I will not let you harm him."

"I…l…I…" Oscar stuttered, my hand shot up to quiet Oscar.

"You think you could possibly do to hurt me?" Maria asked with a hollow laugh.

"It's apparent I already have," I growled. "Maybe you could enlighten me as to what my crime was against you."

The fear of her killing Oscar had given me the strength to fight back. No matter what he'd done to me, I couldn't let him be harmed.

"It's not your crime, it's your mother's. But seeing as you're someone she cares for and I'm not allowed to touch her, I shall torture you to get to her."

"What did she do?" I asked. I needed to know why I couldn't just have the life I wanted. A life without complications. A life where I could succeed and know happiness. I had to know what caused my pain.

"She refused my husband," Maria hissed.

"You wanted her to be with your husband?"

I couldn't imagine that could be possible as the thought about Oscar and Mya was enough to make my heart close off entirely.

"I don't care one way or the other, but my husband has been obsessed with her since she told him no. She wanted her husband and not him. Now my love, Gaap, spends every moment with her."

I shivered thinking of my mother with another man -- a demon and he was with her every moment.

"Why'd he do that?"

"Gaap controls love and hate, since they're one and the same. Your mother's refusal of him was unprecedented. Women always want him and he has them, then throws them away, so they can then spend the rest of their lives yearning for him. Your mother had him, then tossed him away. He didn't like that. I didn't care at first, until I realized by her refusing him, he refuses me."

"What does that have to do with me?"

"She loves her children so much, the only way I could punish her was to torture you. I went a little far a few times but, hey, accidents happen."

"I think you have the wrong family. My mother has never loved me."

"You're a stupid, little girl…Ugh…"

Kelly stabbed Maria in the back, the sword pierced through her chest, right below her shoulder. Kelly was incapacitating her, not killing.

"Run!" Kelly screamed. "Don't wait for me or Max. It may be awhile before you see us again."

Maria's roar shook the snow off the trees. She turned around to face Kelly as Max ran to help her. Oscar grabbed me and ran to the limo. He told the driver to get out of the park as he wrangled me into the vehicle.

"Where to, sir? I need to know where to go?"

"Just drive around the city," Oscar said, raised privacy glass and turned to me. "What just happened?"

My body began to thaw in the warm car. Oscar noticed my condition, became concerned and told the driver to take us to his house. Oscar wrapped his coat around my legs, slipped my shoes off and placed my feet on the floor heater while his hands rubbed the top of them.

"You're close to hypothermia, Ellie, I need to get you warmed up, but I can't have it come up to quickly or you could go into shock," Oscar said. "Ellie, Lil' Girl are you still with me?"

"Uh huh."

"Why did you walk to the park?" Oscar demanded. "Why weren't you at the house?"

"Jordan," I said, trying to remember back that far.

"Jordan what?" Oscar asked as anger crossed his face at the mention of Jordan's name.

"Jordan, showed me a video on my phone."

My eyes glazed over as I tried to remember how this nightmare had all started. *You need to see past the illusions.* I could hear Kelly's voice.

"A video, what video? I found your phone in a snow-bank in front of your house."

He handed me the iPhone.

I fumbled to pull up the video again. The beginning was the same. I saw Oscar was undressing. I closed my eyes for a moment and looked again, that time trying to see past the illusion. Kelly's voice ran in my head. A noise from my phone confused me. I didn't understand what I was hearing. *"do, da, do, do, do, do, do, da,"* Didn't match the Oscar and Mya video. Closing my eyes I told myself focus, Ellie, you need to focus, while I breathed deeply. Opening my eyes, again I saw a hamster dancing.

"This is what upset you? The hamster dance video?"

Oscar looked at me like as if I lost my mind and maybe I had.

My lower legs stung as blood flowed back to them. I arched my back, my head hit hard against the headrest and I held my breath no wanting to not scream from the pain. A deep breath later, I'd blocked out the pain enough to say, "Oscar, we need to talk."

As he carried me into his house, his father came to see why we were home so soon from the dance.

"What the hell happened?" he asked.

"She got attacked and was outside too long," Oscar said, as he carried me thru the spare bedroom, to the attached bathroom, setting me on the toilet as he swaddled me in a blanket. Reaching over to the tub he started to run a lukewarm bath.

"I'm calling the police," Mr. Jeffreys said.

"No," I screeched. "There's no point."

"We need to get you to the ER."

"No, I'll be fine," I said as my teeth chattered.

"Look, you're a minor and you need medical attention. This isn't up for debate."

I looked at Oscar, my eyes begging him to help me.

"I'll be fine. I just need to warm up."

My shivering was a sign I was warming up.

"Ellie, why are you trying to be a hero?" Mr. Jeffreys asked as he and Oscar wrapped another blanket around me.

"Dad, she said she'll be fine," Oscar said, his voice sounding torn.

"What did you do?" his father asked, shooting an accusatory glare toward Oscar.

"I didn't do anything," Oscar yelled. "I stood there doing nothing. I didn't protect her."

He was mad at himself, feeling that he failed me, when it was me who failed him. I doubted him. I believed a simple illusion just because someone I trusted…was it even Jordan at my door? I couldn't remember that clearly.

"So can I please just do as she wishes?" Oscar asked, his voice lowered. "She wants to be warmed up. Can I at least do that for her?"

"It's not your fault, it's mine," I said, trying to relieve his guilt.

"How could it possibly be your fault?" he asked.

"I promise I'll tell you everything," I whispered. "I didn't want to keep it from you but I had to. I can't tell you in front of your dad."

Mr. Jeffreys already wanted to take me to the hospital. If I started in with the whole story I'd be in the psych ward within the hour.

"Dad, she needs to get in the tub if I'm going to raise her temperature. Can you please go heat up some soup or something, so we can warm her up from the inside."

My legs were too cold to move so Oscar carried me to the edge of the tub. Removing the blankets and coat, Oscar then unzipped my dress. It fell to my waist. His eyes were wide and full of guilt when he saw my panties were gone. The warmth stung, it was as if a swarm of bees were crawling and stinging me. He stood me, up steadying me as he held me knowing my legs would be giving out any second. My dress dropped to the floor. Picking me up, he slowly dipped me in the water.

"Ahhhhhh," I screamed.

The water felt as if it was boiling against my skin.

"I promise you it's not as hot as if feels."

Oscar's dad was at the door and I pulled my knees up to my chest to cover myself.

"Dad. I don't think she feels very comfortable with you in here."

He turned quickly away.

"Sorry, I heard the scream. I was just worried. I brought some cream for the burn on her face."

I'd forgotten about Maria scratching me. I looked at Oscar. He gently stroked my face, trying to soothe the burn from left side of my forehead to the bottom of my jaw. The feeling came back to my extremities, but my body was still freezing. The care from the Jeffreys' family couldn't be matched by the top hospital in the country. After my warming bath Oscar brought me into the spare bedroom, covered my body in coco butter and dressed me in warm flannels and woolen socks. He then pulled out a small, familiar looking white jar with a yellow lid. My grandfather always had Carmex and here Oscar was lightly dabbing it on my lips.

"I have lip balm in my coat," I said.

"That won't heal you," he replied. "That's more for flavor than protection."

I knew he like both my Dr. Pepper-flavored and my cherry lip balms. In truth, I liked the flavor of Carmex. The scent always brought me back to my childhood before Caleb's death.

"How bad are they?" I asked feeling my lips sting from the ointment.

He gave me a light, healing kiss and I tried not to wince. I could feel my lips crack a little and he pulled back.

"Not too bad," he smiled. "But I've had better."

I sucked my lips in and lightly licked them.

"Stop that," he scolded and reapplied the Carmex I just licked off.

"Sorry."

I hung my head and he placed his finger under my chin, lifting my face up.

"You have nothing to apologize for."

His dad came in with soup. The bowl felt wonderful on my freezing fingers.

"I should call your parents," Mr. Jeffreys said.

"They're not home."

"They left you alone?"

His voice disapproving, although Mr. Jeffreys might leave Oscar when he's on a tour at the fire station, he can always be reached. Oscar liked to say his dad was a few hours away from earning his pilot's license as a helicopter-parent.

"You don't know my parents, they…"

I was about to say something disparaging, when I remembered Maria saying my mother loved us above all.

"I was going to stay at Kelly's tonight, but she got sick. Can I just stay here?" "Okay" he said.

"Dad, I really think I should stay with her tonight."

"Come out here and talk to me."

Oscar didn't move, his arms remained locked around me.

"If you really think I'm going to try to have sex with her tonight, you're insane. So what other reason is there to not let me stay with her?"

"I don't know I…" Mr. Jeffreys said, throwing up his hands. "Never mind. You'll keep her warmer than a pile of blankets anyway."

Oscar was better than any blanket. Without his shirt on, his body heat radiated to mine. I started to drift off, exhausted and wanting to escape into nothingness.

"Don't even think about it. I need to know what the hell *is* going on."

Chapter 29

Not knowing where to start, I closed my eyes and took a deep breath. Without Kelly there, I didn't know how to explain this to him.

"Have you ever felt something was always out to get you? The deck stacked against you?"

"A lot of people feel that way," he said. "It's called paranoia."

"You were in the park when Kelly went all *Kill Bill*? This is hard enough to try to get out without sounding delusional, please."

He sighed.

"Kelly told me you wouldn't be able to understand," I said, frustrated that I couldn't explain myself. "She made me say I wouldn't tell you."

"You've been keeping this from me?" he asked, sounding upset with me.

"Kelly's not human, Max either. They're angels, or gods, or something immortal sent to protect me from myself," I said.

I paused, not knowing what order to tell the story in.

"God, gives us free will," I said, feeling his arms loosen around me, "but there's a demon that has been plaguing my family, I guess from what happened in the park, because of my mother."

Shaking my head, I wished my brain could be like an Etch-A-Sketch and I could clear everything and start fresh.

"Really, I'm still trying to sort all of this out myself. But basically, demons have been giving my family members options, but pushing them toward the wrong ones. Jennifer chose to skip a game and met an abusive man, sending her down the wrong road."

"Your fear," Oscar said. "Of choices."

"Yeah, I don't know the stories of the rest of my family yet. But Caleb, according to Kelly, wasn't going the wrong way, so a demon used an illusion to block out the train and whistle."

Thinking I had to look at Oscar, I sat up. He took my hands in his, bringing them to his lips. His hot breath warmed them. I found the flannel pajama top and put it back on.

I saw Oscar wasn't judging me, he was listening. He was more confused than doubtful.

"Tonight Jordan told me there was a video circulating the school that I had to see. I don't know if he saw the illusion or if it really was him. But it…It was you."

I looked in his eyes and felt so guilty that I believed it and not believed in him.

"You were having sex with Mya, saying how you really needed it, and I…I…I don't know why I believed it."

He brought a hand to my face and gently stroked my tears away.

"Kelly told me that the demon would try an illusion again, and I had to see past it, just like I did at homecoming, but I couldn't and I'm so sorry."

"Why are you sorry?" he asked, as he blew on my chapped hands.

"I doubted you. I should've never done that. I should've never thought you'd have done that. I should've told myself it wasn't real. I was weak."

More tears fell.

"Kelly's trying to help me see…to fight. It just came out of nowhere. Last time someone weakened me before the illusion. Being happy makes them come after me, but it also makes me strong."

My eyes scrunched trying to explain to him I was happy, I was secure, I did love him, but I couldn't get the words out.

"What do you mean last time?" Oscar said, as his body tensed. "How many times have you been attacked?"

"Just twice, that I know of. Last time was homecoming. Mya weakened me…"

"Mya's part of this?" He growled.

"No, but she put doubt in me and then the demon threw an illusion of you making out with Sharyn right in front of me. Kelly stopped me in the hall and told me all this. She's really better at explaining, I don't understand really and …"

I needed Kelly, but she said she'd be gone for awhile. Could she have been killed? What did she mean?

"So there's a demon thing attacking you? Like a *Constantine*-type demon?"

"I know it sounds crazy, but you have to believe me. It's real."

"And Kelly and Max know who this demon is, and are here to protect you from it," he said, checking off what I just explained.

"Only Kelly, Max can't protect me only her, but now I don't know. We thought it was Gaap, but now it's Maria. I don't know who Maria is, that's why I need Kelly. Look, I know it sounds…"

"I was in the park tonight."

"Well, then you know why I think we should break up, at least until I can figure out how to beat this thing."

I couldn't believe the words spilled out of my mouth. How could I be saying that, but then I thought about Maria's threat and the nightmare I had with Oscar's lifeless body on top of me.

"I'm not going to break up with you. I want to protect you. If you're being attacked, I need to be there to stop it."

"Maria said you'd be in danger. I'd asked Kelly a thousand times if you'd be in danger, because I wasn't going to destroy your life. Kelly didn't know. Now we do. We can't be together."

I knew as much as pulling the hook out of my heart from Oscar being my soul mate would hurt, the thought he was still alive could keep me going. I tried to make him understand.

"If you get hurt or killed I wouldn't be able to live with myself…" I said.

"Do I get a say in this? Do I get to choose?"

OMG. I was being Mya. I was taking away his choice in the matter. But he didn't really understand.

"I can't put you in jeopardy. Do you understand that? I mean, yeah, I suppose you should've the right..."

"We're staying together and that's all there's to say about it. I refuse to let a little thing like a demon get in the way of our happiness. You won't be your sisters or brothers. I'm the right choice for you and I can tell you know that, too. They know it, too, or they wouldn't be attacking you, trying to separate us."

A tear fell from my eye and rolled down his chest.

"Lil' Girl, why are you fighting it? You know how much I hate to lose. This is just another roadblock we're going to have to get through. I'm not worried about being hurt. I'm only worried about you being hurt, and me losing you. I couldn't protect you today and I've never felt more useless. I never want to feel that way again and if you love me, you'll let me help you."

He kissed the top of my head.

"Let's finish getting you warmed up and you can tell me more," he said.

He placed a hand on a knee and started sliding it up my thigh. Petrified, I gasped and snapped my legs together.

"I'm so sorry, I forgot. What happened before I got there? You don't have to tell me, but I saw you lying in the snow your dress ripped..."

"I don't know how I got there," I said, my voice cracking. "I just started walking and somehow I was at our swing. My body was paralyzed. I could feel them around me, but I couldn't see them. I couldn't fight them. I swear I tried…"

"It's not your fault." "They were saying they were going to take turns with me. Kelly and you stopped them in time. I swear to you, I wanted to fight…"

The tears ran down my cheeks once again. His arms surround me and he gently stroked my back.

"It's okay, you didn't do anything wrong. I love you. They aren't going to win. You're mine and no one's going to take you away from me. I promise you this will be the last time you ever feel pain."

I believed him, I don't know why, but his words felt true. I was no longer in this battle alone. I had a partner.

Chapter 30

The next morning my muscles were stiff and every movement hurt. Red splotches dotted my skin. Mr. Jeffreys told me it was common and would take a few weeks to get my skin back to normal. The outer layer of skin froze and died. The damage wasn't permanent, so he said he wouldn't contact my parents. I could tell that was difficult for him. If anything ever happened to Oscar, he'd want to know immediately. He couldn't understand parents who weren't like that.

Oscar brought me some lotion to try to make my skin feel a little less burned. He also gave me a pair of his sweatpants with a drawstring as well as a t-shirt and boxers. I looked like a five-year-old dressed in his father's suit. It was the first Sunday in two months Oscar didn't work. We needed something to make yesterday go away. We needed our day together. Mr. Jeffreys understood that. He could see the pain in Oscar's eyes. That was why he didn't insist he take me home to change.

"He sees my mother and him when he looks at us."

Oscar helped me apply lotion to my skin. Ella Fitzgerald was softly singing *Someone To Watch Over Me* from an iPod on the nightstand.

"Something about how I am with you makes him feel like we're more than just a couple of twitterpated teenagers. We don't talk much, but when we do, it's usually pretty intense. At least since…"

"Mya," I said, not wanting to make him have to say more.

"Yes," he replied. "He said he could tell by the way I looked at you the first time you came over that you were something different. He would never try to tell me who to be with, but he did tell me I'd be a damn fool to let you get away. As much as he likes to make a fuss about you being here, it really is just for show. If he could figure out a way to get you to move in without it looking too weird, I think he would."

"I know it's weird, but this feels more like home to me then my house," I confessed. "Maybe it's the demon that lurks at my house," I joked, "But I feel safe and protected here."

"You are, Lil' Girl."

"What's on the agenda for the day? Bad movies in bed or on the couch, followed by Sunday dinner, so we can try to block out what happened."

"I think my dad would prefer the couch and I haven't picked up anything for dinner so I'll have to go out and get groceries."

"Ooh, great can I make the list? I've been cooking."

"Really? Aren't you sore and tired?"

A knock on the door stopped my complaint about his lack of belief in my culinary skills.

"Hey kids, I just got a call from work. They need me for a few hours. Are you two going to be okay if I take off?"

"How soon do you have to get there?" Oscar asked.

"They need me in the next hour. I was just going to hop in the shower. Why?"

"Oh, Ellie was going to give me a list of food to get since she's cooking tonight."

Mr. Jeffreys raised and eyebrow.

"I just didn't want to leave her here alone," Oscar continued, "and I don't think she's up to going out."

"Well, I'll be around. It shouldn't take you too long at the store."

I got up to go to the kitchen for a piece of paper and pencil. Each step brought a new definition of pain to my brain. I wrote the list out quickly from the one recipe I could remember without a cookbook, clam chowder.

"That will be okay, right?"

"You know, I don't think I've ever eaten clam chowder. This should be an experience."

Oscar took off, as Mr. Jeffreys headed to the shower. I crawled onto the couch to put on the show that Oscar and I'd be watching movies there all day. I knew we'd probably end up back in the guest bedroom.

Othello with Lawrence Fishburn played on a cable movie channel. The only thing I knew about it was it's a Shakespearian play. The movie just started, so I curled up and watched.

I wasn't far into the movie when Oscar's dad came down fresh from the shower. He was wearing his tight, blue SPFD shirt and cargo pants with what seemed like a hundred pockets. My mind was drawn into the movie, seeing the realness of Desdemona and Othello's love.

"So."

I jumped.

"Sorry, I didn't mean to scary you," Mr. Jeffreys said, sitting down in his chair. "I need one of you to tell me what happened. And I have a feeling my own son won't do that."

I was formulating a story, but I kept going back to the truth, a watered-down version, but the truth anyway.

"Someone lied to me." I began. "They lied about Oscar. I shouldn't have believed it, but I did. I was upset and wanted to get away. I wasn't dressed appropriately, but I just started walking. Before I knew it, I was all the way to Como."

"You walked all the way to Como?"

"I was really mad," I continued. "Obviously, I was really cold. I was attacked from behind. I never saw their faces."

My body shook as I remembered the head falling off the body and rolling on the ground.

"They? How many were there?"

"Three. Oscar got there just in time to scare them off, but they had already ripped my dress and..."

I didn't feel like telling him about them removing my underwear.

"Oscar just feels bad because he focused on me instead of running them down," I said. "He thinks he failed me, but if he'd have been a minute later, I don't think I'd ever be the same."

"How did he know to find you there?"

"I don't know. It's where we had our first date. Maybe that's why he went there. I'm just happy he did."

The front door opened.

"Well, that's my cue. I got to get going. Thank you for telling me. I'm sorry you had to go through that. You can talk to me anytime. I hope you know that."

"I do, thanks."

I turned back to my movie, just as Lago started plotting with Cassio. Planting seeds of deceit. This movie was hitting too close to home, but I was drawn to the story, hoping it would end with Othello and Desdemona's love prevailing.

"Othello?" Oscar asked. "Do you really think this will help your mood?"

"What'da ya mean?"

"I had to watch it last year in English. It doesn't end well. Shakespeare doesn't always have a happy ending. You haven't had to read any of his plays yet, have you?"

"No, we've been working through the American writers. Frost, Fitzgerald, and Hemingway."

"How 'bout we go back to bed and I give you a massage? I saw how slowly you walked in here. Unless you want to see the end to this tragedy."

Thinking if I turned off the movie now, the love of Desdemona and Othello would continue forever, I said, "I don't think we need any more tragedy this weekend."

"So you aren't cooking today?"

I stood up and slapped him on the chest.

"I'm going to surprise you."

He spent the day massaging my body, working out all my sore muscles. He even refused to let me rub his shoulders. By five o'clock, we had watched three movies, occasionally falling asleep in the middle. The sleep was restless, however. I'd thrash or scream, and Oscar had to duck to avoid my fists. Oscar woke me and reminded me I was safe.

I went into the kitchen and put a large pot on the stove. I diced onions to sauté. I cut and added all the ingredients to the pot. Carrots, potatoes and parsley, I checked them off in my head. The clams. The cream bubbled lightly as I turned down the heat and covered the pot. I cooked to block out my nightmares. Oscar came in a few times, but I shooed him away. I acted it off as if I could cook by myself, but really I didn't want Oscar to see my tears. My nightmares played like a movie across the screen in my head. Feeding my fears of Oscar's death and me walking the planet alone forever trying to escape myself.

We'd eaten by the time his father came home, and I was getting ready to go home. I stayed long enough to hear he liked my soup and I could cook anytime at his house. I wished him a good night and Oscar drove me home.

"I can't help but be worried about you," he said, as he pulled his car in front of my house.

"I'll be okay," I said. I stroked his neck in my usual attempt to take some of his scent with me. My body probably smelled like him, anyway, as his hands had been all over me that day.

"You can't watch me 24/7," I said.

"That doesn't give me any comfort. I don't want to lose you."

It was strange for me to think he wasn't the strong one in the relationship. His physical size alone made him seem invincible to so many things, but this was something neither of us could control.

"The only thing in this world we can control is our love for each other," I said. "Everything else we have to put our faith in God he will protect us. He sent me Kelly and he will send me protection again. She'll be around."

He sighed, not satisfied with my answer.

"You can't keep me hostage. Eventually, even my family would notice if I never came home."

He nodded, kissing me, not wanting to let me go, and I didn't want to be let go. I finally pulled away.

"I'll see you in the morning, less than twelve hours from now. I'll stay safe and I'll call you if anything happens."

His face looked pained as I held his palm to my lips.

My house was silent and I curled up in a ball on my bed. I took my phone out of my pocket and dialed Kelly. I got her voicemail. She was gone. I didn't know how I was going to protect myself. I breathed in Oscar and imagined his arms were still around me.

Chapter 31

Two weeks passed before Max came back to school. The official story was he and Kelly had meningitis so no one visited them. I wasn't sure if she would ever come back. Oscar was on edge, afraid every person that looked at me was trying to hurt me. He looked exhausted, as if he hadn't been sleeping.

Oscar and I were in the darkroom, eating lunch and processing a photogram I was trying to get right. A photogram was a method of shooting light onto photographic paper with an object, such as a wine glass, placed on it. The outcome was a magnificent x-ray showing the most intricate details hidden to the naked eye. The best part was depending on the length of time and intensity of the light you would achieve a different color.

Ms. Finch taught me color printing because she wanted me to advance and felt I could handle it. The room had to be completely black, not even safety lights. I could hear Oscar lightly snoring. Knowing he was in the room with me put him at ease enough to rest. I moved slowly and quietly not wanting to wake him. The revolving door spun and Oscar jumped. His arms flayed and he knocked me against the counter.

"Hey, hey, calm down, it's just me," Max said.

Oscar released me from the vice he created with his hand and the counter.

"What's going on?" I asked. "Are you okay? How's Kelly?"

The questions spewed out of me because we hadn't known he was back.

"Kelly's on trial for killing the demons."

"How? Why?" Oscar barked. "They were going to rape her. Isn't Kelly her damn guardian angel?"

"She is. But I am, for the time being. Maravia was the issue, damn royal brat, and they're sayin' Kelly didn't give them a chance to stop the attack. It always amazes me killing a demon is a crime, but if they kill one of us they're celebrated. She's going to be there for another month at least. You know, sometimes I think it'd be easier to not be held to such a high standard."

"How can we be protected?" Oscar asked. "Can you teach us something, anything?"

"You really think I should teach you anything? I mean, look what happened when we opened Ellie up enough to try to protect herself."

I could feel Oscar looking at me in the dark. I put away the color paper and switched on the safety lights. Angry at Max's loose tongue, I pursed my lips as I looked at him.

"You said you didn't know how to protect yourself," Oscar said accusingly.

"I don't. It was a failure last time. I just … ended up… hurting myself," I said, holding back the description of what happened.

The dim yellow lights encircled Oscar's head. I remembered when I could see his bright aura and hear his inner voice without his knowledge. I remembered the pain that coursed through my body when my mind was overwhelmed.

"Are you going to tell me what happened? Or am I just going to have to torture Max?"

I took another look at Max, his face appeared older, as if he was no longer the fun-loving teenager he had been just a few weeks ago. He was showing his age and wisdom.

"You should tell him it's not my story to tell," Max said.

Breathing in, I could smell the chemicals in the room. They were starting to give me a headache.

"Remember when I had the flu?"

Oscar nodded, as guilt suddenly crossed his face.

"It wasn't the flu," I continued. "Kelly had been teaching me to see people's auras, you know, the lights around them. It was supposed to help me defend myself by seeing when people were really demons and when they were lying to me."

A month ago, Oscar would have thought I was crazy, but now he just looked at me and nodded for me to continue.

"I got too good at it," I said, gloating. "I was too perceptive and I started hearing voices. I thought it was Gaap attacking me, yelling at me in a thousand voices, but it wasn't. I really heard the peoples voices. My brain fried, for lack of a better word."

"So do you still see auras and hear voices?"

"Sometimes. I've learned to control the auras. The voices, thankfully, haven't come back."

"I didn't say anything, bad, did I?"

"Let's just say your dream hasn't come true yet," I said.

"What's my aura like?"

"It was extremely bright and pure."

"Was?"

"I can't see it anymore. Kelly said it's because we're too close."

I reached for him and wrapped myself up in his arms.

"Max, there has to be a way to protect ourselves, besides waiting for you and Kelly to swoop in."

"You did hurt Kelly the day Ellie got sick," Max said.

Oscar looked shocked.

"What're you talkin' about?"

"When you demanded to take Ellie, you emanated a pulse that burned Kelly's skin. It wasn't more than a first-degree burn, but you did that without knowing it and without focusing. Human love can bring about great powers. It can make you stronger than any immortal if you focus it."

The bell rang and I jumped.

"Maria made the mistake of waiting too long," Max continued. "If she'd have gotten to you in the beginning, if Kelly hadn't stopped her…she could've destroyed you earlier, but I don't see how she could now. As long as you don't let her separate the two of you, the love you have will be enough to strengthen you. I just haven't been on this plane of existence for a long time and teaching you will be hard."

I could hear the class gathering in the other room.

"Let's go," I said, getting my books.

"Yeah, let's go," Oscar agreed. "We're all going home sick and talking this out."

"There's no rush. Maria's on trial too. She can't hurt you. Finish your day, go home and sleep, Oscar. I can't do anything with you unless your body has recovered."

Max acting like a father figure made me miss Kelly, the mother who showed that she cared about me.

I was late to my next class, not that that was unusual. I'd been late every time I came from the darkroom. I slid into my desk and stared at the blackboard, but hoped Oscar would take Max's advice.

Chapter 32

Oscar actually listened to Max. It must have been a guy thing. Lord knows, he wouldn't listen to me. I was just a little defenseless girl. He was my big protector, or at least he would be by the time we were attacked again. It's strange because most victims fear being attacked again, but with me it's a certainty. Oscar's biggest fear was he'd fail me and I'd be killed.

I curled up. While sleeping, my mind was lost, running through a maze I was unable to escape. I heard a tap as I looked at the walls of the maze for a way to bust through. The tapping continued, as I clawed at the wall in front of me. The walls closed in air being sucked from the room. The floor dropped off and I reached for anything to hold on to, but to no avail. The tapping was now pounding. I sat straight up, my eyes opened, but my lungs had not, as I gasped for air. I was unaware how or why I was no longer falling, but still no breathing. My hand still grasped for something to hold onto. Panic set in, as my breaths got shorter and shorter. I turned. The light through my window burned my eyes as I kept searching for something to ground me. A figure blocked part of the light and fear came over me that something was trying to attack me.

My hands felt the bed beneath me as I scrambled to the edge and curled up in fear.

"Lil' Girl."

I heard Oscar, but couldn't see him, my mind still in the dream. His voice was muffled and I couldn't find him. I turned and fell off the bed. The fall hurt my elbow, but was enough to jar me into taking a deep breath. I laid on the floor. My mind no longer fought my body for control. I pulled myself back up on the bed. My eyes were clearer and I could see Oscar outside my window. Racing, I slid open the window and messed with the screen.

"What is it, what's wrong?"

Oscar talked over me, "What just happened? Are you okay?"

I finally realized Oscar was afraid for me, not about some outside source. I calmed down enough to remove the screen and notice the time was six-thirty-six.

"No, no, I'm fine I just was having a dream and why are you here so early. And why didn't you use the front door?"

"I didn't want to wake the whole house," he said, as he squeezed through my window.

The dew as well as the cold followed him. I wrapped myself up in my blanket.

"Max said he'd help us today. I just wanted to get an early start."

I nodded okay as I yawned and rubbed the last of the sleep from my eyes.

"You could've called me to give me some warning."

He picked up my cell phone.

"That would mean you'd have to charge your cell phone." "Oh, I forgot to charge it last night."

I took the phone and scanned the room for where I last tried to charge the phone. One day I was going to have to be organized enough to actually have a spot in my room for charging my phone. Frustrated with the general disarray of my room, Oscar picked up a pile of clothes, and found my charger buried underneath.

"Can you get ready now?" he asked.

"Can you shut my window?" I asked. "We can go out the front door."

As I walked down the hall over, I tripped over Adriana asleep on the floor. It was then I realized she wasn't sleeping.

"Adriana," I said, shaking her.

Her lips were light blue and her skin was colder than it should've been.

"Oscar!" I screeched.

I felt her chest. The movement was slight.

"She won't wake up," I said. "She's turning blue. I just found her on the ground."

"Call 911. Go get a phone."

He pushed me away and opened Adriana's mouth and stuck a finger inside.

I ran upstairs, screaming for Jennifer, as I found the portable phone on the cradle in the kitchen.

"Jennifer, come now."

Everyone else in the house was slow to move, but Jennifer came out quickly, sensing the terror in my voice. I ran back downstairs. Oscar started rescue breathing. A piece of a toy was on the floor beside him.

The emergency dispatcher came across the phone, as I relayed what was happening. Jennifer and her swollen belly moved as fast as she could, and she was now screaming. She tried to push Oscar away. He stopped her with a hand and had an ear to Adriana, listening for breathing. She coughed, and her body twitched. Oscar rolled her on her side, as she vomited all over the carpet.

I ran up to the front door and opened it. The sirens screamed through the light morning air. My body shook as I heard Oscar asking Adriana questions. My parents in their robes, finally came from their bedroom. I pointed downstairs. We could hear Jennifer sobbing uncontrollably.

The ambulance arrived and Oscar's dad was one of the paramedics. Relief swept over me, as if it was divine intervention sending me the two men I trusted most in the world to protect my niece.

"Ellie, what happened?" he asked.

"My niece, I tripped over her on the way to the bathroom, she wasn't breathing, if it wouldn't have been for Oscar…"

We were now downstairs.

"She was initially breathing, but stopped. I swept her throat and found this."

Oscar held up a piece of a plastic toy.

"I then started rescue breathing because she still had a pulse. After two rounds, she started to cough. I rolled her on her side and she vomited. I still haven't been able to get her to respond to commands. I feel she had a slight seizure. Her whole body started to shake."

He was so official in his report, so calm as if this happened everyday and he knew how to handle it. I didn't know how he could be so calm. My whole body was shaking and I was crying uncontrollably.

As Mr. Jeffreys' and his partner took over, he turned to Oscar.

"I'm not even going to ask why you were here so early."

He noticed I was just in a pair of shorts and a tank top.

"You did a good job here, son."

Oscar got out of the way. He put his arms around me to keep me warm as the cold air rushed in from the open door. Adriana's body looked so small and fragile. Her eyes fluttered, but she hadn't opened them yet.

"Come on baby, please wake up for mommy," Jennifer pleaded, she stood at my side and clutched a hand for support.

Drew came out of a bedroom and saw all the activity. My mom snatched him up.

"We're going to take her to Children's Hospital, if that's okay with you," Mr. Jeffreys said to Jennifer. "Okay, let's load her up."

A mask helped Adriana breathe and an IV ran fluid into her arm.

"Ellie, why don't you get dressed and Oscar can drive you to the ER. Jennifer, is it? You can ride in the front with my partner. How are you doing?"

He looked at her stomach.

"Ellie needs to stay here with the kids," my mom said. "I should go to the ER."

My mom didn't want to miss her chance to play the poor victim whose grandchild was on the verge of death.

"That's your choice," Mr. Jeffreys said, "but I really think Oscar and Ellie should go, since they found her. They can give the best story to the doctor."

His firmness sent my mother back a step.

"Fine, but call me with updates," she said, defeated.

I picked up my clothes that were strewn about the floor and headed for the bathroom. Oscar waited outside the door. I cracked opened the door. Tears streamed down my face.

"Can you please help me?"

“What’s wrong?” he asked, coming into the bathroom.

“I can’t button my pants.”

My hands were shaking so bad. Hell, my whole body was shaking. I could barely get my words out.

“How are you so calm?”

“It wasn’t you,” he said, as he too fumbled with the button on my jeans. “I can separate myself in situations. If it would have been you, I don’t think I could’ve done that,” he finished buttoning my pants. “There. You ready to go?”

He wiped my tears away. I turned to the mirror; my hair was going in a hundred directions. I ran a brush through my hair and pulled it up into a ponytail.

In the hospital elevator I turned to Oscar and kissed him, hoping that would calm me down.

“I don’t know how I could ever thank you for this.”

“Promise me I’ll never have to do that to you, because I don’t know if I could.”

In the ER, we checked in with a nurse.

“Martin said you would be coming in.”

Martin? That was Oscar’s dad’s name. It was strange not having the deference of Mister before his name.

Down the hall Mr. Jeffreys, I’d never be able to call him by his given name, had his hand on Jennifer’s shoulder. She was breathing heavily, a nurse was assessing her. Maybe she was going into labor.

"Ellie, why don't you go in," Mr. Jeffreys said. "It might be scary. There're a lot of tubes everywhere and she hasn't woken up yet. You can hold her hand. Her mom's probably going to have to go next door to United."

He took my hand and escorted me into the room. Mr. Jeffreys stopped Oscar from entering.

"You and I have to talk."

Mr. Jeffreys' hand landed on Oscar's chest as he pushed him into the hallway.

Adriana had a mask on over her nose and mouth. A nurse was shining a light into Adriana's eyes one at a time. The only noise in the room was a beeping from a machine with numbers flashing.

"Hello, are you the aunt?"

I nodded.

"Let me get you a chair so you can sit by her." The nurse crossed the room and brought me a chair. I took one of Adriana's hands in mine. It was now warm and soft. I brushed her light brown hair away from her face.

Mr. Jeffreys' voice was loud enough for me to hear, and he sounded agitated.

"That's not the point."

"We were going to be meeting Max at seven to work on my car. I'd just gotten there."

"She didn't look dressed like she expected you to be there. You're making choices now you will not be able to come back from. You just better be sure you know what you're doing."

I think they walked further down the hallway, because I could no longer hear them.

Oscar came back into the room. He smiled as if the conversation in the hall never happened. If I could've seen his aura, there would have been huge cracks from the mask.

"How's she doing?"

"I don't know. She's warmer. Oh god, Oscar, she's so little."

"They took your sister to labor and delivery. They had to, her water broke. She told 'em you could make any decisions concerning Adriana's care."

"What?" Why'd she give me such a big responsibility? "I can't make those decisions."

"I'll be here for you."

He held one of my hands as he pulled another chair from the wall and sat down next to me.

A doctor walked in. He was a shorter, Hispanic man with glasses.

"So you're Martin's boy?"

He shook Oscar's hand.

"He's a great paramedic. I wish he did it more often. So he said you found," he looked down at the chart, "Adriana this morning unconscious."

"Ellie found her," he said, signaling to me. "Then she called me when she couldn't get her to wake up."

"I tripped over her in the hallway. I thought she had been playing and fell asleep."

"Does she usually fall asleep in the hallway?"

"No, but I'd just gotten up. I was still half asleep."

"What time was that?"

I turned and looked at the clock in the room. It was only 7:20 it felt as if five hours had passed, but it had been less than an hour since Oscar woke me from my dream.

"I don't know, about 6:40," I said.

"That sounds about right," Oscar chimed in.

The doctor showed us a clear biohazard bag with a small piece of plastic in it. "You found this in her throat?"

Oscar looked at the bag and nodded.

"You have a visitor," the nurse said, popping her head in the room. Max was in the doorway. Oscar squeezed my hand. I wondered how he knew we were there, then realized that was a stupid question.

"Is CT ready?" the doctor asked.

"Yes, I'll grab someone to come with me," the nurse answered.

"By the way, I'm Dr. Herrara, if you need anything. I think I have enough history to try to piece this together. It was a good thing you were there young man. You saved her life."

The nurse came back with another person so they could move all the equipment attached to Adriana. I got up to go along with.

"It's okay. We'll only be about ten minutes. Why don't you rest or get something to eat? It'll be awhile before we can determine what's going on with her."

I collapsed into Oscar's arms.

"I'm sorry about this," Max said.

"You did something to help her please say she'll be okay," I pleaded.

Max looked at me confused.

"I didn't do anything," Max said.

"You had Oscar come over, and his dad was on the paramedic crew. You can't tell me that wasn't divine intervention."

"Sometimes it's just dumb luck," Max said.

"So was this an attack?"

"No. Bad things just sometimes happen. You two are fighting more than demons. There's life you have to deal with. You have to fight yourselves and your everyday actions. The world's full of challenges you need to face, those you'll have to do together. People will die, be born, you'll have injuries and illnesses, your prides and egos will get the better of you, you'll be told no when you really want something, and you'll have to work extra hard for something, then be denied. I don't know how this will turn out with the child, but how you both react to it will determine who you are as people.

The truest test of a champion is how they handle adversity. It will make your bond stronger or pull you apart. That has nothing to do with demons, that just has to do with life."

Oscar and I looked at each other, suddenly overwhelmed. I hadn't thought about the little, everyday things that everyone has to deal with. My head lay on Oscar's chest and I wanted to just give up, I wasn't ready to have this responsibility on my shoulders. But then Oscar wrapped an arm around me, encircling me in safety.

"I'm not giving up, so don't think I'm going to let you," Oscar whispered, so sure of his decision.

"Look," Max said. "I can help you with the extra things, but you need to learn to take responsibility for your actions and your feelings. Everything can't be blamed on a demon."

The nurse brought Adriana back into the room.

Max said, "Hey, I'll catch up with you tomorrow when it's less hectic."

Oscar stiffened. I placed a hand on his leg. Without words I told him it'd be okay.

"Thanks, Max. We can work on the car in the morning, and Oscar's cooking tomorrow, right?"

"No, it's your turn," Oscar said.

Chapter 33

Adriana was still in the intensive care unit at Children's, but she was awake. Jennifer delivered her fourth child, another girl, only a few weeks premature, Sophie. My mother was in full drama mode and said I was being insensitive wanting to spend the day with Oscar instead of another day at the hospital. I was upset she hadn't acknowledged Oscar saved her grandchild's life, but that would have shed light on someone other than herself.

Oscar picked me up around eight. This time he used the front door this time. My mother answered the door, as she was up and about getting the other kids ready to go see their mother.

"Hello, Oscar, Ellie's downstairs."

I was already on the stairs on my way up.

"I'm here," I said, not wanting Oscar to even come in the house. "I'll be back later tonight."

"What should I tell your sister?"

"Nothing. During the eighteen hours I spent with her and Adriana yesterday, we talked," I snipped.

As I pulled Oscar by a hand, but jerked back because Oscar hadn't moved.

He started walking and I tried to readjust my slightly dislocated shoulder.

"She's still your mother. You could show her a little bit of respect."

"No, I don't?"

"Quit being such a child. It's not fair you don't get to be a normal child, but you have to grow up."

I let go of his hand.

"A child," I said angrily. "A child? So what does that make you, a pedophile?"

"That's not funny. It's just what Max said yesterday. We have real challenges we need to deal with. Your mom will come back to you someday."

I sat pouting in the passenger seat. I'm allowed to hate my mother. I have that right. How dare he tell me what I can and cannot feel? Then I remembered what Max said about pride and ego. My pride was getting the best of me. Oscar was just trying to help me change my perspective.

"I'm not saying you have to like her. But she's an elder and you do have to show her respect."

I sighed.

"I'll try."

"That's all I'm asking. Remember what Maria said in the park? Her love for you and your father was so great she refused Gaap. He torments her every day. You don't know what she goes through. Just try to see the world through her eyes."

I thought of the past six months of torment, it was more anticipation of than the actual torment. I couldn't imagine how hard it would be to go through it every day, never having those wonderful moments Oscar and I carved out of the darkness.

"I guess she does have it hard. At least I have you."

Max was waiting on the front steps of Oscar's house as Oscar pulled his car into his driveway. He opened his garage full of tools. Oscar got the care when he was fifteen. He found it in a junkyard. I'd seen original pictures of the car. He worked on it whenever he could, but he rarely had time. He liked to tease me that his car would be done if it weren't for me distracting him.

"Okay," Max said, picking up a socket wrench. "Here's what I know. Your aura can be used as a shield or a sword. The sword's mightier than the shield, historically."

"Good," Oscar said.

I knew Oscar wanted to be the force giving the blow, instead of just sitting back waiting to be attacked.

"The reason I need the two of you here is because the love between the two of you hasn't been seen in centuries. That power's amazing."

We looked at each other, enjoying the knowledge that what we both felt for each other was special and unique. We weren't just lost in the newness of our love. How we felt was shared by the other and it was true. My hand instinctively reached for his.

"Pass me the trashcan, 'cause ya'll are about to make me puke," Max said, slipping into his childlike attitude. "For offense, you need to focus your feelings for each other and then project them out. Like you're screaming out to the world of your love. You won't harm me or her. I'll help you, but only in the beginning. I don't want you killing me."

"We could actually kill you?" I asked.

"Yes, I told you Oscar burned Kelly. You could turn us into ashes. And I didn't stick around this many years to just die teaching you to fight. Now I need you to try to push me away."

Max stood with his arms crossed right in front of Oscar. Although Oscar was physically much larger than Max, it was like Oscar was pushing against a concrete building.

"No, push me from inside, with your mind," Max instructed.

Oscar focused his eyes on Max, breathed deeply and stared him down. That kept up for five minutes.

"You know, Ellie's looking kinda cute today," Max said, looking at me sitting on the hood of the car. "Hey, Ellie, could you go put on a bikini and stretch yourself out on the hood. A red thong would be the best."

I stared at him confused. Oscar looked over at me and then back to Max.

"Would you focus on me and not Ellie's sweet apple butt? God just makes me want to take a bite out of it. You know what I'm talkin' about, don't you. You tapped that, right? Bent over praising me. Oh, my, god. Oh, my, god," Max moaned. "Mmmm tasty. I could imagine just holding tight…"

Max gestured as if he was groping my ass.

"…mmmm and her legs wrapped around, me as I ram my…"

With a loud smash Max was against the garage wall. The drywall had slight indentation from his broad shoulders. Oscar's right hand pinned Max around his throat.

"That was great, Ellie, but Oscar you have to work harder."

I hadn't even known what I'd done.

"You better not have meant one word of that," Oscar said through gritted teeth.

Oscar released Max and he shook the dust off himself.

"Come on, I was just trying to get your real feelings to come out. Ellie's are just a little stronger. Am I that unattractive?" Max asked, winking at me.

I reached out to calm down Oscar, but as I touched his shoulder, Max flew down the driveway and landed in the street. He just missed a passing car by inches. He stood up, unscathed, and walked back to the garage.

"Well, that's interesting," he said as he reached the door. "What changed?"

“I don’t know,” Oscar said, shocked at what he’d done. “I was still really pissed with you and Ellie came over.”

“Did you touch him?” Max asked me. “Did you touch him?”

“Yes, on his shoulder,” I answered.

“Great. This is going to be harder than I thought. You need her.”

I smiled at the thought. I always felt I needed him. He made me stronger. Telling me he loved me and I was worth something built up my confidence. It was nice to know he needed me for strength.

“Kelly would love this,” Max said. “She’s always pickin’ with me about how women are ruled by their brain and men are physical. You just had to prove her right, didn’t you? You need Ellie to touch you for your strength. Ellie just needs to be ticked off.”

“Be careful or I’ll touch him again,” I warned.

Oscar leaned over to me.

“Oh, you’ll touch me again,” Oscar whispered. “That felt awesome.”

We practiced the rest of the day to get Oscar to project without me. By two o’clock, Oscar was really frustrated. This was the first time he hadn’t excelled at a physical challenge on the first attempt. To make him feel better, I slid my arms around his waist, Max flew across the street and crashed into a neighbor’s metal fence. He bent it back quickly before the neighbor could make it outside.

“Don’t touch him again,” Max demanded. “That one actually hurt a little. Let’s call it a day. I don’t want what happened to Ellie to happen to you. Her brain’s still not right.”

“Hey,” I said, annoyed he said my brain was messed up. I hovered my hand above Oscar’s. “Let’s see if I can get you to the alley this time.”

“Okay,” Oscar said as he stepped away from me. “You need to start cooking anyway. My dad has to be to work by seven.”

I went inside to start preparing chicken and Oscar talked to Max for a few more minutes. Through the window, I saw Oscar shake Max’s hand and hug him. They both grinned. The door opened and Oscar bounded into the kitchen, picked me up and spun me around. This was the happiest I’d seen him in weeks. Finally, he no longer felt helpless. He kissed me.

“We’re gonna be okay. I can protect you.”

“Protect her from what?” Mr. Jeffreys asked.

“Salmonella. She’s cooking chicken tonight.”

“Fine, lie to me. That’s always worked so good for you in the past. Has he told you the big news?”

“You have big news,” I asked.

“Yeah, he’s signing with the U. Instead of…”

“Instead of skipping college all together.”

“You know, I still need to sign your contract. You’re a minor.”

I realized I was in the middle of a fight and I didn't know all the details.

"Did you know he could've gone to two other division-one schools on a full ride? But no, let's go to the U on a partial. They don't even see your ability."

"What schools offered you a full ride?" I asked.

"Florida and Notre Dame," Oscar said.

I hadn't even know he applied to Notre Dame.

"But it doesn't matter, 'cause I'm staying here."

For the first time, I felt animosity from Mr. Jeffreys. I was keeping his son in Minnesota and not letting him go with the best deal.

"You know, she'll be fine being here without you. Won't you, Ellie? You could live seeing him on long weekends and holidays, couldn't you? What if I allowed you to move into his room when he comes home?"

Wow, he really wanted Oscar to move away to school.

"Dad, I'll be on campus at the U. I won't come home until Christmas. Would that make you happy?" Oscar said, obviously tired of having had the same conversation over and over. "Is it okay if I choose a school for academics?"

"Really? Notre Dame doesn't have good enough academics for you? Making a choice based on some girl…"

His dad was against the wall faster than I could've imagined. Oscar's forearm was pinned against his father's chest. The hairs on my arms stood up. "If you ever call her *some girl* again, it'll be the last time you see me," Oscar growled. "Do you understand?"

"Boy, if you don't get your Goddamn hands off me…"

The air in the room must have dropped twenty degrees.

"…I brought you into this world and I can take you out of it."

"How long do you have until you declare?" I yelped.

They both looked at me.

"April first," Oscar said, giving me a look that said didn't matter, he wasn't leaving me. He released his father, but both kept an eye on the other.

"Okay then, let's just calm down for now. You can sign in a month, and between now and then you two can discuss the pros and cons. And I don't have to be a part of it."

I smiled and hugged Mr. Jeffreys and kissed Oscar on a cheek as I left the room and turned on the TV in the living room.

Low, angry voices still came from the kitchen, but after awhile Mr. Jeffreys joined me.

"You aren't just *some girl*," his father said as he sat down. "That was wrong of me to say."

"Thanks. I'm sorry Oscar…"

He put his hand up.

"I'd have done the same thing. You're special to both of us. I just want the best for him."

"And I'm not *it*?"

"No. You are. It's just school's a big choice. He needs to make that choice…"

"Not based on me. But based on what he wants."

"Yeah."

"Did ya ever think he was?"

"No. He's not known for thinking with the right head, if you know what I mean."

"Why did you become a fireman? I mean you have a degree. A bachelors, right?"

"Masters actually."

"How many…what do you call yourself again?"

"Smoke jumper."

"Right. How many smoke jumpers have a degree outside of the firefighter academy?"

"What's your point?"

"I've found…now you can tell me if I'm wrong, but Jeffreys' men are bullheaded…"

He laughed.

"…determined and not subject to persuasion."

"I beg to differ with you on the last point."

"I respect your opinion, but I'm right. There isn't one thing I could talk Oscar into he hasn't already decided he wants. Trust me, there're things I've wanted him to do that he's refused. No matter what I used for persuasion."

"Why is it I don't believe you?"

I looked at him, breathed in deeply and decided I needed to make peace between Oscar and his father. My face flushed, my stomach knotted and my fingers dug into the sofa.

"You know, we've never slept together. Not once."

Okay, I'm gonna puke. Why the hell did I just say that?

"I'm a virgin. Is there anything more persuasive?"

Shoot me! Shoot me! Shoot me!

"My son? The whore of Babylon?"

"Don't ever call him that in front of me again! Ever. He isn't the only one who can put you in a choke-hold. I'll get a ladder if I have to. I don't care if he lined girls up on the fifty-yard line and bounced from one to another. He's not that person anymore. And…and…I love him. More than…do you hear me!"

I was shaking, not from fear, but anger. I didn't care what Oscar did in his past. He's mine now and he's a good man. I refused to see this screw-up his father was trying to fix. He fixed him. He was perfect now.

"I'm sorry, Ellie. It's just hard. He's got priors."

"Yeah. Well I come from poor white trash and got two whores for sisters. You don't see me...People change. I've changed because of him. Six months ago I could barely look you in the eye. Because of him. How he is. How he treats me. He's good. Better than good, he's perfect. Whatever happened before me is gone. That's not who he is anymore. Just like I'm not a mousy, scared little girl. He's told me he's wanted to go to Minnesota since we got together. Something about the head of Carlson he respects. I don't think I was even a factor."

"I hope not," Mr. Jeffreys said holding his hands up to stop me from interrupting. "Because I want him to go for him and what he wants. Carlson? Really?"

"Business school. Is that you or me?"

I wiped away some tears of frustration.

"I don't want him to feel trapped by me. Trust me. As much as I love the idea that he'd be close…I'd never be able to live with myself if I thought he chose based on me alone."

Oscar finished cooking supper alone and then brought plates to his father and me. His father finished and left for work. Oscar turned off the TV.

"What the hell was that about? I'm going to the U and that's final."

"I know you are, but see it from your father's perspective. How many NFL players are picked from the U of M compared to Florida.

He wants the best for you. If I have to be nice to my mom, you at least have to hear your father out."

Knowing he couldn't win this argument, he turned the TV back on. I leaned in and nuzzled his neck. He to rubbed my back, then stopped. He hadn't touched me in a non-protective way since the night of the dance. I pressed the subject by moving towards his lips. He gently pushed me back on the couch and placed a hand on my leg.

"So how long am I going to be *punished*?" I asked, knowing that word would at least get his attention.

"Punished? I'm just really into this movie."

"You know I feel *Blazing Saddles* is one of the best cinematic masterpieces created by man. But your father's gone, there're no demons here right now…"

"Are you sure?" he snipped, cutting me off as he cut me with his eyes.

"What's this about?" I asked.

"You need to support me in whatever I do. How could you stand up for my father? I spend every lunch hour in a damn darkroom because it's something you love doing?"

He pulled his hands back crossing his arms.

"I support any decision you make no matter how stupid I think it is."

A hundred questions ran through my head. I tried to help him and he was mad at me, questioning our entire relationship. I went against him once and he bit my head off. How was that fair? I hadn't even gone against him. I sat there mad. How dare he treat me like that? I stormed off to the kitchen. As I rinsed the last dish, a hand reached in and grabbed.

"We have a dishwasher, you know."

"I know, but then I'd have to be in the same room as you. Since there's something wrong with that lately, I figured I'd give you some room. Are you ready to take me home now?"

"No, I'm not."

"Fine, I'll walk."

It was a nice day and my house wasn't really that far away. Truthfully, I wasn't in the mood for any more attitude.

"You're not the only one who was attacked in the park, you know," he said, stopping me at the door.

His arms wrapped around my waist as he held me from behind and talked softly in my ear.

"Physically you were, but I felt so useless. You stepped in to try to save me. Do you remember that? I'm not used to having someone protect me. It kinda cut me down as a man. I'm sorry I've been so standoffish, but I didn't want to push you either. You were seconds from being raped. I don't know how you've been able to block that."

"I haven't, but how they touched me is so different from how you touch me. When you touch me, I feel safe, like nothing can hurt me. I feel like…"

I paused, not knowing how to explain in words the way he made me feel. My body was alive, but the world was quiet, as if everything went away and we were the only ones. He didn't make me have to say it. He turned me around, kissed me, holding me tightly, he carried me to his room.

Chapter 34

Oscar had been trying to get me to run track. I told him it wouldn't work. Running wasn't my forte.

"Come on, we get to practice at the same time and sometimes we have meets together."

"We have meets if we're both on varsity. I don't see that happening, unless there are no other girls going out for the team."

"Just try it, please. It'll help your vertical and at your height…you really need it."

"You know, short jokes aren't going to win you any points. And I've grown a half an inch, I'll have you know."

"I can't help it you're a midget," he joked.

"Or you're a mutant?"

"Both are good possibilities. That's why we're perfect for each other."

He kissed me, threw me over his shoulder and carried me towards the track.

"Coach Trenton, I have a new recruit."

I wasn't dressed for track. That was the one time I regretted wearing sneakers to school.

"She doesn't look too excited or willing," Coach said.

"Her? She's never been so excited," Oscar said as he sat me down.

"Do you have any shorts?" Coach Trenton asked.

Coach Trenton was the youngest coach in the school. He was only two years out of college. He was an attractive man with light brown hair. I knew most of the girls that went out for track went out for him. I could see why. He had a young face with just a little bit of stubble and he always wore the tightest looking sunglasses. Oscar towered over his five-foot-nine frame. Being a running coach, his body was lean and fit. I could see the other girls coming in their shortest, tightest pairs of shorts.

"Yeah, I'm sure I have some in my locker."

"Well, go change."

He leaned in, his breath hitting my neck as he spoke, "Don't worry, I'll take it easy on you. If you really don't want to do this, maybe Oscar would let you be the manager."

That sounded better than actually running, so I went into the school so I could change into my shorts. I'd only have to do this for a day, then I could be the manager, and I'd be able to be with Oscar when he ran. I thought about Coach Trenton and what he said. Actually, it was how he said it. Suddenly, Coach replaced my visions of Oscar. What was I doing? I loved Oscar and he loved me. How could I think about anyone but him? He's my soul mate.

While changing, I tried to figure out why my thoughts betrayed me, and more importantly, Oscar.

When I came back out, Oscar ran up to me.

"Wanna warm up?"

"Take it easy on me. I haven't done anything since October."

We jogged around the track. Oscar was talking, but I couldn't hear him. My eyes kept wandering to Coach. He caught me once and smiled.

"Alright everyone, stretch out and let's split you up. Seniors, please lead. Those of you who are new, I'm Coach Trenton."

Some of the girls giggled.

"If you know what you want to run, please follow the seniors into the groups. Oscar you take the boys, Serina please take the girls."

Serina was lean and blond with long legs. Her face was stern, but attractive. She had gone to state in a few events over the past two years.

Serina asked us to split up into groups; sprinters, mid-distance and long distance. Everyone knew where to go but me.

"What do you think you want to do?" she asked, sounding annoyed.

"Really, it doesn't matter, just not long distance." The last thing I was going to do was run a mile.

"Fine, we'll put you in mid-distance."

I joined the group of about a dozen other girls. We warmed up some more, then Serina lined us up and told us we were running a four-hundred. I raised my hand.

"What's that?"

Serina sighed and glanced at Oscar, knowing he was the reason she was stuck with me.

"Once around the track. Make sure you save something for the final curve."

"Right, thanks."

The other girls scoffed looking back and forth with each other with mocking glares, they knew I wasn't a challenge. I was in the eighth lane. I thought that seemed good, I was in front.

Serina stood with a stopwatch.

"On your marks."

I looked back to see what the other girls were doing.

"Set…Go…"

Everyone took off. I hesitated but then I took off. I had no form. I was just running and trying to remember what Serina said, *save something for the final curve*.

No one seemed be next to me. Until I took the second turn, everyone was by my side and passing me. My competitive nature blocked out the fact I hated running. I turned it up, running as fast as I could as we passed the last turn.

"That's my girl, keep it up, Ellie, you got this."

Oscar's voice made me move faster. I saw him standing at the end of the track, like a carrot dangled in front of me, begging me to go faster. Suddenly, I couldn't see anyone next to me and I was in Oscar's arms and he was laughing.

"What was her time?" he asked Serina.

The other girls looked mad I finished first.

"Not bad," she said, "fifty-six seconds. Not great, but obviously we don't have much competition this year."

Coach Trenton came over.

"So much for being a manager. Good job, Ellie."

He placed his hand on my shoulder.

"You'll need to get you some decent shoes," he said.

"I'll take care of her," Oscar said, happy he won, but I was now stuck on the track team led by a coach who suddenly was invading my thoughts.

Instead of going straight home, Oscar took me to the mall.

"You need metal spikes and we need extras because they'll fall out and dull." He was talking a mile a minute, "Since you're running fours, you'll need this tiny heel, but if you go down to twos, you'll need this one. Which pair. They'll both work, but do you think you may do an eight or a two?"

"A what or a what? I have no idea what you're talking about. I thought I just had to run."

"There's more to track than that. You have to learn to react and start correctly. You have to pace yourself even in something as short as a two hundred."
"Aren't you a football player?" I asked, surprised he cared so much about track and field.

"Yeah, but in track you're truly competing against yourself. Outside of relays, you're the only one responsible for the outcome. If I don't have my best day or I'm off, no one gets hurt. I'm responsible for only me. Do you know how much pressure's removed? Didn't it feel good running as fast as you could? Didn't you get some sort of runner's high?"

"Are you high right now?" I asked.

His eyes were sparkling. I kissed him.

"You pick the shoes. I don't know what I'm doing."

He bought me a pair of Nike Zooms, promising me they'd be versatile. He seemed to believe I found another outlet.

"I promise you after you run at a few meets, you're going to love it."

That night I was sore from actually moving, something I hadn't done in months. I took an Advil PM and hoped to get a goodnight sleep. However my mind wouldn't let me forget coach's breath on my neck.

Oscar called and told me all about what to expect over the next few months. Bus rides together and sitting in the middle of the field together in our team's camp. As he hung up, my eyes weighed a thousand pounds. I drifted, imagining being camped out in the middle of a football field with Oscar's arms around me. He was kissing my neck and telling me all about how he was going to help me stretch out. I turned around and kissed his mouth. He laid me down on the ground. Everyone around us seemed to fade. I opened my eyes and saw Coach Trenton. I didn't stop kissing. My kiss got stronger, wanting to know more about this stranger. I allowed his hands to feel every part of me. I started to pull off his t-shirt. He pulled my shorts off, then his pants. I could feel his hands between my legs as he slowly kissed and licked my body. He kissed my inner thigh slowly inching up my leg. I arched my back in anticipation. I opened my eyes and saw Oscar staring down at me.

I sat straight up, more awake than I'd ever been. My body was flushed with heat.

Chapter 35

On the ride to school, I brought my new cleats so Oscar could return them. I refused to put myself in a situation in which I wasn't dreaming about Oscar. I was quiet and hoped for a song on the radio that could capture my mood. Unfortunately, the Black Eyed Peas were coming soon in concert, and *Don't Lie* wasn't the song I really wanted to hear.

"I need to quit the track team," I finally admitted as we pulled up to the school.

"Why?"

"I just don't think I'll like it."

"You're too competitive to be the manager."

"You're right I guess I was just nervous I wouldn't do well."

"You're so cute. "

He didn't see in my face the betrayal I felt. Walking into the school, I made him hold me close, hoping his arms could protect me from my own thoughts.

As the season progressed, my dreams persisted, making me feel guilty with every kiss Oscar gave me. Although I didn't feel Coach Trenton singled me out, he was always there to help me stretch or to whisper a strategy or a joke in my ear or to be there with a congratulatory squeeze after my race. There seemed to be to be more and more meets without the boy's squad. Although Oscar and I were back on track, I felt every word I was saying was a lie. As he touched me, I couldn't help but think of Coach. I became afraid to close my eyes, to speak or even breathe, somehow I'd show Oscar the betrayal I felt.

Inside I was dying. Max was working with Oscar as often as he could, but Oscar wasn't very strong without me next to him. Max looked at me differently, as if he could see my guilt. I tried to stop the feelings, but each night Coach was in my dreams, no matter how hard I wanted to kick him out, I couldn't.

The worst part was I enjoyed running. With all of the abs and back exercises, I actually started to get a washboard stomach, not like Oscar's, but there was definition. And the adrenaline rush, the way it made me feel inside, was as close as I'd ever been to an orgasm, or at least what I imagined one was. My body trembled, and if anyone touched me, I'd shiver as if lightning bolts were surging through my body. That didn't help the situation with Coach.

I wasn't the best on the team, but I more than held my own. What I really needed was Kelly to come back. Max promised me she'd be back the next week, but it just wasn't soon enough. To take my mind off Coach, I decided I had to try to see auras again. Max worked with me building up my strength.

One practice I actually got time with Oscar. We were conditioning, instead of focusing on our events.

We locked our feet together and raced each to see who could do fifty sit-ups first.

He won.

We did parachuters to strengthen our backs. I won, but I cheated. It was his fault, I told him, since he had us do the exercise facing each other.

"How could I possibly resist?" I asked, after I kissed him.

"Try harder. If I can resist, you can."

His resolve was stronger than mine. But maybe it was because he was less attracted to me. I know it was crazy to think that way. He always told me how much he loved me, how much he loved my body. But I still couldn't believe it was real.

Push-ups came next.

"Are we racing again?" I asked, lying on the track.

"Of course. You're my favorite opponent."

I knew he was feeling less than a man because he still couldn't use his powers without my touch. As much as he loved when I touch him and Max would go flying, he wanted to do it on his own.

"What are you doing?" he asked after we had done five push-ups.

"Quit trying to distract me," I said and kept going.

He stopped all together.

"Time out," he said. "Really, where did you learn to do push-ups?"

"What? My body's straight. No butt in the air, five-year-old style. What am I doing wrong?"

"Your hands," he said, pointing to my fingers, which were fully extended. "What's with the fingers?"

I dropped flat, tucking my arms under my chin.

"I'm a setter. I always do fingertip push-ups. What? Not man enough to handle it?"

I joked, trying to be cute, but then I realized his manhood was the last thing I needed to question right now.

"Sorry, I didn't –"

"Don't worry about it. Let's just finish, okay?"

****

We had a conference meet at our school, which meant we had to do all the prep and clean up. Coach asked me to pick up an extra race. Agnes twisted her ankle and couldn't run her leg on the relay. We needed to fill her races to avoid losing points. At least this meet was co-ed. I had Oscar there to catch me at the end of my race, his hands would be on me when I achieved my runner's high and not coach's sending surges through my body.

The races were great. I cheered for Oscar as he easily won the hundred-meter dash and the two hundred later in the night. He was there for me. Screaming for me to turn it on in the four hundred and two hundred. The last race of the meet was the four-by-four. I was taking Agnes's leg. It was just another four hundred. I could do that, I told myself. Coach wanted us all to get together to practice hand offs.

"No, no, no," Coach scolded. "Ellie, you have to put your hand back on the third step. She'll get it to you. Trust her."

He held my arm back to make sure I had my hand opened correctly. My breath quickened until he dropped my arm.

"Try it again."

We practice three more times until I got my spot right. When the race was about to start, I was so scared, standing on the side of the track.

"Remember," Coach said right next to my ear, "Cindy's cutting in, you're in the first lane the whole time, only pass on the straight-aways, not on the curves. It just wastes energy and don't get boxed in, nothing good comes of that."

He put his hand on my back, Oscar's spot.

"Don't worry. You'll do great."

Cindy took off and I waited until the rest of the field cleared to step out on the track.

The runners I stood with all kept shuffling, our line-up as the places kept adjusting in the race. Cindy was neck and neck with the runner from Johnson High when she yelled "Go." I took off, throwing my hand back on the third step. Coach was right. The baton was there. I took off full speed. I was one stride behind Johnson's third runner in the curve. I cut out of the first lane at the back straight-away and I passed her as we got to the curve and I ran down the final straight-away to Serina, our anchor leg and fastest runner. She took off before I said go and I had to push myself extra hard to get the baton to her before we were out of the exchange zone. Her strides lengthen as she entered the first curve. I was out of breath from my final surge. I gasped for air. I raised my arms above my head and tried to watch the end of the race. Serina was extending our lead and we should win. I looked for Oscar, but only saw Coach coming over to congratulate me. The adrenaline rushed through my body as the lack of oxygen made me lightheaded.

"Where's Oscar?" I asked, gasping as Coach approached.

I knew he would find a way to touch me, the way only Oscar should.

"I had to put him on the boys four-by-four, too, so he's warming up," he said putting an arm around me. "We may have to put you on relays. That was great."

Serina crossed the line cementing what I already knew. We won the race. Coach's arm didn't moved from my waist.

After the meet was over, Coach asked the team to bring in the equipment. Oscar and I were the last ones walking equipment in.

"Ellie," Coach called from his office. "Can I talk to you for a minute?"

Oscar kissed me.

"I'm going to take a shower," Oscar said when he left me alone with Coach.

I held his hand not wanting to be alone with the Coach, but not wanting to tell him why.

"Yes, Coach?" I asked.

Coach closed the door. No one was in the hallway, so I wondered why the extra privacy was needed.

"I think we need to talk about something."

He took off his sunglasses and for the first time I saw his green eyes. Coach sat on the front edge of his desk and I sat down in the chair across from it. I gripped the arms on the chair to try to calm down.

"There seems to be something that I know is wrong going on here."

I became confused. Did he think I was cheating?

"And I think you know what I'm talking about," he said, as he brushed a lose strand of hair behind my right ear and slid his finger down my neck before he pulled it back.

I shivered. My neck instinctively turned into my shoulder to try to stop the sensation. I stood up, my mind and body fighting each other. My physical desire for his kiss tried to overpower my love for Oscar. Standing up backfired. We were now face-to-face and the chair blocked my escape.

"I assure you, I don't know what you mean," I said.

I tried to pull myself away as he wrapped his arms around my waist and pulled me close.

"I think you do."

His velvet tongue opened my mouth. I felt a rush, but not like when I was with Oscar. My body became warm as if a fire was burning inside my chest and Coach flew across the room, knocked the desk over and slammed against the wall. His skin was slightly smoldering.

His eyes were ablaze with rage. I looked at him. Really looking at him, there was no light around him.

"You little whore, you know you want me. You have done nothing but put yourself in my way, throwing your body at me."

He stepped over his over-turned desk

"Why are you trying to deny it? You want me. Your desire for me is greater than that little child you're playing with. If you loved him, I would have no effect on you and you know it. It's been eating you up inside you couldn't find a way to be with me. Now why don't you just do what you want to?"

My hand was on the doorknob, but I couldn't turn it. Somehow he locked it. I fumbled, trying to figure out how to unlock it. I felt him behind me.

"I chose someone that you would find attractive," he said. "When Maria put out the orders to my legion I debated with myself for a year before I came here. Dealing with these idiotic children just to be with you. Avoiding those nasty protectors of yours. Now I'm just asking for one night, then you can go back to your little boy you seem to think is so perfect."

His tongue licked me from my neck up to my ear. He started to suck my earlobe. My body was betraying my mind. The hormones enjoyed the feelings even though I was disgusted by the person touching me. My moistened skin was causing my body to tremble and my muscles relaxed. Something deep inside me wanted to just fall back into his arms and let him take me.

No, I told myself as I tried to focus on Oscar's face. Coach tore me away from the door.

"Help," I yelped at the top of my voice. "Oscar, help."

"Don't waste your breath. He'll never be able to help you again. A friend's taking care of him."

Coach flew back against the wall again from my power, because I knew Oscar couldn't use his powers without me beside him. The trance Coach had me under was broken. I wouldn't let Oscar die for my weakness.

The door exploded. Splinters flew everywhere. I had an escape. The stillness of the hallway was too unsettling. Oscar's being killed just down the hall. I'd be the cause of his death. His death would be my doing. My inability to see through the illusion now brought about his demise. Oscar, my love, who never hurt me, who helped me become strong.

But I was unable to move fast enough to save him. I allowed another man into his world and mine. A man who wanted nothing more than to destroy us. I would be doomed to walk this planet alone forever. Unable to save Oscar's life, I wouldn't be unable to take mine, afraid of who else I would leave behind to die if I wasn't there to save them.

Breathless, I ran through the hallway. The lockers and posters were a blur as I tried to reach my destination in time. My feet slipped as I rounded the corner. I sprawled on the ground. I felt every inch of me hit the hard concrete floor. I scrambled, unable to get my footing, as I heard the footsteps slow and methodical behind me.

Why had I chosen to fight? I could've just let myself fall and allowed Oscar to live. But there I was running to save a life I'd thrown into the fire. My heart lurched again as I saw visions of his lifeless body. Oscar was strong, but not strong enough to stop the curse I bore.

My hands reached for the locker room door. Pushing with all my might, I prayed Oscar was alive, and I could help him save himself, if from nothing more than me…

Unable to fill my lungs with air, I tried to scream out. I breathed in deep, the steam from the shower caused the air to be thick and soupy. I hoped with each breath I could find my voice to call out to Oscar. As my head spun from the loss of oxygen, the footsteps were coming closer. I finally screeched out "help," the word Oscar should've been yelling to me.

****

I gulped a lung full of air and with a little more power, I yelled, "Oscar, help." With that cry, the wall to the shower exploded. Water and cement flew everywhere. A large chunk hit me in the head. Blood flowed down my face. Wet, dust-like particles flew in my eyes blinding me, temporarily.

Oscar's wet, naked body emerged from the shower stall. He gasped for air, as if he'd been choked.

"Coach's a demon," I sputtered. "Please say you're okay."

Oscar coughed and tried to regain his breath.

"I can't see him," Oscar said. "I can only feel him."

"Coach was attacking me in the office," I said. "Someone else is here with you."

I brought my hand to my head to stop the bleeding. The room seemed to spin. A block flew across the room and smashed right above Oscar's head. I ran across the room and grabbed Oscar's hand as he pulled me close. This time a rush of heat came over my whole body, not just my chest. A tingling, electrical charge seemed to shoot from Oscar's skin to mine. I gasped and buried myself more into the glistening skin of his chest. The room seemed to explode around us. Lockers flew as the smell of sulfur penetrated the air. We were stood together in fear of this invisible creature attacking us.

"Didn't Max say you burned Kelly?" I asked in almost a whisper.

I tried to make sense of the new odor. I was afraid if I let go of Oscar, the shield we created would be gone. I looked across the room at a smoldering scorch mark on the wall. I slowly slid out of Oscar's arms.

"It's okay," I said.

He didn't want to let me go, but I stepped away from him. I walked across the shattered locker room as Oscar snagged some shorts from a pile of debris. I touched the wall and felt the soft powder ash stained the wall. My fingers ran across what I assumed was the remains of whatever attacked Oscar.

Fear shot through me again as the door opened and I could once again hear footsteps.

"Oh, that's a shame," Coach Trenton said, looking at the black mark on the wall. "Ellie, you're bleeding, do you need me to take care of that?"

"Don't touch me. You'll never touch me again."

The memory of his touch and my rage again flung him against the wall. His chest caved in as if I punched it directly. The impact cracked the wall. He bounced off the wall and landed face first on the ground. He got up. He still was only slightly scathed. He came toward me again.

"Now why don't you tell him the truth about us? How you have wanted to do nothing more than be with me even if it was just one night. You know it's true. Tell him if I'm lying about it. You know you've been dreaming about me touching you."

I couldn't lie anymore to Oscar. I just hung my head in shame. I cried as I thought of my betrayal played in my head for the last month. My throat closed on in me from the shame that was ripping through my body.

"See, she really wants me," Coach Trenton said as he looked at my body with a smile that oozed lust. "She never said no when I kissed her. Why do you think that is Oscar?"

His eyes cut to Oscar's.

"I threw you across the room when you kissed me. I'd say that was a pretty clear *no*," I yelled as his body flew across the room, again landing on a pile of lockers.

Jumping up he wiped off the dust. He stumbled a little as he climbed across the floor littered with rubble.

"Oscar, why don't you just leave me alone with her? I'm sure she'd be happier with someone who can fulfill her needs, instead of an impotent neophyte that cannot even get past his childish issues to do his manly duty."

His voice was like a snake slithering his lies and poisoning the air.

"She wanted it and you weren't giving it to her," he continued. "That's why she wanted me. Hell boy, the bitch just wanted to get laid and you didn't have the scrot to do that."

"It's not true! I was having nightmares about him," I shrieked trying to force his lies back at him.

That was true. My guilt made them nightmares. I hated myself every moment of the past month. I looked at Oscar and hoped he believed me.

Oscar closed his eyes. I prayed he still wanted me. His hand twitched and reached for me. I stepped closer to him only to fly back as Coach ensnared me around my waist and pulled me towards him.

"No, let me go," I screamed.

Coach's arms burned against my skin as I tried to pull away.

Oscar's eyes shot open. They were dark, as if his soul had been ripped from his body. His eyes stared directly into mine. My feet left the floor as I flew ten feet in the air. The world spun around me in one second as all the memories of Oscar flew through my mind instantaneously. My skin felt as if it'd been ripped open as I crashed into the wall. He was attacking me now! Oscar was trying to kill me! I screamed in pain. My back felt as if it exploded and I passed out.

Chapter 36

"Oh my God, please say you're okay."

I could hear Oscar's voice in my ear.

"Please, Lil' Girl, please wake up."

My eyes fluttered and I made out Oscar's figure above me. He cradled my upper body as I lay across his legs on the floor.

"What happened?" I asked, my voice scratchy.

"Thank God. I called Max. He's on his way."

Oscar gently stroked my hair.

"I did it, Lil' Girl. I saved you. The demons are gone. I did it without you touching me."

His voice full of pride, while his eyes were full of worry.

"Please say you're okay. I'm so sorry. I'd have never done that, but I couldn't stop myself. I'd no idea you'd…"

I lifted a hand to his lips to quiet him.

"It was my fault," I said in a strained voice. "I tried to quit when I first found Coach attractive. I'd have never done anything, but he kept invading my thoughts. I'm so sorry, I never cheated on you, I swear."

"He's a demon and he was manipulating you."

Oscar gently kissed my forehead.

"Max warned me this could've been a possibility," Oscar confessed. "It's a cheap shot and they're pure evil. They're not going to play fair with us. All I care about is you're safe."

He embraced me as I held in a screech from the pain in my back.

"But…"

"Ellie. You can find other people attractive," he said, tracing my lips with a finger. "That's allowed. As long as you don't act on it. That's how a relationship is."

"Are you attracted to other girls?"

"Of course not. I'm perfect in every way and utterly devoted to you," Oscar said, but couldn't hold back his smile. "Not like I am to you," he admitted. "I'm human."

I thought about that. Lorenz Tate got me going when we watched *Love Jones*. And Orlando Bloom caused my stomach to stir a little.

"I'll always love you," Oscar said. "And there's a difference between attraction and love."

"Just because you're so much older than me doesn't mean you have to act like I'm a child," I said, laughing. "But I see what you mean."

Stroking his face, I curled into his chest.

"Because you showed me love," I said.

Max came running into the locker room.

"Now how am I going to clean this up? There were two of them?"

Max pointed to the two black streaks on the wall. He surveyed the broken walls with lockers strewn everywhere.

"Yes," I said, trying to sit-up but still unable to move. "You might want to poke your head in Coach Trenton's Office, too. I'm not as destructive as Oscar, but it isn't pretty in there either."

"Look at you two, I'm so proud of you," Max said, like a father just who's children won some coveted prize.

"Will Ellie be okay?" Oscar asked. "Coach…it…whatever was holding her when I threw him. She hit her head pretty good."

Oscar's eyes were trained on me as I found myself becoming lost in the worry and love in his eyes. Max came over to look at my head and back. He touched my stomach and I winced.

"It was a lower-level demon. Ellie will be fine, but you're going to have to find a way to cover these bruises and burns. I can only fix insides, bones and internal organs. Skin's demon realm, so we better find a way to hide these. I can't think of any cover story that wouldn't put Oscar in jail. Your hair should be able to cover this cut. Nothin' permanent. "

"Thank God," Oscar said.

Max smirked.

"You're welcome. Is there any chance she can stay at your house tonight?"

"Yes. My dad's working." Oscar looked at me as I sighed knowing he had been fighting with his father about keeping things from him. Finding me and then seeing I was beaten wasn't going to help the situation.

"But I better call him. I'll tell him you got hit in the head with a discus or something, so he'll be fine with you being there.

"Well, I don't want you to see what I have to do to clean this up," Max said. He looked at the second streak of ash.

"Ellie, did you? No, couldn't be? Could it?"

"What? Did I do what?"

"You said he was holding her?" Max asked Oscar.

"Yes, but I wasn't able to calm myself down enough to stop," Oscar said remorsefully.

"You worked together."

Oscar and I looked at each other. We were confused, of course. How was that significant? I replayed the attack. Oscar touched me and he turned the demon to ash. Wait, that was the first one.

"Ellie, what's the last thing you remember?"

"A ton of pain and I thought Oscar was attacking me."

A look of shock and shame crossed Oscar's face.

"Then I remembered everything wonderful we had together."

"See this," Max said, pointing to some red streaks intermixed with the black ash. "You didn't just burn him. One of you ripped him apart as he was burning."

Max's voice was quiet as if we succeeded in a painful torture he'd only heard of in myths. Breathing in and shaking his head, he returned to the little kid we had come to love.

"I'll no longer be your practice dummy. Yeah and I'm staying on your good side from now on."

Oscar found the rest of his clothes among the rubble. Then he gently picked me up.

"This isn't the end, you know," Max said. "Gaap has sixty-six legions of demons, which are currently subject to Maria's whims. Until a decree comes down from on high, they won't stop."

He surveyed the damage and with one hand picked up a row of lockers.

"At least you know you can beat them."

"How many are in a legion?" Oscar asked.

"In Hell. Six thousand."

As we drove home, Oscar called his dad at work. He then passed me the phone.

"At least let your sister know. They do care they just don't know how to show it."

I called Jennifer and she told me she would cover for me with Mom and Dad and she was glad one of us found someone who truly made them happy.

Oscar turned on the shower for me and got some ibuprofen.

"You know, I should buy stock in Advil. Between you and these demons, I'll make a million easy."

"I don't know if I'll ever forgive myself for bringing this into your life."

"I knew you were a handful when I first met you and I still made the choice to be with you. I've always had the free will to walk away."

He pulled my hair back behind my ears. I cringed, then I relaxed, realizing that history would repeat itself if I didn't learn from it. Oscar's touch wasn't the monster I just had in front of me. His touch was right and gentle. And exactly what I needed.

"Do you ever think we'll have a time when we can just be?" I asked.

"I don't know," he said, "but what fun would that be?"

He enjoyed the damage he had done at school. He noticed the look of sadness creep across my face.

"If peace is what you want," he said, brushing my cheek with his fingertips, "peace is what I'll get you. There's nothing in this world I wouldn't do for you."

I let the water wash over me as I tried to clean the dried blood from my head and hands. Oscar would take care of my burns after I dried off. My body was now becoming a story in itself. I didn't know which burn would leave a scar. My skin still hadn't recovered from my last attack. Oscar always gently touched each imperfection.

Maybe if I could see the scars as proof I'd survived instead of marks of a victim, Oscar might be able to do the same.

He was my protector. He made me strong enough to fight and gave me something to fight for. Now it's my turn. I had to let him know I never saw his shortcomings, but only the beauty, strength and security that was inside him.

He wrapped me up in a giant towel as I left the shower.

"I'll go get you one of my shirts to wear."

As he turned to leave, I reached for him. We dropped back on the bed.

"I love you," I said, "and there is no one in the world I'd fight for more than you."

"As long as we're fighting together, Lil' Girl, we'll always win."

His mouth found mine with the most tender of embraces.

In the soundtrack of my life, I never thought I'd be hearing *Halo* by Beyonce playing. The walls in my heart built up as each year passed. No one could get in. It was a hard journey to get here, but as his arms enclosed me in the cocoon of his love, all I could hear was *I'm surrounded by your embrace. Baby, I can see your halo. You know you're my saving grace.*

The End

About the Author

Michel Prince is an author who graduated with a bachelor degree in History and Political Science. Her novel Chrysalis is the first in a "cross-over" series following the demon plagued Ellie Chisholm. Michel writes young adult and adult paranormal romance as well as contemporary romance.

With characters yelling "It's my turn damn it!!!" She tries to explain to them that alas, she can only type a hundred and twenty words a minute and they will have wait their turn. She knows eventually they find their way out of her head and to her fingertips and she looks forward to sharing them with you.

When Michel can suppress the voices in her head she can be found at a scouting event or cheering for her son in a variety of sports. She would like to thank her family for always being in her corner and especially her husband for supporting her every dream and never letting her give up.

Michel is a member of RWA Pro and lives in the Midwest with her husband, son, and cat.

Chrysalis